# DESOLATE

# GARDEN

# DESOLATE GARDEN

Book Two of the Reclaimed Saga

SAM ODIORNE

www.samodiorne.com

First Edition: March 2024

Desolate Garden / Sam Odiorne
ISBN: 978-173-787-5925

10 9 8 7 6 5 4 3 2 1

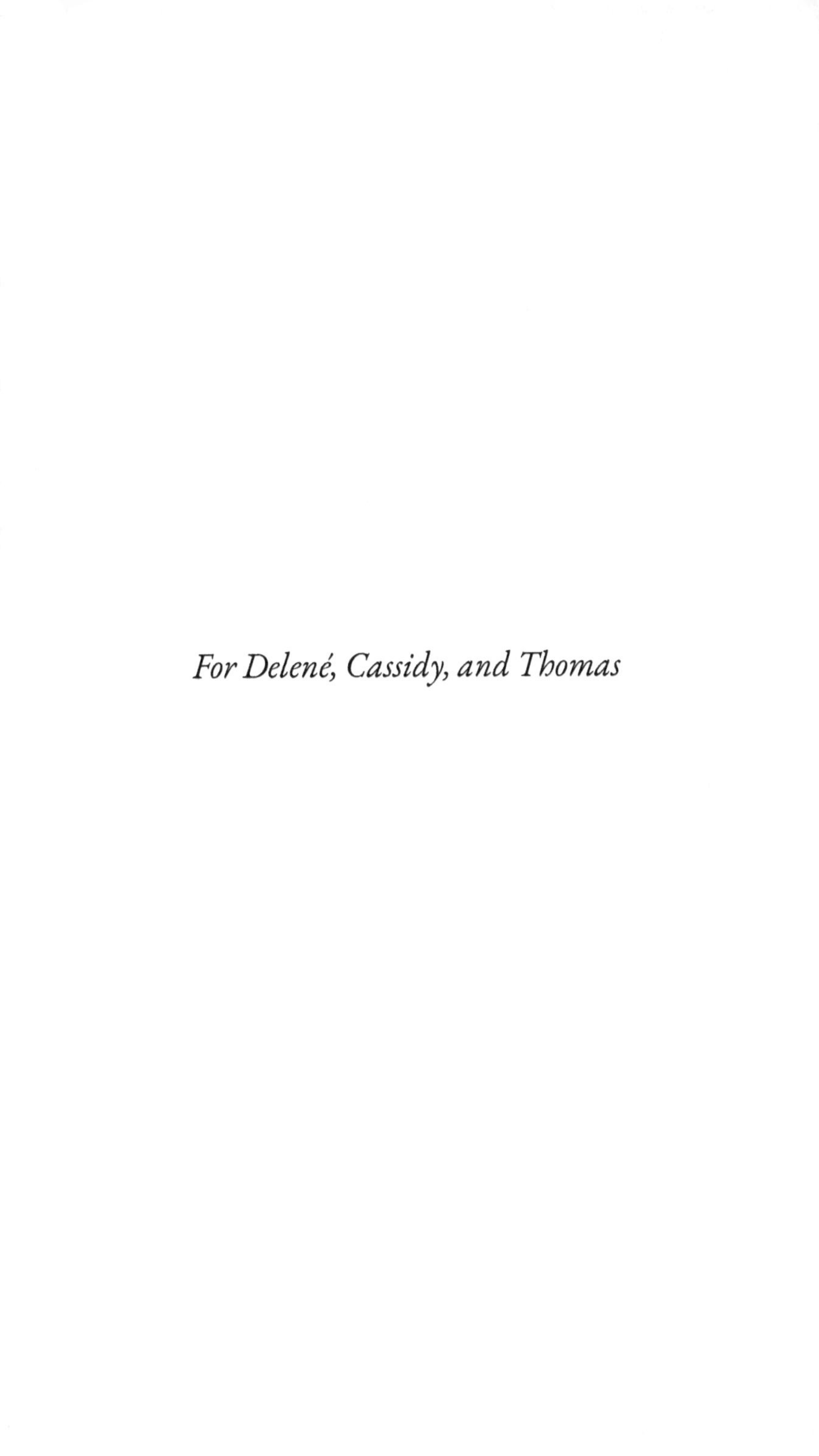

*For Delené, Cassidy, and Thomas*

# ONE

Hyatt stalked Bex through the Reclaimed with his Cern blade low, keeping them at the threshold between a full silhouette and almost concealed by the encroaching, frost-bitten foliage. He placed every step with intention and froze when they stopped to tip their nose skyward, smelling and tasting the air. Bex tilted their head and Hyatt held his breath, willing his jacket and boots to blend with the branches and deadfall around him as his heartbeat battered the inside of his chest like a caged creature. After what felt like an hour, they resumed their walk through the scattered rays of dawn light, and Hyatt exhaled a low breath. He waited until they were almost out of view again before taking another step, avoiding any brittle branch or hardened clod of earth that might draw their attention.

From his right, the brush burst apart in a flare of scattering leaves that left him just enough time to raise his weapon in defense as Rellah tackled him at waist-level. Hyatt's air left him and he brought his elbow down hard on her shoulder, but not hard enough to break her clasped grip around his midsection. They hit the ground together and the impact knocked Hyatt's Cern blade from his grip. He pulled his forearms together to shelter his stomach and face from the three-quarter's strength fists and elbows she rained on him as she slung a leg over him to straddle his hips.

"Okay! Okay!" Hyatt shouted as Rellah's knuckles caught his temple around his guard. "I'm dead!"

Rellah drove a closed fist into his ribs and when he dropped his elbow to protect them, she cuffed the exposed side of his face with her open hand. "Why are you dead, Hy-att?"

"I don't know!" The handprint on his face stung and he tried to shift his arms to shelter his head, wincing at her ongoing assault.

Rellah slid four more strikes through his clumsy defenses, then sat back on his hips to keep him pinned as the rustle of dewy leaves announced Bex's arrival. His attacker rolled off him, collecting his lost weapon in a fluid motion as she tumbled into a crouch and rose to her feet. For a moment, Hyatt lay where Rellah had tackled him, catching his breath and staring up at the canopy of the massive trees that surrounded them.

"Fixation. Your stalk was good – I heard her, not you." Bex offered him a hand and he took it, his shoulder nearly dislocating as they propelled him to his feet with a forceful jerk. "You didn't hear her, though."

Hyatt coughed as his lungs acclimated to air moving through them again, brushing the moisture and dirt from his jacket. "I love these exercises. Do you think we can do them again?"

Bex smirked at his sarcasm and lowered their head to hide it, turning away from them to study the scenery as Rellah tossed Hyatt's weapon at his feet. Hyatt rubbed the side of his face to ease the lingering sting before picking up the blade.

"You'll like them less when it's a Haleu weed trying to kill you – or an Iron." She turned to Bex and nodded in the direction they had been moving. "Wait for us at the six-pillar ruin, see if you can catch him sneaking in."

Bex nodded and gave Hyatt a supportive clap on his shoulder before turning and setting off at a light jog, their boots making almost no noise as they navigated the space between trees and brush. In a moment they were out of sight, swallowed by the sprawling wilderness with no trace they had ever been present. Hyatt attached his blade to his belt and shoved his hands into his pockets, sheltering his fingertips against the crisp air not yet warmed by the creeping sunrise.

"Am I at least getting better?" He asked without looking over at Rellah.

"You're not getting worse," she replied with a shrug.

Hyatt rolled his eyes, clenching and unclenching his fingers to force blood through them. "Great."

As they walked together in silence, morning crept forward and the spreading daylight turned the frost-bitten leaves damp and limp. Hyatt felt the ground tack against his boots and glanced back to see the prints they had left in the dirt not protected by deadfall. Somewhere deep in the forest, beyond his line of sight, a starling called out to alert other wild things of their presence. He was reluctant to give up the warmth of his pockets but pulled his hands free anyway, unlatching his blade from his belt.

Beside him, Rellah nodded her approval. She didn't speak and kept her eyes on the spaces between the trees ahead of them and on her side, and after six months together in the Reclaimed, Hyatt knew which parts of the wilderness to focus on to compliment her search. He studied the branches above and the fallen leaves below as he walked, trying to see what she saw and catch anything out of place before she did. Nothing reached him but the rustle of shifting brush and the distant flurry of wings or scurry of small creatures, sounds to which he had become accustomed.

"Are you still dreaming about it?" Rellah climbed over a fallen trunk with broken shards where branches had been and spared him a glance to be sure he'd heard her before moving forward on the other side of the natural obstacle.

Hyatt mantled the sturdy tree less gracefully than his pack-mate but landed neatly on the balls of his feet on the far side. Four steps behind Rellah, he wondered what answer she expected and how she would feel about the truth as he lengthened his stride to catch up. The very question brought the strange metal terminals and shattered glass of the laybrair to the forefront of his memory. The gut-wrenching scent of decay flooded back to him, but none of the bodies he'd found slumped at their desks lifted their heads in his reverie to stare at him with empty, accusing eye sockets as they did in his dreams.

"Not as often." He used the flat of his blade to push aside a low, encroaching branch and stepped around it. "You?"

She shook her head. "Not much."

*And that's all we ever say about that.* Hyatt fell into step behind her before rolling his eyes when he was certain she couldn't see him. "Good."

Hyatt pictured the rest of the conversation scattering like mice across the forest floor as they walked, scurrying away in every direction until they were alone in the Reclaimed. Silence filled the remaining space between them, broken only by Hyatt's occasional misstep that disturbed a leaf or twig and the rustle of branches as the wind passed through them. There was no marked path, but Rellah moved with the certainty of someone who was native to the sprawling wilds he still struggled to learn.

Rellah glanced back to make sure he was following her and made a slight gesture low by her hip to tell him to catch up. Hyatt grit his teeth, forced to choose between moving quietly and moving quickly, and his concern was validated by the leaves that shifted under his steps as he chose speed. Rellah lingered as he navigated the terrain between them, and resumed her movement as soon as he reached her.

"When we get there, what side will you approach from?" She ducked beneath a low-hanging branch, her gaze sweeping the Reclaimed to their right.

Hyatt glanced in the direction of the cresting sun and immediately regretted it as a million specks of frost refracted the light like needles through his eyes. "From the east, if the sun is this low, and I can find a way in."

She didn't reject his reasoning, and Hyatt took that as a small victory. He followed her around a cluster of low, thorny brush that interdicted their course. The leaves ahead were wet but under the shelter of the thicket, blue-white frost persisted in the shade, and tiny animal tracks trapped there held Hyatt's attention as they passed. As they ended their arc around the thicket, he felt the first splash of warmth as a sliver of daylight broke free of the horizon.

"Look." Rellah's single word made Hyatt freeze.

He followed her gaze to a massive tree with unevenly spaced, fist-sized holes punched into its trunk. "Veshtrue?"

She nodded and kept moving. "They're old."

*Just a nod – couldn't bring yourself to say I was right, huh?* Hyatt bit his tongue to stop his thoughts from becoming words and he veered from the path Rellah created to get a closer look at the marred tree. The exposed wood inside the massive punctures had browned and faded with time, and the moss that grew on the trunk encroached on the perimeter of the holes. The irrational but powerful urge to slip his fingers into the gaps came over him, but he knew Rellah would somehow sense his violation of the don't-reach-inside-anywhere rule of surviving in the Reclaimed, and resisted his compulsion.

"Leave them alone, Hyatt," she said without looking back, confirming his suspicion.

He narrowed his eyes and stuck his tongue out at the back of her head but changed direction to converge with the wake of her movement. They moved together over the uneven terrain, the thicket becoming denser around them, and the deadfall more prevalent. Hyatt focused on the way Rellah planted her boots when climbing over fallen trunks or slipping beneath splintered timbers that hung low over their path, a casual deftness to her motions that reminded him how new he still was to the Reclaimed.

Rellah reached a cluster of stumps and stopped. "Drop your pack. Bex needs more lead time."

Hyatt slipped the straps of his pack from his shoulders and joined her, tucking it beside hers against one of the broken stumps. By the time he turned around, she'd drawn an arrow from her quiver and faced him with two paces between them.

"Not just taking a break, then?" He knew the answer, but asked all the same.

"You can rest when you're dead," she replied, "and the way you use that blade, it will be any moment now."

Hyatt rolled his eyes as he lowered the tip of his Cern blade to a ready position, trying to remember when the feeling of Rellah's shots at his competence shifted from a sign of friendship to relentless criticism. The leather-wrapped grip of his weapon felt better in his hands than it had when he first held it and there were more scratches along the flat sides of the dark metal blade than when he started, but as he stared through it at his companion, he couldn't shake the memory of the unskilled Haleu he'd been when he first picked it up. He fumbled with his two-handed grip along the handle, trying to find the place where his closed hands formed together around it.

Rellah lifted her arrow to point the tip at him, then lowered her hand to hold it like a makeshift blade. "Five, five, six, four."

Hyatt nodded, memory of the dozens of times he'd run that drill flashing through his mind. He stepped forward and brought the curved blade down like he was going to cut from her right shoulder to her left hip and when she deflected it with the shaft of her arrow, he let the weapon carry through its arc and follow the same angle again. Rellah batted it aside and he let her, shifting his grip to bring it down in the opposite direction toward her left shoulder and across her body.

She took a half-step back and Hyatt didn't miss his step in their dance, closing half a step toward her as he spun to bring the blade around parallel with the ground. The edge caught on Rellah's arrow, not the glancing deflection of his first three swings but the hard resistance of a perpendicular strike that told him he'd done it correctly. They froze, matching force in their arms and legs keeping them stable.

"Where next?" she asked, meeting his eyes over their locked weapons.

He tried to hold her gaze while searching his periphery for an opportunity. "Six?"

"Are you asking me?" Rellah didn't blink or shift her intense, focused attention from his face.

He gritted his teeth and spun away from her, lining up his next overhand strike. Halfway through his turn, Rellah cracked the shaft of her arrow against his exposed ribs with enough force to raise a welt. He hissed and stepped away from her out of reflex, and it was all the space she needed to extend her arrow at arm's length with the tip pressed to his sternum. Hyatt froze.

"You lived two minutes." Rellah lowered her arrow and returned it to her quiver as she started toward their discarded gear. "Try to kill whatever is trying to kill you in less than that – easier to kill when you're not dead first."

Her annoyance with his performance was all Hyatt could taste on the cold air, and he spat it out. "A little encouragement wouldn't hurt, you know – I'm trying."

Rellah's reply was a distinctly Cern sound, a whispering hiss that ended in a hard press of her tongue to the roof of her mouth that clipped it short. "Wanting to live isn't enough?"

He caught up with her as she knelt beside her pack, cinching drawstrings and adjusting straps with deft motions. Hyatt dropped to his knees on the other side so he could do the same while regarding her over their gear. He knew she could feel him staring a hole in her forehead and when she didn't look up, it churned the acidic feelings building in his chest.

"Maybe it's not." He yanked one of the straps on his pack harder than he needed to, just to give the pent-up energy somewhere to go. "Maybe I want to feel like you want me to live, too – is that so fucking much to ask?"

She looked up at him then, her eyes as clouded with anger as he'd seen them since the day they'd met. "And when an Heir or an Iron kills me tomorrow, what then? What happens to you, when you don't have my attention to keep your heart beating, Hy-att?"

The question of how they got to where they were from the moment he decided to face the world with her washed over him like a lackluster tide, and he broke their locked gaze to focus on the grip of his weapon. The wrap around the blade's handle was snug and well maintained, but the sweat from his hands had begun to color the sides of the leather. He moved his hand over the ridges where the layers of the wrap overlapped, feeling the calluses on his palm slip over them on their way to the weapon's hilt.

"We'd better keep practicing then," he replied with a sigh that turned into a grunt as he forced himself to his feet.

Some of the ire dimmed in Rellah's eyes and she stood without Hyatt's labored noises, picked up her arrow again, and took three measured steps back from him. "Two, six, five, six."

Hyatt started toward her with his weapon low, and gripped the handle with both hands to launch himself into the drill she'd called out. The rising sun caught the edge of his blade as he drove it through the air, and Rellah parried the first three strikes. As he brought his weapon overhand to complete the sequence something shifted in her expression and she stepped toward him, planting her palm over his mouth and taking his legs out from under him with a fluid sweep. Rellah caught him on the way to the ground and they reached the forest floor in silence, her palm pinning his head to the dirt and her head up to listen.

Hyatt heard it then – the sound of metal on metal from the direction Bex had headed. The realization drove his heart up into his throat to choke him. Rellah released him and by the time he rolled to his knees, her pack was settled on her shoulder and her bow was tucked under her arm.

"Run."

# TWO

Against the natural sounds of the Reclaimed, the clash of metal against metal was stark and out of place. Without a word, Rellah rolled her shoulders back to shed her pack and took off at a sprint without breaking stride or looking back to see where it landed. By the time Hyatt started after her, she was a dozen paces ahead of him. He struggled to free himself of his pack while swapping his blade from one hand to the other, stumbled over a root and almost tumbled to his knees, but caught his balance and ran after her. Branches lashed as his jacket and the uneven ground threatened to trip him, but months of footraces with his pack-mates gave him the endurance to keep pace with her and he began to close the distance.

The crash of weapons grew louder as the first glimpses of the ruin appeared through the thick forest, and Hyatt's heart plummeted. He thought he had run as fast as he could, but growing certainty that Bex was fighting for their life poured fuel into his legs and he surged forward. He severed a branch that threatened to block his way with a violent swing of his blade and the resistance of the wood against his weapon reverberated down his arm to his shoulder, igniting something in his blood that burned white-hot. The sensation of twigs and leaves clawing at his face became inciting instead of inhibiting and he ran harder. He was shoulder to shoulder with Rellah as they reached the gap in the ruin's broken wall, and Hyatt heard an unfamiliar voice roar in agony.

He vaulted the knee-high fragment of stone without slowing down and landed on the other side, willing his sight to expand from the tunnel vision it had become so he could take in the scene. Bodies lay scattered around a courtyard space, crumpled against standing pillars that had once supported a roof and splayed across stone floors covered in moss and dirt. A gap in the canopy poured buckets of daylight into the walled courtyard, gleaming on the frost-turned-dew that clung to the vines and saplings that claimed every surface as their own. Bex lay on their back at the center of the open space between two pillars, their weapon discarded and wrestling with the man sprawled across them for control of the jagged-ended pipe he was trying to drive through their face.

"Hey!" Hyatt roared, changing directions to run toward his pack-mate and their attacker.

The telltale thwack of Rellah's bow sounded behind him, but Hyatt barely noticed. He raced toward the man over Bex and didn't slow down when he reached them, driving his boot into the man's ribs with a savage kick that sent the attacker tumbling. Bex crab-crawled backward as Hyatt closed with the man again, bringing his weapon up to end his life, but paused as he saw lifeless eyes looking up at him and an arrow that entered one side of his temple and exited the other. Hyatt's heaving lungs rushed searing hot blood through his body, almost demanding he bring the blade down in a vicious slash, but after a steadying breath, he lowered it to a ready position. The haze retreated from the edges of his vision as he turned, focusing on each body scattered around the courtyard to ensure they were dead.

"That's it, I think." Bex grabbed the pillar beside them and used it to haul themself to their feet.

Rellah moved along the perimeter of the courtyard toward crumbling and rusted stairs along the far wall that led to a decimated second floor, a new arrow nocked. "What happened?"

"They were all dead when I got here, except those two." Bex picked up their blade and used the point to gesture to a body crumpled against ancient twin doors at the back of the courtyard, then to the man Rellah shot. "This one ran at me as soon as I crossed the wall."

Hyatt stepped closer to the body leaned against the nearest pillar and pressed against the woman's shoulder with his boot until she tipped over, then knelt beside her head. Seeing her slack expression and her still form, he couldn't imagine how she'd found herself in a fight among the ancient ruins that ended with her dead. Without the slash that opened her clothes and flesh from her sternum to her pelvis, Hyatt wouldn't have known her from any other Haleu walking the pathways of a Garden. He grabbed her hand and turned her arm over to examine her braid, then lowered her arm to the ground as if she would feel him drop it otherwise.

"These aren't security workers, or hunters – this one is an apprentice metal worker." Hyatt rose to his feet and moved to the next body and checked their braid. "This one is an apprentice speaker. None of this is right... there's no reason they should be this far from home."

Rellah paused her ascent halfway up the stairs as one of the metal steps groaned under her weight, the bolts that anchored it to the wall threatening to pull free. She pulled her leg back and turned toward the vine-covered wall, gripping the woven vegetation for balance as she stepped over the unstable stair to the one beyond. With a grunt of effort, she pulled herself across.

"Everything makes sense if you find all the parts." She kept her attention on the landing above her, but her voice filtered down to them in quiet, clear tones. "They didn't attack a Cern in the wild for no reason."

"I think it was all of them against him," Bex added, walking toward the dead man by the doors.

Hyatt approached the third body and noted the dead man's apprentice builder braid and the deep chain marks around his throat and forearm that spoke of a violent, painful death. He traced the imprint of the man's flesh up from his wrist to his palm, then frowned. He peeled the corpse's fingers open and turned them upward towards the daylight, then dropped it and checked the dead man's other hand.

"This one has an Apprentice Builder's braid, but no calluses..." He dropped the man's arm and turned to scan the courtyard until his gaze fixed on Bex's discarded backpack. "And none of them have packs with them. What the rot is going on?"

"Maybe they dropped them somewhere outside the ruin before they fought – oh, shit." Bex's sudden halt and grim change of tone drew Hyatt's attention, and he looked over to see them holding up three linked silver bars.

"Shit," Hyatt echoed, his voice quiet and the corpse before him forgotten as he stepped over it to join them at the back of the courtyard.

Morning light tangled in the links of the chain and ran like water along the hard edges of the silver slats before Bex folded the three bars in on themselves in a neat stack. They held them out at arm's length towards Hyatt as he approached and he reached for them, but the cold knot of dread he felt as his fingers drew close to them made him hesitate. Bex raised an eyebrow at him and he grit his teeth, wrapping his fingers around the cold metal even as a frigid vice gripped his stomach and spine, but he forced himself to unfold the bars and look at them. The cuneal markings on the flat faces of the bars made no sense to him, but they reminded Hyatt of the characters etched on the bars he'd seen carried by Iron Delores and Iron Sawmet.

"That explains how one-on-seven ended like it did." Bex pried open the dead Iron's hand and pulled the grip of his chain-weapon free, doubling it over itself with care so they could toss it aside without being snagged by the barbs that adorned the last third of the weapon's reach. "I didn't think Irons could be killed."

Hyatt flashed back to the memory of Iron Sawmet on his knees and the perfect, brutal arc of Delores' strange blade as she beheaded him in a clean stroke. "They can. It's just very hard."

Bex shot a sideways look at Hyatt but didn't ask whatever question had risen to their mind. Instead, they pulled the strange serrated blade from the Iron's other hand and held it up so light caught on the blood that lingered on the weapon's teeth. They nodded in what looked to Hyatt like begrudging approval for the blade's design.

"The Iron comes across these ruins, and there's a bunch of Haleu scavenging..." Bex began working through their theory in slow, halting statements as they unbuckled the Iron's sword belt, pulled it free, and fastened it around their own waist beneath their jacket.

Hyatt glanced around again at the bodies scattered through the walled-in space and shook his head. "I don't think so. Look where he died... I think he was here first, guarding the door."

"And they were willing to face him to get whatever is behind it?" Bex slid the dead Iron's blade into their sheath with a warm hiss and a matted click as the hilt settled into place. "Even seven against one..."

Hyatt shrugged as Bex pulled open the man's jacket, revealing a dozen violent gashes in his chest and stomach that revealed bone through his butchered flesh. "No, they don't have anything to carry whatever is behind it, no tools to pry it open... I think he was the goal. I think they came here to kill the Iron."

"Rot," Bex said again, stretching the syllable out for the length of a breath that ended in a dry chuckle. "Now I wish he hadn't come at me. This feels like a good thing for all of us – one less Iron in the Reclaimed."

Their humor was lost on Hyatt as every alarm in his head and body rang in a confusing thunder, everything about the grisly scene telling him he should run somewhere, anywhere but where he stood. He didn't realize his fingers had uncurled from around the Iron's bars until he heard them land on the stone floor with the sound muted by intervening moss, but as he looked down at them, he lacked the motivation to pick them up again. His guts and veins felt like they were clogged with cold mud and he swallowed hard to clear the warm saliva pooling on his tongue.

"Yeah," he managed in response, staring with unfocused eyes at the Iron's bars.

The sound of a backpack hitting the ground across the courtyard jarred Hyatt from his budding shock. The top closure of the backpack flapped open as it landed, dumping rations wrapped in wax paper and an assortment of tools into the dirt and stone. He looked up from the scattered gear to the stairs where Rellah was descending with careful, purposeful steps, her bow in one hand and a wad of crumpled fabric in the other. When she reached the warped metal step that had threatened to collapse on her ascent, she turned and dropped off the edge of the stairway into the courtyard below.

"This isn't trouble we need." Rellah rose from her crouched landing and dusted her palms against her jacket. "Irons and Haleu killing each other isn't our problem. Lessons are done for today – take what's worth taking. We're leaving."

Bex nodded their agreement and began frisking the dead Iron for anything of value.  Rellah stopped at the nearest corpse, grabbed the arrow she'd put through the dead man's head from just behind the tip, and planted her boot against his neck so she could pull it through his skull. The fletchings dripped red and gray as they came free on the other side.

The way Hyatt's stomach turned over as Rellah slid the arrow back into her quiver told him that his time in the Reclaimed hadn't fully erased his response to gore, but he swallowed hard to clear the lump in his throat. "It might be our problem, if another Iron comes looking for him."

Though Bex continued to search the body in front of them, Hyatt caught their flicker of a glance at the rare moment of disagreement between Hyatt and their pack-master. Rellah looked up from her quiver in a fluid motion that ended in a crisp stop like a predator fixing on prey, but Hyatt forced himself to meet her gaze even under the intensity of her undivided attention. The silent moment swelled like a cresting wave and Bex averted their gaze, hunching lower over the dead body they were searching.

"If an Iron comes looking, our odds are better with the rest of Hollow Bone Pack at our backs... unless you wanted to fight one of the Butcher Queen's assassins, one at a time?" Her voice managed to communicate a thousand shades of challenge without changing inflection at all.

"No," he replied, crouching next to the body in front of him and stripping their Apprentice Builder braid without looking away from Rellah, "but we should be as sure as we can be about what happened here, in case we're asked to answer for it..."

Hyatt trailed off as his hands brushed something beneath the dead man's shirt that crinkled under the pressure of his hands. He frowned and set down his Cern blade in favor of his belt-knife, pulled the corpse's shirt taut with one hand, and sheared the fabric open in a long stroke. Underneath, folded parchment protruded from the man's belt and clung to his ribs with the aid of drying blood.

Hyatt worked his fingers around the edges to peel the paper free and tugged it out of the dead man's belt, then held it up for Rellah to see. "Something like this."

Her locked gaze doubled in weight and almost made Hyatt lean back to create more space between them, but he unfolded the paper and smoothed it across the dead man's form as she started walking towards him. The lines and arcs that covered the paper brought the same wash of dread that seeing the Iron's bars had flooded through Hyatt, and his eyes were drawn against his will to the corners. Like the map fragments that had led them to the Laybrair, the outer edges of the parchment had anchor marks to overlay it against other partial drawings.

His pack-mate's steps slowed as she recognized the markings too, and Hyatt squinted up at her in the morning light as she hooked her thumbs in her belt and stared down at the paper. "... fuck."

Across the courtyard, Bex tied the retaining band around the handle of their new blade and rose to join them. "What is it?"

"Keeper maps," Rellah answered with a sigh through her teeth. "Secrets that they break into pieces – dangerous places and things."

Bex nodded as if her explanation was as obvious as a sunrise, turning in a slow circle to look over the dead bodies around the walled-in space. "So these are all... Keepers?"

A non-committal cock of her head was the only answer Rellah offered. They looked to Hyatt and he searched for a better response, but the words were mired in all the things Rellah and he had chosen not to tell the Claimed they welcomed to the pack one after another. A shadow crossed between them as a starling streaked through the morning sky above, having found the bravery to investigate the noise and scents of the courtyard at last. Hyatt looked up just in time to lose it in the branches on the far side and then studied the parchment again, trying to imagine the lines that would connect the pieces in front of him and make it complete.

Bex leaned a little closer to take a last, long look at the markings on the paper, then set off towards another dead body to strip of their worthwhile possessions.

"We should at least–" Hyatt watched Bex pick over the corpse like a discerning carrion bird.

"Rellah's right." Bex shook their head. "This is trouble we don't need."

"Go," Rellah added with a directional jerk of her head. "Find the rest of them if there are any. We'll destroy them and be done."

Rellah walked away before he could reply, and Hyatt opened his mouth to call after her, but saw no chance to argue with her without Bex overhearing him. In the time it took his pack-mates to discard weapons and clothes that were of no use to them and collect the things that were, he found three more parchments stuck in the boots and belts of the corpses that littered the courtyard of the ruin. Hyatt unfolded them one after another against one of the pillars, pinning them in place with one hand as he rotated them with the other until the anchor points aligned.

"Do you recognize it?" Rellah asked from over Hyatt's shoulder, who flinched in surprise at how near to him she'd come without him noticing.

"I don't..." He paused, tilting and rotating the pile of pages clockwise, then shook his head. "I don't think so."

On his other side, Bex extended another page covered in markings. "I found it inside the woman's jacket lining."

Hyatt unfolded the new sheet and laid it over the others, adjusting it until its anchors matched with the sheet underneath it, but frowned. "These could stack in any order, and the anchors work at least two different ways. I don't know where... wait a second."

Rellah crossed her arms and looked over her shoulder at the breach in the wall where she and Hyatt had entered the courtyard. "We should go... now."

Hyatt only half heard her, focused on turning over one of the pages and realigning them. Still unsatisfied, he rotated the bottom sheet counterclockwise to realign the anchors, then stopped as realization dawned on him.

"They're not pins... they're points," He muttered, turning the sheets until the marks on the edge of each were evenly spaced in a circle around the perimeter of the drawing made by the interior marks. "This is just... fuck. It's a map of the Gardens. There's Brathnee, and there's Ceojic."

"Let's go," Rellah repeated, her voice lowered into the matted tones Cern raiders used to blend with the sounds of the wilderness instead of standing out against it, "now."

Hyatt growled and started to crumple the pages into a wad capable of absorbing his frustration in the crushed ball of paper.

"Why were there ten?" Bex asked.

"What?" Hyatt turned the sphere of smashed parchment over and compressed it again, driving every pocket of air inside with his palms.

"Why were there ten Gardens?" Bex repeated. "Aren't there only nine?"

Confused, he started to pluck at the exposed edges of the decimated map fragments, but Rellah snatched it from his hands. "I said destroy them, not figure them out – and then I said we need to leave. Is today the day you want to become pack-master, Hy-att?"

His reflexive response to her snatching the ball of paper was to turn toward her and reach for it, but he stopped with his hand low and his face inches from hers with the full force of her challenging glare boring through the space between his eyes. Outrage and fear fought for control as he stood very still, tunnel vision closing in around his sight until he could focus only on the flecks in Rellah's irises. He knew her hand was hovering over her quiver, open and fingers splayed, ready to move if he did.

*Would you really do it, Rellah?* He let his breath become shallower, and the unsummoned question of how fast he could pull his knife from his belt bolted from his brainstem to his sternum. *After months, are we only here? Really?*

Slowly, he took a half-step backward so he could lower his gaze without staring into her collarbone. "No. I don't want that."

The space Hyatt created between them let the tension drip from the moment, even as Rellah continued to stare him down as if he might rethink his choice. "Then get your things and let's go – quietly. There's something out there, and you would have heard it, if you were paying attention to what mattered and not some Keeper secrets that don't concern us."

She closed her hands around the pages, packing them back into a ball. The force Rellah used to compress them raised tendons of muscle along her forearms and her hands shook with exertion, as if she was strangling them and ensuring there was no meaning left anywhere in the pages. When she was satisfied, she handed them to Hyatt.

"Destroy them, and forget them," Rellah told him, her eye contact with him direct and unwavering.

# THREE

Hyatt stepped over the wall that separated the courtyard from the world beyond, and he knew Rellah was right. He couldn't place if there was a difference in the sounds of the Reclaimed or the way the wind moved through the branches, but he could feel something in the wilderness watching them. He fell into step with Bex as Rellah moved toward the landmarks they'd followed from camp to the ruin, moving with silent steps across the damp forest floor. As they walked, Hyatt searched the right side of their route for any sign of movement that could warn of whatever stalked them. He peered into the depths of every shadow and tried to penetrate the leaves and overgrowth with his gaze.

Bex reached the space just before a fallen tree where Hyatt and Rellah had shed their packs, and Hyatt searched through the low brush for a moment before finding his. By the time he shouldered his backpack and adjusted the straps, Rellah had recovered hers and crouched beside it but had not yet put it on. He thought he had been quiet, but her silence and her stillness made Hyatt acutely aware of every leaf or twig dislodged by his jacket or his boots. He tried to move slower, scanning the branches above him and the trees back the way they had come, wishing he was able to imitate skills that seemed innate to his pack-mates.

He moved towards Bex with four careful steps before they brought their hand up in a single, silent motion that caused neither their jacket nor their pack to make a sound. Hyatt froze every muscle below his collarbone, turning his head in a slow arc to search for the threat Rellah and Bex were trying to track but unable to pick up a trace of it. The perfect quiet seemed to congeal around him until he wasn't sure he could move his arms or legs if he wanted to, and even the slight motion of continuing to search his periphery without moving his neck seemed a risk. He parted his lips so the sound of air passing in and out of his nose wouldn't distract them from their effort to find something he couldn't see.

Then, he felt it.

A single thump ran through the ground beneath Hyatt, as if the earth had formed a heartbeat for a solitary pulse. The force of it ran from the soles of his boots to the cavity in his chest, like he'd been punched. In the distance, a dragging sound like a tree-trunk being hauled over the ground ended in another solid thump. He turned to look toward the dragging sound, gripping the handle of his weapon so tightly that the tip of his blade began to tremble. He couldn't see it, but on the gentle shift of the morning air, he smelled it – the scent that lingered in his dreams and woke him in a cold sweat.

"Run." Bex slid the dead Iron's weapon from their sheath in a slow, smooth motion, and their whisper didn't sound any less determined for its quiet notes. "I'll distract the Heir until you're safe."

Hyatt opened his mouth to reply, but Rellah cut him off. "Bex is right. Get as far from here as you can–"

"There's no rotted way—" Hyatt protested in the loudest sound he could still call a whisper.

"—stay low, and quiet, and move fast—" Rellah continued as if he hadn't spoken.

Bex was the first to abandon any effort to be quiet, a steel edge in their tone. "I meant both of you. It makes no sense for all of us to die when one of us will do."

In Hyatt's line of sight, saplings began to crack and fall like cut grass as the quaking earth became a constant rumble. He dropped his pack again and grabbed the handle of his Cern blade with both hands, watching the destroyed foliage form a direct line toward them through the Reclaimed.

"Fighting Heirs is what the Claimed do," Rellah growled without looking at him, fitting an arrow to her bowstring, "but you're not Claimed. You don't have to die here, Hy-att. Get back to the—"

The line her words drew between them felt like she'd cut his arm off, but Hyatt grit his teeth and forced the molten feeling in his heart deeper into his gut. "After this, until we die – that's what you said! If you're fighting, I am too!"

Before she could fire back a retort, the Veshtrue broke into view. Branches and trunks of trees scattered like kindling as it barreled through them, teeth gnashing. A gnarled, reddened scar wrenched one of the beast's eyes closed but the other radiated hunger and hate as it thrashed its head from side to side, trying to see them all at once. The massive creature lunged forward and stepped on the fallen trunk between them, mashing the wood flat in a single step that closed its branches around the Veshtrue's leg like teeth, only for them to snap and break with splitting sounds.

"Scatter!" Rellah shouted, sending her arrow flying at the beast's giant skull. "She can't see us all at once!"

Hyatt didn't consciously process her instructions, but his body responded all the same. He dashed right and forward, flanking around the enraged creature. The Heir started to turn toward him but Rellah's arrow buried inches into the bridge of her nose and she thrashed back the other way, snapping the shaft of the protruding munition as it connected with a tree. Hyatt caught a glimpse of Bex climbing into the forked heart of a nearby tree and looked for one close enough for him to do the same, but the trunks around him had no branches low enough to jump for.

"Hey! Hey, right here!" Rellah roared at the creature two-hundred times her size, taking a step backward to draw the beast further between Hyatt and Bex as she nocked another arrow and fired it into the Veshtrue's chest.

The arrow's tip barely broke the beast's skin and the rest shattered, scattering splinters and indigo fletchings across the ground. The Veshtrue's spiked tail lashed back and forth, ripping bushes out of the forest floor by their roots as it passed through them. She surged forward to close the distance to Rellah, but as it did Hyatt saw it lurch as one of her back legs failed to fully support her weight.

Hyatt focused on the giant muscles shifting under the thick hide of her back leg and started running toward her. In his periphery, he saw Rellah dive behind a tree as the Heir exhaled a wet, noxious cloud that hung in the air around its mouth like morning mist. A flash of understanding that he was about to die flared through him, white-hot and crystal clear, and he felt more than he saw the creature's tail curling so that he was caught between the Veshtrue's massive body in front of him and the vicious spikes of her back end behind him. He shouted, a primal sound that ripped out of his throat almost faster than his mouth opened to let it escape, and brought his Cern blade down on the Heir's injured leg as hard as he could.

The creature screamed and her leg folded under her, taking his blade with it and almost crushing him under her full weight as she crashed to the ground. The force knocked him back and he landed on his shoulders as the massive beast thrashed inches from him, and he crawled backward away from her. From somewhere on his right Rellah's bow fired again, and suddenly Bex was on all fours atop the fallen Heir, driving their serrated blade into her hide and forcing it deeper with their arms and shoulders against the weapon's hilt.

"Die! Bleed to death, you fucking beast!" Bex shouted, rising to their feet in an unsteady stance before stomping on the weapon's crossguard to push it another inch into the Veshtrue.

Whatever the blade found inside the Heir made it spasm and jerk, lurching back to its feet. Bex began to tumble from the creature's back but grabbed the handle protruding from the Veshtrue's body like a climber clinging to a handhold. The Veshtrue bolted forward and Bex hung on for four steps before the reverberations through the embedded weapon became too much and they lost their grip, plummeting to the forest floor with a crunch before laying still. Hyatt scrambled to his feet and raced towards Bex, and Rellah roared from somewhere nearby, firing two more times at the fleeing Veshtrue as it tore into the Reclaimed in search of escape.

*Don't be dead, don't be dead, don't be dead!* Hyatt's race to Bex's side ended in an uncontrolled dive that churned earth under his boots and knees as he crashed into his pack-mate's body, frisking frantically for blood and broken bones as he mantled over Bex to get a look at their face. *Don't be fucking dead!*

Bex opened their eyes and a flood of relief coursed through them, and they coughed and moaned in pain as Rellah reached them. "Where is she?"

"She ran off – you did it," Hyatt answered quickly, brushing Bex's hair and sweat from their face with rough smears of his palm. "You won."

They rolled on their side and pulled their elbow to their ribs as they coughed again, blood tinging their spit as it soaked into the disturbed earth below. "I hope I hit her third heart. If I did..."

"She has three hearts?" Hyatt's question sounded more like outrage as he looked up at Rellah who was unwrapping the band around a packet of herocaine. "How do you kill something with three hearts?"

"They same way they kill you. Trauma." Rellah knelt beside Bex who forced themself to their hands and knees before sitting back on their heels and accepting the wrapped packet from Rellah's hand.

Hyatt found nothing about her answer complete, but the absurdity of it reminded him that his question wasn't the most important thing in their shared moment. Instead, he looked in the direction the Veshtrue had escaped, marked by the newly formed path of uprooted saplings and trampled brush. His hands began to shake and it spread as the quiver moved up through his arms, and he felt the contents of his stomach begin to rise. As Bex inhaled the herocaine dose, Hyatt crawled far enough from his pack-mates to let the welling vomit in his throat break free with two hard heaves, spattering the grass with yellow bile and the remnant of his last meal.

"I think..." Hyatt sat up and paused as the motion made his stomach clench again, but continued when he was certain he had nothing else to surrender to the forest. "Was that the same Veshtrue we...?"

"No. Heirs don't migrate, and we're weeks from there." Rellah's answer was quick and certain.

Hyatt opened his mouth to argue but saw Rellah's caustic look over her shoulder at him, and fell silent. Beside her, Bex shook their head in a spasm as the herocaine flushed through their bloodstream and turned their pupils to pinpoints. After a deep breath, Bex nodded their agreement with Rellah's statement. Hyatt's memory of the effects of the powder made his fingertips tingle and his mouth water with warm saliva, and the aches from his last encounter with an Heir throbbed as if their phantom visitation could justify him using it again. He spat into the damp leaves, crawled over to his discarded pack, and rose to his feet.

"Where did you see an Heir before?" Bex spoke and moved with more surety than their brush with death should have allowed, and Hyatt marveled all over again at the potency of the drug.

"South." The tone of Rellah's answer left no room for follow-up questions. "Hyatt – your turn up front. Let's go."

"Me?" he asked, earning a bladed glare from her. "Um, I mean – okay."

Hyatt dressed the strap of his pack against his shoulder as he looked around, trying to get his bearings in the aftermath of the fight. As his gaze swept over Bex, they offered an almost imperceptible tilt of their head to orient him. Hyatt looked in the direction they hinted toward until he picked out one of the unique trees that had marked their way from camp to the ruin. Unwilling to risk a nod or wink that might have given away Bex's help, he settled for a slow exhale of relief and started walking.

From one remembered point to the next, Hyatt moved to the next landmark and hesitated long enough to search the wilderness for something familiar. His pack-mates moved like wraiths behind him, no misplaced step or whispered word to tell him they were still in tow or even existed. The height of the sun limited the reach of shadows, pooling them in dark, contained spaces beneath leaves and branches low enough to the ground to cause them. Only the shifting of leaves broke the silence as Hyatt stepped over the smaller deadfall and walked around the larger features of the Reclaimed that stood between him and his destination.

In four hours' walk, he glanced back twice to ensure he was not alone. Both times, he saw Bex and Rellah side by side, their mouths moving in an imitation of conversation that expelled no sound he could hear as they navigated the uneven terrain with deft strides. Hyatt focused on the way forward, fighting the urge to dwell on what they discussed and why he wasn't a part of the conversation.

*Someone needs to be up front. It's my turn. That's why.* He ducked beneath a massive trunk that had done its best to reach the ground, only to be caught against the stronger body of another. *This is an important skill. Rellah wants me to learn it.*

Hyatt couldn't help but doubt his rationalizations, less noble alternatives pulling at the edges for his attention, but he committed to his optimistic construct. A cluster of tall bushes with slender, brown stalks that blossomed pale yellow flowers stood out against the green and gray foliage that surrounded them, and he slowed to a stop as he recognized the last landmark before Hollow Bone Pack's encampment. He didn't hear Rellah or Bex approach on either side until they appeared beside him, and Rellah put her hand on his shoulder.

"Good." Her compliment was succinct and she didn't look at him while she said it, but it felt to Hyatt like her hand on his jacket radiated her acknowledgment in waves of cascading warmth. "Call them."

No sooner had Rellah's approval blazed to life in his chest, than her next instruction poured water over it. The idea of attempting their recognition signal seemed twice as daunting on the tail of his noted success, and he stalled as he searched the limits of his vision for any sign of his pack-mates. No movement or sound gave them away and he frowned, fighting the sweat that threatened to break out on the back of his neck and run down his spine.

Hyatt cupped his hands and pressed his thumbs together, tilted them towards his mouth, took a deep breath, and exhaled through his pursed lips into his cupped hands. The result was a sound like wind across the mouth of a bottle instead of the low whistling sound he hoped for. He frowned and unfolded his hands, cupped them again, and blew his hot breath into the cavity created by his hands, with the same result. Disappointment welled up in him and he tried to wrestle it into submission as he changed the angle of his hands and tried again.

Beside him, Bex cupped their hands and created two short, low tones and a higher one on their first attempt. Hyatt dropped his hands and suppressed a growl that started in his throat and tried to keep his face neutral as an answering call sounded from the forest ahead. Rellah's hand dropped from his shoulder and she started toward the still hidden pack-mate who answered them, and the space where her touch had warmed his skin through his jacket cooled and faded. As Bex followed her, Hyatt looked back toward the ruins as if he expected the Veshtrue to be stalking them at a distance, but nothing in the wilds moved and he fell into step behind his pack-mates.

Ahead, Rayce emerged from behind a large tree draped with vines and hanging moss, and waved with an open hand in a single gesture. "How was training?"

Rellah and Bex passed him without a reply and Rayce walked beside Hyatt, who shoved his hands in his pockets. "It was easy. We killed some people and fought an Heir. We're planning to go back this afternoon if you want to come. Good times."

The stocky man laughed, a gravelly chuckle that ended in a stalled breath as no one else joined in or even smirked. "What... the rotted fuck?"

They passed the edge of their camp as a group, a perimeter of deadfall that looked natural from the outside but carefully constructed from within. Amidst the sparse trees and low brush where Hollow Bone had made their home, Hyatt caught sight of charcoal gray guidelines that held pale green tarps in place above one of their preparation areas. The leaves and twigs that blanketed their chosen space were matted flat from dew and the pack's repeated passage, the only sign that separated their camp from the sprawling forest in every direction. Despite fearing for his life twice in a morning, his confusion at the scene in the ruins, and his tension with Rellah, a sense of familiar comfort coursed over him as he found himself in camp again and not yet dead.

Bex reached the edge of the preparation area first and stepped beneath the tarpaulin before dropping their pack on one of the makeshift tables under it. "First Haleu at the ruins, then a Veshtrue on the way back."

As Rellah and Hyatt found space on another table to unload and break out their equipment, Rayce switched his attention back and forth between the three of them, his face a carving of confusion. "You fought an Heir and lived?"

Hyatt was surprised by the bristle under his skin at the realization that a band of garden-dwellers at the ruins didn't strike Rayce as a threat. The thought of what his pack-mates would think of the men and women he grew up with in Brathnee Garden intruded on his consciousness without his permission and refused to let go when he tried to banish it. Images of Rayce casually gutting his childhood friend Gorman or the hunter Omalara flashed through his mind and Hyatt grit his teeth against the tension those images added to his shoulders and gut. He almost replied that one of those Haleu might have killed Bex if he and Rellah hadn't caught up with them, but the tense expression on Rellah's face dried the words to dust on his tongue and he swallowed hard to clear them.

"The Heir was wounded already, and it still almost killed us. With five Claimed in one place, I'm surprised one hasn't found us yet." Rellah didn't look up from the tools and clothes she was laying out in neat piles on the table, her eyes clouded and distant. "Who knows how long it will take to find us again – it's a good thing our sentry is at his post and keeping a look out."

Rayce's mouth curved down in a disapproving frown at her barb, but headed toward the edge of camp. "I'm on it – but it's not five anymore, there's a new Claimed in camp. She's with Veck, setting her sleep space."

Rellah didn't answer him and Bex shot Hyatt a concerned look before setting off after Rayce at a pace somewhere between a walk and a trot, closing with him and walking by his side. Hyatt watched them go until their details began to fade into shadowy outlines of people he knew, their heads turned toward one another in quiet conversation. With a glance at Rellah to see if anything changed with their departure, he upended his pack on the table to dump its contents with an unnecessary clamor as tools clanged together, and dropped his bag so the buckles of his straps clacked.

Rellah's head snapped up, her eyes full of accusation. "What is wrong with you?"

His pulse began to spike in anticipation of the argument he knew he was starting, and he felt his hands become clammy, but he turned his whole body toward her and glared back at her. "What's wrong with you, Rellah? Taking swings at Rayce, trying to fight me for pack leadership, snapping at everybody – what's your problem?"

Hyatt watched her pupils darken from black to murder, something sharp glittering at their edges and hardening through her irises. Her look sent wires of ice spiraling between all the vertebrae of his spine and he thought she was going to punch him, and he hadn't realized he'd closed his fists to defend himself until her gaze darted down to his hands and then walked slowly back up his torso like her eyes were cutting him open from his stomach to the bridge of his nose.

"You think you have the roots for this, becquerel?" Her voice was a whisper without any softness. "You want to tell me how to lead this pack – how to keep these Claimed alive?"

Hyatt willed his knees not to buckle and fought the overwhelming, primal urge to back up and create a gap between them. "That's not what –"

He never saw Rellah's hands move. They went from resting at her sides to flat against his chest with such speed that he had no time to prepare for her shove that drove him two staggering steps backward, and only colliding with the supply table allowed him to keep his feet. He brought his open hands up in the ready-to-fight stance Rellah had taught him and sidestepped, trading the table covered in gear for open space at his back.

The anger in her words battered him but the hurt and sadness in it drove through him like a barrage of needles, and it stole his ability to form words. His mind went blank and lancing pain punched through his heart and lungs, and the thought that he hadn't known how hard everything was on her felt like being buried under a pallet of bricks.

"If you want to do better, you're going to need a blade to fight me – where's your blade, Hy-att? Oh, that's right – you lost another one, you dumb fucking weed!" Her voice rose another level, somewhere between a snarl and a yell.

Hyatt locked his jaw to stop himself from wincing at her personal attack and the venom she infused it with. "Fine, I'm a dumb fucking weed – what else? Get it all out, Rellah! Let's hear it!"

"You're not learning!" She shouted at him. "You can't stalk, you can't hide, you can't call, and you can't fight! How the rot am I supposed to keep you alive when you are set on not growing the skills you need to not die? Tell me, since you think you have it figured out!"

A twig snapped beneath the pressure of a boot in their periphery and even on the receiving end of Rellah's rage, Hyatt recognized it as intentional, a mistake no member of their pack would make. "I wouldn't push him too far, langevia – that's Hyatt of Brathnee, Slayer of Cern. He lives through fights that should have killed him, all the time."

Rellah turned with her whole body, squaring herself against whoever was suicidal enough to interrupt her tirade, but froze solid. Her eyes flashed between recognition and confusion, and her mouth hung open. The silence was so sudden that even the rustle of swaying branches seemed reluctant to intrude upon it and Hyatt tracked Rellah's gaze until he saw Jenna, carving into a honeyfruit with her paring knife as she leaned against a tree four paces away. His thoughts tangled as he tried to place her familiar face in a setting she shouldn't have been in, and he opened his mouth to speak but like Rellah, words refused to form for him.

Jenna looked from Rellah to Hyatt and when neither uttered a word, she turned her attention to the fruit in the palm of her hand and slid her blade under its hard shell again. "Hey there, Rel."

"Hi – uh," Hyatt replied before it registered in his mind that she'd spoken to Rellah instead of him, adding another bucket of broken thought-shards into the pile of debris forming in his head. "What?"

"How..." Rellah started, but her words got lost halfway between her and Jenna, and she took a half-step forward as if she could catch up to them before they melted into the air. "How are you here, Jae?"

# FOUR

Jenna sheathed her knife and grabbed the honeyfruit in her cupped hands, prying it open with her thumbs until the shell and meat of it ripped away from its pit into two halves. She held out one half of the pale fruit toward Rellah, her upturned forearm host to pocked scar tissue that began just above her wrist and disappeared under her pushed-up sleeve near her elbow. Rellah's gaze traveled along Jenna's arm over the cratered, hardened flesh and continued up to meet her gaze, his pack-mate's expression something Hyatt had never seen in her before.

"Claimed by a Skarren," Jenna confirmed as Rellah took another tentative step toward her, as if she was feeling her way across a bridge that might give way at any moment. "I heard a rumor there was a pack of Claimed, so I thought I'd go–"

"You know that's not what I mean." Rellah's words hardened to stone, but the spaces between them sounded like they were crumbling.

As the two women stared each other down, Hyatt felt like he was eavesdropping on a conversation not intended for him. He only realized he'd looked away from them when he discovered himself studying a tuft of grass in the shadow of a nearby tree, and consciously returned his attention to the two of them.

"You know each other?" He hoped his interjection would dilute the strange tension rising between them, but Rellah's knuckles remained white, and Jenna's eyes had the dangerous glint he remembered most from the first time he'd met her.

"We –" Jenna started.

"No, we don't." Rellah cut her off, stalking past Jenna toward the interior of the pack's campsite. "You can sleep here, but this is not – it will never be your home."

Hyatt watched Rellah walk away, expecting the acid in her tone to singe the leaves in her footsteps, and Jenna kept her posture without following Rellah with her gaze or body. After a moment, she took another bite of the honeyfruit still dripping in her hand, pushed away from the tree she was leaning on, and walked toward Hyatt.

"It's good to see you, Hyatt." She lingered as she passed him, looking him over from his boots to the top of his head before her vision tracked downward to meet his gaze. "This life suits you."

He dug for something to say, but untangling his condolences for her encounter with an Heir from his gratitude for her compliment took too long and by the time he formed words, she was six steps past him and moving between slender trees beyond the reach of his voice. He found himself standing alone, looking back and forth between receding silhouettes as Rellah and Jenna moved away from him in opposite directions.

*What just happened?* He ran his fingers through his hair.

Following Rellah seemed like he would be reigniting their fight, so Hyatt turned back to the gear table and picked up a pair of pitons. He checked the spikes for pitting and rust and brushed the dark dirt from the thumb-sized eyelets through their heads, then returned them to the bag he'd dumped them from. He uncoiled his bundle of rope and ran it through his hands, fistful after fistful, to ensure there were no cuts or frays. Satisfied, he coiled it again and dropped it into his pack. One tool after another, he inspected his gear and returned it to his bag, then fastened the clasps that held the top flap closed. By the time Hyatt was finished checking his equipment, he was certain enough time had passed for Rellah and Jenna to reach their destinations in camp.

He slung the pack over his shoulder and set off toward his shelter but found Bex on the way, seated with their back to a massive elm tree and repairing their jacket with a needle and thread. They glanced up just long enough to identify Hyatt before turning their attention back to the folded leather in their lap, their needle flickering in the light as it plunged through the thick fabric. Hyatt eased himself into a seated position beside them, crossing his legs and watching them work.

"Fixing a tear or adding a stitch?" he asked.

They peeled back a fold of the fabric to reveal the dark yellow thread they were sewing into the flap over the jacket's buttons. "You okay?"

The question wasn't what he expected, and he looked up sharply at Bex. "What? Yeah – of course. Why? Yeah."

His torrent of clipped responses brought a faint smile to Bex's lips, and they shrugged as they kept their eyes on their stitching. "Dead Haleu, a dead Iron, fought an Heir... just another day in the Reclaimed for Hyatt?"

He chuckled, a dry note that sounded tired even to him. "No... but I'm okay. We're all still here."

Bex cocked their head to the side, conceding his point as they made two quick turns with their needle to knot the thread. "How many of your branches did Rellah break?"

It took Hyatt a breath longer than he felt it should have to realize Bex's first question had been a gentle primer, adding momentum to the conversation before getting to their point. "It's fine."

Bex's silence felt like a complete repudiation of Hyatt's reply, but he preferred it to the conversation they seemed inclined to have, so he changed the subject. "How long did it take you to get good at fighting?"

They chuckled at the question but considered it for a moment as they coiled their leftover thread around two fingers to store it. "I'm okay at fighting, but not great – not like Rellah. I just... I grew up Cern, so it was always there since I was a sprout. I was learning to fight when I was learning to talk. Why?"

Hyatt leaned forward over his crossed legs to stretch his lower back, then planted his palms in the dirt to support himself. "I keep drilling with Rellah and Veck, practicing, and I'm learning the movements... but every time I get into a fight, the world gets blurry and it's like... it's like I'm seeing everything in flashes. Like a flip-book."

Bex slid their needle into their sewing kit. "We call it flood sight. Your eyes send what you see to your head, to make sense of it, but not wanting to die isn't a thought – it's a feeling. It floods the connection between your eyes and your head with wet, suffocating feelings that compost the message, and all you see are the parts that make it through."

"Huh." He tried to visualize the explanation, messages running around inside him like the Lines that Brathnee Garden was famous for. "How do I fix it?"

"Care less about dying. You can't control that anyway, so worry about standing in the right place and fighting the right way." Bex replied with another shrug. "If you die, you won't have to worry about it anymore – and if you don't, what were you worried about?"

"That's... insane." Hyatt shook his head. "How am I supposed to stand in front of an Heir and not think about dying?"

Bex smirked as they tucked their sewing kit away. "If you were really trying to avoid dying, what were you doing, standing in front of an Heir?"

His pack-mate's logic was so absurd that Hyatt couldn't find the most important part to argue amidst everything wrong with their point of view, and was surprised to find himself laughing. "Okay, good point."

Bex tapped the side of their head twice with a slow nod, emphasizing their wisdom. "Now pay for it – go see if Kenna has any meat cooking that you can bring me."

Hyatt chuckled and forced himself back to his feet. The afternoon breeze moved through the branches above him, quietly shifting the leaves. The crisp, dry scent and feel of the gust made him pull his jacket closer around him as he headed toward the center of camp, letting go of his fight with Rellah and Jenna's jarring arrival for the moment. Instead, he focused on the firmness of the earth beneath his boots, the dashes of blue sky and white clouds that appeared intermittently between the forest canopy, and the smell of smoked meat that corrected his course toward Kenna's shelter.

*I am growing.* He drove his hands into his pockets, rolling his shoulders forward to keep the unsecured front of it closed against the wind. *Brathnee Hyatt would have spent days seething and simmering over that fight. I am getting better at living this life.*

Even though his shadow stretched out behind him, and he disturbed no leaves or branches as he walked, Kenna still glanced up from her stump as he approached. He waved in greeting and took care to step over one of the guidelines of her shelter, and she returned his greeting with a warm smile and an upward tilt of her chin.

"Veck grabbed the first batch, but these are almost done – want some?" Kenna asked, nodding to the skewered meat cooking over a bed of amber coals.

"Thank you, one would be great – can I grab a couple for Bex, too?" Hyatt glanced back the way he'd come as he eased himself down on a log beside her.

"If Bex coughs up the roll of thread they owe me," Kenna replied, but the smile didn't leave her lips and she tucked away the strands of her hair that seemed ever-present in her eyes.

He laughed, more exhalation than sound. "I'll ask them about it."

They sat in silence together for a moment, watching the pulsing colors of the coals in the bottom of Kenna's pit. She turned the skewers one at a time, exposing their opposite sides to the warmth that rose to meet them. Droplets of juice plunged into the embers and released bursts of delicious scent, hinting at whatever paste she had massaged into the strips of meat before cooking them. The smell made Hyatt's mouth water, and he realized he was hungrier than he thought.

His stomach growled to emphasize the point, and Kenna's smirk widened. "You can have a couple, too."

Hyatt rocked to the side to bump shoulders with her in silent gratitude, then settled forward to rest his elbows on his knees. "How are you healing?"

Kenna touched her thigh where her canvas trousers hid two long trenches in her flesh, left behind by a Drashvoy claw. Touching the swollen, red welt along the edge of the wound through her pants seemed to brighten her eyes and smile instead of dimming it, and Hyatt felt the familiar tension in his stomach and dryness in his mouth as he became aware of how close they were sitting to each other. He planted his palms on the log on either side of himself and shifted just enough to install another handspan of space between them, and Kenna didn't seem to notice.

"The welt is still pretty tender, but it's not causing the muscle spasms anymore, and I don't feel crazy." She looked over at Hyatt and alternated wiggling her eyebrows and bugging her eyes out of her sockets while her tongue darted in and out between her lips. "Do I look crazy?"

He chuckled and shook his head. "Not that I can see."

Kenna kept up her antics for a moment, wiggling her arms erratically and shaking her body like she was struck by lightning, then gave up her act with a laugh that collapsed into a sigh. "I guess I'll live, then. Meat's ready."

Hyatt stole one of the skewers from over the coals and bit into the succulent, dark meat. "Don't rush it, okay? We'll miss your cooking when you're back on sentry duty."

She rolled her eyes and punched him in the leg, sending a tingle down to his knee from the nerve she struck. "Go bring Bex their food. I'll get started on more."

He grabbed three more skewers and stood, stomping his boot to demand blood return to his lower leg and drive the tingle from it. Kenna waved as he walked away and he returned the gesture, but he couldn't stop himself from looking over his shoulder at her after a few paces. She was still smiling as she punched skewers through filets of meat, and her hair had fallen into her eyes again. Hyatt let his gaze linger as long as he dared before the flush in his cheeks and the thought of her looking up to notice overcame him. He searched the camp for Bex instead.

Hyatt found them with Rayce, who was listening with visible focus to Bex's recounting of the morning's adventure. He joined them without a word, handing two skewers to Bex who continued to talk with their hands while holding the sticks.

"It looked like the Haleu thought they could take on the Iron – and the Iron killed five of them before somebody buried an axe in his neck." Bex pointed with the end of the skewer to the side of their neck to illustrate the point.

"Rot... the Iron took down five people?" Rayce asked, eyes wide. "By himself?"

Bex nodded. "Cut them down like saplings."

Their recounting of the events resurrected Hyatt's memory of the corpses throughout the ruins. He held the details still in his head, focusing on the braids the Haleu wore that were wrong for the men and women who wore them, and weapons with too few notches and scratches to belong in the hands of seasoned fighters. The scene shifted and he recalled the dead Iron slumped against the sealed door of the ruin, but the lack of pry-marks on the door or tools to breach it made no sense. Everything about the scene seemed wrong to him, and the Keeper Maps with the strange markings added another layer of mystery that he couldn't lay to rest.

"I'm exhausted," he interjected, patting Bex on the back. "Thanks for the help with training... I'm going to get some sleep."

Their brow knitted in concern. "Are you okay?"

"Just tired," he assured them.

"Well, hey..." Bex held both meat-sticks in one hand and used the other to free the clasp of the sword-belt around their hips. "Take this – it'll do until we can trade with a pack for a new Cern blade."

Hyatt reached for the belt and blade in their outstretched hand but hesitated just before he touched it. Taking the Iron's weapon felt like one more line between him and his pack, but he knew they were right – he didn't have a weapon, and he needed one.

"Thanks." He grabbed the belt and pulled it around his hips, fighting with the awkward weight of the sheathed weapon. "Just until then. See you in the morning."

He started towards his shelter, and the voices of his pack-mates receded to near silence behind him. The draw of his sleeping bag and thick, waterproofed muslin to block out the remaining daylight sounded more than welcoming, but he knew he wouldn't be able to sleep. His eyelids felt heavy and all of his major muscles demanded rest, but he could feel his brain still racing like an animal trapped in a cage.

Outside his sleeping space, he sat on a log to unlace his boots, and Rellah's words came back to him. *You can't stalk, you can't hide, you can't call, and you can't fight.*

He tried to push them aside by focusing on Bex's strange logic or how pretty Kenna was when her smile reached her eyes, but as he crawled into his shelter, it was Rellah's words that climbed on top of him to hold him down and make themselves heard. *Destroy them and forget them. This isn't trouble we need.*

# FIVE

The giant chain in Hyatt's hands was cold. The ridges where the links closed bit into his hands and the backs of his legs as he hung upside beneath it and clung to the frozen metal. He contracted his stomach to pull his knees inward, and tipped his head back to look toward the next broken concrete pillar. It looked impossibly far given the way his shoulders and forearms ached. A gust ripped through the chasm below and buffeted him, reminding him how little traction the frosty metal offered as it twisted in his grip.

"You're never going to make it," Shelara called from her perch atop the shattered top of the pillar, one knee pulled to her chest and the other leg dangled over the edge, her boot swinging back and forth above the terrifying depth against the smooth side of the square structure.

Hyatt loosened his grip with one hand, just enough to slide it along the chain without letting go, then clamped down on the links again. "Shut up."

"The chain won't hold. Why else would Rellah have made you go first?" The dead Cern woman picked up a handful of debris and tossed it into the open air like she was scattering ashes, and it made no sound as it plunged into the chasm below. "You're going to fall, and you're going to die, and my jacket will be lost forever."

Hyatt hung his head back to take stock of her, then looked up at the sky where the low, heavy clouds were darkening. A lone raindrop landed on his face, bursting hard against his cheekbone and tracing a trail up past the corner of his eye before absorbing into his hair. He held his breath, hoping it was only one, but after a long moment, he felt the next one splash against his bare neck. Thunder growled, low and resentful at the lack of lightning that should have accompanied it.

He pulled at the chain and pushed with his calves, dragging his body another handspan along the underside of it. "You're dead, and it's not your jacket. It's mine."

Shelara laughed, a joyous expression made macabre by the drizzle of blood that poured from the corner of her lip. "Your bones are going to break on the rocks down there. It's going to take you days to die. The scavengers are going to eat your flesh before you stop feeling."

"I'm so fucking glad I killed you," Hyatt tried to block out the feeling of his muscles buying into her prophecy and begging his mind to let the strain of his body end by releasing the chain.

The pelting rain picked up, spattering his face with cold droplets. He shook his head, trying to clear it, and he felt his trousers start to cling as they began to soak through. Runnels of rainwater formed miniature streams from the back of his collar and the heels of his boots, creating waterfalls that plummeted into indiscernible depths under him. Each grasp of the chain was more slippery than the last and Hyatt felt one of his calluses shred, but when he looked towards Shelara's perch, he seemed no closer than when he started.

"But you didn't, did you?" she sneered. "Jenna killed me – you didn't have it in you, did you? Jenna, who didn't want you – Jenna who sent you away with an Iron to die so she wouldn't have to deal with your pathetic crush."

"That's not what happened!" Hyatt shouted against the rising wind of the growing storm.

He flung his arm out for his next grasp of chain and slipped, his heart spiking in panic as he flailed for the wet metal until he managed to close his fingers around it. As he turned his head to clear the rain from his eyelashes, he caught the outline of Iron Sawmet standing on one of the broken columns that paralleled the ones near his chain. The decapitated figure knelt on the canted cap of the slanted pillar, his head held in his lap with its eyes staring back at Hyatt.

"Leave him alone, Shelara," The words that left the lips of the beheaded Iron's face were clear and stern. "He's not going to fall to his death."

Sawmet's defense sent a burst of energy through Hyatt and he used his legs to drive along the chain, but he froze as he felt a jerk reverberate through the metal and change in the tension of the section in his grasp. He contorted his midsection to look back towards the edge of the chasm where he began and saw a silhouette through the rain, wrapped around the chain and surrounded by fabric that snapped and fluttered like pennants in the windstorm. The figure moved with rapid, erratic grabs at the chain, closing the distance towards Hyatt with horrifying speed. A crack of lightning illuminated the flapping fabric in the shades of Keepers' robes and a destroyed visage of ground meat where their face should have been.

"He's going to kill Hyatt," Sawmet said, and Shelara laughed in malicious delight.

*Fuck! No!* He tried to cross the chasm faster, his soaked pants snagging on the links of the chain and his hands slipping.

The Keeper continued to gain on him, grabbing fistfuls of links faster and faster. Hyatt knew he couldn't outrun the corpse pursuing him and looked around frantically for another option but instead found every pillar within his sight with a dead body standing on it like a statue, unidentifiable outlines that watched him, waiting to see him die. Hyatt screamed and both of his hands slipped from the slick chain.

His eyes snapped open and he bolted upright to a sitting position in the dark, his arms flailing through the air in front of him in search of something to grab. Sweat matted him and it took the length of a frozen, foreign moment for him to realize he was in his bedroll in camp, no longer suspended above the ravine between the Laybrair and the wilderness where he'd killed the fanatical Keeper. His lungs heaved and he wiped the clammy sweat from his forehead. Even as consciousness spread through him, his layered sheets felt too much like the memory of his drenched trousers crossed over the chain, and he kicked them free.

Hyatt eased himself down onto his back again but as soon as he lay flat, he knew he had neither chance of sleep nor any desire for it. He sighed and focused on the way the memory of being exhausted in his dream clung to his shoulders and legs. He let his head roll to the side and his calibrating night vision focused on the side-pocket of his pack where he'd stashed the crumpled pages from the ruin. Staring at the pocket made his stomach tighten and he grit his teeth, unexpected reluctance and drive competing for control. With a grunt of resolve, he crawled across his tent to his pack and opened the strap that held the pocket closed. Hyatt shoved his bare feet into his boots, grabbed his jacket, and slipped out through the flap of his shelter with the compressed wad of pages in hand.

Gaps in the canopy let a million pinpoints of starlight puncture the night air, with more than enough illumination for Hyatt to make out the scattered shelters of his pack-mates amidst the preparation areas and the two unlit firepits based on the felled-logs-turned-benches that surrounded them. He slipped his arms into his jacket's sleeves against the sharp chill of the dark and walked towards the closer pit, picking at the edges of the crumpled wad of paper sphere to pull the pages apart.

*Rellah expected you to die in the chasm. Jenna sent you away so she wouldn't have to deal with you. You didn't have the guts to kill Shelara.* The dead Cern's accusations in his dream sloshed around the bottom of his mind like the dregs of a spiced honeywine in the bottom of a mug and were joined by unwelcome, waking additions. *You can't stalk. You can't hide. You can't call. You can't fight. You can't go back to Brathnee. You don't belong anywhere.*

He smoothed the pages across the tops of his thighs and took hold of the top layer, working the pads of his fingers along individual creases to flatten them. A tear welled in the corner of his eye and threatened to fall onto the paper, and he tucked his cheek into his shoulder so he could grind his eye against his jacket to clear it. The night's chill was biting without fire or sun to drive it back, but he was grateful for the cold's grip on the bones of his fingers because it gave him something to focus on. He burrowed his thoughts into the sensation of the chill as he worked out the folds of the second page, dwelling on the gnawing ache that felt like it came from his marrow and the sharpness of the pulses of cold that swirled in his flesh like eddies as the night air moved over his skin.

Leaves cracking behind Hyatt caught his attention and as he looked back to see Jenna walking towards him, and he realized she'd done it on purpose to avoid startling him. She held up her hand in recognition and he returned her gesture before turning his attention to the papers in his lap, hoping the light wasn't enough to show the thoughts he was certain were written across his face. She chose a seat on the log closest to him and hunched over, working the twin cinch straps at the top of her boots.

"The skin suits you," she said without looking up from the fasteners of her boot's straps.

Hyatt nodded without a word and as he smoothed the third sheet's creases, he realized she was talking about his jacket. He didn't know what to make of her statement and knew it wasn't reasonable to apply the condemnations of a dream to the real woman beside him, but couldn't disentwine the idea of her sending him away from the conversational notes in her quiet words. Jenna grabbed the heel of her boot and pulled, and did the same with her other one, then set them together neatly with their backs against the log beneath her.

"In Brathnee, they say you're a hero. The Iron of the Eastern Reach says you saved the world." Jenna held her forward-leaning posture, her fingers working into the hems of her trousers to roll them to her mid-calves. "Gorman's version is... more."

Hyatt moved the last wrinkled sheet to the top of his pile, weighing his lack of a meaningful answer against the stand-offish feeling of failing to respond to her second effort to start a conversation. "How is he?"

"He is exactly like you remember. Talkative. Loud." She crossed her ankles and sat up, slipping her knife free from her belt.

They sat together in the quiet, Hyatt working out the dozens of tiny folds in the paper on his lap and Jenna cleaning the dirt from beneath her short fingernails with the point of her knife. He tilted the stack of pages to maximize the starlight against them, but it wasn't enough to see through the top sheet to the layers below. With a frown, he cursed the moonless night and held them up to the sky so the stars could shine through them, but it was no use.

"You didn't come back to the Garden." There was a question in Jenna's statement but she didn't ask it and Hyatt didn't answer, so she changed tacks. "Are you paired with Rellah?"

Her ask brought Hyatt's head swiveling around to meet her gaze. "No. Women like you don't Pair with me."

"Women like me?" Even in the dim light, he could make out the raise of her eyebrow.

"I said women like her." Hyatt looked down at his encrypted map again, his cheeks burning.

Whether or not she believed him, Jenna didn't press her advantage. Instead, she switched her knife to her opposite hand, setting to work clearing the sediment under the second half of her fingernails. As the flush faded from Hyatt's face, he rotated the top page as if it would change how easily he could see through it.

"Are you Claimed?" she asked.

Her direct candor wove cracks through the version of Jenna that Hyatt had built in his memory since he'd seen her last, and in that moment she was the team leader who had kept him alive in the ambush at Vohk Bridge again – practical, succinct, and tactless. "No. I'm Cern."

Hyatt didn't know what kind of reaction he'd expected from her, but her nod of acknowledgment wasn't it. She laced her fingers and stretched, tipping her shoulders from side to side to engage her lower back, then leaned forward to touch her toes with her forehead almost resting on her knees. When she was done, she adjusted the beaded blue string tied around her left ankle and plucked at the stray strands wisping from the ends of the knot, then sat up and leaned closer to look at the papers in Hyatt's hands.

"What has you up before the sun?" she asked, nodding to the stack of pages.

Hyatt hesitated, weighing how much to say, then handed the stack of map fragments to her without a word. She tilted them a few ways until she found the best light, then flipped through each page as she squinted at them.

After a moment, she shrugged and handed them back. "What do they mean?"

"They make a map when they're stacked on top of each other in the right way, with light behind them." He held the pages up to demonstrate despite the failures of the dim starlight, then set them in his lap. "It was important enough for people to die over, so I want to know what it leads to."

"Then let's make light," Jenna replied.

Hyatt shook his head. "We don't light fires until the sun is up."

She shrugged and melted from her seat on her log to a crouch where she collected a fistful of tinder, then crawled the two paces to the edge of the fire pit and started piling the twigs in a pyramid shape and stuffing dry leaves into the center of it. After fishing in one of her hip-pockets she produced a match and struck it against one of the rocks that surrounded the bed of cold coals and ash. It flared to life with blue-violet fire and a moment later, the little structure of dry sticks was ablaze.

Jenna sat back on her heels, watching the twigs burn as Hyatt hurried around the firepit to grab the rolled light shield from the far side. He unfurled the non-flammable fabric until the attached stakes dropped free so he could plant two on the near side and the other two on the far side, letting the fabric stretch taut between them and the sides fall like tent-flaps around three sides. Dark gray smoke wafted up through the fabric but it blocked nearly all the light from the fire except through the side left open.

"Is that enough light?" Jenna asked, and in the flickering glow from the pit, it looked to Hyatt like she was fighting a smirk.

He scowled at her and glanced in the direction of Rellah's tent even though it was out of sight with a stand of bushes between them. "We could have waited for sun-up."

Hyatt turned to hold the papers between the fire and himself. As he worked to align them with the aid of the fire's light, Jenna stood and dusted the earth from her shins before padding barefoot around him so she could see the papers over his shoulder. The glow from the fire was barely enough to help him see through the layers, but as it caught a new leaf or one of the dead buds at the end of a twig flared in sudden ignition, it was enough for Hyatt to make out the design.

"What are we looking at?" Jenna asked, inching closer to him until they were almost touching.

"It's a map of the Gardens. Here – hold this side." He turned a little and Jenna stepped up beside him, grabbing the offered edges of the papers so he could point with his free hand. "Brathnee, Ceojic, Leshtara. This is Mescwar, Relcora, Vengehl, ad Wayleh... and these are the twin gardens, Jemtagen and Toshgovoy."

"And that?" She pointed at the last matching, seven-sided symbol comprised of shapes etched on each layer.

Hyatt nodded, more to himself than to her. "That's a Garden where there is no Garden. Bex was right... there are ten Gardens on this map, and there shouldn't be."

Jenna waited as Hyatt studied the map all over again, and when she spoke, she sounded neither surprised nor concerned. "What are the symbols down the side?"

Hyatt tilted the stack of pages to angle the edge of them into the firelight. "They're a glyphic shorthand – artists learn them in the Trades. This one is rope, this one is hammer, and this one is ladder."

"Climbing gear?" she asked, her brow furrowing in confusion.

Hyatt barely heard her, because his gaze had continued down to another symbol at the bottom-left corner of the paper. Three pie-wedges with missing tips pointed inward to a filled circle like the blades of a fan, and the image made him clench the paper tighter. The urge to crumple the pages again and chuck them into the fire flashed through him in an instant, urgent and insistent. Instead, he shifted the pages to misalign them, turning all the marks on the pages into disconnected fragments, and rolled the pages together into a tight cylinder.

If Jenna cared that he hadn't answered her question, it didn't show in her tone. "So what are you going to do, becquerel?"

He tucked the pages through his belt. "What do you mean?"

"Well, now you know what it means." She eased herself down onto her log and crossed her legs again, the band around her ankle catching and holding the firelight in the stones trapped between the woven strands. "Do you really think you can forget about a tenth garden? On the other hand, your pack-master wants nothing to do with it. What wins, your Haleu curiosity or your Cern loyalty?"

He looked down at the hard angles the fire's glow created on her face and the way she looked up at him with eyes devoid of amusement, and it struck him how different he'd become since he met her last. His Cern jacket, the jacket she had insisted he keep, fit him as if it had always belonged to him. He heard nothing in her words that called him unskilled or a liability, and the realization that she was trying to understand who he was felt surreal and unnerving.

"We're not Cern, we're Claimed." It felt like an evasion, even to him. "We call ourselves a pack because it's what they know."

"They're not, but you are - you're not Claimed," she replied, apparently happy to follow him whichever way he wanted to take the conversation. "You said so."

"I'm not." Hyatt turned to face the fire and fanned his hands to absorb the heat radiating from it, but he shot her a sideways glance and wondered if she'd asked him as a setup for a conversation she knew she wanted to have.

"And you're not Paired," Jenna continued, unphased by his momentary glare.

"I'm not." Hyatt felt her boxing him in with her statements but in the early hours and with the map's symbols on his mind, he couldn't find his way out.

Jenna shrugged and turned her focus to the bed of red coals beneath the burning kindling. "So, what are you going to do?"

# SIX

Hyatt hesitated at the flap to Rellah's shelter, the pages of the map rolled in his hand, trying to imagine how she would react to learning he'd kept them. He flashed back to her barely contained rage in the preparation shelter and the feel of her palms slamming into his chest, not the three-quarters strength shove of a training session but that of a Cern warrior getting ready to fight to the death. The rising sun bled color into the camp and washed warm rays over the back of his neck, trying to leech the cold that still clung to his bones.

"Rellah, it's Hyatt." He did his best to bury his words in the raider-tones she insisted he learn, hoping it bought him a little credit.

"Only you sound like you, Hy-att." Her reply was coated in the cobwebs and gravel of having just woken. "Come in."

He lingered a moment longer and looked over his shoulder into camp where Rayce and Jenna were seated together on a log by the firepit, the light shield discarded scattered embers hanging in the air above the small campfire's flames. As if she could feel his eyes on them, Jenna looked over and gave him an almost invisible nod, and he chose to take it as encouragement. With a deep breath, he pulled aside the flap to Rellah's shelter and stepped inside.

The darkness inside momentarily blinded him and he blinked to adjust until he could make out the mussed sheets of Rellah's bedroll. She was seated on an upended log on the other side in her trousers and jacket without a shirt beneath. As soon as he recognized the slender strip of bare skin from her belt to her collarbone, he averted his eyes so quickly his neck twinged and he winced.

"I can come back—" he started.

"Why?" Rellah looked down at herself and then up at him, realization dawning on her. "For compost, Hyatt – we're pack-mates. Do you need to Pair that badly?"

Mortified, he looked at her to protest but found her in the same state of dress, and looked away again as he blurted out the first thing at the forefront of his mind. "I kept the Keeper map and I found the Garden and I think we should go there."

He grit his teeth, waiting for her to explode, but the tent fell silent. He studied the wall of her tent until the moment stretched out too long and he couldn't bear it, and turned to face her. Rellah had risen to her feet and turned her back to him, and was pulling her shirt on over her head, twisting her head back and forth so her braid could clear the garment's collar before letting the fabric cascade down her back. She grabbed her jacket, the leather crunching as she bunched it in her fist and her free hand tucking the front of her shirt into her waistband as she faced him.

She started walking towards him and Hyatt locked his core in preparation for whatever was to come, but she only clapped her hand against his shoulder as she passed him. "Okay."

He stared at her as she stooped to collect her boots from just inside her shelter's flap and then ducked through it, vanishing behind the wall of canvas. Bewildered, he looked back at the log she'd been seated on and then at the flap, at a loss for what had just happened. The flap chose that moment to fight him as he tried to duck through it and by the time he freed himself of the twine lacing that snagged him, he was five paces behind Rellah who was walking across camp toward their pack-mates. He broke into a jog to catch up with her and matched her stride a half-step ahead of her so he could look at her face as they walked.

"I kept the map," he repeated, watching for any reaction.

"Yes." Rellah nodded twice and gestured in greeting to Bex, who was just entering camp on the far side  from one of their patrols around the perimeter.

Hyatt scowled in confusion. "I disobeyed you."

"You did." Her tone was neutral but not flat, ceding his points without investment.

Something in his head told him to stop, but Hyatt couldn't bring himself to leave it alone. "You're not mad?"

Rellah sighed and stopped, just out of earshot of Rayce and Jenna who were caught in their own conversation. "A dozen corpses tried to keep this broken in parts. That Iron died over it. You're ready to go up against me over it. Let's go see what's there."

She started walking again and Hyatt found himself staring after her, no less confused than he had been, and forced to jog again to catch up to her as they approached their pack-mates around the firepit. Rayce and Jenna turned to her with expectant expressions, but Rellah waited as Bex made their way toward her between the solitary trees and tarp-sheltered spaces of camp.

"During our Working Hours, we're going to break camp." She made eye contact with each of them before continuing. "We're going to trade for supplies in Mescwar Garden, or with Timber Shade Pack if we find them first, and then we're going to a new part of the Reclaimed. Pull Kenna and Veck in from the edges, pass the word – we're moving at sundown. Bex, help Hyatt make the travel plan."

Without waiting for a question or complaint, she turned and walked back toward her tent. Hyatt took a step toward following her with the dozens of questions he needed her to answer, but

Bex's penetrating gaze through the side of his head pinned him in place like he'd been speared through his temple. Jenna stood and kicked over the burning kindling in the firepit, stomping the flames into the bed of ash beneath them until they were extinguished, and Rayce set off for the edge of camp.

Hyatt sent another conflicted glance after Rellah's disappearing silhouette, but Bex stepped into his line of sight and shoved their hands in their pockets. "Ready?"

"No, I'm not fucking ready," he replied, his low tone doing little to mitigate the growl at the core of his words. "I don't know anything about making a travel plan for a pack."

"She knows that. Let's start easy – how long will it take us to get to Mescwar?"

"I don't know – why would I know? You and Rellah plan the routes and I follow one of you until we get there, or you say it's time to camp. I don't even know what direction Mescwar Garden is from here!" He turned to look to his right and then all the way around to look the opposite way, and he shrugged.

"But you decided it's time to go?" Bex asked.

Hyatt turned to face them and found something gleaming in their eyes, an unspoken thought that made him feel penetrated and judged. "So she's going to let me risk the lives of the whole pack to teach me a lesson?"

"Is that what you got from this?" Bex managed to shake their head without breaking eye contact, which only redoubled the layers of extra meaning in their gaze. "She's not ripping up your roots for trying to grow, Hyatt. She's trying to make them deep enough so you can live when you get there."

Bex's revelation was so contrasted with Hyatt's thoughts that he had no idea how to respond. He opened his mouth because he needed to fill the silence, but words wouldn't form so he closed it again. His pack-mate stood silent before him, waiting for him to digest the insight, until Hyatt nodded in base acceptance.

Satisfied, they pointed in the opposite direction of the sun's partial ascent. "Mescwar is that way, and it will take us six days to get there unless someone is injured. You need to find out if we have enough stored food and water, or if we're going to have to find food on the way. Decide how often we're going to rotate who is in the lead, and if we're moving single file or in pairs. Choose the direction and distance from our last landmark that you want us to move if we get separated. Check weapons and medical supplies."

As Bex listed the parts of the travel plan that Rellah would expect from him, he flashed back to the things he'd seen her do before moving the pack but hadn't understood the significance of. They continued to enumerate components of Hyatt's assigned task, but their words diffused behind Hyatt's realization of why Rellah was so out of sorts. The tension in her face and the sharpness in her tone came back to him in flickers and he physically flinched as he realized he'd lost track of Bex's instructions.

He knew Bex must have seen it too because they stopped and stared Hyatt down again. "You have to do all of these things, every time the pack moves. The one you skip is the one that will get your friends killed."

Kenna appeared beside him without a sound, stepping into his periphery and bending down to adjust the straps of her boots while squinting up at him in the mid-morning light. "They're right – the travel plan and the guard plan are the most important things we do. Don't get us all killed, okay Hyatt?"

Her smile through the strands of hair that dangled in front of her face added just enough satire to her request that Hyatt didn't feel like she was doubting him, but all he could do was shrug. "I'll do my best."

Kenna rolled her eyes as she straightened and pulled her errant locks back to rejoin them with her ponytail, then leaned towards him like she was going to whisper something in confidence but spoke in a regular tone. "We won't let you mess it up."

He knew he should feel relieved to have their help, but he couldn't escape the feeling that he was awash in a river and they were throwing him twigs to help him float. Memories of every time the pack had moved since he formed it with Rellah came back to him in jumbled fragments and he felt a headache forming in the center of his forehead. In place of any useful ideas, every possible thing that could go wrong on a six-day trek cascaded into his mind.

"If you're not up to it, just say so." Veck's condescension coated every syllable. "You haven't been doing this as long as we have."

*Yeah, you're great at everything. That's why you're Claimed, and not Cern.* Hyatt gritted his teeth and watched his pack-mate stroll toward his shelter to begin breaking camp, resisting the urge to spit the silent words into existence and invite the rest of his pack to take Veck's side. *I don't see Rellah trusting you with the rotted plan.*

"I'll get him started," Bex offered to Kenna, who nodded her agreement. "Come take over when your gear is packed?"

"You'll be fine, Hyatt." She punched him in the shoulder, hard enough to radiate the impact through the thick leather and sore muscle, into his joint.

Kenna headed toward her shelter, and he turned to Bex. "Okay... can you walk me through it again?"

They found a log and sat down, and Hyatt listened as Bex recounted the parts of a travel plan as if it came naturally to them. When they finished, Hyatt repeated it back to them, and Bex interrupted to add details. The sun moved higher and threw long beams of pale-yellow light through the gaps between the branches above, leaves tinging the daylight green as it passed through them. The sounds of the forest transitioned from the sounds of small birds and animals waking and searching for food to the more persistent noise of breezes through the Reclaimed and the almost imperceptible noises of his pack-mates assembling their things.

As they went over the structure of the plan again, Hyatt began to fill in his answers. Bex replied with nods of approval or questions that led Hyatt to adjust his decisions, and when they reached the end of the plan, they started over.

He was on his third repetition of the plan when Kenna returned. "All set – your turn."

Bex stood and dusted themselves off. "Okay. Hyatt, are you set?"

"I think so." Hyatt tried to hold a mental picture of all the steps in his head, rows of words etched on parchment with the parts of the plan in black and his answers in blue. "Thanks."

Bex smiled and headed toward their shelter, and Kenna took Bex's place on the log across from him. "Okay then, tell me the plan."

They ran through it again and Kenna nodded along as he covered each part, and when finished she was smiling too. "That's a good travel plan. Try again, but only include the words you need."

He frowned at her, confused. "Huh?"

She tumbled her hands, one over the other, like a waterwheel. "You explained everything with a lot of detail – and it's good that you thought of everything, but your pack doesn't need all of that. We've all traveled before. Cover everything and provide your decisions but leave out the why and most of the how."

He started over, pausing after every step to cross out and rearrange words in the mental picture he was still holding. By the time he was finished, it looked like one of his papers in Trades training, but he managed to cut the plan in half without missing any parts. Kenna favored him with a full grin, and the silent praise filled him up until he felt like he might blow apart in rays of daylight.

"That's it – just like that," she said, her eyes shining. "Do it just like that when we get ready to leave, and you'll be all set."

Her validation flooded his head with fog. He wanted to say something to return the feeling for her, but all the words in his brain melted and churned when he tried to grab ahold of them. She seemed to feel his fluster and it made her smile widen, but she looked off into the forest to take the spotlight of her attention off him so he could recover.

"Thanks, Kenna," Hyatt replied, the best he could fish out of his mind-soup.

"You don't have to thank us." She turned back towards him, put her hand around the back of his head to pull him forward, and headbutted him with just enough force to rattle his sinuses before releasing him. "We've got you."

# SEVEN

Hyatt had convinced himself he was ready to lead Hollow Bone Pack's travel until they were standing in front of him, six Claimed survivors with their backpacks loaded down with everything they intended to carry to their next destination. Behind them, it was as if the camp had never existed – he couldn't spot a single stray end of twine or displaced rock to show they had spent weeks there. He wondered, as his pack waited for him to speak, how many people had crossed through that same strip of wilderness and left no mark before them.

He cleared his throat and hooked his thumbs in his belt, a subconscious mimicry of Rellah's position of dominance when she gave the Hollow Bone Pack's new travel plans. "We're leaving for Mescwar Garden, and it's going to take us six days to get there. Travel in pairs – Jenna and Veck up front, Rellah and Kenna at the mid, and Bex and I in trail. Find landmarks every hour, point them out as the other pairs pass though, and take up trail behind them – if we get separated, track back to the last landmark and head fifty paces south of it to rally. If we have the choice between fighting and hiding, we're going to hide – this is a travel to supplies, not a travel to stake ground."

"And if we can't hide?" Veck asked from behind Kenna and Bex.

"Quick, quiet kills," Hyatt's words jerked a knot in his gut, but he said them with authority. "We don't need carbines and war cries calling down every Heir on us while we're weighed down with camp gear, and no one gets away to bring reinforcements."

Veck nodded, a grim smile touching the edges of his thin lips.

"If I get killed the travel plan goes to Rellah," he continued, searching his mind for any other parts of Bex's list that he might have forgotten. "If we run into ruins, we go around them."

"What about Heirs?" Jenna met and held his gaze, amusement lingering at the corners of her lips.

Hyatt let the question hang between them long enough for the other members of Hollow Bone Pack to exchange glances and return their attention to him. "We can't outrun a Veshtrue or a Skarren with our camp gear. We fight, and they die or we do."

The humor lines around Jenna's mouth faded and melted out of existence, replaced by something else in her eyes. "Okay, becquerel – them or us."

Her response brought nods and murmurs of agreement from the rest of Hyatt's pack-mates, and he felt like he'd just passed a test he hadn't realized he had been taking. A cool breeze cut between the trees and washed over them, and he glanced up at the sun through the canopy where it brought the thinner edges of leaves to life with almost neon colors. Veck stood up his collar to block the cold air and Bex shoved their hands deeper in their pockets, rolling their shoulders as far forward as the broad straps of their backpack would allow. Hyatt locked his jaw to keep his teeth from chattering at the unexpected gust and looked over his shoulder in the direction he was about to send his comrades, then turned his attention to Rellah where she stood at the center of their pack-mates with her arms crossed and her expression unreadable except for irises that sparkled with intent.

He took a deep breath and recalled words he'd only heard a few times before and never expected to be the one speaking. "If you have a fight in you, say so now – leave the blood in this camp before we travel."

His pack-mates looked around and he waited for one of them to raise an offense that needed redress, and when no one did, he focused on Rellah. Her eyes narrowed and Hyatt was certain she was about to call him out for disobeying her, but she turned and slipped the straps of her pack from her shoulders so it slammed to the ground as she stepped out of it towards Jenna, who crouched to ease her backpack off but held her ground as she straightened again.

"You let me think you were dead." Rellah spoke through clenched teeth and her right hand tightened into a fist. "You fucking let me believe you were dead."

Hyatt watched the two women square off, less than a handspan between the tips of their noses. He only became aware of the way his body tensed in anticipation when Bex stepped beside him to press their shoulder into his and take his hand, supporting him and warning him not to interfere at the same time. The others backed away from Rellah and Jenna, forming a loose arc around the side of them that faced toward the space where their camp had been.

"I did." Jenna didn't nod or lean away from Rellah, letting her words fill up the space between them in clear notes that offered no defense or explanation. "Now what, langevia?"

The word Hyatt didn't recognize made something savage flare in Rellah's eyes but after a moment, it faded to a controlled blaze and she bowed her head. She started to turn away from Jenna and Hyatt let out a breath that had begun to ache in his lungs, but it caught again as Rellah started to gain speed in her pivot and her arm came up. Her spinning backfist caught Jenna square on her cheekbone and took the woman off her feet, her body turning like a screw in the air on her way to the ground.

She landed hard and rolled to a stop on her back, arching and pressing her palm to the side of her face. When she turned her head, she spit blood onto the ground and a wet ring of crimson ringed her nostril. Jenna coughed and winced as she forced her elbows under herself to prop herself up, one eye clenched tight and the other squinting up at Rellah.

Rellah's face was a conflicted tangle of anger and pain. "You never came back."

"No, I didn't." Jenna lifted her palm to blot the blood dripping from her nose, then planted her hand back on the ground.

That same look of maniacal rage flickered over Rellah's face as she stepped forward, and Hyatt pictured her driving her boot through Jenna's head, but Bex's fingers tightened where they were interlocked with his. "Wait."

The two women continued to stare each other down and, in the silence, something in the intensity of it ebbed. Jenna let her head hang back and pinched the bridge of her nose, then sat forward and extended her free hand toward Rellah. For a moment she stood motionless, then nodded and grabbed the fallen woman by her forearm. They both pulled and Jenna found her way to her feet, wiping her bloody fingers on the hem of her shirt. They turned their backs to each other and recovered their packs without a word, but Hyatt noticed Rellah steal a furtive glance at Jenna as they adjusted their straps.

Bex let go of Hyatt's hand and the sudden absence of their warmth made everywhere their fingers had touched feel colder than the rest of his skin, and he shoved his hand into his pocket to drive the chill away. Rellah and Jenna settled into places on either end of the rest of Hollow Bone Pack, shifting the weight of their loads with their shoulders until they found the right distribution. Hyatt turned to look at Bex who didn't return the gesture but nodded once, almost too slight to be seen, and he took their meaning.

"Anyone else?" Hyatt searched the expressions of his pack-mates and saw something he didn't expect, a kind of relief and content that surprised him. "Okay... Jenna, Veck – let's go."

The lead pair headed toward the wilderness in the direction of Mescwar, Veck reaching out to bump knuckles with Hyatt as they passed him. When they were twenty paces ahead, Kenna and Rellah followed them. Bex stood beside Hyatt until the pair moved far enough ahead for the foliage to start obscuring them.

"Ready?" they asked.

"Yeah." Hyatt nodded and started after the pair ahead of them, his body flooding with anticipatory aches as it tried to convince him that four days through the Reclaimed was too far to travel. "Hey, what's the word Jenna used... langie-something?"

Something crossed Bex's face, a flicker of a thought that told Hyatt his pack-mate realized a truth that they were stalling to find a way around. "It doesn't have a clear definition."

"Bex... is that the first time you've lied to me?" Hyatt asked.

"Oh, rot no," they replied with a dry chuckle.

He rolled his eyes and focused on the trail they were making through the forest, and the broken silhouettes of Rellah and Kenna ahead. When he looked over his shoulder in the direction they'd come from, he couldn't find a single feature that reminded him of the camp they'd worked and slept in. Bex moved beside him, not as silent as their stalk but still quieter than the sound of Hyatt's boots hitting the ground.

"What's the word mean, Bex?" he asked again.

His pack-mate tipped their head one way and then the other, then looked skyward through their eyelids as if the branches above might have an answer. "Rellah could probably say better."

Hyatt shook his head. "I'm asking you. Is it an insult?"

"It's not an insult." Bex sighed and gave him a sideways glance, then sighed again. "It's like... first-and-forever."

*Your arrows are fletched blue because your first love wore a blue, beaded anklet...* Realization slammed into Hyatt like a hammer as words of the Iron of the Eastern Reach appeared in his mind from behind shattering, smoked glass, and he flashed back to the string he'd seen around Jenna's ankle by the firepit. "Oh, fucking compost."

If Bex heard the sound of understanding crashing over Hyatt, they didn't seize the opportunity to soften or strengthen it. Hyatt stared ahead at the partial silhouettes of Kenna and Rellah, losing them in the forest and then regaining sight of them in the spaces between low branches and tall brush. He tried to wrap his mind around the information Bex had just surrendered. Hyatt didn't know if it was the idea of Rellah and Jenna in love or the thought of an entire life Rellah had been living before he met her that seemed more surreal. Those twin notions refracted into other realizations – he tried to summon things he knew about Rellah's life before he met her and could count fewer than five facts that seemed definite to him.

*She doesn't talk about her past.* Even as the rationalization filtered through his head, it felt weak to him. *Who was she, before I knew her?*

He walked beside Bex in silence, a torrent of new questions churning in his head and daring him to pay attention to them instead of his surroundings. He fought the instinct by focusing on details, his gaze fixing on the way individual leaves shifted in the air and the different shades of earth that were exposed by leaves that had been disturbed without a sound by his pack-mates ahead. A bottomless reservoir of curiosities about Rellah tugged at the edges of his thoughts like Bex's explanation had plucked a cork free, but he kept his eyes on the spaces between the trees and the intermittently visible backs of the pair ahead of them as they navigated the wilderness.

*Was Rellah born in Moss Wall pack? Did she ever have children?* He winced as the sight of Rellah stepping over deadfall let questions begin to slip past his defenses, but as he forced them out of his mind, more replaced them. *Did she have any brothers or sisters? Who taught her to shoot her bow?*

Ahead, Kenna appeared and didn't vanish again, but crouched so close to a cluster of bushes that Hyatt knew he'd lose her if he looked away and back again. He covered the ground between them and caught sight of Rellah again a dozen paces beyond them, and turned outward to watch the Reclaimed in the opposite way her traveling partner faced.

When Hyatt and Bex were close enough, Kenna pointed to the gnarled remains of a massive tree, split open by a long-forgotten storm and host to moss that clung to the exposed interior of the trunk. "Landmark."

He looked over the distinct hardwood, committing the shape to memory. "Got it. Can you go ahead with Bex?"

Kenna frowned at the change and looked to Rellah for confirmation before she caught herself, and gave Hyatt an apologetic shrug as her traveling partner nodded in agreement. Bex looked up at the branches that blocked the mid-day sun to avoid making eye contact with anyone and when Kenna started off in their direction of travel, they fell into step beside her without a word. Rellah waited as the pair moved deeper into the wilds before stepping away from the decimated trunk of the landmark tree. Hyatt kept pace with her.

They walked together without speaking as the terrain became more broken. Larger rocks rose from the earth and roots of trees broke the surface like fish jumping from rivers. Trees on either side of them had fewer low branches, and the hanging moss that draped from their higher limbs seemed more tattered than the blankets of green draped over the boughs where they had camped. Hyatt started to notice the other changes, a gradual increase in the grade beneath their boots and the sound of burbling water somewhere in the distance to their right. He realized he liked the region of the Reclaimed before him more than the one he was leaving and slowed his stride, taking in the cool air and the paler colors of the foliage.

He was surprised when Rellah broke the silence first. "Your travel plan will probably not get us killed."

"Bex and Kenna helped me make it," he replied before he could stop himself from deflecting her version of a compliment.

"If everyone dies, will it be your fault, or theirs?" she asked.

The question sent a spike of anxiety through Hyatt's chest. "Mine."

Rellah shrugged. "Then it's your travel plan."

He couldn't get around her brutal, simple logic, so settled for a shrug of his own in response. They'd walked another hundred paces before he realized she'd sidestepped his reason for trading travel partners with Kenna, and he shot her a sideways glare as he became more and more certain she'd done it on purpose.

"Tell me about Jenna." He tried to imitate Rellah's knack for making a demand seem irrefutable, lowering his pitch on his last word and ending it on a crisp note.

She scoffed and extended her stride, forcing Hyatt to work to keep up with her. "No."

"Just, no?" Hyatt frowned. "We're just not going to talk about it?"

"The details don't matter, the result does – and we resolved it. Focus on keeping the pack on track – that's your job until travel is done." The way her fingers tapped in a rhythm against the edge of her quiver betrayed the deeper current in her mind, but her words were firm.

Hyatt fought the urge to look down at Rellah's irritated gesture but let it linger in his periphery as he weighed pressing the matter. They mantled a fallen trunk that blocked their way and on the far side, Hyatt regained sight of the traveling pair in front of them through the thinning underbrush between tall, straight timbers. Rellah's bow snagged on a sapling and she let out a low grunt as she tugged on it once to free it. The fact that she let her weapon catch on anything tipped the scales for Hyatt.

"It doesn't feel resolved. You said my job is to keep the pack on track, but you're distracted – so tell me about Jenna," he replied.

Rellah sent him a sideways glare laced with poison, but sighed. "We knew each other when we were Cern, after she left Whitefall Pack. We haven't seen each other in half a History. We heard she died."

"Have I ever told you what a great storyteller you are, Rellah?" he asked.

Her features sharpened in confusion. "No?"

"Huh," he replied, earning a glitter of realization and an unimpressed eye-roll from Rellah. "I wonder how I managed that."

She continued to shake her head and they walked in silence. Hyatt lost track of time as moments bled into hours and they rotated through the traveling order, passing landmarks and exchanging nods and knuckle-bumps with the rest of Hollow Bone Pack as they moved. As they moved together, his thoughts strayed to the symbols on the map in his pack.

"When we find where the Garden is marked on the map—" Hyatt started, glancing at Rellah.

"If we find it," she interrupted without turning her attention to him.

"—there is something else marked on the map. Something bad." He hesitated, sounding his next words out in his head before saying them out loud. "Something that could destroy the world."

He expected something from Rellah, concern or outrage, but she said nothing and continued to watch the depths of the wilderness as they walked.

"Did you hear me?" he asked.

Rellah nodded. "Yes."

Her answer gave Hyatt no conversational steppingstone to continue from, so he settled for a bewildered shake of his head. When darkness drained the daylight from them, he waited until it was his and Rellah's turn to choose the next significant feature along their route, and brought everyone together to camp.

The following morning they resumed their trip, Hyatt with Bex and Rellah back with her travel partner. It felt to him like the sun was reluctant to rise and struggled to gain distance in the sky, and the cold of the night clung to them longer than he would have liked. The hanging moss dwindled and vanished, and the low brush broke apart into smaller clusters. Leaves that shone like gloss still dragged their jagged edges across any skin or fabric that came within reach, but they were too few to gain much traction. Hyatt moved through the lingering morning fog before the sun worked up the strength to melt it, only to be replaced by a scattering of snowflakes that managed to navigate the canopy to reach him below.

"Great." He squinted at the gray-white sky and searched his jacket-pockets for his fingerless gloves. He pulled them out and forced his cold fingers into the knit fabric and leather knuckle-guards until he could close the straps at their bottoms around his wrists. "The travel plan didn't call for snow, you rot."

"Your Sklodowska likes to find her way around our travel plans. This is how you know you did okay." Rellah's chuckle was dry but amused as she held out her hand, letting the floating flakes of snow land on her palm before melting in an instant.

Her tone made Hyatt dwell on how long it had been since he'd heard her laugh or compliment anything, and the fact that he couldn't recall it worried him, but he couldn't find the words to extend the moment. "I don't think it will last when the sun gets higher."

She shrugged, wiping the snow-turned-water on her hand against her jacket. "The Reclaimed is quiet and still when it snows. It will help you learn it if it stays—"

A crash behind them cut her off as if it was summoned by her mention of quiet. Hyatt spun in time to see the forest giving way, trampled flat and blown apart by immeasurable force, as tremors began to rip through the ground beneath his boots. The heat at his core that had been fighting to keep the cold morning air outside him gave way as his heart turned to ice and his spine ached in anticipation of a fight. He watched branches rain from the canopy and heard massive trunks releasing cracks that sounded like peals of thunder as they snapped like twigs, and he pulled his borrowed blade from the sheath at his hip.

Rellah slipped two fingers into the corners of her mouth and whistled, a piercing sound that punched through the air for the space of a breath, then pulled an arrow from her quiver and showed Hyatt a dangerous half-smile. "Two Veshtrue in four days – how did we get so lucky?"

He swallowed hard and fought the urge to let his knees buckle. "Lucky us."

# EIGHT

The short, fat blade in Hyatt's hand felt entirely different than the Cern blades he was used to, and he swung it back and forth in front of himself in short, unsatisfying slashes as the charging Heir continued to race toward them. He caught sight of Veck running through the woods to his left, moving abreast of him and Rellah with his twin axes in hand. The Veshtrue barreled toward them, destroying trees and pounding the earth beneath her massive paws, and every impact sent a jarring jolt through Hyatt's entire skeleton.

Two more trees broke apart like kindling as the Heir came into range of Rellah's bow, but she lifted her eye from the round sight embedded in her bowstring to look squarely at the beast before resetting her aim and releasing. "We're days from there..."

Her words were hushed but Hyatt heard them, even through the stampeding roar of the Heir and the reverberation of Rellah's bowstring. "Rot, seriously?"

He could see it then, the indigo fletching of an arrow buried in the creature's cheekbone just beneath its left eye and the lopsided gate as it favored its rear right leg. The Veshtrue's tail smashed back and forth, uprooting the sharp brush and flinging entire tree limbs through the air in every direction like wake behind a boat. Her front claws churned the earth as she galloped towards Rellah and Hyatt, ripping deep gashes into the forest floor as she propelled herself at them in a reckless charge. Clouds of her noxious breath hung in the cold air before parting as she dashed through it.

Rellah drew another arrow, nocked it, aimed, and fired with uncanny speed. The Veshtrue planted her paws hard with an agonized roar as the new set of fletchings appeared in her pupil above the older one embedded below. The Heirs' momentum carried her over her locked front legs and she flipped, landing on her side so hard that deadfall jumped from the earth below. Her legs flailed and her torso wracked with pain as she thrashed her head back and forth, unable to free herself of the arrow fully buried in her eye. She roared again.

Hyatt sprinted toward the fallen Heir. He vaulted a jagged rock and dove beneath a destroyed tree, rolling on his side and up to his feet in his desperation to reach the beast before it found its legs. Kenna appeared on his left, her bladed polearm glittering in the late morning sun. They reached the massive beast at the same time but the sheer size of her even laid on her side staggered Hyatt as he looked up at the rise and fall of her chest, four times taller than him. The sheer absurdity of attacking an Heir with a blade less than the length of his arm crashed into his consciousness and he looked down at the blade's point as if he'd never held one before.

Somewhere blocked from his view by the thrashing beast, Veck's raging cry was followed by the wet sound of his ax blade finding purchase in the Heir's hide. The creature's roar changed pitch and she buried her nose in the forest floor in front of Hyatt, the feathers of Rellah's arrows close enough for him to touch as she tried to use her neck and head like another leg to push herself to her feet. He staggered back as she began to rise in front of him, the full strength and terror of her shoulders and back beginning to undulate beneath her thick hide.

The Heir's movement was enough to jar him free of the shock that paralyzed him, and he lifted his weapon over his head. "Kenna! The back leg!"

He spun and brought the serrated lower section of his blade down across the Heir's nose as she began to lift her head, and the teeth of his weapon grabbed the wet, suede-like flesh and caught. Hyatt yanked hard and chunks of meat came with his blade as he wrenched it free. The Veshtrue's mouth opened wide and Hyatt crushed his eyes closed as he pulled his arms close to his chest to avoid having them bitten off, just before the beast let out a blood-curdling scream and engulfed him in a cloud of her wet, deadly breath.

Hyatt felt every exposed part of his skin react like he had been lit on fire, nerves in his face and neck and hands sending bolts of pain through him that drove him to his knees. He threw himself on his face and ground his body against the earth, trying to cover himself in enough dirt and leaves to stifle the wrenching agony that seemed to get worse with every breath. He couldn't open his eyes and his lips felt like they had salt crushed into every microscopic crack, daring him to open his mouth and let the wet breath of the Veshtrue onto his tongue and down his throat.

Without his sight to make sense of it, the sounds of the fight between his pack-mates and the Heir were even more terrifying. Splintering and shattering wood combined with shouts and the ground shook every time the beast moved. Hyatt couldn't discern what was right beside him and what was far away. He scraped dirt into his hands and scrubbed it against his closed eyelids and lips, then began to crawl across the ground without any sense of which direction was safe. Rock and hard roots attacked his elbows and knees as he moved, punishing his body for his blind movements.

A hand curled into his collar and Hyatt lost control of his motion, his legs scrambling for purchase as he was dragged on his back. Instinct drove him to reach for the arm attached to the hand pulling on him, but his flail missed. After a dozen paces, the grip released and he dropped into a slump against a tree, the jagged bark rough against the back of his neck. He dragged his hands across his face to rid his eyes and mouth of debris and grit his teeth as he opened his eyes, waiting for the searing burn that would signal the end of his vision.

The wash of fire and darkness didn't come, and Hyatt watched through blurry vision as Bex and Veck fought with the wounded Veshtrue. The beast spun to snap at Bex and Veck took the chance to close with the Heir, hacking at her until it whirled to face him by exposing herself to Bex. Hyatt searched for the others and found Rellah on a branch in a nearby tree, her bow drawn and waiting for her next precise shot, but couldn't make out any of the others amidst the forest and the fray.

"—here!" The voice of a child shouted in his ear, but Hyatt couldn't make out every word. "—swim, okay?"

Hyatt turned to search for the owner of the voice but caught only the small silhouette of a boy running toward the Heir with a wire-weapon in hand. The unlikely realities of a child alone in the Reclaimed and the thought that he dragged Hyatt to safety combined with a primal need to protect the boy forced Hyatt up to his knees. He reached for the sheath on his belt before he remembered his borrowed weapon lost in the fight, but the thought of letting the child die without trying to stop it was all the determination he needed to find his feet and start after him.

"Wait!" He shouted after the boy, coughing as he staggered in his direction. "Stay back!"

Ahead, the Veshtrue turned all the way around with its vicious tail coming around in a decimating arc. As it lashed through the air, Hyatt saw Kenna impaled on one of the Heir's spikes. The tapered end of a white spike protruded from her sternum and her body hung limp around it, her arms and legs swaying as the Heir's slashing tail carried her with it.

"No!" Hyatt forgot the boy and changed course, running toward the Veshtrue's tail. "Kenna! Kenna!"

He ran full-tilt, his lungs demanding air in blazing hot contractions and vision narrowing to a tunnel around his pack-mate's impaled body. He was so focused that he didn't see Jenna until she connected with his rib cage in a spearing tackle, hitting the ground with him and tumbling together into the decimated brush. Desperation and rage made him flail to free himself and for a moment he did, but Jenna grabbed him from behind with her hands clasped across his chest and dragged him backward away from the fray.

"She's dead, Hyatt!" she shouted in his ear as he thrashed to break her grip before throwing him to the ground and landing on top of him to pin his chest and shoulders. "It's done! You can't help her!"

Hyatt barely heard her and he twisted his body under her, his elbow connecting with the side of her head with a bone-jarring impact that sent her sprawling with a grunt. Free from her restraint, his hands and feet scrambled for traction like a feral animal free of a snare until he was on his feet. He'd just oriented himself to the fight and taken a step when Jenna was on him again, her legs scissoring his and sending him crashing to the ground. Hyatt planted his palms against a patch of wet dirt and a jagged twig and he started to push up from the ground, only to be knocked over backward by a concussive wave and a blinding flash of green and violet in front of him.

The sky was beside him as his vision swam and his equilibrium upended. Hyatt clung to the rim of his consciousness to stop himself from plummeting into the dark, crushing his eyes closed as a splitting migraine blossomed in his head and the daylight became unbearable. Nausea and vertigo ripped through him as he doubled over and his hands clawed at the ground for traction. It was only as the waves of disorientation faded that he realized the ground was no longer shaking with the stomping and thrashing of the Heir. Hyatt forced his eyes open, wincing at the sun's piercing brightness, but the Heir was gone.

Instead of victory or even relief at their survival, dread ripped through Hyatt at the thought that the Heir might have fled with Kenna still impaled on her tail. He tried to run, staggering like he was drunk. The ground seemed to rock and toss under him, and the shattered ends of branches grabbed at him. By the time he reached the decimated space where the Heir had cleared the trees with her thrashing and charging, Rellah and Bex were kneeling beside Kenna's body.

"No – no, no no!" Hyatt was unable to stop his momentum and crashed into her, his hands frantically feeling over her hips and stomach as if he could find a way to plug the giant hole ripped through her center. "Kenna!"

Bex tried to pull Hyatt's arms away but he shook himself free of their grip. It wasn't until Veck joined in, grabbing hold of Hyatt's shoulders and shoving him backward like a plow driving snow, that Bex was able to get themself between him and Kenna's body.

"Hey – she's dead, Hyatt. You can't – you just... can't." Bex's words were soft at the edges but unflinching at their core, and they wove back and forth to keep their head in front of his as he tried to juke around them.

He didn't know when he went from fighting to get past Bex to embracing his pack-mate with his head buried in their shoulder, but a moment later he was crushed between Bex and Veck in a restraining embrace. The sob that ripped through him was raw and unchecked, and it rose to a scream before collapsing to a wracking whimper again. He lifted his head and brought it down on Bex's shoulder again, and Veck's arms tightened around both until Hyatt could barely breathe. Every other sound in the Reclaimed seemed to fade as if it was bearing witness to the moment.

"I'm sorry about your friend," the boy's voice broke in, and Veck loosened his grip around Hyatt and Bex as he turned to look down at the little face looking up at them.

"And exactly what kind of weed are you?" Veck barked, his fingers curling over the head of his ax.

"I'm Iron Tobin," the boy said, shoving his hand out in a greeting too mature by years for his age.

"Oh, compost – no, you're not." Veck spat and shook his head. "You're a twiggy little sapling."

"I am so an Iron!" the boy insisted, digging through the folds of his shirt beneath his jacket to produce the three linked bars hidden there. "See?"

Hyatt released Bex and took an unsteady step backward, dragging his sleeve across his eyes to clear the blur of tears from them. He looked down at Kenna and Rellah beside her, immune to his emotion or the argument between Veck and the strange child. She'd rolled Kenna onto her back and laid her legs flat, and the dead woman's unseeing eyes stared skyward like they revealed something the living couldn't see. Rellah's unspoken thoughts moved like shadows on her features and she didn't move except for a single fingertip on the hand she rested on Kenna's collarbone, tracing an oscillating arc back and forth on the bloodstained fabric of her shirt.

"Bitter fucking seeds, Sklowa must be short on choices if she's Calling sprouts," Veck snarled, taking a step toward the boy.

Jenna put her hand on Veck's arm, just above his wrist so he couldn't pull his ax from his belt. "Leave it, Veck. We need to clean Kenna and keep moving."

"It'll only take a minute," he replied, his fingers tightening around the metal head of his weapon.

"Oh yeah?" Tobin tucked his Iron links away and clenched his fists. "I saved your life, Cern! I can punch you in the nose just as easy!"

"Let's go, then!" Veck snapped and lunged toward the Iron just as Bex and Jenna latched onto him to restrain him.

Hyatt lost track of the boiling point between his pack-mate and the young Iron. He couldn't tear his gaze away from Kenna, motionless on the ground, and tried to fathom what they needed to do. The handle of the knife on Rellah's belt snared his attention as she reached for it, and he  was unable to break his fixation on her fingers curled around the polished handle. He eased himself to the ground beside his dead friend's knee, resting his hands on her shin and the top of her thigh and wishing with everything in him that they still gave off warmth. Tobin's shouts at Veck and his snarling responses faded to background noise as the reality before him settled like a terrifying blanket of wet despair and horror.

He wanted to tell Rellah he couldn't do what needed to be done to Kenna's corpse, and he looked up at the side of her face to meet her gaze if she turned toward him. When she did, the look she gave him put him back in Moss Wall Pack the day they met, refusing to face Shelara's children and tell them how their mother had died. There was a tension in Rellah's face and her eyes were vacant, save for a caution that lingered around the bases of her lashes, warning him not to make his weakness her problem in that moment.

*If everyone dies, will it be your fault, or theirs?* Her question hammered his memory like a metalworker folding steel, and tears without sobs started to burn trails down his cheeks. He nodded, and she nodded back.

"Help me," she said.

Rellah pulled Kenna's body to a sitting position and Hyatt wrapped his hands around the back of her neck to hold her upright. While he kept her in place, Rellah stripped Kenna's jacket from her shoulders and fought it down her arms until it was free of her body. She folded the garment and set it beside her, then braced Kenna as Hyatt let go so she could ease their pack-mate back to the earth. Her hand trailed slowly across the dead woman's stomach as if she was reluctant to lose touch with her, and when Rellah's fingers fell away from Kenna's form, they curled around the handle of her knife.

"Did Kenna have..." Hyatt didn't know whether to ask about children, parents, or pairing, and his pause caused him to choke before he could finish the question.

"Just us," Rellah's tone was blank and flat.

Excarnating Kenna separated eighteen pounds of bone from one hundred and forty pounds of muscle, fat, and skin. Hyatt's gut clenched and his throat closed over and over as he followed Rellah's lead, while she worked with no expression on her face as if Kenna had been an animal killed instead of a packmate they had loved. Tobin sat nearby, watching them work with the horrified fascination of a child, but said nothing. By the time Hyatt and Rellah were finished, they were soaked in their friend's blood.

Rellah used her waterskin to rinse the bones and Rayce appeared with an armful of boughs from tarn-ferns, and he dumped them in a pile beside the cleaned bones. "I'll degrease them. Go change."

Numb at his core and feeling hollow to his extremities, Hyatt moved in the direction Rayce pointed until he found himself standing over his pack. He couldn't be certain if his fingers were clumsy or if the buckles of his pack were harder than usual, but the disjointed thought appeared in his head that getting out of his shirt and pants took longer than it should have. He pulled his Cern jacket back on over his fresh clothes, and the waft of blood on the leather filled his nostrils. It fired his gag reflex but even that response felt muted, a half-hearted attempt to expel something but finding nothing left to give.

Hyatt dropped to his knees and then struggled to swing his legs in front of himself so he could lean his back and head against the broad trunk of a massive tree. When he was stable, he stayed, his arms hanging by his side and his head tilted slightly back to look up through the branches overhead toward the sky beyond. He didn't know if his eyes were open or closed, but all he could feel were the tears on his cheeks and all he could see was Kenna impaled on the Veshtrue's spiked tail with her body limp and lifeless.

He didn't remember falling asleep but woke to a nudge from Jenna's boot. "Food's ready. We're going to eat, and then we're going to keep moving."

She moved away without another word, and Hyatt blinked and looked around to orient himself. He squinted into daylight that had shifted further than he expected and made out the shapes of his pack-mates, seated in a circle as Veck passed a wooden bowl to Rayce. The little Iron was looking back at him and seeing his eyes open, struggled to his feet, and walked over.

"Are you okay?" Tobin asked, shielding his eyes from the sun with his little hand as he squinted down at Hyatt.

He had no idea how to answer that question but settled for a shrug and a nod. He pushed away from the tree and found his way to his feet. Tobin followed him back to the circle of Hyatt's pack-mates, and settled down beside him when Hyatt took a seat next to Rayce. Across the circle, Jenna offered him the large wooden bowl filled with mushroom caps, berries, and dark red tubers. The sight of food made his whole body ache with deficiency, an overt demand to fuel his muscles despite having no appetite.

"Eat." Jenna pushed the bowl into Hyatt's hands for emphasis. "The berries should help with…"

Her sentence trailed off, leaving Hyatt to wonder what the little tan spheres could be made of that would help. His eyes swept over the rest of his pack and there was no sign of Kenna anywhere, except her jacket where it lay folded in half on top of her pack between Rellah and Bex. He accepted the bowl and scooped a fistful of its contents into his hand, but suspected nothing in their nutrients would help in any way he needed them to.

Tobin took the bowl from him, picked a few berries out of it, and passed it to Rayce before squinting up at Hyatt. "Your friend was brave."

He didn't know what to say, so he said nothing. Hyatt could feel the way Tobin's compliment drew the eyes of his packmates from across the circle, but it was more akin to remembering something faded, as if they had looked at him once years ago and he could still recall what that experience had felt like. Hyatt knew he was detached from the moment, but his mind couldn't find his way back to the space his body occupied in the circle.

The little Iron waited for an answer Hyatt was unable to form, then shrugged. "I told the mean woman I was going with you to Mescwar, in case the Veshtrue comes back. She said I had to talk to you about it."

Tobin's unasked question drifted through Hyatt's head like a cloud, and he didn't know whether Jenna or Rellah was the mean woman in the Iron's opinion, but the reason they sent the boy to him was clearer. *My plan. I still have to get us to the end... the rest of us, anyway.*

*Not Kenna, though.* Hyatt clenched his teeth, and the sensation felt new against the hollowness and the numbness that saturated him. *Kenna is dead because my plan walked us right into an Heir. She's a handful of bones in a bag and it's my fault.*

"Except – we don't have to talk about it," Tobin continued, measuring imaginary weights in his little palms in a gesture that exceeded his years, "because the Accords say you have to let me go with you if I want to."

He felt himself nodding, but even as he answered, the sound of a thrush fluttering through the leaves overhead sounded closer to him than his own voice. "The Accords. You can come."

# NINE

Hyatt had never seen stone as white as the walls of Mescwar Garden. The tendrilled ivy that climbed the tall barricades and spread like veins over the full expanse appeared almost black in contrast. He was so stunned by the majesty of the garden's perimeter that he didn't notice the swath of burnt earth between him and the gate until he felt the charred dirt shift under his boot. To either side, the last thirty paces between the edge of the wilderness and the white walls of Mescwar were pocked with shallow craters where trees had been torn out by their stumps and vegetation had been burned away. The wide perimeter where nothing grew made Hyatt move with slow, intentional steps, and he was surprised by the rising urge to fall back to the Reclaimed where he felt safe.

Iron Tobin strode by Hyatt like he owned the whole world, beckoning him forward with short, rapid gestures. "Are you coming?"

As Hyatt followed him, he marveled at how the boy's irritated tone could dampen his awe at the sight of Mescwar Garden without having any impact at all on his reservations about leaving the Reclaimed. Rellah fell into step with him, and Bex joined them as they trailed the young Iron across the tilled and burned earth toward the gate. As they got closer, Hyatt could make out the heads and shoulders of silhouettes above the wall's broken upper edge.

At the gate, two men with security braids stepped into their path but seemed to hesitate as they identified them as Cern and then caught sight of the Iron bars on Tobin's belt. Hyatt watched their struggle to divide their attention between the boy and the five of them, and self-awareness crackled through him as he pictured what they saw – Cern jackets and wild hair, smeared with the grime of combat and life in the Reclaimed. He didn't realize the corners of his mouth were turning up in a smirk until it was too late to stop himself, and he knew by the wolfish grin Veck gave him that he'd seen it too and known why.

"Their nightmares will be full tonight," Veck made no effort to subdue the smug tone in his voice, and on his other side, the corner of Rayce's eyes crinkled in amusement.

He instinctively glanced to Rellah and then to Jenna for their reaction, but their faces were neutral and neither made eye contact with him as they advanced towards the Haleu at the gate. *My travel plan, my problem.*

Hyatt extended his stride, forcing the dirt to churn where his heels planted to drive him ahead of his pack, until he was standing between Rellah and Jenna as they reached the men blocking the path. He caught the white weave of their braided bracelets and as he registered the caution and tension in their faces, he was grateful neither were apprentices. The man on the left unslung his flechette carbine as they approached, tucking it under his arm so it was ready to use but still pointed at the ground.

"Easy now." Hyatt opened his hands and kept them low, palms pointed towards them. "We're traders, on our way north. No trouble here."

"Heavily armed and light on the goods for traders." The taller man on the right crossed his arms and set his jaw, but didn't reach for his weapon, which Hyatt took as a good sign. "Which pack are you with?"

"Hollow Bone," Bex answered, catching up with them and adjusting the strap of their pack.

The Security Journeyman on the left narrowed his eyes. "That's not a Cern pack."

"We got a Keeper here," Rayce replied, bemused. "He knows everything about Cern."

Veck laughed in a condescending tone. "What makes you think we're Cern? Don't we look like garden weeds?"

Hyatt felt like he was back on the iron chain in his nightmares, surrounded by people trying to get him killed while the chain itself threatened to dump him to his death in the ravine below. He clenched his fists before realizing he'd done it, then opened them to avoid showing aggression to the guards. Instead, he pressed his tongue to the roof of his mouth and hissed before clipping the sound with his teeth.

To his surprise, his attempt to make the sound worked, and his companions fell silent as if he'd snatched their voices from their throats. In his periphery, he caught the sparkle of raw approval in Rellah's eyes like dew on her lashes and had to contain the concussive explosion of pride in his chest as he tried to avoid the brewing confrontation. He gestured to Tobin, who walked to his side like he owned the whole of the Reclaimed including the city before them.

"Hollow Bone isn't a Cern pack - we fight Heirs to keep Cern and Haleu safe." He put his hand on Tobin's shoulder. "This is Tobin, Iron of the Broken Mountain. We're here to trade for supplies, and then we'll be gone - no fights, no trouble, and we don't want to stay here. Are you going to refuse hospitality to an Iron, or are you going to let us through?"

The man on the left began to reply, but his partner raised his voice to talk over him. "No, of course not - welcome to Mescwar Garden."

He crossed in front of them to herd the other Security Journeyman backward, and Hyatt led his comrades through the great gate of the garden with Tobin at his side.

"I would have killed him," Tobin said, glancing back at the silhouettes of the two guards.

Hyatt dug an herb-twist out of his jacket and peeled away the wax wrapping, taking the time to bite and chew the end of it before answering. "Have you killed many people?"

"No," Tobin admitted, but his voice gained a quieter, confessional note as he continued, "but I would. Iron Coraline said people only do what they're supposed to when they're in danger, so sometimes they have to know they're in danger."

Hyatt tilted his head back and forth, weighing the advice, then shrugged. He couldn't entirely disagree with the little Iron's premise, but confirming the Iron's bias towards murder felt wrong, too. Instead, he led the way a few dozen paces further into the garden before stopping and signaling for everyone to gather close.

"I meant what I said to the guards." Hyatt regarded his pack-mates who had had formed a half-circle in front of him. "No fights, no trouble. We have enough trouble behind us, and probably enough trouble ahead of us - we don't need enemies here, too. We're here to get supplies, maybe some information if we can, and get back outside the walls where we belong."

Rellah and Jenna nodded, and Bex murmured their assent. Rayce scowled and looked to the side, finding sudden interest in the rooftops of the nearest building, and Veck crossed his arms with a scowl as he studied the ground.

"Everybody understand the plan?" Hyatt asked, alternating his attention between them until Rayce felt his stare and grunted his concurrence.

"Yeah, got it," Veck nodded, but didn't uncross his arms.

*Good enough.* Hyatt looked over his shoulder to take in the lay of the garden, but it gave him no indication of where to begin. Instead, he saw Haleu watching them. Children stared in unsubtle fascination and adults crossed the path to keep space between themselves and the strangers in their Garden. Lips moved as they murmured to each other, inaudible remarks about the outsiders. As Hyatt planned his next move, Iron Tobin shifted to stand in front of him.

"I protected you and your friends all the way to the Garden, and you're inside now." He stuck out his hand towards Hyatt. "You're welcome."

He felt the corner of his mouth tugging upward into a smirk but fought it as he grasped the Iron's forearm tightly, then released it. "Thank you."

The boy's nod felt like a parody of a gesture he'd seen an adult make, and he turned on his heel toward the broad path into the Garden. Tobin stopped a dozen steps away and turned to face him again, studied his shoes for a moment, and squinted up at Hyatt.

"Sorry about Kenna. She was brave." He nodded again, more to himself than to Hyatt, and turned away again.

Hyatt felt Veck stiffen beside him in a way that seemed to distill the air into a void where only danger could live. "What does that weed know about being brave?"

"Leave it alone." Hyatt watched Tobin turn down one of the walkways that broke from the main path like streams diverging from a river, happy to have space between the boy and the members of Hollow Bone Pack. "He's not our problem anymore."

"Every living Iron is a problem." Veck spat into the grass, then turned his back toward the vanishing Iron. "Now what?"

Hyatt didn't have a good answer, but the possible alternative of Veck coming up with his own spurred him toward an acceptable one to keep everything on track. "This way."

He glanced back at the towering gates of Mescwar Garden and led his companions toward what he hoped was the middle of the settlement. He started down the path away from the Iron's direction, and the shadows of his pack-mates that stretched out in front of them told him they followed his lead.

With every Haleu they passed on the street, Hyatt felt his past and his future intersecting along jagged lines. His life inside Garden walls was not so distant that he had forgotten what it was like, but far enough behind him that the clean fingernails and carefully brushed hair of Mescwar's residents felt foreign to him. He led the pack past a man with a Journeyman Petaler braid on his wrist and it made Hyatt feel his own faded and worn Journeyman Artist braid sewn into the lining of his Cern jacket, how proud he had been to earn it, and how little it meant to him in his life outside Haleu society.

"Home is more a time than a place, huh?" Bex dropped into step beside him.

Their question didn't quite speak to the feelings and thoughts that Mescwar tangled in his mind, but they were close enough that he could shrug in acquiescence without feeling like he was lying. They walked together in silence as they passed a group of children hurling tarrow nuts at one another in a parody of pitched battle, ducking and skittering to avoid the fist-sized orange projectiles, but lowered their throwing arms in hesitation as they caught sight of Hollow Bone pack.

"Don't do it," Rellah muttered behind Hyatt, and he looked back to see Veck roll his eyes as he dropped an overripe tarrow-nut that splattered rotten goo when it hit the ground.

On the other side of the street, lattices blooming with climbing winter flora framed a grassy park in a half-circle where wicker benches surrounded low, masoned fire pits. Men and women sat near the fire, their cheeks and fingertips blushed from the chill but smiling and happy as they talked in unquiet tones and ate little meals from crisply folded wax-paper wrappings. Hyatt took in the scene as he led the way beyond the park's entrance and caught himself wondering why none of the Haleu in the park were armed and what they would do if an Heir stampeded through the Garden's wall.

At the next intersection, a signpost made of stacked blocks emblazoned with descriptive glyphs gave Hyatt the information he needed. He led his companions to the right, and homes and parks began to give way to workshops and yards for construction. The sounds of tools replaced the sounds of conversation, and the doors and windows of the structures were taller and wider. More and more, braids for builders and artists took the majority away from the more diverse professions of the central Garden area.

"What is this Garden known for?" Rayce asked.

Hyatt wracked his brain, trying to recall his lessons as a child, but all he could recall was the legendary white walls of Mescwar they had already seen. "I don't know. I never lived here."

The rows of workspaces on either side of the path ended at another signpost, and on the far side of the cross-street, larger buildings with sliding barn doors dominated the Garden space. They reminded Hyatt of the warehouses in Brathnee, and he was relieved they'd chosen the right section of Mescwar to search first.

"They'll have what we need here." He nodded towards the four-story buildings with their shallow-pitched roofs.

Rayce stopped beside him and began counting on his fingers as he looked over the rows and columns of buildings but gave up before he reached the total he was trying to discern. "Does it take all of this to run a Garden?"

"Yeah." Hyatt shrugged as he crossed the intersection and headed down the street on the other side. "Some of it is daily supplies, but most of it is either set aside for major tasks like wall repairs or water storage, or reserves for the months when trade and gardens provide less than they expected."

"How weak do you have to be to need this much, just to live?" Veck scoffed in open disrespect, resting his hand on the head of his axe and shaking his head. "More proof Gardens are just compost piles with structure."

*We're here because they have supplies we don't have but need.* Hyatt felt a faint, prickling need to defend the refined logistics and contingency plans that High Rangers presided over, but as soon as it rose in his mind, he realized it was a barb from Veck to make Hyatt sound more Haleu than Cern. *Not today, rot-head.*

"We're looking for someone with a green and blue braid." Hyatt gestured ahead down the road. "Let's get what we need, and get out of here."

# TEN

"I'm Journeyman Provisioner Heidi Kesh, in charge of Warehouse Eleven. Welcome." The young woman's gaze moved from one face to another as if unsure who she should be addressing.

The large building behind the woman was constructed differently than the storage houses of Brathnee, but the oversized doors and the shallow pitch of its roof were similar enough to Hyatt. When he caught Rayce's questioning glance, he gave a small nod to confirm they were in the right place.

Rellah stepped forward and looked Kesh up and down, visibly assessing her before locking eyes with her. "We're from Hollow Bone Pack. We're short on climbing gear. Do you have any to spare?"

She smiled like she was excited to be able to help and nodded with overeager enthusiasm. "I do, yes! Come on in!"

Provisioner Kesh grasped the iron handle of the door and leaned to throw all of her weight into driving it aside, metal rollers on the top and bottom grumbling from the friction as she slid the barrier out of their way. Her stride into the building was more bounce than trudge and Hyatt watched Veck and Jenna exchange a look, but whatever agreement they reached was never spoken aloud and they followed her inside. Hyatt trailed behind them, blinking to adjust from the brilliant daylight to the relative darkness of the building.

Rows of shelves divided the yawning room into aisles. On either side of each one, the shelves held gear that was neither identical nor perfectly stacked, but a system of organization ran through it all that was immediately apparent to Hyatt. The provisioner moved along one of the aisles, tracing the shelf with her fingertips as she moved.

"We don't get many Cern in the Garden." Her voice was clear but low, and Hyatt was unsure if she was talking to herself or to him until she continued speaking. "I always wondered – do you live in the ruins, out there?"

The question took him by surprise, and he was grateful that her eyes were focused on the piles of supplies on the shelf in front of her. By the time she looked over to ensure he had heard her, Hyatt had managed to chase the bemusement from his features.

"We live in camps – like where you live, but without walls or roads." Rayce picked up a shovel from the opposite shelf and inspected its shaft and handle, then returned it with a dull clank. "Sometimes we live near ruins."

Provisioner Kesh nodded and her breath suggested she had another question to ask, but instead she grunted in satisfaction as she pulled a ladder into place against the shelf in front of her. "Found it."

She climbed with quick, sure steps on the ladder's narrow rungs, glanced down to ensure none of her visitors were directly beneath her, and started tossing gear off the shelf. Lengths of rope landed in front of Hyatt, followed by muslin bags that made clattering sounds as they struck the hard-packed earth of the warehouse floor. He took a step backward to create more space between himself and the falling equipment and bumped into Jenna.

She put her palm between Hyatt's shoulders to steady him. "Miss garden life yet?"

He hadn't been able to place what felt claustrophobic about Mescwar, but Jenna's question brought it into focus as he looked at the stockpiles of equipment that covered every horizontal surface on both sides of the aisle. There was so much of it, compared to the pack he had lived out of for months, that he couldn't imagine what it was all used for.

"Not at all." He kept low and turned his attention back to the provisioner who had climbed two shelves higher to reach different gear. "The sooner we are out of this Garden, the better it will be for everyone."

Jenna followed his gaze up the rungs of the ladder to the woman near the top of it. "Soon, but not too soon?"

It took Hyatt a moment to realize what she meant, and he met Jenna's smirk with an eye-roll that failed to dim the rising flush in his cheeks. "As soon as we can."

Sounds of heavy items shifting across dusty planks filled the warehouse as Kesh looked through her stores. She grabbed the ladder and hopped, using the absence of her weight on it to pull and shift it a few finger's widths before her boots landed on the rungs again. She performed the stunt two more times, and the ladder's top clicked into slots on the shelf's face. After a tug to ensure it was stable, she moved to the edge and slung her leg up onto the shelf so she could roll onto it.

"Hey," she called down to them as her head popped into view over the edge of the shelf, "do you want spring-loaded anchors, or manual ones?"

Hyatt had no idea what it took to climb an unscalable cliff and paused to see if anyone else spoke up, but no one filled the gap he left for them. "If you have both to spare, we'll take both."

The provisioner disappeared into the depths of the shelf and reappeared a moment later with a pair of satchels. "Look out!"

The leather bags hit the warehouse floor with a reverberating clank. A moment later, Kesh was climbing back down the ladder, rung after rung in practiced motions until she was standing in front of Hyatt and Jenna again. As she dusted herself off with her palms, she looked around the men and women that surrounded her and scratched her head.

"Can you carry all of this?" she asked, studying the pile of gear she'd pushed off the shelves where it lay scattered around them like fallen stars.

"Yes," Rayce replied behind her.

For a moment Kesh looked skeptical, but her expression melted like a cloud falling apart on a summer afternoon, and she shrugged as she shouldered a bundle of rope and headed toward a table near the front of the warehouse. "Okay. Grab the gear and pile like-stuff together, so I can account for it all. We'll have you on your way in no time – where are you headed?"

Bex adjusted their backpack and slung one of the coils of rope across the top of it, and followed Kesh. "Northeast."

The Journeyman Provisioner had begun flipping through an open book to find the latest entry but at Bex's response, she paused and turned to face them and understanding blossoming in her dark eyes like ink in water and certainty in her voice. "Oh, no – you're climbing Bloodstained Mesa."

Hyatt swiveled his attention to Provisioner Kesh, and in his periphery he caught every one of his pack-mates pulled to her the same way, as if tethered with string. The unison of it was enough to drive the Haleu woman back a step and she searched their faces as if she couldn't make a connection between what she'd said and how they'd reacted.

"Oh, the fuck we are!" Veck set down his bundle of climbing anchors and crossed his arms, amplifying the tension in the warehouse like it was a claustrophobic shack.

Kesh's face paled a shade, and Hyatt stepped between her and his pack-mate, trying to keep his voice tranquil and inquisitive. "What, uh… what's Bloodstained Mesa? Why is it called that?"

She shot a sideways glance at Veck and bit her lip in indecision, but Hyatt nodded in silent encouragement and she found herself nodding with him. "It's unscalable. Not with this equipment, not by our best climbers – it can't be done. Hundreds of people have tried, and almost all of them fall to their deaths, so the rocks around the base are…"

She trailed off as she became more and more aware of the four other sets of eyes staring a hole through her, and Hyatt couldn't stand in front of all of them to keep her attention. Veck laced his fingers behind his head and he kept them there as he walked outside, his eyes turned skyward and his breathing intentional.

"Bloody. And that's why they call it Bloodstained Mesa," Bex finished for her, taking a bite of their herb-twist and grinding it between their molars with a thoughtful expression. "Not very creative."

"No one's ever climbed it?" Hyatt asked, hoping he'd misunderstood her.

Kesh looked like she was going to answer his question, but glanced around to see if doing so might upset the four of them left in the warehouse, and settled for shaking her head instead. Jenna put her hand on Rellah's shoulder, who continued to stare at the provisioner as if the lore around the terrain feature was somehow Kesh's fault, but allowed herself to be pulled away. Hyatt followed them with his eyes until they stopped between two of the tall warehouse shelves, leaning close to talk in low tones he couldn't make out, then Hyatt turned his attention back to the provisioner.

"What's up there?" he asked, and when she started to shrug and shake her head, he held up his hand to stop her. "What do they say is up there?"

"There's nothing up there." Kesh's voice was low but insistent. "With field glasses, you can see trees growing from the top, but – here. I'll show you."

Hyatt followed her to a nearby gear table and waited while she shoved aside a backpack with a broken strap and a pile of detached jacket-sleeves to clear space on gridded paper underneath. She sketched a crude design with her wax stick, concave on two sides and lightly arched across the top. Kesh drew short, vertical lines from the top that looked like spikes until she added branches in the form of downward-slanted hash-marks in both directions. Hyatt could tell Kesh was no artist, but he began to see the rudimentary design take form.

Hyatt tapped the trees at the top of the design. "How high is this?"

"Higher than carrion birds fly." Kesh pursed her lips like she was searching her mind for something to compare it to, and she pointed to the side of the drawing where her line bowed inward before swinging back out beneath the cap of the mesa. "You can't climb this, not with everything in this warehouse – not with all the climbing gear in Mescwar."

Bex stepped closer to join them around the table, taking in the provisioner's drawing. "Maybe that's not where we're going. What else is out there?"

Hyatt entertained a moment of hope as he considered the possibility, but something inside him ground that flare of optimism to dust. For no reason he could put words to, he knew without a shred of doubt that the Keeper's map pointed to the place Kesh called Bloodstained Mesa. His certainty felt like a claw-trap clamped around him, teeth sunk in and inescapable.

"Nothing. There's an Iron Hold beyond it, a lake…" the provisioner trailed off, her eyes unfocused in her search for other details to offer before sharpening again as she shrugged. "That's it. After that, it's the Rim."

"Compost," Bex replied dourly, then shrugged. "If that's where we're going, then that's where we're going."

"Not with my gear, you're not." Kesh's nervous tone didn't match the decisiveness of her words, but she said them anyway and she got louder as she talked. "I'm not giving you rope and stakes just to get you all killed. Give it back."

Her tone drew attention from Rellah and Jenna, who started back their way as Bex favored the provisioner with a raised eyebrow and a lopsided, amused smirk. Hyatt stared at her, unable to recall any time in his life that a Haleu provisioner had denied anyone supplies that were stocked and available. Kesh looked from one of them to the next and her fingers tightened around the edge of the table beside her like it was holding her upright, but she didn't withdraw her demand.

"What's going on?" Rellah asked, standing inside the provisioner's personal space but ignoring her as she talked to Hyatt.

"Journeyman Provisioner Kesh believes we're all going to die at that mesa," Bex volunteered, just nonchalant enough to sound bemused, "and doesn't want to lose the equipment she gives us to climb it with – so she wants it back."

Rellah looked from Bex to Hyatt as if looking for another version of the story, but all he could do was nod. She spun on her heel to face Kesh, so close their noses were almost touching.

"Explain it to me." Her instructions to the visibly nervous provisioner left no space for Kesh to misinterpret her.

Kesh leaned back against the table behind her, and Hyatt saw her pulse thumping in her throat. "I'm not giving you gear for that. Not without the High Ranger's say-so."

"We can take it," Veck called from the doorway behind them, silhouetted against the afternoon sky beyond.

"We're not taking it unless she gives it to us," Hyatt replied before the option could gain traction with their pack-mates, and he rested his hand on Rellah's shoulder for a long moment before she took a step back from Kesh. "Is that what it will take – an order from your High Ranger?"

The provisioner swallowed hard and looked grateful for the space to breathe as she nodded. "I'll give you the gear if High Ranger Genshei tells me to."

"This is a waste of time," Veck growled from the door, but when Hyatt shot him a look, he turned his attention to the Garden outside the warehouse. "Fine."

"Let's go," Hyatt said. "Leave the gear. Provisioner, we'll be back for it."

For a moment, he wondered what Rellah would do in his place, and decided to leave the warehouse without looking back to see if the others agreed, argued, stayed, or followed. Veck pivoted away from the door's frame as he approached, clearing the way for Hyatt's purposeful stride. He heard the rustling sounds of Bex, Jenna, and Rellah setting aside the equipment they'd already stashed in their packs and as Veck joined him at the edge of the street, he broke out an herb-twist to chew on while he waited. When the others joined him, he wrapped the wax-paper over the remainder of his snack and shoved it into his pocket.

"Gardens are so..." Bex began, looking up and down the road with a mixture of fascination and concern as they came to a stop beside Hyatt, but abandoned the thought. "What's the plan?"

Hyatt looked around, trying to see what Bex saw. The layout of Mescwar Garden was different than Brathnee or Ceojic had been, but the lampposts and building styles along the crushed-rock pathways made it familiar. The Haleu that moved to and from their homes and jobs gave Hyatt and Bex a wide berth and long, lingering glances, but they wore clothes that reminded Hyatt of where he had grown up. The walled settlement bore no resemblance to the Cern camps he had seen or the ones he had made with his pack-mates, and he wondered if being inside the Garden was as strange to them as his visit to Moss Wall Pack had been for him.

"No change," he replied with a shrug, before returning his attention to his pack-mates. "We get High Ranger Genshei to give us the okay for the supplies, and we head to the mesa."

"You think this Genshei is going to just give us the gear?" Rellah sounded doubtful. "His provisioner was pretty set against it."

Hyatt had no idea what the High Ranger would decide, and he hoped his face didn't say so. "Provisioners are supposed to keep supplies stocked so the Garden doesn't go without – she's doing her job. The High Ranger is going to want unpredictable Cern travelers out of their Garden so they can keep the peace – that's their job."

Bex frowned. "Is he going to just meet with us?"

The question staggered Hyatt's confidence and he paused, remembering when he'd spoken with the leaders of Brathnee and Ceojic Gardens. The memories brought with them an unexpected wave of self-awareness as he realized that the first time had been less than a year prior. It felt like he'd grown a decade since then. For a moment the intervening months and moments seemed to wash over him like a waterfall and threatened to drown him, but just before their current dragged him under, he caught hold of the one thing both of his discussions with High Rangers had in common.

"No, not with us – but I know who the High Ranger will talk to." Hyatt glanced left and right to get his bearings, then started walking.

# ELEVEN

Veck took one look at the end of the path and stopped in his tracks, his arms crossed and his forehead drawn taught with disbelief. "No – no rotted way!"

Hyatt kept walking as if he hadn't heard Veck's protest until he reached the end of the path between two clusters of trees on either side. Beyond them, the ground was carpeted with Low Flowers. Their blue petals glittered with frost that clung to them like impossibly delicate rime and created a blanket broken only by dark gray steppingstones that picked up where the walkway through Mescwar stopped.

"Rellah, you can't be okay with this!" Veck protested behind him, no closer than where Hyatt had left him standing. "Jenna?"

"Trust Hyatt – he knows what he's doing," he heard Rellah answer with the sound of her hand clapping against Veck's shoulder in reassurance. "If he says this is the way, this is the way."

Her simple, direct validation felt like someone had flooded his system with herocaine and Hyatt felt heady for a moment. He couldn't fight the urge to glance back at her, and she matched his gaze with a smile that was as bright as any he'd seen from her.

*Where has that been?* He turned away and hoped it was quick enough to mask the relief and fulfillment he felt bleeding across his features, and pointed his attention across the stepping stones. *That is what I need.*

He stepped into the field of Low Flowers, keeping to the flat stones between hexagonal plots of blue petals that had been curated to leave two fingers' widths between one section and the next. Six-sided columns rose unevenly throughout the space, some taller than Hyatt and others as low as his knees, but all formed from the same ash-gray material and topped with garden beds that held still more Low Flowers. Every few steps, divergent paths of stones moved away from the central line that bisected the space and led to white metal benches or parts of the curated flower garden that were out of sight.

By the time he looked back to signal his companions to wait, Bex was already a few stones behind him and sending the gesture back to the rest of the pack. Satisfied that no one would stomp through the flowers to make a point, Hyatt continued along the flat stones toward the heart of the elevated flower beds.

Beyond a wall of raised columns, Hyatt found Tobin seated on a bench with his back to the tall divide and his feet hanging inches above the ground. The Iron's pack rested against one of the curved arms on the end of the bench, and his three linked bars lay expanded on his legs. His eyes were closed, and he was as still as a statue.

Hyatt hesitated and wrestled down the clench forming in his gut. He tried to banish the sensation of cold water in the crevices of his brain that cascaded down the vertebrae in his neck like a babbling brook that insisted he was somewhere he shouldn't be, seeing something he shouldn't see. The feelings of intrusion and danger moved inside him like a coiling snake, and he imagined wrapping two hands around their twisting form to squeeze them from existence.

He opened his mouth to call out to the boy, but the air in his lungs caught and refused to make sounds. He closed his mouth and swallowed hard as he thought through the basic components of greeting another person and tried again.

"Tobin?" Unable to choose between whispering and raising his voice, Hyatt winced at the way his voice cracked in the space between.

If the boy heard him, he gave no indication. Hyatt looked back at Bex, who only shrugged and waited with each boot on a separate stone. They stood as still as Tobin was but looked ready to move as fast as they might need to. Hyatt grit his teeth as the thought that he was neither as serene as the boy nor as prepared as his pack-mate rattled through his brain.

"Iron Tobin, it's Hyatt," he called again, only slightly louder than before.

Tobin's head turned in a slow, steady motion until his unfocused eyes settled on Hyatt. The slack in the boy's features and the way his eyelashes remained still without blinking unsettled him, and when the Iron's eyes lit with recognition and his face reanimated, it sent a shiver down Hyatt's spine that almost buckled his knees.

"Oh - hi, Hyatt!" Tobin called out with a half-hearted wave.

He returned the low gesture. "Is it okay if I come over there?"

The Iron nodded, and Hyatt made his way along the series of stones that broke away from the central walkway until he reached the bench. The metal arm was cold as he leaned on it to ease himself down onto the seat, and the interwoven metal bands of the back offered support but no comfort against his back.

"What were you doing?" Hyatt glanced back at Bex, but his packmate had chosen to stay on the primary path of stones through the flowers.

"Waiting for her to tell me what to do," Tobin replied, fidgeting with his linked metal bars, shifting the connecting rings back and forth.

"What did she say?" The boy's answer sent the same feeling through Hyatt that he remembered from telling scary stories with his friends as a child.

"She didn't answer yet." He sounded matter-of-fact. "Sometimes it takes a while."

The Low Flowers that blanketed the ground in front of them quivered in a breeze that was enough to shift their blue petals but barely enough for Hyatt to feel, and he focused on the thought that the rustle of the tiny blossoms was coincidental until it felt stable and reliable. He found himself looking at Tobin's fingertips instead, turned pale around his little nails by the cool air and their contact with the bars of metal in his lap. Hyatt curled his own fingers to gauge how cold they were by the flex of his joints and wondered what kind of divine being would call a child their champion.

Their conversation had faltered again, and he cleared his throat to restart it. "Would you like to help me with something, while you wait for your answer?"

Tobin cocked his head to squint up at Hyatt. "With what?"

"We are leaving Mescwar tomorrow, and we need to talk to the High Ranger – a man named Genshei – before we go." As Hyatt talked, his desire to simplify the story for the boy wrestled with his caution about sharing too much with someone outside his pack. "We need his permission to take climbing gear from here with us."

The Iron's fingers stopped fiddling with the linked bars in his hands, and competing thoughts played out on his delicate features as he considered the request. Hyatt waited with intentional patience, resisting the urge to pour more words onto the scale of Tobin's deliberation.

"No." Tobin shook his head. "I have to stay here."

Hyatt felt his mouth opening in surprise and forced himself to close it. "You do? Why?"

"I don't know what Sklodowska wants yet," he replied, "but if I wait here in the flowers, she'll tell me."

Hyatt didn't know what to say. He ran his fingers through his hair and looked back at Bex, but their back was turned and the sight of them offered no help, so he nodded as he let his arm fall to his side.

"Okay. I hope you get your answer." He stood and shoved his hands in his pockets, his eyes moving from the iris of one Low Flower to another.

He crossed the steppingstones to Bex, who looked past him at Tobin still seated on the bench before turning their attention to Hyatt. "We're on our own?"

He put his hand on Bex's arm as he stepped around them onto the broader row of flat stones that led away from the tended field of blue flowers. "We're on our own."

They made their way along the walkway and had almost reached the edge when the Iron called out from behind them. "Wait!"

Hyatt looked back to see Tobin fumbling to attach his metal bars to his belt as he half-stumbled, half-jogged across the stones after them. Bex stepped off the path to the street beyond. By the time the Iron reached Hyatt, he was out of breath.

"She says... I need to go... with you." Tobin panted beneath each part of his statement, his cheeks flushed.

*Compost.* Hyatt hoped his face gave off more curiosity than alarm. "To see the High Ranger?"

Tobin shook his head as he waited for his breathing to balance. "No – to the climb."

"Did she say why?" he forced himself to ask. *Rotted compost.*

"She said I'll find out when I get there." The Iron reacted to Hyatt's dubious expression by doubling down. "I trust her, and she trusts me. If she says I need to go with you, I'm going!"

"Okay – I hear you." He held his hand up in mock-surrender to Tobin's insistence.

The Iron nodded in resolute confirmation and dusted his palms against each other in a comedic prohibition on future discussion. "Good. Let's go."

*This is going to go over badly.* Hyatt began to turn over the possible reactions from his pack and it led him to realize that his companions were no longer gathered nearby waiting on his return, a reality that set off a different set of alarms in his head.

"There." Bex pointed down the path to where Jenna leaned against a wall beside the door to a large building.

Above Jenna on the wall, a sign with three mugs marked it as an Assembly and caused his stomach to clench as visions of the mayhem Hollow Bone could wreak inside flashed through his head. He started with a walk that turned into a brisk stride before surrendering to a full jog that left Bex rushing to catch up with him and the Iron trailing behind them.

She hooked her thumbs behind her belt and rolled her head against the wall to focus on Hyatt as he approached. "They're inside. Rellah is keeping an eye on them."

Her assurance took some of the urgency out of Hyatt's rush, and he slowed to a walk. "I thought you were going to wait at the intersection."

"You didn't say wait – you said you'd be right back." Jenna shifted her attention over to Bex and then down to Tobin who had just caught up. "Veck is going to love this."

Hyatt rolled his eyes and pushed the door to the Assembly open, with Bex close on his heels. Sounds of conversation and the thud of wooden mugs had been trapped inside but hurried to meet them as they traded the chill of the street for the warmth of wall radiators and congested bodies. The scent of sweet, stale honey mixed with mint and autumn berries hung over the space.

He searched the crowd of clustered Haleu drinking and playing games on the tall, long tables that divided the open floor into segments, and found Veck on the far side of the room. Rayce was seated at the end of the table looking disinterested in the conversation between his pack-mate and a woman wearing a Haleu jacket but whose face was hidden from view. He didn't see Rellah and he scanned the crowd in search of her once more before starting across the room toward Veck and Rayce.

Hyatt had almost reached their table when he felt a hand curl around the grip of his belt-knife. He brought his elbow down to pin the thief's arm in place against him, but their other hand grabbed his wrist and rotated it away to strain the joint of his elbow and shoulder.

"Fixation," Rellah said from behind him, releasing his arm.

Hyatt pulled his arm free with more force than he needed and looked around to see if their almost-altercation had drawn any attention, but couldn't tell who was looking at them because they looked like Cern and who was paying attention to them because of her practical exercise.

"I was going to save that Haleu woman from Veck," he argued in a low but vehement whisper.

"Your enemies don't care what you were about to do, or why you thought it was important." She strode passed him, and Hyatt glared at Bex for letting her sneak up on him. "Right, Iron Tobin?"

"I would have double-stabbed you," he agreed with authority, as if double-stabbing was a practiced skill of his.

"Yeah?" Hyatt flung his exasperation at Rellah in a single word as he caught up with her, just before they reached the near end of the table where Veck and Rayce were seated with several empty mugs around them.

" ... ruin you forever. You wouldn't survive it," Veck was saying as Hyatt came within earshot.

The Haleu woman across the table tucked her hair behind her ear and then reached across the table to trail her fingers down along the seam of Veck's jacket. "I could try..."

"Hey," Hyatt began, and felt immediate regret for starting with such a soft interjection. "Finish your drinks. We're going."

At the other end of the table, Rayce gave a single, stiff nod that said he heard and understood the instruction, picked up his mug, and threw his head back to gulp down the last third of its contents with loud quaffing noises. When it was empty, he set it down firmly next to four other empty mugs. His cheeks and the bridge of his nose were reddened by consumption but his eyes looked clear and alert to Hyatt.

"It will take me a while to finish." Veck kept his focus on the woman in front of him, his gaze shifting from her eyes down to her lips and then back up to her eyes again. "I'll meet you at the gate tomorrow morning."

The Haleu woman visibly blushed at his insinuation, and Rayce shook his head as he passed behind her on his way to Hyatt's side. Bex gave Hyatt a sideways glance to see how he would respond. Around them, wooden mugs clacked and voices rose and fell in conversations and arguments that seemed to be the pulse and lifeblood of the establishment.

Rellah moved around the table until she was shoulder to shoulder with Veck, and rested her forearms against it as she regarded her pack-mate and then the woman across from him. She picked up Veck's mug and when he started to reach out to recapture it, she fixed him with a blank gaze that threatened to pull his entire existence into it and consume it if he looked over at her. His grasp fell short and he let his hand rest on the table in the shadow of his mug as Rellah picked it up, emptied it in two gulps, and put the mug back down where it had rested before she touched it.

"Let's go." Her voice was no louder than Hyatt's had been but seemed to weigh ten times as much.

Hyatt felt a twinge that surprised him as Veck sighed and nodded, shrugged an apology at the woman across the table, and turned to leave. His pack-mate's willingness to challenge everything he said wove a bitter web through Hyatt's nerves, and watching Veck cede to Rellah after her two words of instruction tugged at the barbs that set inside him. He ground his teeth and tried to stop his frustration with Veck from bleeding over to Rellah, but found himself wishing she hadn't stepped in before he had a chance to handle the confrontation on his own.

Hyatt turned around to see Tobin with both arms outstretched over him, his hands wrapped around the body of a mug that he was helping himself to. The Iron had just raised the lip of the vessel to his lips when Veck passed Hyatt and caught sight of him. From behind, Hyatt caught the waft of the honey-mint liquor on his pack-mate's breath and watched his back stiffen, his shoulders rise, and his fists close.

*Great. Here we go.* He stayed close to Veck's left side and he didn't know if Bex followed his lead or reached the same conclusion on their own, but they shadowed Veck on his right as they moved toward the door. *If we can just get outside...*

Tobin took a solid gulp from the mug in his hands but his eyes moved across the rim to lock on Hyatt and his companions, and he set the cup on the table again. As they approached, the Iron headed toward the front door of the Assembly. They'd almost reached it when two older children stepped into Tobin's way, both with their arms crossed.

"Who are you?" the taller one demanded, his brow darkening his eyes into caves of distrust and aversion.

Tobin stopped and looked him up and down, then did the same to his companion. "I'm the Iron of the Broken Mountain. Who are you?"

The shorter boy scoffed, an explosion of air that fluttered his lips and blew up the strands of hair on his forehead. "No such thing as a kid Iron. You're a liar."

*Well, rotten fucking wet compost.* Hyatt stepped closer to Tobin and in his periphery, he saw his pack-mates spreading out in a pattern that should have frightened everyone close to them if anyone in the Assembly had ever learned Cern fighting techniques. *We made it most of an afternoon without a fight.*

The second between the Haleu boy's challenge and the Iron's response seemed to last the space of two-hundred heartbeats, enough time for Hyatt to conjure a ghastly image of Tobin's wire-weapon whistling in an arc around the busy room and slicing limbs and necks that set off geysers of blood. He even had time to wonder if the Iron would discriminate between Haleu and Claimed, or if the boy would trust Sklodowska to guide his aim and kill only those she wanted dead.

Instead, Tobin pressed both of his hands to his chest with his middle fingers almost touching, arched his back so far he was at risk of falling over backward, and let out an uproarious laugh that reminded Hyatt of a fat, old man and seemed entirely out of place coming from the boy. When he finished, he leaned forward and gestured with his little hand for them to lean closer as well.

With their heads all together, Tobin said something that Hyatt couldn't make out. Whatever the boy said, it drained the color from the taller boy's face and darkened the shorter boy's features in embarrassment. The Iron straightened his posture as the two boys took hesitant steps backward, their eyes fixed on

Tobin as he walked between them and continued to the Assembly's entrance.

Hyatt followed the Iron onto the street, and a moment later the rest of Hollow Bone stood around them in the waning afternoon light. His curiosity demanded an answer to what Tobin had said to the two boys, but the glower Veck pointed at Tobin forced itself into a higher priority.

"Hyatt says you need to talk to the High Ranger. He'll talk to me," the boy said with absolute certainty as he crossed his arms and looked around at the adults who encircled him. "He has to."

The tone Tobin ended his sentence with all but screamed there was more to the story and Hyatt opened his mouth to explain the rest, but Rayce beat him to it. "And?"

"After we talk to the High Ranger -after I'm going with you to the rock place." Tobin's voice lost none of its resolute tone.

"Out of the question. No," Veck barked from across the circle. "We're not taking an Iron with us."

Hyatt felt a flash of aggravation, but it came with a thread of pride when he realized what he needed to do in the moment before any of his companions caught hold of the opportunity to help him out. "It's not up to you, Veck. This is my travel plan, and I said he's coming – so he's coming."

He watched the anger rise in Veck like a pot filling with water.

*This can't go on. We can do it the Cern way if you want, Veck.* As his pack-mate turned to square his body to Hyatt with his lip curled to expel a retort, Hyatt took a half-step backward so he was equally square to Veck and pulled his jacket open with a shrug of his shoulders so that the handles of his belt-knife and his blade were visible and within inches of where his hands held the front panels of his coat open.

"Hey, come on—" Rayce's voice was padded with the comforting assurances of a warm blanket.

Hyatt's Cern hiss-click cut off Rayce's entreaty with such force that the empty space where the rest of his pack-mate's words would have existed felt like the air would be too thin to breathe. "Veck wants to fell trees and see where they land. Go for it."

The embers that lit Veck's eyes were blazing coals that promised the kind of violence that Hyatt had spent most of his life terrified of and avoiding at all costs. The same tension he knew well pulled at the long muscles on either side of his spine and made his legs feel heavier than they were, but deep within that anxiety another sensation began to radiate that was less familiar – the primordial thing he had felt outside the Laybrair when he had stabbed the rogue keeper over and over until the man was dead and Hyatt had been drenched in his blood. Instead of trembling, his fingers became the most still he had ever known them to be capable of, as if the marrow in every digit had become as placid as the surface of a lake with no wind to move it.

Hyatt felt his elevated pulse crest a plateau and then begin to descend, and his vision felt sharper and clearer. He was aware at some subconscious level that none of his pack-mates had spoken since he cut off Rayce, but he could no longer see them as his periphery collapsed to lend extra acuity to all five of his senses' attention to Veck. He felt like he could see the blond hairs on the side of the man's neck, smell the matted oils in his hair, and taste the quality of the air that spanned the four paces between them.

"Look who thinks their roots are deep enough –" Veck started.

"You're still talking," Hyatt cut him off, the movement of his lips to form words the only motion in his body. "Do something."

Veck's hand drifted toward the head of his axe, but stopped just before his palm and fingers made contact with the metal. He stared at Hyatt like he was trying to see inside him. Hyatt didn't blink or shift his weight.

The moment broke and Veck, rather than lifting the weapon from his harness, let his hand drop to his side. "This is a mistake… but it's your mistake to make."

Hyatt held his ground and continued to fix his gaze at Veck across the space between them until his pack-mate averted his eyes. The dark, potent thing inside him that had filled up his body from his heart to his fingertips seemed to lap against his outer husk like the water sloshing around the rim of a mug, and it refused to recede as abruptly as Veck had capitulated to Hyatt. As he watched his pack-mate shift his focus, Hyatt could picture himself pulling his knife free as he rushed toward Veck to bury it in his kidney over and over with the frenzied violence of a varmint clawing to escape captivity.

"You made your point." Bex didn't lean closer or reach out to him, but somehow seemed to reduce the space between them with their low, unintrusive tone. "Let it go."

Bex's voice drew Hyatt's attention off Veck and as he turned to face them, their attention was on something else. The way their profile shed the murky poison in Hyatt like a ridgepole on a rooftop shedding water surprised him, but he felt it become watered down and seep into the cracks of his being, back to whatever dark well offered it safe harbor.

He took a deep breath and let it out slowly, as he became accustomed to the hollow feeling that remained in the spaces vacated by the sensations that had overcome him. "Iron Tobin will get us into the Gloratt, to see the High Ranger. Once we have the climbing gear, we'll leave for the mesa."

# TWELVE

The Gloratt at the heart of Mescwar Garden reminded Hyatt of the seat of governance from his childhood in Brathnee, but larger. The white stone and green-black ivy of the Garden's outer walls also comprised the columns, steps, and structure of the Garden's center. Their contrast, both serene and sinister, let awe and trepidation compete for control of Hyatt's mind.

He climbed the flat, broad steps toward the two guards posted at the entrance to the central chamber, the rest of Hollow Bone Pack fanned behind him like they were patrolling the Reclaimed in search of dangers. The carvings on the nearest columns held his attention. Angular lines at the top and bottom became more fluid and streamlined as they came together at the center of the pillars as if they were unfinished on either extreme but artistically perfect at their center. Iron Tobin didn't seem to notice them at all as he stomped up the stairs in front of them.

"Is this our best plan?" Bex asked from a step behind Hyatt, their voice just loud enough to reach him but go no further.

"No," Veck replied before Hyatt could. "We are counting on a child to get what we need. It's a rot plan."

"I'm not a child!" Tobin snapped at Veck, glaring up at him in raw indignation. "I'm the Iron of the Broken Mountain!"

"You're a stupid fucking weed –"

Hyatt tore his attention away from the advanced craftsmanship and glared at Veck. "That's enough."

Veck wore censure in his narrowed eyes and bands of tension in his neck, but he said nothing. Hyatt continued climbing the steps beside Tobin, lagging a step to stop his shadow from enveloping the young Iron. When they neared the top of the stairs, the two guards descended a step with their gloved hands on the grips of their long-handled cleavers, but Tobin held up his Iron bars and they uncurled their fingers from their weapons' wooden handles.

"Where'd you get those bars, sapling?" The corner of the more lanky guard's mouth barely twitched upward as she lost her battle to keep confusion and amusement from her face.

"Sklodowska." Tobin looked down at his belt to fasten his identification to it, immune to the woman's skepticism.

Hyatt watched her expression falter and she glanced at her partner, who could only offer a helpless shrug. By the time Tobin finished working the clasps on his bars, the woman's face had adopted a more cautious expression.

"Is the High Ranger expecting you?"

"No." Tobin resumed his climb and walked between the two guards without giving either one another glance. "These people are here with me – let them through."

Hyatt followed Tobin up the last three steps, and the stockier guard hurried to outdistance them toward the entry of the Gloratt. He pulled the lever on the right side of the large, embossed metal doors, and they swung to reveal the large meeting room beyond. Hyatt lingered to let the guard move in ahead of them, and watched the melting frost from the man's boots leave wet boot-prints on the pale green tile beyond the threshold.

"High Ranger, an Iron is here to see you." The guard drew himself as tall as he could as he spoke but when the High Ranger looked up from the far end of the table that occupied most of the large room, the guard halted in his tracks as if he had run into an invisible wall.

"Journeyman Topher, that introduction does no credit to the Iron and gives me very little to work with." The High Ranger set down the papers in his hands and moved along the length of the table with a comfortable, confident stride. "Show them in."

Hyatt stepped over the threshold into the Gloratt and in his periphery, he saw Rayce follow suit on his left while Bex moved in on his right. As the High Ranger continued toward them, Hyatt could play out in his mind the movements of the rest of his pack, crossing the entryway and sidestepping to occupy more space in the room while standing clear of the doorway itself. By the time the High Ranger reached him, his companions owned enough space to contest it and the guard had a Claimed fighter behind him no matter which way he turned unless he retreated further into the room.

The guard realized the situation and shifted uneasily before taking a step backward toward the wall of the chamber, while his companion lingered on the steps outside rather than try to find space just inside. Hyatt glanced back to track the second guard's movement and he caught the glint of approval in Rayce's eyes as his companion saw him do it, and by the time Hyatt looked back at the High Ranger, the leader of Mescwar Garden had focused on him.

"I don't know you, Iron – but you are welcome here, of course." The man extended his hand towards Hyatt. "I am High Ranger Genshei. Which Hold are you from?"

Iron Tobin popped out from behind Hyatt and moved around him like a varmint circumnavigating a tree. "Hey- he's not the Iron! I am!"

Hyatt clenched his jaw to fight the smirk he felt forming, but if the High Ranger was surprised or amused, his face was the perfect mask of diplomacy and let nothing but courtesy bleed through. He lowered the angle of his hand toward Tobin and when the Iron wrapped his little hand halfway around the High Ranger's forearm, Genshei returned the greeting with a firm grip around the child's arm too.

"Of course. I had heard that there was an Iron who was called before he found his trade, but did not expect the privilege of meeting you." He released Tobin's arm and took an almost imperceptible step backward as part of the same motion, creating enough space between them that Tobin wouldn't have to tilt his head all the way back to look up at him. "Welcome to my Garden."

"I'm Tobin, Iron of the Broken Mountain," he replied, beaming with pride.

From the far end of the table, the three Haleu that Genshei had been conferring with started to make their way toward them. The High Ranger made a curt nod toward the door, and the guard who had shown them in took his opportunity to make his escape. Hyatt tracked him across the chamber for a moment and felt a spike of anxiety as images flickered through his mind like firelight – the guard finding a Security team, the team bursting through the door of the Gloratt with flechette carbines roaring, and the savage fight in a confined space as Hollow Bone pack tried to survive not only the ambush but their race to the walls of the Garden and into the safety of the Reclaimed beyond.

*And... that's who I am now. The safety of the Reclaimed.* Hyatt pursed his lips and banished the thoughts to the edges of his awareness, and turned his attention back to the High Ranger.

"These are my advisors – Master Speaker Matau, Master Provisioner Tarrent, and Master Hunter Rasheeb." The High Ranger gestured to the three men who were attempting to navigate to their leader's side without coming too close to Rayce. "Who are your friends?"

Tobin looked up at Hyatt and over his shoulder at everyone he could see. "This is Hollow Bone Pack. We met in the Reclaimed."

Hyatt watched Genshei's gaze shift from one face to the next, taking the measure of everyone before him, and it was jarring to imagine how differently he would see Hyatt than he might have six months before. The High Ranger met his eyes and Hyatt stared back at him, wondering if there was anything left in his face that spoke to the Haleu he had been in Brathnee Garden. When he completed his inspection, he turned his attention back to Tobin.

"You've brought seasoned Cern raiders with you, Iron – but you'll find no reason to fight in my Garden. We honor the Accords here, and we tend the Low Flowers that grow here. Three Irons have been Called from our home in my lifetime, and we are proud of them."

Veck coughed at the High Ranger's assurance, and Hyatt watched Jenna drive her elbow into his side. He searched his periphery for reactions from the others, but their faces were masks of apathy. If the High Ranger noticed Veck's derision, he starved it of fuel by ignoring it.

"I knew the Iron of the Broken Mountain who came before you," he continued, gesturing toward the table. "What became of her?"

Tobin turned and walked beside the High Ranger. Hyatt watched the Iron's purposeful stride the boy probably hoped would convey maturity but instead made him seem more like a child doing an adult's job. As they reached the long, marquise-shaped table, Genshei pulled a chair aside for the Iron.

"She said she was going to be a Keeper." Tobin climbed onto the high-backed seat. "I think she went east."

"Well." The High Ranger made his start of a reply sound like an entire thought while adjusting a chair for himself and sitting across from Tobin.

"We don't want to fight – we just need stuff to climb with." Tobin scowled in a way that made him look exactly his age. "Kesh told my friends no."

The High Ranger's brow creased in confusion and he looked across the table at Master Provisioner Tarrent, who had been rotating his braid on his wrist in an idle, halting way but stopped at Tobin's mention of Kesh. "Is Mescwar short on climbing equipment?"

Hyatt watched the stocky man's expression but caught only the subtle shake of his head. "No – in fact, we should have a surplus. I'll find Kesh, see what's going on."

Genshei nodded and returned his attention to Tobin. "I assure you that my Garden is aware – that I am aware – of the hospitality afforded to you by the Accords. If you can provide me with a list of what you need, I'll have it assembled for you and your friends."

The tension in the High Ranger's voice sounded new to Hyatt and as he watched the fifty-year old man make promises and commitments to the young boy, the familiar tightness in his stomach set in. *Is he... afraid of Tobin?*

The Iron beamed at his accomplishment and spared a moment to smile at Hyatt and then stick his tongue out at Veck. "Thank you."

"May I ask where you and your friends are intending to climb?" Genshei offered no reaction to the sidebar between Tobin and Veck, his attention fixed on the Iron and his question devoid of judgment.

"Um..." The Iron's smile faltered and he touched his fingers to his lips in thought before frowning as he realized nobody had told him.

"Your Provisioner called it the Bloodstained Mesa," Bex chimed in, hooking their fingers in their belt. "It's a few days north and east of here. Do you know it?"

Hyatt was again surprised by the lack of change in Genshei's expression, but the Master Provisioner's surprise and amusement was as evident as the alarm written on the Master Speaker's face. They both recovered quickly, but their reinforced neutrality only solidified the authenticity of their spontaneous expressions in Hyatt's mind.

"I do." The High Ranger paused. "I'm sure that Sklodowska has a reason to ask such a difficult thing of you, but... that is a very hard climb, Iron Tobin. I am beginning to understand why Provisioner Kesh was reluctant to send you with Mescwar equipment—"

Veck slid his chair back. "You are full of understatements. You said it was hard – Kesh said it was impossible. You said she was reluctant – she refused. You talk and talk, but say nothing. We are wasting our-"

He had started to head for the chamber's exit, but Jenna's hand on his shoulder held him in place as she directed her words at Genshei and Tobin. "It has been a long road to your Garden, and not all of us are familiar with Haleu customs."

Across the table, Master Hunter Rasheeb lifted his index and middle fingers from the polished surface as he spoke. "Is Hollow Bone pack deep in the Reclaimed, far from the Gardens?"

Hyatt only realized he had begun relaxing into the conversation when the man's tone drew his nerves taut like a bowstring again. He couldn't place what it was in the Master Hunter's words that made his question feel intrusive and set off alarms in his head, but he felt the muscles in his shoulders and neck tighten at the possibility of giving him an answer.

"No," Jenna replied without missing a beat.

Rasheeb waited as if he expected Jenna to elaborate on the topic but the pause started to gain gravity as she offered nothing more, and Master Speaker Matau broke the silence before it could roll in an unfavorable direction. "Master Rasheeb is only concerned for your safety, honored guests. The Reclaimed north of here is unlike the wilds nearer the center of the valley – there are no other Gardens that way, so fewer paths and the wild things have no fear of us."

"Have you traveled the Reclaimed much?" Rayce raised an eyebrow in a parody of heartfelt curiosity. "To compare the different parts of it?"

Matau's fluster was limited to a quiver of the space between his eyebrows and when he smiled, it looked authentic instead of a mask for his response to Rayce's barb. "Surely not as much as you have – but we listen when we welcome visitors to Mescwar. Is your experience in this area different than that?"

The continuous shifting of their conversation's center of gravity built a tension in Hyatt that seemed lost on the High Ranger, whose features remained animated but soft as he focused on Tobin. "No one is questioning your judgment, or Sklodowska's will – an Iron north of the Garden can only be good for us. We lose more Hunters in that area than in any other part of Mescwar, and we have seen no Keepers from the Cloi north of here in a season."

"What? Why didn't you send for an Iron?" Tobin interjected.

Hyatt watched the way the High Ranger's fingers stayed motionless where they were half-curled against the table's smooth surface, but in his mind, he saw Genshei move them in a single rolling tap of constrained irritation. "As Master Matau said, the edges of the Reclaimed tend to be more savage than the heart of it. We only find trouble in the northern reaches, and so we do not go into the northern reaches. Why bother an Iron with a problem we can avoid entirely? There was no dispute with another garden, no violation of a Warning – just the Reclaimed, reminding us that the valley belongs to her."

Tobin's expression shifted from astonishment to something more petulant, a darker cloud lingering around his eyes and beneath the edge of his lower lip. The Iron looked up at Hyatt with unspoken expectation but he hadn't expected the boy to turn to him for a remark, and by the time he managed one, Tobin had turned his attention back to the High Ranger.

"My friend Hyatt will finish the talking now." He slid off his chair and landed with both knees bent and his feet planted as if he expected the floor to shift beneath him, then stood. "I am going back to the Low Flowers to think about this Garden's problems."

The High Ranger stood in deferent courtesy and watched as the Iron stalked from the large, central chamber of the Gloratt. Hyatt looked over his shoulder as well and waited until the massive doors to the room closed before easing himself into the seat that Tobin had vacated.

"Kesh will give you the best gear we have." Genshei punctuated his decision with a nod to Master Tarrent. "With the blessing of Sklodowska and Mescwar climbing equipment, I am certain you will reach your destination."

"Enough with the Butcher Queen compost." Veck rolled his eyes at the astonished look from Tarrent and the glare from Matau that his remark earned him.

"Thank you, High Ranger – the gear will help." Hyatt paused as he looked from Genshei to his Speaker and Hunter, and searched for words he hadn't expected to exchange with the leader of the garden. "Can you tell us anything about the space between here and the mesa?"

Master Hunter Rasheeb frowned. "It is unwelcoming, even by Reclaimed standards. There are six or seven Heirs that stalk that region, and the Cern pack there consider any Haleu they encounter to be advance scouts for an expansion of the garden."

"Are they?" Bex asked in their favorite, non-committal tone.

"No," the Master Speaker replied, "but that can be difficult for Cern to believe, since we expanded our walls to accommodate our people ten years ago."

"What kinds of Heirs?" Rayce asked.

"Skarren and Clastryne. We hear rumor of a Drashvoy, but none of my Hunters have seen it." Rasheeb paused and his eyes became distant for a moment, as if he was recalling a scene so graphic it took precedence over his vision. "We have been lucky in that way."

Hyatt flashed back to the creature that had chased him and Rellah through the tunnels of an ancient ruin. He heard the strange hiss of the creature moving in the corridor and its deafening roar as it came for them, and the stale smell of the long-forgotten space filled his nose as if he was still there.

"I hope your luck holds," he replied. *I hope ours is as good as yours.*

# THIRTEEN

Under the shadow of the massive gates of Mescwar Garden, Provisioner Kesh oversaw the work of three Apprentices as they stacked climbing gear on the ground in organized piles. When the last bag of pitons was opened, inventoried, and resecured, she walked around the arrayed equipment to join Hyatt.

"This equipment is all surplus," she said as she crossed her arms and surveyed the gear one last time, "so we can afford to lose it – but since you have nothing to trade for it, we'd like as much of it back as you can recover."

Hyatt didn't miss the way that the end of her sentence seemed to hang in the air between them. "If we live, you mean."

She shrugged and tilted her head back toward the warehouse district, releasing the apprentices who needed no second invitation to get as far away from the men and women of Hollow Bone as they could. "Some of you will survive, but if you lose two or three to the rocks, I don't expect you can carry all the gear back. I included some cache markers – you can collect the equipment and leave it marked for our hunters to look for."

The candid way she talked about his companions dying should have jarred him, and he chose not to dwell on how little defensive resistance it raised within him. "We'll see what we can do."

He clasped arms with Kesh and held onto her forearm for a moment before releasing it. As she headed back the way she'd come, he joined the rest of his pack in picking over the climbing gear and adding things to their backpacks where they fit. When he had taken what he could carry, he shouldered his pack and shook his shoulders to let the gear settle. It felt lop-sided, and he worked the buckles on his straps until it set properly on his back. He jumped once to listen for rattles or rustles and when he heard none, he smiled despite the extra weight.

Rellah moved between Rayce and Veck to join him, her thumb dressing the strap of her pack against her shoulder. "Ready to go?"

"Almost." He looked around to ensure no climbing equipment was on the ground, and that everyone had finished securing their packs, then raised his voice. "Hollow Bone, listen up."

His pack-mates turned at the sound of his voice and moved toward him until they were gathered at the side of the main street of Mescwar Garden. He waited until they had dropped their packs and directed their attention to him, and glanced over his shoulder at the sound of Tobin's rapid and light footsteps hurrying down the path to join them.

"We're leaving Mescwar Garden for the Bloodstained Mesa, and it's going to take us three days to get there." He paused as the Iron found a spot between Jenna and Rayce to stand and listen. "Travel staggered and solo – Rayce up front, then Jenna, Veck, and Rellah. I'll be at the back, and Tobin will move with me. Find landmarks every two hours and point them out as the lead peels to the back. If we get separated, track back to the last landmark and head twenty paces west of it to rally. There are Heirs, a Cern pack, and Mescwar Hunters on our path, and who knows what other rot, so go slow – favor awareness over speed. Hide if we can, and fight if we have to."

Nods and general murmurs of acknowledgment rippled through his companions, and he continued ticking off parts of the travel plan on his fingers as he talked. "If I get killed, the travel plan goes to Rellah. We'll use ruins to camp or take breaks if we find them but go around them if it's not time to rest."

"What's the rest cycle?" Jenna asked, one hand on her belt and the other resting idle on the handle of her Cern blade.

Hyatt paused to consider the temperature, extra weight, and unwelcoming terrain that the Master Hunter had told them to expect. "Every hour, offset between landmarks."

She pursed her lips and nodded. Hyatt looked around, focusing on each face in the pack for signs of confusion or concern, and saw none. Instead, the clear eyes and attentive expressions of his pack-mates reassured him that they approved of the plan.

His visual check-in with everyone ended with Veck, and he held his gaze without blinking as he concluded the plan. "If you have a fight in you, say so now – leave the blood in Mescwar before we travel."

He expected a longer stand-off, but Veck looked down and then out toward the gate as soon as the words left Hyatt's lips. After another long moment, Hyatt looked around to make sure no one else was on the cusp of airing a reason to brawl. He saw his companions doing the same, looking to their left and right to ensure everyone was ready and no one had anything to say.

He didn't know how long he should wait but after a moment, he decided that it was enough. "Okay, Rayce – lead us out."

Around the semi-circle they had formed, his companions checked their boots and picked up their packs. Hyatt waited as they began to move toward the opening in the Garden's white walls, Haleu men and women moving aside to make way for them. As he fell into step in the back of the column, the way the residents of Mescwar watched them depart with degrees of fascination and relief reinforced in him how much he belonged with Hollow Bone and how little he belonged to the world he had grown up in. It wasn't until he was beyond the gate and felt the rush of cold wind across the clearcut terrain between the Garden and the wilderness that he wondered if somewhere in the scattered men and women who witnessed their departure, there was anyone who wished they were going with him into the world beyond.

The way the Reclaimed closed in around them as they left the tall walls and cleared fields behind them was so comforting to Hyatt that he let out a deep sigh. He watched the silhouettes of his pack-mates ahead of them as they became a part of their environment, their shoulders and hips shifting in ways that aligned with a rhythm with no obvious meter, but made sense and combined in seamless ways all the same. Even the brisk, cold air and the potent quiet of the Reclaimed seemed more right than any other condition.

Tobin's strides and sounds didn't match the wilderness in the same way, his short legs hurrying to keep pace with Hyatt. His footfalls disturbed branches and churned up the deadfall that carpeted the forest floor, and the leaves would have crunched under his boots if not for the way the fading frost had softened them. His pack jostled louder than Hyatt's did, and Hyatt wondered if he had sounded the same on his first trip outside Brathnee.

The foliage became denser, encroaching on Hyatt's visibility. He kept occasional sight of Rellah ahead and to his right, but Veck disappeared amongst the brush. Only the sound of the breeze through branches and leaves kept them company. As he walked, he thought of his friend Gorman from Brathnee Garden and how much his friend needed to talk, and how easy it had become for Hyatt to walk for hours without a word.

The terrain began to undulate into almost imperceptible crests and valleys marked by the persistency of dark leaves where moisture lingered longer. As Hyatt stepped over a low log, he caught sight of Rayce crouched by a large bush with clusters of green berries beside pastel orange flowers. As he passed it, his pack-mate made the hand gesture to mark the bush as their first landmark.

"Those will make you sick." Tobin emphasized his declaration with a grave nod, and when Hyatt nodded instead of speaking, the Iron fired another conversational volley at him. "Did you grow up in a Garden?"

Hyatt sidestepped a gnarled root that rose from the ground and plunged back under like a sea monster and nodded again. He felt Tobin's repeated glances at the side of his face, searching for more of an answer than he offered, but Hyatt stuck to his silence.

"Which one?" the Iron pressed.

Hyatt bedded his voice in the matte sounds of a Cern raider. "Have you ever seen a Clastryne?"

Tobin shook his head, a confused look on his face.

"A Clastryne is twenty paces long and as tall as the trees, with a scaled hide that flechettes won't penetrate and jaws that will crush boulders to dust. Their claws are barbed and their four rows of spines are poisonous. A Clastryne's sweat is a paralytic that feels like a cheese grater from the inside of your body out, while your muscles are frozen and your brain becomes hyper-aware." He paused for effect and looked down at Tobin, who was staring up at him with rapt attention. "They have very, very good hearing – so stop talking."

When Tobin heard the moral of Hyatt's story, his eyes narrowed like he had been tricked, but he said nothing. They continued together, Hyatt managing his distance so that he intermittently lost and recovered sight of Rellah while Tobin worked to keep up. The wind picked up the scent of the conical white flowers and carried it over them as they moved between trees and brush on a general northeastern course.

Rellah's path diverted to the left and Hyatt changed his route to give the same wide berth to something ahead he couldn't see. As he crested a small knoll and moved past an obscuring wall of brush to his right, he made out a rended metal structure that shared no characteristics with the twisted tree trunks and gently rolling terrain around it. From a distance, it looked like three boxes the size of small buildings, inter-connected by large and rusted hinges. As he circumnavigated the site, he tried to reverse engineer the structure in his mind and imagined the boxes sitting in a line, the hinges allowing them to flex like a whip as they moved like the flatcar rail of Ceojic. From that image came the thought of how much force would have been required to rip the ends off the boxes at either extreme, twist them forty-five degrees from one another, and slam them into the ground with enough force to bury the bottom third of one in the earth. It wasn't until he examined the open, sliding door on the third box's dented and half-crushed face that he saw something dark brown move dark brown inside.

Hyatt flung his hand out to grab the front of Tobin's jacket, and Tobin froze. As slow as tree sap in winter, Hyatt bent his knees and began to melt toward the ground with his eyes fixed on the opening where he had seen a flicker of motion. Tobin followed his lead, crouching down so the slope of the terrain partially broke the line of sight from the metal structure to where they hid.

Rellah reappeared between two trees in the direction they had been moving and when Hyatt spotted her, her gaze locked with his. With his hand low to the ground, he touched the pad of his thumb to the tips of his index and ring fingers, and gestured twice in the direction of the damaged metal boxes with his index and middle finger.

She matched his sign to acknowledge she had seen it and faded back into the foliage, and as Hyatt turned his attention back to the structure, he saw the dark brown silhouette shift again.

"Are they Keepers?" Tobin whispered, stretching his neck as he tried to peer over the sloping ground at the twisted metal boxes.

Hyatt shook his head as the figure of a man with a short jacket and a bald head climbed through a break in the third box's siding with a bag over his shoulder. *No robes, no hoods. Scavengers.*

As they stayed low, time seemed to grind to a halt. Hyatt watched the stranger move around the rended metal with his crowbar and a satchel of tools. He was too far from the site to make out the man's distinct actions, but Hyatt could tell that the man was using his gear to remove things from the structure and shove them into his pack. Realizing that the stranger probably believed he was alert to the dangers of the Reclaimed as he looted the structure but had no idea that he was surrounded by Hyatt and his companions sent a shiver down Hyatt's spine.

Tobin fidgeted beside him, disturbing a branch that dragged over several leaves. It sounded like rolling thunder to Hyatt in contrast to his curated silence and he watched the scavenger for any sign of alert, but the man continued his work. He shot a withering glare at Tobin, but the Iron wasn't looking at him and so absorbed Hyatt's silent censure without effect.

The longer Hyatt held still, the less sure he became of the passage of time around him. By the time the scavenger dismounted the structure and pulled his sack over his shoulder, Hyatt had no idea whether he watched the man for one hour or three. The bald man gave a cursory look around but saw no one, and started on his way south.

Even with the man out of sight, Hyatt waited. He counted his breaths as he listened to the clank of the man's bag and tried to estimate his distance, and whether he had traveled far enough to pass wherever Rayce had chosen to hide behind them. He half-expected to hear the cry or gurgle of the scavenger's life ending because he had stumbled upon Hyatt's pack-mate without realizing it, but no such sound echoed through the forest.

He rose in a slow, intentional movement and waited until he saw Rellah do the same, then tapped Tobin on his shoulder. "Come on, time to move."

"What do you think he took?" The Iron asked as he scrambled to his feet.

Hyatt shrugged. "Not our problem."

The answer seemed to satisfy Tobin. They walked together without a word, taking in the colors and sounds of the wilderness. The evening bled into night and dwindled the meager warmth of the day to a hard chill, fading the edges of every feature that would otherwise be familiar.

With the last light, Hyatt reached the place where Bex had chosen to set camp. The location was empty enough for all of them but with sufficient scattered vegetation and a natural rise in the terrain to hide their presence. Hyatt nodded his approval and found a space beside a chest-high bush to lay out his bedding. As soon as his blanket came free of the bottom compartment of his backpack, fatigue washed over him from his eye-sockets to his toes.

He finished preparing his strip of ground and waited as the rest of his pack-mates did the same, then pulled them all together. "Good travel today. We'll take hour-long shifts, one person at a time, in order of names from bottom to top. Keep fires low and covered, and break camp at dawn."

Bex grabbed their weapon and headed for the northern edge of their camp, and Hyatt knelt on his bedding to dig through his pack for one of his rations. The draw of sleep was stronger for him than the draw of heat, and as he unwrapped the wax paper from around his prepared meal, his mind lingered on the thought of how good it would feel to lay down and close his eyes.

He'd just taken his first bite when Rellah dropped to a crouch beside him, and she waited until he had chewed and swallowed his food before speaking. "What do you have left to do?"

The thought of having anything between and sleep started to blossom a flower of despair inside him, but he worked to stamp it out. "Check everyone for supply shortages and injuries. Walk outside camp to see how much of it can be seen."

Rellah gave him an approving clap on his shoulder, and Hyatt thought he saw the hint of a smirk at the corner of her mouth. "Good. I'm not hurt or missing anything. I'm going to sleep."

*Fuck you, Rellah.* He took another bite and glared at her over the wrapper of his ration, then folded it around the remainder of his meal and talked with his mouth full. "Get good sleep."

He didn't know if it was the extra weight of their climbing gear, the tension of evading scavengers, or being unused to having additional responsibilities after camp was set, but getting up from his bedding felt like a monumental effort. He planted his hands on the ground and stifled a groan as he pushed off to break the pull of the earth and get his legs under him, but realized he was grateful that his boots were still on. The thought of adding one more step felt like it would have been too much.

Hyatt made his way over to the space where Bex and Rayce had laid out their bedding near a jagged, prickly brush that hid their packs from view. Rayce had already slipped beneath his blanket, but his eyes were open and he spotted Hyatt as he approached.

"No shortages, no injuries," he offered before Hyatt could speak, a knowing smile pulling at his lips that made Hyatt realize he must have looked as spent as he felt.

"Bex?" he asked.

They looked up from their pack where they had been quietly rifling through its contents and gave him two thumbs up. "All set."

He returned the gesture and moved on without a word to where Veck had set up alone. His pack-mate had piled tinder into his metal cup and lit it, and flickers of red and orange light escaped the cup's cover through round perforations to deepen the shadows around his eyes and under his cheekbones. Veck held his hands close to the makeshift fire for warmth, and his expression didn't change as he recognized Hyatt.

"Do you have everything you need? Are you injured at all?" Hyatt asked.

"I'm short a pack-mate, and we have an extra Iron." His tone didn't rise or fall at all, which somehow made his implication penetrate deeper. "Other than that, I'm fine."

"You had your chance to fight before we left Mescwar," Hyatt replied, and he meant to match Veck's tone, but he could hear his own exasperation creep in around the edges. "Sleep it off."

Veck stared at him for a long moment with only the light from his cup-fire to show each other their expressions, and to Hyatt's surprise, Veck nodded in agreement. "Okay. No shortages, no injuries."

Hyatt headed toward where Jenna and Rellah had set down their gear but after the strange interaction with Veck, he couldn't resist the urge to glance back. His packmate had turned his focus to the flickers of firelight escaping the filter over his cup and seemed to stare through it as he held his palms toward the heated metal. Hyatt didn't know what to make of Veck's acknowledgment, and wondered if he was as tired as Hyatt was.

He found Rellah sitting with her knees drawn toward her chest and Jenna kneeling behind her, Jenna's fingers pulling free the tan twining that laced through Rellah's braiding. She leaned forward as if she was saying something into Rellah's other ear as her fingers extracted the string, and Hyatt's hesitation to intrude caused him to slow his approach. The unexpectedly intimate moment caused a strange collection of responses in him, like watching a dozen metal pans clank together without the ability to hear them. It didn't feel like confusion, jealousy, or alarm, but something else he couldn't normalize by naming.

Hyatt glanced down and saw a slender branch within reach, and crushed it with his boot. The green wood cracked as he expected.

"You can come here, Hyatt," Rellah didn't turn to look at him as she spoke, and he was certain there was a smirk on Jenna's face that he couldn't see with her back to him.

He finished his walk toward them and in his periphery he noticed the placement of their bedding, laid out closer together than he remembered it being on their travel from their camp to the Garden. Even as interpretations began to form in his head, he glanced back at Bex and Rayce's space and recognized they were almost overlapping.

*Not that it matters. Why is this strange? It's not.* His brain spun faster with every link in the chain of his thoughts, and he focused on the way that the crimps left behind in Rellah's hair as Jenna pulled coil after coil of the binding twine from it cascaded along Rellah's cheek and down her neck. *Well rot, that doesn't help!*

Hyatt looked away, focusing on the depths of a shadow beyond the edge of their temporary camping area. "Jenna – any gear you're missing, or any injuries?"

"I never imagined the man I took outside Brathnee Garden would ask me that," Jenna said to Rellah, before glancing over at Hyatt. "Making travel plans, doing checks... but still can't be too close to women, huh?"

He opened his mouth to answer her but found himself at a loss for words, and he hated proving her point for her.

Jenna returned her attention to her work releasing Rellah's hair, and filled the space for him. "No shortages, no injuries."

"Okay," he replied, relieved. "Get good sleep."

He made his way outside their camp and started his slow walk around the perimeter. He searched through the dark for the outline of backpacks or the texture of bedding, but he finished his circle around their space and saw only the flicker of Veck's little cup of fire. Satisfied, he crossed back into camp next to Bex who was settling into their position for the first guard shift.

"Good job today," they said as Hyatt passed.

He lingered next to their position, taking a moment to savor the compliment. "Can I ask you something?"

Bex shrugged. "Sure."

"Having Tobin with us..." Hyatt hesitated as he realized he hadn't fully formed the words for the question he was trying to ask. "Do you feel any way about it?"

Bex shook their head as they looked out into darkness between two mid-sized trees that concealed their position from the outside. "I guess not. It's hard to see him as an Iron."

"Yeah, I get that." Hyatt looked across the camp towards where Tobin had set up his sleeping space near his own. "Have a quiet shift."

When he reached his bedding, the pull to collapse onto it was just as strong as when he'd first laid it out. As he worked his way free of his boots, he felt himself dozing off. He had no recollection of laying down as sleep swallowed his awareness in one full gulp.

"Hyatt." The whisper that woke him wove through the barrier that separated his sleep from his waking mind, lingering like the scent of campfire smoke.

He squinted against the expectation of daybreak but as he let his eyelids part just enough to let sunlight filter through his lashes, he realized it was still dark – so dark that he couldn't make out the little head in front of his face for a moment. When he realized how close the Iron's nose was to his own, he blanched.

"Tobin?" Confusion and irritation fought for control over the single, whispered word.

"I have to go now," he whispered back. "I'll meet you at the rock place."

"What?" Caught in the disorientation of his unexpected waking, one part of Hyatt's brain processed what Tobin was saying while the other had no idea what the boy meant.

"Sklodowska needs me to do something, so I have to go now." The Iron patted Hyatt's shoulder through his blanket in an imitation of a reassuring gesture. "You will be okay."

Hyatt propped himself up on his arm, willing the fog to recede from his mind as the outline of Tobin's nighttime silhouette began to become more distinct against the darkness behind him, and he could make out the shine of the boy's sclerae. "Tobin – you just had a dream. It's not real. Go back to sleep."

When Hyatt woke next, he didn't remember what the Iron had said, or going back to sleep himself. He startled awake with a flinch and sat up quickly, crashing into the morning glow that flooded through the wilderness around him. As he climbed to his knees and feet, he looked around and tried to remember where Tobin had chosen to sleep the night before. When he found it, the leaves were still disturbed where the Iron had bedded down, but the boy was gone.

"Where's Tobin?" Instead of questioning anyone in particular, he asked it loud enough for everyone to hear.

Rellah was just rising and looked around, and Jenna shook her head as she knelt over her pack and shoved her bedding into it. Rayce walked over to where Tobin had slept and looked around like he'd lost a belt knife that might have tumbled under a bush or pile of leaves.

"Left in the night." Veck shrugged.

A frustration Hyatt couldn't articulate began to build in him over the confluence of the Iron's choice to leave and Veck having the last guard shift before daybreak. He ran his fingers through his hair and turned in a slow circle, searching as far into the forest as he could see for any sign of the Iron, but there was nothing to indicate which way the boy had headed.

Hyatt's concern over Tobin wandering the Reclaimed on his own and his relief at the Iron's absence coalesced in Hyatt at the same time, and he allowed himself a moment to linger on the conflict between the two feelings. He wiped the sleep from his face with his palms and reminded himself that they had met the boy on his own in the wilderness and he had been alright, but it did little to alleviate the stress that the situation caused him.

"One less Iron," Veck added. "Good for us, good for the Cern."

"Maybe, but that wasn't your call," Hyatt snapped at him. "This is my travel plan, and you should have woken me up."

The amount of acid in his tone sounded foreign in his own ears, but he didn't regret it. Veck's attention riveted to him and it felt like he was about to retort, but settled for a clipped Cern hiss as he walked over to his backpack. He knelt beside it and began collecting his bedding, but looked up as Rellah's shadow fell over him.

"Answer Hyatt." Her words were barely above a whisper but carried in the quiet of the early morning, and left no room for misinterpretation or argument.

Veck let go of his crumpled blanket and stood to face Rellah, but being taller than her gave his willpower no advantage. Hyatt watched his pack-mate visibly deflate in concession to her, but Veck rolled his eyes as he turned to face Hyatt.

"Okay. I should have woken you." He paused as if he was trying to hold back the rest of his words, and when they came out, they were strained and taut. "Do you want us to go after him?"

Hyatt considered it, but shook his head. "He's not Hollow Bone, and he chose to go. We continue on to the mesa."

Around him, his companions continued to break camp. Hyatt put his hands in his pockets to stave off the biting cold of the air without the first rays of sun to warm it. His thoughts chased after Tobin through the Reclaimed but he chose to focus on Rellah's promise that with few exceptions, everything in the Reclaimed conspired to keep its inhabitants alive.

*He'll be fine. Sklodowska will keep him safe, the Reclaimed will keep him safe, and he'll meet us at the mesa.* He nodded to himself, as if the motion of his skull could hammer the thought into reality like a stake.

He packed his things and coated the blade of his weapon with oil to stave off rust and frost, and by the time he was ready to move out, the rest of camp had been erased as if it had never existed. The sun had just begun to filter over the horizon and across the ground, and it brought with it a brisk wind that knocked loose the dead leaves that had clung to almost barren branches until that morning. He stood at the outer edge of the space Hollow Bone had claimed for their campsite and watched as Rayce and Bex took the lead followed by Rellah and Veck. Hyatt gave their campsite one last glance before taking up the trail end of their departure.

# FOURTEEN

Hyatt caught sight of the white shape in the brush on the right side of the trail, a line that contrasted with the natural pattern of the shrub's growth, but it took five more steps before he realized what he was looking at. A segment of bone caught the light differently than the deep green leaves and the olive-brown sprigs around it.

He let his next footfall land and stopped as he stretched out his left hand to stop Bex from continuing beyond him. Their chest bumped into Hyatt's arm and they stopped like they had collided with an immovable wall, and they followed his nod in the direction of the brush. He could tell they found it when the skin on their cheekbones tightened and they turned away, searching the surrounding foliage for another marker. When they identified one hanging from an overhead branch with twine, they nudged Hyatt and tilted their chin up toward it.

Rellah appeared behind and between them without a sound, and with Veck close behind her. Her lips parted in the formation of a question and Hyatt felt a swell of pride at the chance to see and know something first, but he saw the glint in her eyes shift as she spotted the marker in the brush and it drained the positive pressure in his chest.

"Good eyes." Rellah's compliment spun him back in the other direction and he felt his jaw go slack, but he closed it before she could turn her attention from the marker to his face.

"Do you know anyone from Timber Shade Pack?" he asked in his best approximation of the low, raider's cant, and fought a wince as he ended his question with a crisp consonant sound.

Rellah shook her head, and Beck matched the gesture. Veck frowned at the Reclaimed that lay ahead of them as Rayce caught up to where the pack had gathered, looking at each of them in askance before he noticed the white bone against the frost-tinged vegetation. He pointed it out to Jenna as she reached the group.

"Timber Shade Pack is big." Veck didn't take his eyes off the unfamiliar terrain ahead of them as he spoke. "They'll know we're here, if they don't already."

Hyatt followed Veck's gaze along the terrain, searching for contrasting movement against the still branches and deadfall, but finding none did nothing to lessen the tension growing in his stomach. *They could be right on top of us, and I'd never know.*

"Going around could take days." Rayce's low tone and rolled consonants left Hyatt uncertain about whether he was reasoning with himself or providing counsel, and his pack-mate studied the buckle of his pack instead of making eye contact as he spoke. "Going through will be shorter, but..."

Hyatt searched his companions' faces for their sentiments, but Rellah and Jenna both wore non-committal expressions and Bex stood with their back to him while they searched the trail in the direction they'd come. "Okay... through. We go through – single file, and nobody fights unless we get attacked."

Even though there was no discernable change in the ground or the air, stepping past the markers and into territory owned by a Cern pack felt like stepping through a wall of cobwebs. The shadows seemed deeper to Hyatt, contrasting harder with the bands of daylight that cut like knives from the canopy above to the ground beneath his boots. Every rustle of brush or warning call of distant animals doubled in his mind as a possible communication between raiders or sentries just outside his periphery.

The cornerstone of an ancient structure swept from the planet Histories ago served as their landmark at the end of the first hour, and Hyatt wondered how many times that knee-high stone with its chipped edges and spoon-leaved moss on two sides had served as the anchor for others passing through the region. He tried to imagine the building it had once supported, but whatever space the builders had cleared to erect it had long since surrendered to the low ferns and taller sprig-bushes that stood around the stone. He let his attention linger on it as he passed, before focusing on the way forward and the silhouette of his pack-mate in front of him.

A tremor ran through the ground beneath Hyatt and as he froze, he heard a sound that reminded him of thunder. He lowered himself to one knee and planted his palm on the ground the way Rellah had taught him, and waited. When nothing else happened and he started to stand up, another quake rippled through the earth under him and he sank back down to his knee as another rumble played out somewhere to his left. He closed his eyes and tried to focus on the sound, but the sound lingered long enough that he wasn't sure if it was fading or changing distance from him.

He opened his eyes and looked in the direction of the sound, and spotted a stained hart with its legs folded under it and its chin resting on the ground so the autumnal colors of the spots on its side camouflaged it with the deadfall and its four antlers stood lower than the surrounding brush. Its milk-white eyes were open wide with alarm, and it was as still as the trees around it.

*You and me both, friend.* Hyatt held his breath as a stronger tremor shocked the ground under him. Somewhere between him and the hidden source of the following rumble, a tree creaked as its roots no longer anchored it to the ground before crashing with the sound of splintering branches and a snapping trunk.

The closer crash changed the hart's survival strategy, and it bolted from its bed-down in a frenzied, bounding gallop into the wilderness. Hyatt watched it vanish into the Reclaimed and found himself envying the animal's speed and dexterity as it put as much ground as it could between itself and whatever was large enough to shake the earth over and over again.

No matter where Hyatt looked, he saw no sign of toppling or shifting trees to mark the source of the noise. In the absence of evidence, his brain began to fill in gaps with a family of Heirs rampaging through the wilderness, destroying everything in their path. He envisioned Tobin amidst the stampeding claws and thrashing tails of the megafauna, clouds of noxious breath churning like ground fog around them.

Another, fainter tremor shook the ground beneath him, and the rumble that followed seemed further than the last one had sounded. He held still and listened, and moments stacked on moments until too many had passed to keep track, but no new quake reached him. The uneasy feeling in his neck and arms reminded him that of all the parts of the Reclaimed that he had grown comfortable with, the transition from imminent danger to continued travel with no finite resolution had not become one of them. He started walking again, but felt like he was dragging the shadow of the unknown and distant horror behind him.

When he reached Bex crouched by a unique tangle of vines that climbed the remains of a stone chimney, he paused beside them. "What was that?"

They shook their head. "I didn't see it – Jenna didn't, either. Big, whatever it was."

Hyatt thanked them with a smile and touched their shoulder as he passed, searching the wilds ahead for the outline of his pack-mate. He spotted the slope of Rayce's shoulders as he ducked beneath a low branch, and measured his pace against his companion's speed. He walked with only the sounds of birds in the treetops and the occasional gust of icy wind to interrupt the silence.

The sun was halfway to its mid-day crest and had driven back the last of the morning's chill when Hyatt found himself walking behind Rellah, who was navigating less and less even terrain. Chunks of rock broke apart the ground into sharper depressions and jagged rises. He watched which changes in elevation she committed to with silent, high steps and which ones she navigated around on the lower ground, and he followed her example. The deadfall covered the forest floor uniformly except in places where twin rises created channeled walkways between them. Hyatt tried to picture the land in the wet season, those channels filled with rapid and frothing runnels of water that stripped the topsoil between the trees and brush. Overhead, the canopy continued to block out the sun and created walls of foliage on either side of him.

He caught sight of Rellah again and realized he had been too lost in his thoughts to keep his distance, but glancing back proved he wasn't the only one. Rayce was closer than he expected, and ahead of Rellah, he was almost certain he saw sunlight catch Jenna's hair before she vanished amidst the moss-covered trunks of the large trees around her.

Hyatt looked back at Rellah to judge his distance from her and watched her fingers begin to articulate the shaft of an arrow in her quiver, rocking it back and forth so it slid in slow and silent movements upward into her hand. He felt his pulse begin to hit harder like an approaching drumbeat, and the space between each thump became smaller and smaller. The way nothing else about her walk or her expression changed only confirmed to him that they had passed a point of no return to a danger he couldn't see or hear.

Just as he glimpsed Rellah's arrowhead at the mouth of her quiver, a voice broke the brush from closer than anyone should have been able to be. "Drop it, becquerela."

Hyatt pivoted in time to see a Cern raider melt into existence from a tree four arm's lengths away, and he heard the hiss of Rellah's arrow slipping between the fletchings of her other arrows until the arrowhead met the bottom of the quiver. He took a half-step backward to conceal his hand as it drifted toward the handle of his weapon, but the unexpected feel of another hand closing around his wrist to stop him from reaching it made him whirl around again. He shoved the second raider who was close enough to breathe in his face, and as the stranger stumbled backward, he took Hyatt's weapon with him in a solid yank.

"Everybody be calm." The raider caught his footing and held eye contact with Hyatt as he spoke, holding the stolen weapon with the point just above the ground between them. "Who's in charge?"

"I am." Hyatt held up his hands as Veck and Rayce appeared in his periphery, trailed by two more raiders with weapons drawn. "Are you in charge?"

"Packmaster Ruthmer is in charge." The raider took his eyes off Hyatt to examine the strange blade he'd taken from him, then drove the tip of it into the ground with enough force to stand it upright in the earth. "I'm in charge of trespassers on this edge of our territory – so I'm in charge of you. What pack are you from?"

Hyatt's mind tumbled and spun around the options they had and the options he might be able to create. He felt opportunities siphoning away like water through a strainer and searched for the best place to be standing when the space to affect change had drained from the moment, but it felt like the gap to come up with their best option was vanishing too quickly.

"We're from Hollow Bone." He stared at the raider's face and willed him to look up and meet his gaze, as if drawing his focus would give his companions the seconds and breaths they needed to act.

The Cern's eyes narrowed and he returned his attention to Hyatt. "That's not a pack. Don't lie to me again, or we'll kill you here and save Ruthmer the aggravation of deciding your fate."

The causal way he presented the option of ending their lives, devoid of anger or haste, made his threat seem more real. As Hyatt opened his mouth to argue the existence of their pack, one of the Cern raiders stepped to their leader's side and tilted their head toward him to murmur something inaudible. The raider kept his eyes on Hyatt as he listened to his pack-mate, and Hyatt caught the moment his pupils adjusted.

"Rot." The man's single word landed somewhere between disbelief and fascination.

"Yeah," Hyatt agreed, with no idea what he was acknowledging.

The speaker for the Cern walked away, giving Hyatt no impression he was welcome to follow. Out of earshot, two of the other raiders converged on him, and they spoke in tones Hyatt couldn't make out. As they conferred, Hyatt glanced around to gauge the expressions of his pack-mates but learned nothing from the tension in Veck's eyes and Jenna's jaw, Rellah's serene features, or the annoyance etched into Bex's forehead.

The trio of Cern broke apart and the speaker approached him again. "Tell your pack to come with us to camp."

Hyatt felt a thread of amusement at the thought of telling Hollow Bone pack what to do in their situation, but he fought the smirk that threatened to break across his face. He watched the man pass to set their path while the rest of the raiders formed a loose column around them to funnel them in the same direction. Hyatt turned and found the remainder of his pack staring back at him, awaiting his instructions.

"Okay, Hollow Bone – change of plans." He kicked his leg out and hooked his thumbs in his belt in imitation of the pose he'd seen Rellah adopt whenever she spoke to the pack, even though it felt like a child wearing his parent's boots as he did it. "We're going back to Ruthmer's camp. Let's play nice, see what he wants, and get back to the travel plan as fast as we can."

His pack-mates nodded, and Hyatt set off after the leader of the Cern raiders. The man had lingered a dozen paces ahead and looked back to ensure they were following, and when he started to move, so did the Cern. The Reclaimed seemed no different in the direction they walked, intervening clusters of brush forming a labyrinth of pathways made identical by the millions of minute differences that somehow created a more uniform and indistinguishable view across the broken terrain. Between the rows of his companions, Hyatt led the way in the man's wake and off their course.

Unlike the invisible sentries, there was no mistaking the perimeter of the Cern camp. Hyatt marveled at the bone structures that formed the entrance before them, six-sided towers made of bones lashed together with twine that cast long shadows on the forest floor. Unprepared for the sight, it caused him to hesitate a step as he imagined the number of Cern represented in the hexagonal monoliths that stood twice his height. The smaller bones suspended on either side of the towers reminded Hyatt of beaded curtains, and the way they extended in both directions promised that generations of Cern were represented amidst the display.

"Move it," the closest raider prompted Hyatt as he lingered to study the structures.

Hyatt complied, but stared up at the towers of bone as he passed between them. Beyond the markers, tents that reminded him of his visit to Moss Wall pack stood in clusters between trees that held wooden bridges taut between them across long spaces of open air. More members of the pack than Hyatt had seen at Moss Wall or Cleft Rock moved through the camp, attending to the duties of their working hours in near silence. The contrast between the large settlement and his own pack of seven people hit him hard as he took in the breadth of their camp.

*Six, now.* The realization snuck into his thoughts like an adder through reeds. *Six of us.*

The Cern in the lead looked back to ensure Hyatt and his friends were still following him, then turned toward a different section of their camp. The path was lined on one side by more tents, and on the other side by cords of wood stacked beneath tarps that wore the matte glisten of animal fat used to waterproof them. Rope nets covered the tarps and ended at heads of stakes driven into the ground until they were little more than hooks sprouting from the dirt. The tension on the nets drew his attention back to the tents on his other side, and he saw the same tautness in the guidelines of each one.

At the end of the row, the path left in the negative space between their disciplined structures and supplies widened to a larger clearing surrounded by trees tall enough and old enough to close their canopies over the vacant ground. A Cern man in dark trousers stood at the center of a field of cut logs, a heavy axe in his hands and his shirt slung over a nearby branch. As they approached, he hefted the axe over his head so the blade caught the sunlight in a blazing flash, then brought it down with a swing that seemed to originate in his legs and carry through his entire body to the end of his tool. The cracking sound as the giant log in front of him split in two was crisp and seemed to echo against the nearby trees. He pulled the axe back to him as he walked around the standing halves until he found the angle he wanted, swung his axe again, and split the closer half into two perfect quarters.

The leading Cern stopped at twice the distance the man could reach with his axe, and cupped a hand beside his mouth to help his voice carry. "Ruthmer, we found the trespassers."

The packmaster reeled his axe in again and walked around the far side of the remaining half of the log with steady, purposeful steps. He looked over the workspace at Hyatt and his companions with the look of someone who was interrupted just before they were about to be free, and didn't appreciate it. Instead of speaking he returned his attention to the task in front of him, squared his body to the log, and split it in half with a single violent chop that launched both fragments of wood through the air in opposite directions as the axe's head buried in a stump beneath where the log had stood.

Ruthmer ran his hand through his hair and shook the sweat from his fingers, sending it scattering onto the cool ground where it clung like dew to the leaves. "If our markers were not clear enough, we could kill a few more of our people to make them bigger."

Hyatt continued to close the distance between the packmaster and himself, and the closer he got, the bigger Ruthmer appeared. He guessed the man was a full handspan taller than his own height, with shoulders broad enough to carry a log on each one. The sight of him made Hyatt flash back to the first Cern raiders he'd ever seen, terrifying but no different in build than he was, and he wondered if the horror stories of those who lived in the Reclaimed began with a giant Cern like Ruthmer.

When he reached the man who had led them into camp, he stopped. Around him, he saw the remainder of their escorts spread out across the edge of the clearing, containing his companions in a loose ring.

Ruthmer looked around his feet and fixed on another section of log, large enough that the bear hug he wrapped around it to carry it only brought his fingers just past the mid-point. He dropped to a crouch and flexed his legs to lift it in the air, walked with the same even strides he had used without the burden of the segment of tree-trunk, and dropped it on the splitting stump.

"They're Claimed," their escort added.

"The Claimed pack." The shirtless man ripped his axe from the stump and slid his thick fist up the handle to grip just beneath the ax-head, then walked toward them. "What do they call you?"

Hyatt felt the familiar rise of word-vomit inside him. The building urge within him to fill the tense vacuum of sound with every detail of the way their pack began and everywhere they had been since then was almost a compulsion, and his body seemed to commit to telling the story before his consciousness could catch up. At the last minute, as his lips parted to deluge the Cern with far more information than he had asked for, Hyatt's mind found its gear and froze his mouth to halt his imminent reply.

*These are Cern. Answer like you're one of them, because you are.* He slid his thumbs behind the buckle of his belt and waited until the man was four steps closer so he wouldn't need to raise his voice. "Hollow Bone Pack."

"Hollow Bone Pack." He repeated it like he was trying the words on, seeing how they fit on his tongue. "Huh."

Hyatt resisted the urge to fill the silence that followed with further explanation, and after a pause that seemed to last for twenty heartbeats, the Cern shrugged. He handed off his axe to a woman who grabbed the handle just below the axe's head and headed into camp. The man brushed his hands against his pants as he looked left and then right in search of something.

When he spotted his shirt hanging from a nearby branch, he nodded in recognition and started toward it. "Why are you headed north?"

Rayce stepped forward to answer the Cern. "We have been in your spaces less than a day."

The man lifted his arms to pull his shirt over his head, the muscles in his stomach and back rippling under his skin like a machine barely contained in a living thing before vanishing beneath the thin fabric. He glanced over at Rayce to identify who had spoken, but nothing in his eyes or posture said he considered him a challenge or a threat.

"You move well." He walked toward them with sure steps and continued through the semi-circle they had formed to the pile of wood he had been splitting without a glance at Hyatt or his companions.

*Are we really just going to make statements at each other without answering anything?* The absurdity of their non-conversation dawned on Hyatt so suddenly that Hyatt forced a cough to mask the chuckle that built in him and almost broke free. He spared a glance at his pack-mates but either they didn't find the same humor in the situation that he did, or they were better at masking their perceptions.

The Cern bent to pick up a quartered log and tossed it onto a nearby canvas tarp under a hanging metal ring, then did the same with another one. Hyatt missed the cue but Jenna caught it and stepped past him to join the man at the pile. It took until she had picked up a log of her own to realize they were meant to help. Hyatt stepped to her side and as the rest of Hollow Bone found space around the edge of the pile, he picked up a wedge of wood and lobbed it into the canvas where it landed with a dull thud.

Something in the Cern's eyes hinted at his approval, but Hyatt couldn't place what it was. As they moved the stack of split wood out of one pile and into another, he glanced around at the man's pack-mates who formed a loose box around them. The two Cern with flechette carbines slung them over their shoulders, and the two with Cern blades held them in their hands but lowered them too far to react quickly.

"You lead this... pack." The man looked up at Rellah and held her gaze as he spoke, and there was no question in his tone.

"Our time in your spaces began mid-morning." Rayce's remark drew the man's attention but again, held it for only the space of a breath before he redirected his attention to the pile of logs.

They worked without another fragmented statement until all the split wood was piled on the canvas, and the man collected the ropes from the corners of the tarp. Without the heat of the labor, Hyatt felt the sweat in his neck begin to cool in the brisk air and rolled his shoulders forward to bring the collar of his jacket closer to his skin. If the Cern man felt the chill, it didn't show as he pulled the ropes together to lift the edges of the canvas around the logs and knotted them to close the bundle. He fastened the loose ends to the ring hanging above the pile and stepped back to inspect his own knot.

When he was satisfied, he turned to face them and crossed his arms. "You being here has changed the pattern of the Heir we track."

*What does that have to do with us?* Hyatt didn't realize his thought had transferred to his face until he saw the man's attention fix on his brows that had come together in confusion.

As the pack coalesced around him, Veck spoke up to steal the conversation and the man's attention. "Your camp hasn't moved much."

The way the Cern turned to face Veck implied an insult that Hyatt only heard in the aftermath, and the tendons in his neck tightened as he watched the man start towards his pack-mate. Grim images and hectic calculations tripped over each other in his mind as he spent the man's next six steps turning over a dozen scenarios of a fight breaking out at the heart of Timber Shade pack, and none of them ended with him or his companions alive.

Rayce stepped closer to his pack-mate but Ruthmer continued until he was toe to toe with Veck. The two men looked into each others' eyes like they were trying to push the air between them into one another's irises but as Hyatt tracked his attention down along their frames, he saw neither of them had closed their hands into fists. Beside him, Bex took a slight sidestep, and in his periphery, he caught one of their guards shifting their weight onto their front foot in a slight but intentional movement.

Ruthmer's tense jaw and narrow lips were devoid of warmth, and he didn't blink or spare a sideways glance for

Rayce. "You can put down your backpack if it is too heavy for you."

Hyatt harnessed the instinctive wince that Ruthmer's barb created and expected Veck to smash his fist into the Cern's nose, but when his pack-mate didn't retaliate with instant aggression, Hyatt seized the opportunity to redirect the pack-master's attention. "I'm Cern, not Claimed."

Ruthmer turned his head to look over his shoulder at Hyatt, and the rest of his body followed suit until he was fully facing him. He retraced his steps through the members of Hollow Bone pack, every step cranking on the coils of tension in Hyatt's body, until the Cern was standing in front of him and frowning in concerned curiosity.

The man looked him up and down, from the tip of his head to the toes of his boots and back up, then shook his head. "Moss Wall?"

The little victory that Ruthmer's question was connected to Hyatt's last statement wasn't lost on him, but neither was the way Rellah stiffened behind the pack-master at the mention of the pack she had left behind. Without time to seek encouragement or warning from his pack-mates, he decided to follow suit.

"Cleft Rock, a raider for Etred." Hyatt met his gaze but screamed in his own head at his lie. *What? Why did I say that? Rotten fucking compost!*

Ruthmer looked back at the rest of Hollow Bone Pack, then at Hyatt with calculating eyes. "What is a Cleft Rock raider doing days from their spaces... in a pack of Claimed?"

*Way to go, Hyatt. You're knee-deep in rot now, you dumb weed.* Digging for an answer through the static of his inner monologue's condemnation felt impossible, so he latched to the first coherent answer he could put together. "We're paired and she's seeded."

The disbelief on Ruthmer's face as he looked at Jenna and then Rellah was hard not to take as an insult, but when he returned his attention to Hyatt, something had shifted in the corners of his eyes and the edges of his mouth. He nodded and dismissed the lingering sentry with an inclination of his head.

"Your child will be lucky to wear such a jacket." His tone was more personable, and he reached out to straighten Hyatt's coat. "You and your... pack-mates can stay until daylight, and we'll send you out with weapons and food."

"Thank you." Hyatt hoped he struck the right note of gratitude without showing too much relief, but adrenaline bleeding from him gave him little control over the way he presented himself.

Ruthmer clapped his palm against Hyatt's shoulder and led him deeper into camp. As they walked, he exchanged a glance with Bex on one side who nodded an affirmation toward him, then caught sight of Rellah on his other side staring daggers into his skull. He mouthed a word of apology in her direction, but she had shifted her focus straight ahead and he was almost certain she hadn't seen it.

The array of tables and pavilions before them was the largest Cern encampment Hyatt had seen, and the men and women that milled through the natural walkways and footpaths between their makeshift structures paid them little mind as Ruthmer led them forward.

"Our sentries found you when the Clastryne left the glen where it wanders in the morning," the pack-leader said as he stepped over a tether that held a tarp over a pile of supplies that formed asymmetrical shapes beneath its cover. "Your pack of Claimed is calling to it."

Hyatt followed him, careful to step over the same strap as he recalled the miniature Clastryne he had carved and placed on the mantle in his home in Brathnee. His body had not replenished enough fear toxins to answer the clench of his brain at the thought of encountering one in person, producing an ache in its place that made Hyatt feel tired instead. He was glad for the Cern tradition of saying nothing more than the moment called for, and hoped his silence was enough response for Ruthmer.

The pack-master stopped at a pair of larger tents. "You can leave your things here, and I'll send someone to get you when we eat. I would let you stay longer as a favor to Etred, but your pack puts mine at risk. You need to be gone with the daybreak."

"We will be." Hyatt nodded as he let his pack drop from his shoulder and eased it to the ground.

Ruthmer looked over the group once more, his gaze pausing on each face as if he was committing their features to memory or comparing them to an expectation he didn't share, then nodded at Hyatt to conclude their conversation and set off into the camp. Hyatt watched him go, turning his head to track the pack-master as he disappeared and reappeared between tents and trees.

"So, which of us is carrying your little Cern baby?" Jenna asked from so close beside him that he flinched in surprise.

Hyatt turned around and found himself face to face with Rellah and her crossed arms, while Jenna hid her smirk behind her palm beside them. "I didn't know what to say!"

Rellah continued to stare at him with a deadpan, unimpressed expression as Jenna laughed, a bemused sound that faded into a sigh as she walked away. Hyatt turned to watch her go, uncertain if her departure was a benefit to him by improving his odds of survival or a threat because there was no one to stop Rellah from stabbing him. He swiveled his head back towards

Rellah and found her still looking at him, and it was clear to Hyatt that it was the latter.

# FIFTEEN

Somewhere between the outskirts of their camp and the northeastern edge of their marked territory, the biting cold of the morning was Hyatt's first conscious thought. As he navigated the channels between broad plates of earth, he found himself grateful that whatever instincts swam in the dark beneath his awareness had managed to close the laces and latches of his boots without his intentional participation.

The two Cern raiders who escorted them seemed to know the exact place to stop, despite the ground being devoid of any recognizable landmark Hyatt could see. He rubbed his eyes and willed his brain to pick up speed, but the churning fog of sleep and the stress of the day before refused to surrender without a prolonged fight.

One of the raiders nodded up at the bones suspended from branches above them that Hyatt had missed, the raider's eyes catching just enough starlight to stand out against her shadowy silhouette. "This is as far as we go. You're headed that way, less than a day's walk."

"Okay." One word was all he could manage as his eyes followed the direction she pointed, unable to make out anything in the dark.

"The Heirs start moving in an hour or two," the other raider said. "You should have a good head start by then."

In the twilight between being awake enough to manage the major motor functions of his body and being awake enough to string together thoughts, it occurred to him as strange that he had never thought about an Heir's patterns before. As the Cern raiders melted away into the wilderness and left him with his companions at the edge of their territory, he realized that the only two thoughts he'd ever had about the massive monstrosities that wandered the Reclaimed were how to escape them, or how to kill them. It took until Hollow Bone pack reached their first landmark of the day's travel and light was bleeding over the horizon that such dichotomy seemed sensible again.

By mid-day, the cold had retreated enough that Hyatt no longer needed his jacket. The pack gathered to rest after a landmark that consisted of two broken trees destroyed at eye level by wind or lightning and he took the opportunity to drop his backpack, shed his outer layer, and feed it through straps on his ruck that he tightened to anchor it in place. His fingers sank into the fabric as he rolled one of the sleeves, turning the brighter stitching from its previous owners inward to conceal it from view.

Bex took his cue and stripped off their jacket as well, wedging the dense material under the top flap of their bag. "Cold yesterday, warm today. The weather can't make up its mind."

From a few paces away, Rayce talked around the half of an herb-twist that he'd bitten into and was working on gnawing into consumable bites. "Better this than cold and colder."

"Yes." The one word from Rellah was the first syllable Hyatt could remember her speaking since they'd left the camp, a thought that jarred him, and he started toward Rellah to check on her, but Veck stopped him in his tracks.

"Rotting fucking weeds." Veck's muttered curse stopped Hyatt in his tracks, and he followed Veck's line of sight to the Iron of the Broken Mountain who was stumbling over uneven ground on his way toward them.

"You move very slowly," Tobin said between bites of a pesha fruit, its translucent blue juices dripping down his chin. "I thought you might need help, so I came to find you."

Hyatt saw Veck's shoulders stiffen at the suggestion, but his pack-mate continued to shake his head as he took a drink from his water canister. Tobin edged by him and walked up to Hyatt, crossed his arms, and stared up at his face with a suspicious expression in his little eyes.

"You're still going, right? Because you have to. Sklodowska says so," he said.

Hyatt had begun to string together a reassurance for the Iron in his mind, but Tobin's last sentiment gave him reason to pause. "This has nothing to do with her."

The Iron didn't seem concerned with Hyatt's protest. Instead, he turned in a circle, counting on his fingers as his attention hopped from one member of Hollow Bone pack to the next. When he was finished, his expression faltered for a moment as he looked at the six fingers he held up, then shrugged and turned to walk the way he'd come.

"It's not much further," he promised. "Come on!"

Rayce looked over at Hyatt as if asking permission, and he found himself tilting his head in the Iron's direction before he'd taken time to finish processing the situation. They re-checked their packs and hefted them onto their shoulders, and Rayce took up the next place in line as they continued north.

"We should have been impossible to find." Hyatt stated his conclusion, half to himself and half to Jenna as she passed. "We're days from where we saw him last."

Jenna nodded, the usual affability missing from her face as she stared into the wilderness after Rayce and the Iron. "Strange seems to follow them. Maybe being lost was too common for the boy."

The logic made Hyatt smirk, even if she didn't when she said it. "Maybe."

Jenna continued to move and Hyatt lingered until Veck passed him. When Rellah followed in his footsteps, Hyatt fell into step beside her. They made their way between the tall, slender brush and the larger trees with thick trunks and lowest branches out of their reach, moving closer to each other than their marching order called for but not close enough to demand a conversation where one was not needed.

As they left the density of the section of Reclaimed that stood behind them, the foliage became more sparse and allowed more bleak morning light pour over them in wider bands that lingered longer and carried warmth. Even the ground seemed drier as the canopy of branches and leaves above them became less robust, letting more and more light bleed through until the ground was awash in it.

Hyatt picked up his pace until he passed Veck and caught up with Bex, then pressed on to reach Rayce where he was rechecking his heading and ensuring he was leading the pack in the right direction. "Hey... it's too thin here. We're switching to arrowhead movement."

"You got it." Rayce started walking again, moving slower to let everyone else settle in.

As the rest of the pack caught up, he pushed his companions left and right to spread out along a wider space. By the time he took up the back-most position with Tobin at his side, his five pack-mates were stretched out far enough that no single danger could catch them all at once.

When the mesa came into view, Hyatt couldn't help the disappointment he felt. It looked tall, but no taller than other cliffs throughout the Reclaimed, and against the sparse foliage that stood between them and the elevated surface made it seem all the more approachable. To fight the anticlimactic view, he assured himself that the climbing gear he and his companions brought with them would be more than enough.

The thought gave him a moment of fortitude, but from within that aura of confidence, the memory of the symbols on the Keeper's map percolated to the forefront of his mind. Having the place marked on his map within sight deposited the sediment of fulfillment in his muscles and tendons, but it also washed away the dirt and frost of the trail that had faded his memory of the dot surrounded by three tipless triangles at the bottom of the pages that led him and his companions to the mesa.

The ground before them declined at so mild a grade that Hyatt didn't notice at first. Only when the descent steepened and the sky-seeking foliage seemed to leave the dirt at a more acute angle did he look back and notice how long they had been on a downhill march. The slope of the terrain undulated in broad swaths, some almost flat and others so slanted that he had to turn sideways and use the sides of his boots to stop himself from tumbling. Large, flat surfaces of dark gray rock broke through the forest floor and made the rich soil and frosted deadfall look like earthen rivers channeled between their immovable forms.

As the terrain sloped downward and surrendered its ability to support brush, the mesa seemed to rise by comparison. Hyatt saw what he had been unable to from the edge of the dense wilderness. In every direction around a core of jagged rock, the earth descended like the walls of an ancient and eroded crater, leaving only the column of stone at its heart amidst a field of shattered earth where nothing more than moss had been able to grow since whatever force had carved into the ground with such savagery. Around the base of the enormous, rough-hewn monolith, darker surfaces of the rock merged with the shadows to make the scene even more foreboding.

*Okay, Kesh. I get it.* Hyatt hopped from one piece of broken ground to the next, his pack swinging and threatening to pull him over. *I see it.*

Tobin lost his footing as he passed Hyatt and tumbled headfirst down a steeper section of ground. He managed to get a shoulder tucked under himself and as he began his fourth revolution, his pack hit the dirt with enough traction to stop himself. By the time Hyatt caught up with him, the Iron was sitting up and dusting himself off.

*The chosen one of Sklodowska, unable to keep his feet under himself.* Hyatt fought the eye-roll that his face demanded to release and offered his hand to the boy. "You okay?"

"Yeah, I'm okay." Tobin took his hand, and Hyatt couldn't help but notice the size difference between their palms and fingers as he pulled the Iron to his feet. "Are you okay?"

"So far." Tobin let go and put his arms out for balance as he made his way down another steep swath of ground until he found a surfaced rock to stabilize against.

They continued in silence, navigating toward the easier descents. Hyatt wondered at how far the terrain dropped in so few paces. Scents of damp rock and standing water surrounded them, and summoned memories of racing through a tunnel in the dark as an Heir stalked them. He took a deep breath to fight the physical response, but couldn't stop himself from searching the open expanses on both sides of him for signs of the monstrous beasts. No sights or sounds of danger reached him, and a wave of embarrassment ran through him at the thought, but the fear of shadowy threats beyond his periphery refused to uncurl from his spine.

As they drew closer to the massive column of stone, it became less open and more jagged. With every new choice, Hyatt felt like he was choosing one path forward at the expense of another, and regretted changing the travel plan to extend his companions further apart from one another. The pocketed depressions in the earth became deeper and the spaces between rose steeper, creating walls of broken rock that were impossible to cross without backtracking.

"It's okay, Hyatt," Tobin assured him as he sat on the edge of a deeper drop before pushing away in a controlled fall to the ground below. "We're almost there."

He didn't know if Tobin had seen the tension on his face or if the Iron had decided to lend his support of his own volition, and he liked less the amount of reassurance he felt from the child's words. The absurdity of it crinkled his nose and furrowed his brow, and he navigated his way to the next flat space without replying to the Iron. When his boots were planted on solid and stable rock, he looked at the rising terrain on either side of the chasm he was descending into and realized he still needed to get Hollow Bone back together.

With a frown that balanced determination and doubt, he cupped his hands and lifted his thumbs to his lips, and blew a stream of air between them. What started as a hiss of air evolved into a warbling tone that surprised him so much that he jerked his hands away from his face, and the sound came to an abrupt stop. His mind raced as he cupped his hands again, working to recall every texture of his thumbs and the placement of his lips against their tops. In a moment of realization, he frowned like he was concentrating, and exhaled through his pursed lips.

A low, unsteady tone radiated from his hands, and with a little adjustment, it became smoother and louder. He let out two shorter bursts of it and stopped to listen, and from across the rocks, calls answered him. Hyatt could feel his giant, overpleased grin spread across his face, and was glad he had a moment to rein it in before Jenna's silhouette appeared above the rocks to his left. Moments later, the rest of Hollow Bone closed in on his location from both sides and dropped into the broad, flat chasm to join him.

Bex looked up at the towering monolith of rock and drove their fingers through their hair. "Wow."

"This cliff is unclimbable." Rayce was out of breath and favoring his left side. "Even with our gear, and strong climbers among us, I don't see a way to make it even half-way up."

Staring up at the rock before him, Hyatt couldn't argue their point. Brief stretches of reasonable handholds and footholds were broken apart by large swaths of flat stone or overhangs that offered no purchase and did every favor to gravity. From where he stood, he could see no fissures deep enough to set the anchors they had gathered in Mescwar, and looking around at the stained and darkened rocks provided a grave reminder of the consequences of falling from any height.

Hyatt took a few steps back and shielded his eyes, trying to gauge how high the top of the mesa was.

"I can climb that." Tobin rested his closed fists on his hips.

Hyatt ignored the Iron and tried to picture how many paces it would take to cross it if it were flat terrain, but a range between five-hundred and six-hundred was the best he could guess. His estimation did nothing to encourage him, but as he felt another rock settle onto the cairn of despair building inside him, he caught sight of a roughly horizontal crease along the cliff's face.

"Hey... I think that's a ledge." He pointed at it and tried to hold his arm still as Bex moved to his shoulder, using Hyatt's arm as a guide.

"Maybe. Do you think that's what the last climbers thought?" Bex paused and stared up at Rellah who was already climbing, with a rope tied to her belt. "Hey – what are you doing?"

By the time she answered, Rellah was already over their heads and searching for her next handhold. "We make it, or we don't. No use talking about it down here."

"Rellah's going to fucking plummet to her death, and Hyatt's going to be in charge forever," Veck growled as he dropped his pack and started pulling at the straps to free another rope. "Might as well all kill ourselves now."

"You go first, we'll be right behind you." Jenna's words carried the same exasperated sarcasm that their pack-mates had, but there was a warning that ran through them like alternating current that dared Veck to try his luck by touching it again.

Hyatt was so focused on Rellah's every moment as she clung to the wall above them that he only caught their exchange as if he had overheard it from another room. Rellah's boot found purchase on an angled surface of the cliff but as she shifted her weight onto it, her foot broke traction and left her hanging by a single handhold. He locked his jaw and watched, unable to do anything to help her, as she pulled herself up far enough to let her other hand find purchase.

On his other side, Rayce let out a slow breath. "That was close."

"She's going to be okay," Tobin said between them, that same child-like certainty radiating from every word.

As Rellah climbed higher, a cold gust cut across the face of the cliff and caused the hem of her shirt to snap and flutter like a pennant. Hyatt looked toward the horizon where clouds had begun to form in low, puffy clusters made gray by carried rain or snow. His heart sank even more as he thought of attempting their climb on wet rock with numb extremities, or the need to escape the crater to avoid soaking their gear in standing water.

Hyatt returned his attention to Rellah and saw her grab the edge of the ledge above her, swinging her hips to land a leg onto it before tumbling out of sight. After what felt like an eternity in the unknown, her head appeared over the ledge again.

"Tied it off – come up!" She vanished again without waiting for their response.

Hyatt set off toward the rope but Rayce beat him to it, so he watched as his pack-mate fed the dangling rope through the metal loops linked around his belt. He knotted the rope with quick, deft motions and gave it a tug to cinch it, then started climbing. Hyatt watched in rapt attention as Rayce made his way to the ledge, hoping to memorize his pack-mate's route.

When his companion crested the ledge, Hyatt stepped forward to be ready when he tossed the rope down. He fastened it in the same way he watched his pack-mate tie it off and grabbed the first handhold on the wall as he felt Rellah or Rayce take the slack from above him. It only took four handholds to realize that the ascent they made look easy was complex, tense, and exhausting.

Two-thirds of the way to the ledge he grabbed a handhold that broke in his hand, and Hyatt fell.

# SIXTEEN

Hyatt's arms strained to reach the cliff's face but found only open air as his feet lost their hold on the rock. In a flash, he saw his back catching the rocks below at a bad angle and snapping his spine in half, paralyzing him.

Instead, he felt the rope snap taut, and his arms and legs flailed as he tried to find purchase on the cliff again. He swayed on the end of the rope until his fingers found enough of an edge to curl around, and he strained with every muscle of his body to apply pressure through his fingertips to right himself. With his heart in his throat and his hands damp with sweat, he continued his climb.

When he reached the ledge, he felt Rayce's grip through his shirt as his pack-mate helped him onto solid ground. Hyatt's tumble onto his knees and then to his back was less graceful than theirs had looked but as he stared up at the sky, he didn't care. His fingers worked at the knot near his belt without the benefit of his sight to guide them. After a moment, he found the right angles to pry at the rope, and it came apart. With a groan of effort, he crawled to the edge of the ledge and hurled the end of the rope into the open air, then struggled to his feet.

The cliff above them made the cliff below look like an introductory climb. The ledge itself was the size of an Assembly and slanted downward toward the cliff, and the majority of its outer edge was rimmed by large fragments of rock that looked like they'd fallen from above and become caught on their way to the ground below. Everything about the ledge and cliff looked inhospitable and grim, and then Hyatt noticed the smears of brown that could only have been the blood of climbers who had aimed for the ledge as their first stop and paid for their mistakes in the moments that followed.

His pack-mates and the Iron had reached the ledge in the time it took for him to become acquainted with his surroundings, and it allowed him to watch their faces shift as they reached the same series of daunting conclusions one at a time. Jenna set to work hauling packs up the cliff-face by their drag-lines, while Bex studied the next expanse of rock with their hand on top of their head. The erratic bursts of icy wind felt stronger, colder, and louder than they had been on the ground below.

"An anchor could go there." Rayce pointed at a place high on the cliff. "If we can get to it."

The thought of climbing to the height his pack-mate pointed to, twice as far as their climb to the ledge, thickened the doubt in Hyatt's heart. He found himself shaking his head before he realized he was doing it, and even though he stopped himself, Jenna had seen it and nodded as Veck began pacing the length of the ledge.

"We can't reach that." She untied the last drag-line from a pack and coiled it around her palm, then shoved it into a side pocket of the bag.

"So we're stuck," Veck concluded without changing his pace or course. "Stuck on a rotted ledge with a storm coming on."

"We're not stuck." Rayce walked to the edge and peered down at the ground below. "We can climb down if we have to."

As Hollow Bone argued about options, Hyatt realized Rellah hadn't said anything. Her face was unconcerned and even lacked the hardness around her eyes and the tension in her cheeks that he had come to know was her baseline state. Instead, she looked like she was standing in the eye of a storm. Hyatt couldn't reconcile it with the most action-oriented person he'd ever met, and moved to stand next to her.

"Is the travel plan complete, since we reached the mesa?" He paused and fished in his pocket for an herb-twist, focusing on unwrapping the wax-paper around it. "Because I could really use your leadership about now."

"You're doing fine." It was strange to hear her voice without either the ring of authenticity or the forced syllables as she told him what he needed to hear.

Her words didn't fit into the place Hyatt wanted them to fill, and felt more like she had tossed him a fistful of spare parts instead of a completed thought. "Okay."

He was wracking his mind for how to crack the shell on Rellah's mood, but caught sight of Rayce cocking his head with a squint that meant he was trying to listen through the whistling wind. His pack-mate's stillness started a chain reaction and he found himself freezing, even as Jenna and Veck stopped moving on the other side of the ledge. Only Tobin seemed unaffected as he shuffled across the stone, kicking loose pebbles in front of him.

The unexpected downdraft that slammed into Hyatt and knocked him to the ground was the only warning that something was above him. His shoulders connected with the rock, and the impact drove the air from his lungs. He opened his eyes to the winged silhouette of a Skarren blotting out a broad swatch of sky and he tried to scream, but his chest seized as his lungs refused to move air either in or out.

Hyatt's next sight was Tobin's little boots running by him and Rayce's head eclipsing the Heir as his pack-mate stared down at him. He hadn't realized his ears were ringing until the sound began to recede and Rayce's urgent and strained tone melted into existence. "Can you move?"

Hyatt nodded and coughed as he forced himself into a sitting position. Beside him, Rellah stood with her bow pointed skyward and at full extension as she tracked the winged beast on its arc through the air above them and loosed an arrow. The Skarren abandoned a full plunge to evade the projectile and banked away as it climbed, flapping hard and slamming gale-force winds against them as it rose out of Rellah's range.

Rayce grabbed Hyatt's pack and used it to half lead, half drag him toward the cliff face and away from the open air. "You good?"

Hyatt sucked in the first breath his lungs would allow, a searing scorch in his chest that made his eyes water and triggered a violent cough. "Yeah!"

The jagged rocks that surrounded them no longer felt to him like an easy position to defend from dangers, but a pen with no overhead cover to protect them from the monstrous winged beast that hunted them. Against the sky-darkening span of the Skarren's wings, six clusters of savage talons gleamed with wicked intention and the beast's rows of teeth inside its open maw promised death as it dove at them again.

Rayce let go of him and mantled the closest boulder. "Spread out!"

Tobin scurried along the edge of the ledge with his eyes pointed skyward, and Rellah brought another arrow to bear on the Skarren as it dove directly over her. As the beast roared, she fired at its open mouth before tucking her bow close to her body and somersaulting across the rock away from it. The arrow missed and raced skyward, and the pitch of the Heir's battle cry rose. It thrashed its head back and forth as Rellah's effort to kill it enraged it instead. Its wings began to pump furiously, and the gust knocked Hyatt onto his back. In his periphery, he saw Veck tumble off a boulder and Jenna scrambling onto a jagged expanse of rock on the far side of their accidental arena, a fistful of rope trailing behind her.

"Right wing, at the wrist joint!" She dropped the coil of rope at her feet except for the segment in her closed fist, two arm's lengths above the grappling hook affixed to the end.

Hyatt watched Rellah nod and nock another arrow. He looked up at the Skarren, time slowing as its ruse of flapping hard to climb high into the sky gave way to a sharp and low arc far too close to Rellah. Its talons seemed to cut the air itself, leaving ripples in their wake like he was watching them through the smoke of a campfire.

"No!" He screamed, a primal defiance of the inevitable as he launched himself into a staggering sprint and ripped his blade free from his belt with a savage wrenching motion.

He could barely keep his feet under himself as his upper body outdistanced his knees with every flailing step, his weapon careening wildly in the air. Ahead of him, Rellah looked up from her bow and stared directly into the spread and razor-sharp talons of the beast, and the tip of her arrow dipped as she realized she couldn't bring it to bear in time and that she was going to die.

Hyatt slammed into her without slowing down and the connection of his shoulder against her back sent Rellah sprawling across the stone and redirected his motion into a spiral like a spun top. As he whirled out of control, he felt the violent yank of his blade biting into something, and it was all he could do to stop the countering force from ripping the weapon out of his hand as he fell. The sound of his impact against the ground was drowned out by an ear-splitting shriek of agony and the roar of the wind that engulfed him.

Hyatt opened his eyes and stared skyward as a rope launched across his vision and snapped taut with a wet, ripping sound. The rope snapped and he threw his arm up to protect his face on instinct. Wet blood splattered over him like hot rain. The sensation forced a spasm through his sternum and he fought the urge to vomit, his throat closing and the taste of copper saturating his tongue.

Tobin was suddenly beside him, crouched with his head tilted to align his eyes with Hyatt's. "It's not your blood – you're okay! Get up!"

By the time he lowered his arm, a quiet stillness surrounded him. Hyatt searched the sky for the Heir, but there was no sign of it. Unwilling to waste the respite, he scrambled to his feet and gripped the handle of his weapon with both hands until his knuckles were as white as clouds. On the ground behind him, Rellah let out a laugh that landed somewhere between euphoria and delirium as she realized she was still alive.

He turned and reached down to help her up, and she wrapped her hand around his forearm as she pulled hard. He planted his foot to anchor himself as he pulled back, propelling her onto her feet. Her laughter subsided and Rayce joined them with Veck trailing behind, while Jenna stayed on the rock above them and coiled what remained of her rope.

"Everyone okay?" Jenna asked.

# SEVENTEEN

"Hey... I think I found something!" Rayce's voice came from the far end of the ledge.

Hyatt looked over to see him kneeling and examining the face of the cliff, tracing the edge of one of the rock's contours with his fingers. "What is it?"

Rayce frowned at the rock and pulled his belt-knife free of his sheath. The blade glinted as he turned it over in his hand so he could drag the back of the knife's tip along the same angle of rock he had been tracing, and a dusting of dark-gray powder drifted away from the surface.

"There's something round here." He squinted at the mark his blade had left in the stone, a trench too deep for the careful pressure he had applied to it.

Hyatt started walking toward him and as he did, he realized he had forgotten the final marker on the Keeper maps that had brought him and his pack to the Bloodstained Mesa. The image of the filled dot with three wedges pointed toward it, and he broke into a dead sprint as the flash in his memory converted to a burst of panic.

"Rayce, wait! Stop!" His body forgot the fatigue of fighting the Heir and propelled him across the narrow shelf at full speed.

Rayce recoiled from the wall like it had tried to bite him, balanced on his toes with his hands up and out and Hyatt almost crashed into him as he tried to stop his forward momentum. As he searched the face of the cliff for the place Rayce had been carving at the stone, he heard the quickened steps of everyone else moving toward them at the end of the ledge. Rayce gestured with his knife to direct Hyatt's attention to the arc he had traced into the face of the cliff. Under the gray, fresh mar of the surface, Hyatt saw what his pack-mate had seen, metal glinting around the right hemisphere of a circle half the size of his thumb.

"What's wrong?" Rayce lowered his hands.

Hyatt took a step backward and reached across Rayce to guide him backward too as he studied the rest of the cliff's face around the single metallic point. He couldn't make out any radiating lines that could form the remainder of the symbol he was terrified would be revealed. Relief tried to grow in him, but with it came a deeper memory and he glanced back at Rellah as she approached.

"I don't know yet. Hang on." Hyatt ran his fingers through his hair and looked back at Rellah, who slowed her stride as he started toward her.

"What is it?" Her attention fixed on the face of the cliff where Hyatt and Rayce had been, then pivoted back to him.

He took a slight step to position himself between Rellah and the rest of their pack to block the movement of his lips from view, and lowered his voice. "Do you remember the panel of broken buttons in the Laybrair, against the back wall by the open shaft?"

Her eyes darkened in confirmation, and he could almost see the images that were surfacing in her mind. "What about it?"

"I think what he found is a button like that." Hyatt reached back and turned his collar up against the sharp breeze that buffeted against his shoulders. "It could be a way up…"

Rellah raised an eyebrow but as she continued to watch his face, it settled again in place of a grim and resigned expression. "Say the rest."

He hunched his shoulders against the cold and looked back at the rest of Hollow Bone pack gathered at the end of the ledge. "The Keeper Map had that other mark on it... one of the world-killer markers. The button could also be for that."

"Okay." She shrugged. "Push it."

Hyatt tumbled her reply in his head a few times. "What?"

"Push it." She walked past him toward their companions as Hyatt turned to follow her. "If the world can end with one button, at least we choose when it's pressed."

"Wait!" Hyatt tried to pack his voice with urgency, without raising it as she shouldered her way between Jenna and Veck to stand in front of the marred rock.

In response, Rellah pressed the button. Hyatt flinched and threw his arm up to shield his face in a raw instinct to survive, but after a moment he lowered it as he heard and then saw Rellah pounding the button repeatedly with the bottom of her fist.

"Sorry, no world-killer—" Rellah turned to face Hyatt, but frowned and looked back at Hyatt as a low rumble began and a permeating vibration reached them through the soles of their boots.

Rayce And Bex bent their knees and extended their arms for balance, and Jenna took a step closer to the face of the cliff to lean against it. Veck knelt on one knee and pressed his palm to the rock beneath him to stabilize himself against the tremors, and Rellah turned in place as she searched her surroundings for changes.

Hyatt stared at her, dumbfounded by her split-second decision to risk all of their lives. Stones dislodged or broken free of the cliff's face above them began to career downward, crashing into their ledge and plunging into the depths beyond its edge. Through the tremors and the hail of rocks, Rellah's face looked disinterested and unaffected, and Hyatt couldn't tear his eyes away from her apathetic expression.

"Why did you do that?" He shouted the question to ensure it carried over the rumbling, but the sound and the vibration stopped as quickly as it had begun, leaving him yelling at her with nothing to compete against.

She glanced at him and shrugged. "It was better than talking."

"It absolutely wasn't –" he started.

"I think there's something here!" Rayce interrupted them as he moved closer to the wall of stone and brushed his hand along the rough surface.

Hyatt settled for finishing his protest with a suspicious glare at Rellah and she turned her attention to Rayce's discovery. A vertical crack started at the ledge under their boots and rose over their heads, too straight to be a natural fissure. In the wake of Rayce's glove, fine white powder wiped away from the cliff face and covered his palm like chalk.

In the heart of the crack, at eye level, Hyatt caught sight of something metal. "You're right – there's something behind the – "

Veck barged between them and slammed his axe into the face of the wall, showering Hyatt with fragments that caused him to throw up his arm in defense and flinch away. He stepped back as Veck hit the wall again with a savage swing that carried all the strength of his legs and shoulders through his weapon and into the cliff. Shards broke free and then a slab the size of Hyatt's chest broke away, shattering into a dozen pieces as it landed on the ledge at Veck's feet.

"It's softer than shale," Veck growled as he lifted his axe again, then grunted and smashed it into the rock.

As the cliff's face broke away, more and more metal began to show through. The surface was pale silver and covered with dents and scratches, and made a hollow sound as the force of Veck's weapon reverberated through it. Every new assault on the cliff's face shattered more stone and exposed more of the metal.

Hyatt took a step back, careful to stay clear of the ledge's edge. "That definitely won't explode or collapse. It's probably fine."

Veck grunted and backed away from the wall, lowering his axe for a moment. "Do you have a better idea?"

Hyatt opened his mouth to reply but had no alternative to offer, and searching one extended his pause into a longer stall, but Jenna broke in. "Can't think of a worse one. Move."

Veck turned his attention to her and for a moment it looked like he was about to argue, but instead he stepped aside to make room for Jenna next to the destroyed rock. She pulled her blade free and tilted it to wedge the steel artificial surface and the rock, then pulled at the handle with both hands to pry against it. A sheet of stone broke away and revealed a seam that separated the metal plate from another one. With a victorious smirk at Veck, she pressed the point of her blade into the seam and threw her weight against it, and it sank into the seam until the hilt of her weapon stopped it. When Jenna shoved her handle to the side, the two plates separated with the whine of metal grinding on metal.

"See?" She pulled her blade back and inspected it before sheathing it.

Rayce stepped forward and peered into the gap between the metal surfaces, then grabbed the one on his left with both hands. It didn't move, and he shifted his stance to throw his weight behind it. He grunted as he strained to move it, but the plate began to slide with the same wailing screech. By the time he stepped back, the space between the plates was big enough to walk through. The daylight behind him revealed the first two tiles of a floor beyond but made it no further into the room behind the cliff's face. Stale air wafted from the chamber before being dispersed on the breeze.

"That... has been closed a long time." Rayce lifted his shirt to cover his mouth and nose.

"Let's go." Rellah wrapped her scarf around the lower half of her face as she moved past Rayce and turned sideways to step into the dark.

*What are you doing?* Hyatt stepped to follow her on instinct but hesitated at the cliff face for the space of a breath. *Well, nothing collapsed or exploded, so...*

Crossing the threshold into the tiled room beyond felt like stepping into another world. Hyatt held his breath as his eyes began to adjust, and when he remembered to breathe, the pungent air clung to his tongue and made him gag. The room was square and smaller than he expected, four paces across with a low ceiling he was sure he could reach if he jumped.

The rest of his companions eased their way through the opening in the cliff's face, and Bex scrunched their nose at the smell of the room. "Anything here?"

Veck turned in a circle and blinked in the dark. "Doesn't look like it."

Hyatt moved to the back wall and slid his hand over the cool metal, perfectly flat except for metal strapping that broke the surface into panels. He worked his way around the perimeter of the room, feeling his way over the scratches and the strapping, until he reached the front. Beside the gap between the two panels, his fingers slid over a pair of buttons like the one Rayce had found outside.

He yanked his hand back like they'd bitten him, and the sudden motion drew Jenna's attention. "What was that?"

"I don't know yet." Hyatt crouched and leaned closer to the wall, squinting to search the buttons for markings or anything to differentiate them. "There's two buttons."

"Press the top one." Rellah's voice came from the back of the room.

He winced at the suggestion, trying to churn through an infinite number of unknowns that could follow her advice. He imagined the room filling with flames and killing all of them, or the roof caving in and crushing them all under the weight of the plateau's stone. Every version of events that he could conjure ended in gruesome fates for him and all his companions.

The grimace stayed on his face as he looked away and pressed the button.

As the metal circle depressed under his fingertip, a pale yellow glow formed in a ring around it. His frantic jump backward was faster than he could get his boots under him, and he tumbled over backward onto his back. Underneath him, the floor began to shake in a violent tremor.

"Rot!" Veck staggered to the wall and braced against it. "Here we go again!"

Hyatt looked up at Rellah where she leaned against the back wall with her crossed her arms as the square room shuddered around them, he scrambled to his feet. No concern registered on her face and she didn't look down at him as he struggled to find his balance. Beside her, Tobin had found a seat on the floor with his back against the wall, and was studying the ceiling of the chamber with a curious expression.

"We're losing our way out!" Bex shouted.

He spun around and almost lost his footing again. The light through the gap in the cliff's face disappeared from the bottom up. The daylight vanished, plunging them into darkness as the room continued to shake and rumble beneath their boots. Hyatt felt like they were moving and hoped they were ascending, but with no point to reference from, he couldn't be sure.

The floor tilted with the sound of rending metal and sent Jenna and Rayce sprawling. Hyatt bent his knees and flung his arm out to brace against the wall, and Veck stumbled into a run across the small chamber to the lower end of the floor's slope to stop himself from falling. His shoulder connected with the wall, halting his momentum with a thud.

"Great idea, Hyatt," he growled as he found his footing and pushed himself upright.

The violent tremors stopped with a sudden lurch, like the last gasp of a dying beast. Hyatt felt his way along the wall and bumped against Bex and Rayce, almost tripping over Jenna as he moved to the side of the chamber where they had pried the panels open before. His fingers found the seam between them and keeping one hand in place to ensure he didn't lose the place, he pulled his knife from his belt and wedged the tip into the crease. When he felt the first inch of it slip between the panels he grabbed the handle with both hands, shoved, and pulled sideways as hard as he could.

Late afternoon light plunged through the gap he created, but his knife wasn't long enough to pry the panels apart any further. He had just begun trying to wedge his boot into the gap when Jenna appeared beside him and slipped her hands into the opening. When she pulled, it relieved the pressure on his blade and Hyatt fumbled the weapon but recovered it before he dropped it. As soon as he returned it to his sheath, he grabbed the other side and pulled the panel in the opposite direction.

The doors groaned in protest at being forced to move in ways they weren't designed and fought being pulled apart, until they suddenly gave way. The change in resistance staggered Hyatt and he lost his grip, but caught himself against the wall to stop himself from falling over. The smell of fresher air flooded into the chamber and began to replace the stale scent. He walked toward the doors with his eyes fixed on the space between them, every step unveiling more of the world outside until he was standing in the gap.

Hyatt stepped through the massive metal doors into the late afternoon light, shades of violet and burnt orange pouring through the trees and across the frostbitten grass and pockets of shallow snow before him. The musty, stale air of the chamber gave way to a cold, alpine breeze that cut to his bones and burned the inside of his nose as he breathed it in. He took a step forward to clear the doorway so his pack-mates could follow him into the outdoor air, the frozen ground crunching under his boots.

"Where..." Bex's half-formed thought fell apart as they reached out, plucking a cluster of pale orange berries from a nearby bush and rolling one of the berries between their thumb and forefinger. "I don't know what these are. I don't know any of these... where are we?"

On Hyatt's other side, Veck crouched down and ran his fingers through the handspan-deep grass, collecting moisture from their flat blades and rubbing it into their skin. "Somewhere old. Somewhere we shouldn't be."

Hyatt barely heard their wonder and concern as he took another step, looking up at the horsetail clouds ablaze with sunset light between the strange, unfamiliar leaves of the scattered trees ahead. The ground sloped upward gently and reached a horizon line against the distant sky, and Hyatt knew with certainty he couldn't explain that what the Keeper's Map marked was just beyond the crest. Bex and Veck lingered on either side of the ancient metal doors while Rellah and Jenna fanned out behind him like an arrow, trailing steps behind him on each side.

"Go slow, becquerel," Jenna murmured, the matte tones of a raider wrapping around the solid sounds in her words. "We don't know this place."

Hyatt heard her, but he felt himself drawn towards the crest and lacked the desire to wait any longer. He stepped into a patch of snow, crunching through the hard crust that covered it to the shifting powder below, and it trailed from the toe of his boot as he continued onward with his pack-mates close behind. The smooth bark of the scattered trees before him cast long, clean shadows, as if their tapered origins were arrows to lead him somewhere.

As he approached the highest point in front of him, the ground beyond turned sharply downward, so that every new step revealed more of the far edge of a deep excavation. Whatever he dreamt he might find in the space marked by the map, the massive and overgrown structure at the heart of a sprawling Garden exceeded the scope of his imagination. Clusters of rooftops divided by honeycombed paths that revealed themselves between long, latticed arbors entangled in flowering vines, and the lingering daylight drenched it all in shades of cream and blood red and pale violet.

"Wow…" Tobin's awe dragged out the center of his whispered word as he appeared beside Hyatt, shielding his eyes with his little palm and stepping closer to the edge.

"How…" Hyatt began, but words failed him and he stood with his mouth open as his mind tried to expand far enough to understand what he was seeing.

Late afternoon light washed over rooftops shingled with dark red and gray slats that looked like scales from where he stood.

Between the buildings, square posts supported cross-hatched lattices that covered large sections of roads made from crushed stone. The Garden filled the depths of the mesa's top for as far as he could see.

At the center, a massive structure dwarfed every other building that surrounded it in asymmetric blocks of neighborhoods, parks, and stands of trees. Its construction was unlike anything Hyatt had ever seen, towered architecture that seemed imposing and elegant at once. Distance hid the details of the large building, but he could make out rows of columns and rings of parapets that made him certain the interior was filled with mazes of hallways and large chambers.

The only thing more surreal to Hyatt than the impossible Garden he overlooked from the outer edge was the absolute stillness of everything before him. The wind tugged at his jacket and pack, but had no visible influence over anything at the bottom of the excavated ground before him. He tried to narrow his focus by choosing specific buildings and stands of trees to give his undivided attention to, but he saw no sign of wildlife or even a window left open to allow curtains to shift in the breeze.

He felt the need to speak but could find no words for the alchemy of experiences that churned in his chest like a whirlpool and flooded his mind like an unstoppable tide. The sight before him defied his understanding and yet was impossible to dispel, and his body felt as though it was uncertain whether to make his heart beat faster or his stomach drop. He laced his fingers behind his head and just let himself absorb what he couldn't express or explain.

"This Garden..." Jenna's voice faltered, and the expression on her face as she tried to process the same experience was surprisingly validating to Hyatt. "It's so..."

Rayce stepped to his side, his gaze sweeping back and forth across the city that sprawled out below. "No fires, no movement... no damage to the buildings. Where is everyone?"

Hyatt had no answer for him. Everything he saw told him the same thing he said – he could find no sign that anyone lived in the Garden. It looked as if everyone had woken up one day, packed their things, and left like an abandoned Cern camp. He lifted his field glasses and searched parts of the settlement, but didn't see any cultivated foliage or tilled earth, and lowered the lenses with a confused shake of his head.

"Dead," Rellah replied, a grim core through her certainty. "They couldn't have lived cut off from the world, and if they came and went from here, someone would have known about it. They're all dead."

Tobin nodded solemnly in wordless agreement and turned to walk along the edge of the terrain's limit. Instinct made Hyatt turn to look where the boy was going but even as his chin shifted after Tobin, his eyes stayed fixed to the city below. He lost sight of the Iron in his periphery and couldn't will himself to turn further at the cost of losing any part of the Garden that shouldn't have existed from his view.

Veck and Bex caught up with them at the edge of the cavernous pit, Bex easing themselves between Hyatt and Jenna while Veck stepped to the edge to get a better look directly below them. When he was done, he took a few steps backward, dropped his pack, and began opening it.

"What are you doing?" Jenna asked.

"Look, somebody is going to say going down there is a bad idea – because it is a fucking rotted bad idea," he grumbled, unloading the coiled length of rope slung across the top of his bag. "Then, Hyatt's going to insist we have to, for some compost reason. We're going to argue, and then we're going to go down there because we came all this way."

Hyatt opened his mouth to protest, but realized Veck was right, so nodded and shrugged.

"Except, it's getting dark, and I don't want to climb down there in the dark. If we're going into this Garden of the Dead, we might as well spend the night under a roof instead of freezing our buds off up here. So, I'm just getting started while you all catch up." Veck tugged at the knot retaining the rope and began to unspool it across the ground.

"Garden of the Dead sounds bad." Bex was nonchalant in their reply but mounted no argument against Veck's version of events.

"Rellah..." Hyatt said, each word moving slowly across his tongue to make sure it landed without any jagged edges, "if this is one of those there-might-be-an-eighth-warning-after-all moments, I'd like to know."

The sharp looks from Veck and Bex at Rellah and her long pause that followed made him wonder if he'd chosen the wrong words despite his careful curation. Rellah held her bow in one hand and put her free hand in her pocket, staring out over the Garden, her breath hanging in pale clouds in the space beyond her parted lips.

"I don't know any stories about a missing Garden." Rellah's reply churned through the translucent mist of her last, lingering exhale. "We have no memory of a place like this."

"Okay." Hyatt stepped closer and looked across the impossible sight before him.

The steps carved into the wall of the garden's carved-out perimeter were broad in places and narrow in others, and their depths varied as if their sculptors had capitulated to whatever shape the rock was willing to accept instead of compelling it to submit to their chisels. No railing shielded the side opposite the wall, so Hyatt kept his shoulder to the solid side as he eased his way down from one stair to the next.

The wind seemed to become quieter and more still as Hyatt descended. At first he thought it was his imagination, but by the time the stone steps switched back on themselves and he rounded the corner, he could no longer feel the movement of the air around him and the only sounds he could hear were the footfalls of Veck's boots on the steps below him. The stairs became narrower, barely as wide as his shoulders, and the rim of the recessed Garden let less and less light pour down to his depth.

He moved with as much care and intention as he could, testing each step before putting his full weight on them. He half-expected every new stair to collapse under his weight and reveal ancient and crumbling supports, or a tunneling abyss that would send him plummeting to the core of the mesa by a shaft like the one they'd used to reach the surface.

He lost track of time as the staircase changed directions four more times, and had no idea how long Veck had been standing at the bottom when he reached him. The last abraded stone step gave way to the familiar feel of hard-packed earth and Hyatt looked up at the sky, a shade of navy against the darker, high horizon line.

By the time his companions reached the base of the steps, the barest sliver of moon appeared above the depression's artificial horizon but gave so little light that it failed to drown out the stars beginning to appear at the furthest reaches of his view. Beneath the expanse with clouds only encroaching on one side, the outlines of the buildings closest to them became indistinguishable except for the massive center structure that loomed high above the jagged rise and fall of rooftop silhouettes.

Hyatt rubbed his hands together to build warmth between them and hunched his shoulders to block the night air from sliding between his jacket and his shirt. He saw Rellah notice and grit his teeth to stop them from chattering as he waited for her to criticize him for being the first to succumb to the cold, but she only shrugged and nodded toward the closest shape of a building.

"Shelter and fire. Nobody goes exploring until after daybreak." She dropped her pack and stared at Tobin as she spoke. and he looked ready to protest, but she continued before he could form an argument. "Bex, with me."

Bex unslung their bag and propped it against Rellah's, and they set up with visible intent towards the nearest building. Tobin struggled free of his little pack and took a step to follow them but Veck buried his hand in the back of the Iron's collar like a cat latched onto a kitten, halting him with a tug.

"Hey!" Tobin reached back to grab for Veck's hand, but couldn't get the right angle to latch onto it.

"Not you, weed." He half-pulled, half-shoved Tobin into the space between Hyatt and Jenna before pointing like he was trying to nail the Iron in place.

The way Tobin's features roiled in frustration and impotent child-rage drew something taut in Hyatt. He recalled everything he'd seen an Irons do, and every story he'd ever heard about the abilities Irons were rumored to have bubbled to the surface of his thoughts. He watched Tobin's eyes flicker with resentment, and Cern stories Rellah had told him about the history of Irons came together like fog forming over a lake.

"We send small groups to check new places, so we're not all surprised by a danger," he told Tobin, resisting the urge to crouch so he was at eye-level with the boy. "If there's a problem, you can help rescue them."

The tempest of red feelings on Tobin's face tempered a bit and he nodded, settling for a glare at Veck. "Good thing he didn't go to check. I wouldn't save him."

Jenna stifled a smirk and cupped her hands over her mouth to hide the part that slipped through, breathing her warm breath across her hands as she composed herself before wiping the moisture from them on her pants. Veck huffed like he was rejecting the idea that he would ever need saving by a child, but he turned to look in the direction Rellah and Bex had headed. Tobin stomped his boots to keep blood flowing to his feet, and Hyatt let out a breath that had begun to ache in his lungs as he moved to stand shoulder-to-shoulder with Veck.

"You good?" he asked without looking at him.

"I fucking hate Irons," Veck muttered in his gruff, clipped cadence, "and the cold, and Gardens – you know what I mean."

No defense rose in Hyatt at Veck's condemnation of the spaces he grew up in, but he buried that thought to dwell on in nights when sleep didn't come. "I don't care. We can't risk anyone getting injured out here – leave the sprout alone."

Veck's head swiveled to stare through the side of Hyatt's head. "You're telling me what to do, becquerel? You don't want to run that by Rellah first?"

Hyatt's instincts ran counter to everything he'd learned in the Reclaimed. Instead of stepping back in the face of his pack-mate's confrontation, he turned and stepped forward so the closures of his jacket and the tip of his nose almost touched Veck. Hyatt focused on an imaginary point three paces behind Veck's head so his eyes wouldn't shift as they searched for a detail to latch onto. He kept his breath level as his climbing pulse started to ask for more oxygen in growlingly insistent ways, and he let his pack-mate's question stall in the air so his answer was his own and not a reaction to the challenge.

"Leave the sprout alone." His words didn't change pitch or falter.

Veck's gaze shifted first, swiveling from one of Hyatt's pupils to the other. The victory, marked by no other word or action, set off an unexpected crackle in Hyatt's blood, and it took everything in him not to smile or nod to bring an end to the moment. Veck shrugged and spat, his saliva eating through the snow like acid.

Hyatt turned back toward the black silhouette of the Garden's outer buildings. A flicker of firelight revealed a window and the sliver of an open door. "It's clear. Let's go."

Even on the frozen ground and scattered patches of snow, the only steps Hyatt heard behind him were the hurried and careless tromping of Tobin's boots. The fifty paces between the base of the steps and the sole point of light in the excavated Garden had nothing to break the wind, and it sliced through Hyatt's jacket and flesh like razors. The edges of his ears had stopped stinging and he pressed his palm against his left one, rewarded by sudden stinging fire in response to the warmth of his hand. He winced and shoved his hands back into his pockets as his fingertips began to numb, quickening his pace toward the welcome glow ahead.

He stepped into the first wave of radiating heat as he reached the acute shard of light that spilled from the ajar door. It carried with it a wash of relief and hope that surprised him, and he couldn't help the smile that spread across the threshold to find Rellah and Bex feeding debris into a crackling fire. The warmth was trapped well by the rough-textured walls and the translucent glass of the window, a strong contrast with the unforgiving cold outside. Hyatt made his way to a free side of the little blaze and held his reddened fingertips and palms toward the flames, grateful for the sparkling pain as they started to absorb heat.

"We'll stay here," Rellah said as Jenna and Tobin slid through the door, Jenna loaded down with Bex's and Rellah's packs, and Veck paused to close it behind them before joining his pack-mates around the fire. "No signs of life in the surrounding buildings. Hyatt, set shifts."

*Is that what you got from this? She's trying to make you deep enough so you can live.* Bex's words echoed in his head, fortifying Hyatt against her clipped instruction and letting him hang onto successful feelings of facing down Veck and the relief of the warm, sheltered room. Her impersonal order jarred him, but he chose to rise to it.

"Jenna, Bex, Veck, me, Rellah," he replied. "Ninety minutes each, no outside checks, keep the door closed and the fire this small or smaller."

"What about me?" Tobin asked, elbowing him in the side. "I can stand guard."

Hyatt paused to see if Veck would defy him by slinging a confrontational retort, but his pack-mate shrugged his acknowledgment of his assignment and turned to prop his backpack against the closest wall. "Only pack-mates can be guards for the pack, Iron. If you want to sit up with me, you can."

# EIGHTEEN

The fire was blue-white and emitted no heat, but the night was nice enough that Hyatt didn't mind. He watched the flames flicker and jump as the pale gray coals pulsed in the depths of the firepit, the totality of the campfire creating a hypnotic rhythm without ever repeating itself. It gave off just enough light to drive the shadows back to the edges of the room, and enough to make him wonder where his pack-mates had vanished to in the middle of the night.

"So this is it, huh?" Kenna asked as she walked through the opaque and bottomless darkness that filled the doorframe on the far side of the fire, her head tilted back to take in the ceiling and the corners of the room. "It's... nice."

The sound of her voice plucked the taut string that ran from Hyatt's heart to his hips and he tried to scramble to his feet, but his legs refused to move. Instead, he watched as Kenna walked around the campfire and took and knelt beside him, sitting back on her heels and holding her hands out as if they could be warmed by the heatless flames. The way she leaned forward exposed the round exit wound of the Veshtrue's spike through her center, and the sight of it grew the seed of terror and anguish trying to sprout in his gut.

"How is everybody?" she asked.

He couldn't answer her, and he didn't know if it was because of the way the sight of the hole through her paralyzed him, or because his dream had forgotten to render him capable. He tried to speak, but no words formed.

After a moment passed, she looked over at him with hollow, distant eyes that still managed to seem exasperated as they rolled in their sockets. "Come on, Hyatt – we don't have a lot of time. Tell me our pack-mates miss me. Tell me you didn't leave my body back there... tell me you brought me with you!"

There was a note of tension in her last sentiment, a precursor to panic that overcame Hyatt's inability to speak. "No – we, uh... you're with the others. We have you with us."

She smiled then, a genuine expression improved by the contrast of the blue-white firelight. She nodded and seemed to relax, rocking back onto her rear and stretching her legs out in front of her.

"Thank you. I'll see you soon." Kenna put her hand on his, and it was ice cold.

Hyatt woke to the temperature change that heralded the last hour before sunrise and for a moment, he had no idea where he was. The scent of the space and the wall and floor closest to him seemed out of place, but as he blinked and took a deep breath, reality washed over him like a bucket of freezing water. His brain began to work like someone had pulled back thick curtains to let light flood into it and he sat up.

None of his companions had woken and no one stirred as he rose to his knees and then to his feet. Rayce waved without a word from the corner he had chosen for standing guard, and Hyatt picked up his boots before crossing the room to join him.

"All quiet," Rayce said in a low, quiet tone.

Hyatt nodded and took a seat beside him to brush the dust from his feet before pulling his boot on. "Good."

His pack-mate shook his head. "Not good. This is too quiet. This kind of quiet is not good."

"What do you think happened here?" Hyatt pulled his other boot on and worked on the fasteners atop both.

"Maybe Rellah's right... maybe they died. A plague, or a poison, or something." Rayce tilted his head from one side to the other, weighing the merits of the theory. "Maybe they left, a History ago... I don't know. It's hard to believe this has been here so long, and nobody knew."

As his companion raised his working theories, Hyatt followed each but didn't hear anything that caused the certainty of undeniable truth in him. "I guess we'll see."

"I guess we will." Rayce glanced over at Tobin where he slept, a ball of blankets and unkempt hair close to the front door. "Does he know anything about this place?"

He followed Rayce's gaze to the Iron and studied the boy's face. As Iron Tobin slept, the weight of his title and the realities of his life seemed absent from his features. Instead, Hyatt saw a child who slept without dreams of the dead or anticipation of the horrors another day might bring. His features were serene and his youth saturated his hair and skin in ways that made him look somehow brighter than the stone beneath him and the rough bedding that surrounded him.

"Who knows?" he replied. "Your guess is as good as mine."

In the shadows that overlaid the pre-dawn darkness, Hyatt found it difficult to reconcile the sleeping boy with the legendary Irons he had grown up hearing stories about. For a moment, as he rubbed his hands together to build warmth in them, he turned over the theory that time had weakened the source of Iron's preternatural gifts and replaced the terrifying and awesome Irons of the past with lesser successors. That train of thought spun off into possibilities he couldn't quantify or reason through and so he set it aside.

The streets were narrower than Hyatt expected, just wide enough for two people to walk abreast beneath the overgrown arbors. He trailed his fingers over the hardwood of the lattices, darker and smoother than any timber he'd seen before. The placement and fit of every intersection drew his attention, no gaps or corrections to mislaid laths. He swept his gaze over the symmetrical, diamond-shaped openings that let vines and flowers interweave through them, but found no imperfections among the closest spaces he could focus on.

Beneath his boots, the crushed rose-quartz pebbles of the path were rough but uniform in size and shifted predictably as he walked. He followed an imaginary path from one rock to the next until it reached the edge of the path, where no stray pebbles revealed themselves between the lush grass beyond. Hyatt reached the far edge of the overhead cover and lingered beneath the dangling, conical blossoms that spilled over, his fingertips still resting against the cold wood and his eyes on the street's edge.

"This is very well made..." he paused and lowered to a crouch, looking along the perfectly aligned border between the path and the grass, "or very well maintained."

His words made Bex freeze and Hyatt rose to his feet in a slow, measured motion to let his pack-mate connect with their environment without distraction. As he waited, he took in everything within his view, from the arbors further along the path to the low-pitched rooftops of the buildings that surrounded them. Searching every window, doorway, and space between the structures seemed as impossible as counting stars but he tried anyway, his gaze moving from one to the next until he lost track of which he'd examined and which were new.

"You think someone is here." There was no question in Bex's remark, and their lips barely moved as they said it.

Hyatt's nod was slow. He listened and heard nothing, and nothing moved in his line of sight. The wood beneath his fingertips was smooth and none of the buds that rose from the vines and branches that penetrated the lattice beside him were missing.

"It's too perfect," he replied. "No weathering to the boards, the crushed rock is even... shouldn't it have sifted in the wind and rain, as old as this place is? None of the rooftops are missing slats. It looks... tended."

Bex nodded. "I think so too... and I think they know we're here."

The same thought had been skittering through the shadows of Hyatt's awareness, but Bex saying it out loud made it real in a way that tightened his chest. "Me too."

They continued along the path, stepping free from the patchwork shadows of the arbor and into the unfiltered light of morning. Hyatt looked and listened as they walked, but everything he didn't see and hear cemented the conclusion he'd reached with Bex. He felt as though the residents he couldn't see watching them existed just beyond his periphery and pressed against him like a persistent wind. As they passed each building, he imagined lurking shapes in the windows opposite where he looked, tracking their placement and communicating it with silent gestures to a hidden clan scattered through the too-quiet garden.

"Should we be in the open like this?" He asked, overwhelmed by the number of places his imagined enemies could lurk.

"Probably not," Bex replied, tipping their head back and forth to weigh alternatives, "but creeping through the buildings might look hostile. With any luck, they'll think we're just curious."

Their logic did little to calm Hyatt, and his spiraling concern was spiked by the low Cern whistle-call from across the garden. He looked to Bex for an assurance he'd heard it, but his pack-mate was already off the path and moving in a low, rapid skulk in the direction of the sound with their weapon out. Hyatt whispered a curse under his breath and drew his blade, hurrying to keep pace with Bex. They moved from building corner to arbor to statue, drawing a zig-zag between nominally defensive positions but lingering only long enough to pick their next mark before setting off again. Hyatt fell into the rhythm, stalling at Bex's last position until they reached the next one, then setting off to keep their range consistent. Just when Hyatt started to lose his sense of how far away the call had come from, it sounded again, a low warble that steadied to the solid note of come-to-me-but-no-danger.

Hyatt and Bex crossed four more streets and caught sight of Veck crouched against the side of a large building, half-obscured by the climbing ivy and tiny blossoms that adorned the wall. He made eye contact with them and stood, and when Veck looked up the street Hyatt followed his gaze to see Jenna approaching at a light jog with Tobin running to keep up.

"Did you find something?" Hyatt asked as he crossed the last street between them, catching his breath in the cold, crisp air.

"Turning Weapons and Untethered Communicators," he replied. "A lot."

He led the way into the building and Hyatt followed him through the doorway, but the sight before him made him stagger and stop. Racks of weapons, stacked two-high and filled with identical models, formed dozens of aisles through the center of the large room. On each end, lockers filled with cubicles held hand-sized devices with keypads, knobs, speakers, and flexible cylinders protruding from their tops. Rellah appeared from between two rows of racks, one of the Turning Weapons in hand.

"The end of the world, in one forgotten building at the top of a mesa," Bex said, pushing past Hyatt and stepping to the side to clear the doorway.

Rellah pulled the box magazine from the weapon and tipped the exposed end towards them, brass casings catching the daylight. "They all have bullets. Thousands."

Hyatt didn't realize he was shaking until Jenna put her hand on his shoulder as she moved beside him, Tobin by her side. Hyatt nudged her with his arm to thank her for her silent assurance, then took a tentative step toward the lockers at the end of the closest column of racks. Picking up one of the Untethered Communicators brought back memories of facing Iron Delores in a clearing, her weapon drawn and intending to cut him down, and he couldn't shake free of it as he turned one of the knobs and a green light appeared above the device's keys.

He twisted the knob the other way until it clicked and the light vanished, swallowing the warm saliva that pooled on his tongue and threatened to summon vomit in his throat. "These have power, but they're different than the ones I've seen."

"These are Warning violations," Iron Tobin said, his voice a mixture of awe and constrained delight.

His pack-mates exchanged glances to read one anothers' intent, and Veck snapped. "We're not seriously letting a sprout decide what we're doing about this, are we? That's fucking compost – he can barely strap up his own boots!"

"I am the Iron of the Broken Mountain!" Tobin bristled with unchecked rage and whirled on Veck, his hand dropping to the handle of the weapon on his belt.

"Draw it, Iron! Pull your weapon so I can rip it from you and beat you to death with it!" Veck snarled, bending at his knees and bringing both his open hands up to a ready position.

Hyatt reacted without thinking. He stepped between them, planted his hands on Veck's chest, and shoved hard in one unbroken motion. The force and surprise of it caught his packmate off guard and Veck staggered backward, losing his footing and catching himself against the wall to stop himself from falling. He sprung off the rough stone in a rebound but Hyatt was ready and shoved him again, and Veck's shoulders connected squarely with the wall in a solid thump.

"I told you!" Hyatt shouted as he used the space between them to pull his knife from his belt. "I told you to stop, Veck – the Iron Accords make this an Iron matter, and it doesn't fucking matter if you don't like it!"

"Hyatt—" Bex tried to break in.

"We're not Cern and we're not Haleu – the Accords don't apply to us!" Veck shouted back at him, pushing off the wall and drawing his own knife.

"You're not Cern, but I still am!" Hyatt spat back.

"This isn't—" Bex tried again, starting toward them both.

Veck turned his knife over and tightened his grip, the fighting stance Hyatt knew from endless hours of training. "Then maybe you don't belong here, Hyatt – you're not fucking one of us! You should be meitnerlise!"

Hyatt's reflexive answer to Veck's outburst had already begun to fade and his accusation battered it down further, like it was trying to smash Hyatt's willpower flat. His rage had felt capable and kinetic but as he stared down the seasoned fighter, both with their knives drawn, it felt hollow and cautionary. Something inside him screamed for him to close the gap and bury his blade in Veck, to do anything before Veck moved and the odds slanted against him, but he hesitated.

"That's enough!" Rellah roared as loud as Hyatt had ever heard her, a primal sound that seemed to shake the walls of the large room and caused Bex to halt their advance.

"Is it Rellah?" Veck shouted, turning to face her and stepping into her personal space. "Are we supposed to listen to you? Giving the weed travel plans, leading us to this fucking Garden – are we supposed to pretend you don't have the Blood Ruin?"

Hyatt didn't know if it was Veck's challenge to Rellah or that he was so unconcerned with Hyatt as a threat that he turned his back to him, but in the space of a breath, he'd dropped his knife and his hands were locked around Veck's wrist as he was stomping on the back of his calf to drive him to his knees. He stepped over his pack-mate's shoulder and dropped, collapsing to the floor with Veck's throat caught between his knees and Veck's hand holding his knife locked between both of his own.

Veck started to roar but Hyatt tightened his legs and the sound broke from a rage to a cough and then a gasp. His body thrashed and he clawed at Hyatt's thigh, yanking hard at his trapped arm, but couldn't free himself. Veck spasmed and arched his back, kicking his legs, and blood began to redden his cheeks and forehead as he struggled to breathe.

Time broke apart into flashes of moments for Hyatt. He heard Bex shout for him to stop, but it took only an instant when the words should have lasted longer. He saw Veck's head twisting back and forth between his knees, the wild look of his desperation to live glinting in his wide eyes. In his next flash he saw Rellah's face, standing over them both without intervening, her eyes narrowing a fraction as they met his. Hyatt could hear his own heart in his ears and his tongue tasted like metal. All the ache in his body decentralized into one locked, tight experience from his ankles to his wrists, and Veck stopped moving.

When the world resumed its continuity Bex was beside him, both of their arms working between Hyatt's thighs to break his clinch. He let them, his legs unlocking as he rolled out from underneath Veck's still form. Bex, exhausted from their sudden burst of effort, collapsed onto their arms and made a half-hearted crawl away from the space where the fight had happened. Hyatt struggled to his knees, gasping for breath, and found Jenna beside Rellah studying him with an expression he couldn't read.

"Is he dead?" Jenna asked, a pragmatic curiosity without judgment.

Her simple question felt like a stone wall collapsing on Hyatt. He crawled toward Veck as he realized that amidst the fight, he hadn't cared if his pack-mate lived or died. That knowledge was so far from who he thought he was that it scared him, and he had a moment to be frightened by whether he would be relieved or resentful when he checked Veck's pulse. His hand slid down the motionless man's neck and he pressed his fingers into the hollow space between his esophagus and the muscle beside it. Two solid thumps answered through Hyatt's fingertips and he withdrew his hand.

"He's alive," he replied as he climbed to his feet.

"Are you going to leave him that way?" Rellah asked, her tone almost indistinguishable from Jenna's.

In his cascade of thoughts about how his pack might react to his fight with Veck, it wasn't a question he had anticipated. "What?"

"When a Cern challenges another Cern's place in the pack, it's a death sentence for one of them, unless the challenged chooses to leave." Bex's tone was a perfect contrast to Jenna and Rellah, full of tension. "He challenged you, so he can't choose to leave... there is only one Cern answer."

Things were moving too fast for Hyatt, and a wave of dizziness flooded through him as he tried to keep up. His memory of wanting to kill Veck lingered but it had become surreal, as if he was recalling someone else's thoughts. Looking down at the motionless form of his pack-mate, the idea of killing him made his stomach wrench tight.

"Killing him lets his bones join Kenna's," Jenna added, somehow managing to provide the information without sounding like she was encouraging or discouraging the act. "He stays with the pack."

"You should kill him," Tobin piped up from where he'd retreated between the rows of Turning Weapons. "He would have killed you. And he's compost."

"You, shut the fuck up, Iron." Hyatt pointed at Tobin and leveled a hostile glare at him, then turned his attention to Bex. "He's not Cern. Those don't have to be the rules."

They paused like they were wrestling with their desire to agree and let it go, but said, "You are."

"Fuck!" Hyatt shouted at the ceiling, turning in a circle. "Isn't being Cern about freedom from structure? Doing what makes sense? Now you're telling me I have to kill Veck because those are the rules? That's just another fucking structure!"

Bex shrugged helplessly, and neither Rellah nor Jenna spoke. Hyatt looked down at Veck as his pack-mate's legs began to shift against the cold floor, his head rolling to the side. All at once, the Cern blade sheathed on his hip felt three times as heavy as it was, and he wrapped his hand around the handle to lessen the way it seemed to drag downward against his leg.

He looked up at Jenna, then at Rellah. "What do I do?"

She shook her head. "Be who you are, Hyatt."

In that moment, he hated her. He hated not knowing what to do, and he hated that she wouldn't tell him. The pressure to make a choice that could end a life without the time to think blossomed in his head like a migraine fueled by a rising frustration that continued to build pressure in his chest. He felt like there was a right answer, and Rellah knew what it was, and she wouldn't tell him. Two new terms he didn't know rattled in his head, and it felt impossible to choose without knowing all the information. He hated most that he was surrounded by his pack, yet he felt alone.

Something in him broke and as Veck rolled onto his side with a groan, he reached down and grabbed the front of his pack-mate's jacket with both hands. He hauled Veck to his feet and, unintentionally assisted by his efforts to find his footing, drove his pack-mate back to the wall and pinned him there. Veck had been blinking and looking around, trying to reorient his consciousness, but as he connected with the stone again he looked directly at Hyatt.

"Why am I alive?" he asked first, his words coated with confusion and resentment.

Hyatt ignored his question as an idea formed, the pounding in his head and the pressure in his chest compressing the thought into a plan. "Veck, once of Hollow Bone Pack – you don't belong here. Choose to leave, so I don't have to kill you... because I will."

"You think you can do it, face-to-face?" Veck's anger was muted by the way he winced as he spoke, but he looked directly into Hyatt's eyes when he said it.

Hyatt didn't answer him. Instead, he released Veck's jacket and pushed off his chest to create space between them. Veck closed his hands to fight but by the time he'd raised them past his belt, Hyatt had drawn his curved blade and stepped in again. The concave blade rested against Veck's throat on one side and his ribs on the other, with Hyatt's weight against the back of the blade pinning it between them. His pack-mate felt it and froze, his hands opening with his palms toward Hyatt.

"I will if you make me, Veck." Hyatt paused so his pack-mate could feel the certainty in his tone. "Choose to leave."

The room felt perfectly still as Hyatt waited for Veck's answer, and could feel four sets of eyes fixed on the moment. He wondered what they all expected, if Jenna and Rellah believed it would end in Veck's blood on the floor and if Bex thought he would hesitate at the wrong moment and find himself overpowered by Veck. Hyatt could feel the rise and fall of Veck's chest, transferred through the cold metal to his own, and his dark eyes searched Hyatt's like he was seeing him for the first time.

"I choose to leave." His words were strained through his teeth and etched with tension across his face, but he inclined his head in acceptance.

Hyatt stepped back, keeping his weapon between them. All eyes followed Veck and no one spoke as he picked up his pack and his discarded knife. When he reached the door he stopped and looked around, studying the face of everyone in the room and settling on Bex.

"Hyatt is going to get you killed, just like he got Kenna killed. Deep down, you know it." Without waiting for an answer, he turned and disappeared into the garden.

The absence of Veck created a hole that carried a quiet, and that quiet spread across the room like a thick fog that couldn't be cleared. The moment became heavier and heavier until it threatened to choke them, and when no one spoke, Hyatt crossed the room to close the door as if it could separate the past from the future. He turned to find everyone looking at him.

"I'm Cern, and I'm bound by the Iron Accords just like all of you used to be – so as long as I am in Hollow Bone Pack, we obey the Accords. We don't need Cern, Haleu, and Irons all coming for us, whether or not some ancient Claimed signed them." He looked to Rellah. "It needs to be pack law, or we'll be fighting forever."

She narrowed her eyes like she was trying to read an unspoken meaning in his words, and she looked at Jenna and Bex for dissent before returning her attention to Hyatt and nodding in slow agreement. "Hollow Bone Pack will abide the Iron Accords for as long as there are Cern among us."

# NINETEEN

"Iron, what do you want to do with all of these?" Rellah asked, gesturing to the columns of Turning Weapons and Untethered Communicators.

The boy put his finger and thumb to his chin like he was stroking a beard that he was too young to grow and frowned as he looked up at the racks of weapons that towered over him in rows. Hyatt caught Bex's eye-roll from the corner of his eyes and Rellah's face said a thousand frustrated words without a sound, but he crossed his arms and waited for the Iron to reply. The absurdity of the moment, exactly as Veck had said, existed in his mind like a kernel that he refused to let sprout.

"Did anyone see Low Flowers in this garden?" he asked.

Hyatt traded glances with his pack-mates before shaking his head. "No."

"Rot. I can hear Sklodowska better near the flowers." Tobin muttered. "Let's leave them all here and see if we can find some. I don't know what she wants."

The Iron's mention of guidance from their god made Hyatt's spine tingle with the tension that folktales of his childhood instilled in every Haleu child. Memories of Iron Delores standing over Iron Sawmet's decapitated body in a field of flowers came back to him but as they resurfaced, they brought eerie mists and rolling storm clouds that Hyatt knew hadn't been there.

"We're going to search the garden for Low Flowers?" Bex straddled the line between verifying the Iron's intention and skepticism.

"Yup." Tobin nodded.

Bex looked to Hyatt for confirmation, and it was an answer he was unprepared to give. Jenna stood with her arms crossed, regarding him with an even and unreadable expression that added the weight of her evaluation to his choice while behind her, Rayce leaned as close to the racks of Turning Weapons as possible so he could inspect their details without touching them.

"I'll go with him." Hyatt shrugged. "I could use the walk."

Bex set their pack down just inside the doorway and rifled through it until they found a water canister. "I'm coming too."

Hyatt nodded and looked to Rellah. "We won't be gone long."

He followed Tobin outside and when the boy reached the path, he looked left and right before turning in a slow circle to survey every possible direction. When he stopped, he pressed his index finger to his temple as if the pressure on his head would help him reach a decision. Hyatt didn't know whether the Iron's method worked or if he decided any direction was as good as another, but he set off at a purposeful pace and Hyatt followed along.

Bex walked beside him in silence, their attention shifting in idle observation from the buildings they passed by to the lattices they crossed under. Against the utter quiet of the Garden, the crunch of the crushed stone along the pathways sounded crisp under each step. The further they walked, the more intentional Bex's wordless companionship felt.

"What?" Hyatt asked.

They shrugged and said nothing until they reached the next fork in the path. Tobin turned left without hesitation and Bex followed him with a lingering gaze in the direction the Iron didn't choose. Soon they were far enough down the walkway that the alternative was blocked from view, and Bex shifted their gaze up over the rooftops of the intervening building to stare at the imposing structure that loomed over them.

"How are you doing?" they asked.

Hyatt felt his instinctive reply rise to his lips but held it. The longer he let the question linger in his head, the more possible meanings it took on. Veck's absence and his part in it were the loudest refrains at the front of his mind, but they built on a dozen other moments he had yet to reconcile and made his thoughts feel like a room too full of clutter with no good starting point to clean it up.

"I'm... you know," Hyatt replied with a deflecting nod.

"I don't know if I do." As they passed by a support wrapped in spiraling vines, Bex reached out and let their fingers trail along one of the stems and leaves that adorned it. "You just put your blade across the neck of a man you've known and lived with for months. You almost had to kill him. How are you doing?"

"I did what needed to be done." He heard the defensiveness in his own voice, but didn't know how to strain it from his response to Bex's question. "He made his choice."

They nodded in a way that seemed to acknowledge his answer without accepting any of his reasoning. Ahead of them, the Iron continued to trudge along the path with abandon, glancing between the buildings in search of Low Flowers.

"It's not like I wanted to fight him. He forced it." Hyatt didn't know why resuming Be's and his silent walk made him feel the need to fill it with defenses and rationale for his actions. "He had his chance to settle whatever was rotting him at Mescwar, and he didn't take it."

Bex shrugged and tilted their head to concede Hyatt's point, but their features remained intentionally neutral. "Okay."

The next decision point for Tobin was a perpendicular path, and he walked to the center of their intersection before repeating his slow turn to look in every direction. He settled on turning to his left, away from the central building of the Garden, and Hyatt couldn't help but glance back at the columns and parapets of the colossal structure before turning to follow the Iron.

"He'll be okay." Hyatt wasn't sure if he was trying to convince Bex or himself but felt like he failed at both.

"Here!" Tobin called out as he turned toward the wrought-iron boundary of a park.

Hyatt's conversation with Bex felt incomplete, but he was glad to be done with it for the moment. He picked up speed to reach the open, hexagonal gate that offered access to a large field of Low Flowers, dense enough to cover nearly all the green of the grass and leaves beneath them in a blanket of colors and broken only by two evenly spaced trees that spread broad branches over the park to shade the Flowers below. By the time he made it to the threshold of the field, the Iron had walked into the center of the field between the trees, and was just easing himself down into a sitting position. Bex joined Hyatt as he watched the Iron lean back on his hands and then settle into a half-reclined position on his elbows, his head tilted to the side to look down at the Low Flowers around himself. The way that the Low Flowers shifted around Tobin made them look like waves on the surface of a lake, ebbing and flowing around him.

"I've never seen an Iron talk to their god before," Bex said, leaning in to speak just above a whisper. "What happens now?"

Hyatt shrugged. "New to me too."

Bex nodded to cede the point. "Do you... is it real? Do you think she's going to speak to him?"

Hyatt opened his mouth to reply, but his answer came slow as it ricocheted back and forth between all the ways he might have answered that question over the course of his life. No matter how many times the changes in his worldview made themselves apparent, it still felt like scrubbing away a scab that wasn't quite ready to be shed when he came face to face with it. He stared at Tobin stretched out amidst the Low Flowers and imagined himself at the boy's age, certain that Sklodowska was the originator of everything and the Irons were her chosen heroes. He remembered Iron Delores, vibrant and fanatical and devoid of some quality that made everyone else feel human, claiming to hear Sklodowska's voice as she walked headlong into danger without a care.

"I don't know if she's real. If she is, I don't know if she speaks to Irons, or anybody – and if she does, I don't know if her guidance can be summoned on the Iron's terms." Hyatt felt like he was working through what he believed as he spoke. "I've seen Irons face down Heirs, survive when no one should have... Tobin is a third my size. He shouldn't have been able to drag me away from that Veshtrue, he just isn't big enough."

"People can do incredible things when they're frightened—" Bex reasoned.

"But he wasn't," Hyatt broke in. "He wasn't scared – he was calm. Composed."

He began to summon other memories of the impossible things he'd seen like Sawmet healing the wounds that should have killed Rellah, and Delores bringing Sawmet back from the dead to do it, but those thoughts brushed up against the things he and Rellah didn't talk about with their pack-mates. For once he was grateful for the secrets they chose to keep because they sounded unbelievable, like the folk tales he'd been raised on. Even reflecting on things he had seen and heard first-hand, doubt crept in around the edges about whether there were other explanations.

"I don't know if it's better if the little Iron hears something, or nothing." Bex's voice was still quiet, but they shifted from talking to Hyatt to talking to themself.

Hyatt nodded, unable to conjure an answer to the implied question and grateful that Bex wasn't expecting one. They watched Tobin lay still amongst the carpet of little blue flowers and time slipped around them like clouds in the sky until Hyatt lost track of how long they had been waiting. At last, the Iron rose and walked back to them.

"Sklodowska wants us to leave the weapons and the communicators – she wants us to do something else, in the big building in the middle of the Garden." Tobin's eyes were wide with purpose. "We have to go there now."

Rellah crossed her arms and leaned against the wall, her eyebrow raised. "We don't have to do anything. We turned the weapons and communicators over to you, stood guard while you communed with the Butcher Queen... we've upheld the Accord. You do what you want, Iron – we're getting the fuck out of this Garden."

Hyatt expected him to protest, and the fact that Tobin didn't have one of his usual outbursts made him uneasy. The boy turned and cocked his head at Hyatt like he was deciding something, then nodded as if it was settled.

"You and your pack can go – but Hyatt is Charged, and nobody released him," Tobin replied.

Rellah shoved away from the wall and stood upright as alarm shot through her. "What?"

"Hyatt broke the rule, and an Iron charged him with service. He has to help me." Tobin replied to Rellah without looking away from Hyatt, the boy's expression triumphant and daring him to say it wasn't true.

*How does he know that?* Hyatt didn't expect the wave of despair that coursed through him at Tobin's declaration. "I was called to kill a Keeper, and I did! I'm done!"

Tobin shook his head. "Nuh-uh. You're not done until you're released."

He couldn't explain why the thought felt like drowning, but it created a despair in him that seemed to take root in his marrow. He looked helplessly at Rellah and Bex, both of whom were looking back at him with tense and wary expressions. The feeling permeated every pore in his skin and frayed the thoughts in his head.

"We are going to go to the big building." Tobin seemed to gain certainty from Hyatt's dread and hesitation.

Something in the way the Iron spoke blended a new emotion into the mix in Hyatt's mind, a kind of defiance that insisted he get control somehow. "Tobin – I'll go with you to the building, but when we leave this Garden, my charge ends. You can go back to the Low Flowers and tell Sklodowska, I didn't come here for her --"

"You mean, you didn't know you came here for her," Tobin interjected, the full weight of his sentence resting on the sixth syllable.

"—I came here because there might be a world-destroyer here and if there is, somebody needs to know about it!" Hyatt finished, not pausing to entertain the Iron's interruption.

"There might be a... what the mold-wrecked fuck?" Rayce's eyes widened in surprise and alarm, but Bex put their hand on his arm to pause his question.

Tobin stared up at Hyatt with as much defiance as Hyatt felt, and a silence hung between them for as long as the moment could bear it before he spoke. "You don't think she knows better than you, but she does. You can't be done until she says so."

Hyatt realized the Iron had no new argument for him, and shook his head at the absurdity of arguing with a child about what his choices were. "Next time you talk to her, tell her I'm done."

Something dangerous sparkled in the Iron's eyes like a match lighting, and he regarded Hyatt with a solemn expression. "I will – I'll tell her. She'll be mad at you."

Hyatt turned and spotted the imposing shape of the large building in the center of the Garden, and started walking. "Tell her to get in line. Disappointing people is kind of my thing."

It wasn't until Hyatt had led his pack three more blocks through the angled and lattice-covered paths that Hyatt began to wonder at his newfound boldness. He didn't know if it had been their journey, or facing Veck, but he knew even though he had his doubts about the Butcher Queen's existence, he never would have challenged her to an Iron a year before. The fact that she came to mind as the Butcher Queen instead of as Sklodowska grew the root of alarm deeper in him, and he felt it twist as he realized that even the Cern who hated her respected the threat of her power.

That lingering anxiety clung to him as he walked. He looked for a signpost at the next fork in the path and when there was none, he realized he hadn't seen any since they set foot in the Garden. Only the central structure of the space served as a landmark above the buildings of similar heights and construction. As he passed a park he slowed to linger and look through the curated trees and the pristine benches, and confessed to himself that he would be unable to tell it apart from any of the other parks he had seen.

With every new angle he expected to see a sign of life, some flicker of motion in his periphery, or the smell of an extinguished and still-warm candle. Instead, every new region of the Garden offered only silence and the kind of foreboding Hyatt always associated with the dark, made more surreal by the daylight.

When the path gave way to the courtyard that surrounded the massive, central structure, it was wide enough and flat enough to halt him in his tracks. Large, hexagonal tiles of marble with perfectly aligned edges spanned the space between the last buildings and the magnificent stairs that led to the building's front doors. The surfaces of each tile were smooth and freshly swept, marked only by mosaic shards of jade, emerald, and peridot that formed a colossal design across the entire expanse of the courtyard.

# TWENTY

It took a moment for Hyatt to recognize the emblem that the shards created and when he did, his heart clenched in his chest so hard he thought it had stopped. Seeing the symbol in his training as an artist in Brathnee had been unnerving and seeing it on the Keeper map had induced a deep terror, but seeing it spanning the range of one of Rellah's arrows before him threatened to rob him of his consciousness until he forced his lungs to function by sheer force of will.

*It's real...* His mind had nowhere to go from there. *It's real... it's real.*

The oxygen he forced into his body and spread through his veins began to break down the paralyzing terror that the symbol caused, replacing it with a mobile and potent fear that soaked into his muscles and bones.

Tobin took a step forward like he was sleepwalking, his eyes wide with wonder and his mouth parted in awe. Hyatt set a hand on his shoulder but when a second step carried the Iron beyond his reach, he didn't move to follow him. When the boy reached the edge of the courtyard, his head tipped back in a slow motion until he was looking at the parapeted roof of the colossal building.

"Two three one three two seven six zero..." the Iron breathed, like he was reciting Trades lessons he wasn't old enough to have completed. "Two-hundred and thirty-one tiles, twenty-seven steps... six days of travel..."

Something about the way the boy let his nonsensical expressions fall from lips like water he had forgotten to swallow made the hair on Hyatt's neck stand up on end, and he tried to speak but his voice refused to rise above a whisper. "Do you know something about this place, Tobin?"

Instead of answering him, the Iron stepped onto the first tile like he was floating in a dream. His little fingers moved in slow, languid motions like he was trying to feel reality in the air, and his feet landed on the marble so fluidly that Hyatt was unsure if he was walking or floating.

Bex appeared by his side and watched until the Iron was five tiles across the courtyard before they spoke. "Did you expect your world-destroyer to be so big?"

Hyatt could only shake his head, unable to reconcile whatever he might have thought or dreamt of finding at the marker on the map with the massive marker before him.

On his other side, Jenna intentionally checked against his shoulder as she passed him with Rayce on her heels, and she smiled back at him over her shoulder as she started across the courtyard after Tobin. "You were right after all, Hyatt. You can be a little happy about it."

He tried to return her smile, but it wouldn't form on his lips. Instead, he watched the boots of his pack-mates and the Iron of the Broken Mountain cross over the polished flakes of semi-precious gems in the dread-inducing mosaic, and wondered what he had done by bringing them to a place none of them would have ever seen without his insistence and direction.

*This could have stayed hidden for the rest of our lifetimes.* Unbidden tears began to form inside his eyelids, searing at the temperatures that only guilt could heat them to. *We could have died never knowing this existed.*

Rellah stopped beside Hyatt and watched the Claimed and the Iron walk ahead. Jenna tilted her head toward Rayce and said something they couldn't hear at their distance, and the Iron had begun to shake free of his daze and was walking with more intention toward the steps on the far side.

"You never become a leader. You never wake up and feel different." She crossed her arms and when Hyatt looked over at her, her eyes were distant. "One day, your pack walks in front of you without you asking them to."

"They shouldn't be here." Hyatt's voice was quiet but he fought to keep it stable, despite the despair that fought to gain ground around every word. "We shouldn't be here."

"I know. They know too, probably." Compassion and sympathy were as unfamiliar in Rellah's tone as if she wore a Haleu braid, and they did nothing to alleviate the building guilt in Hyatt's chest. "Now, go see it through."

His legs responded to her command before his mind did, and he found himself walking across the marble square toward the building on the far side. Rellah stayed with him, almost close enough for their shoulders to touch, with her bow tucked under her outside arm. Their footfalls made muted sounds on the stone courtyard that seemed to carry in every direction like fog across water in the morning.

By the time they reached their companions, Tobin had begun to climb the steps. The giant gray stairs tapered toward the landing at their top, funneling them closer together as Hollow Bone ascended them. The landing beyond the steps was framed by a stone railing and columns that bore no marring marks or ivy. The doors to the massive structure were twice Hyatt's height and wide enough for six people to pass through side by side. The designs molded into their dull copper surface caught the light like honey as it poured along the raised outlines and pooled in the embossed recesses. Hyatt climbed the wide, low steps that rose to the door, passing between the pillars on either side and transfixed by the artwork that adorned the building's entry.

"What is this place?" Rayce wondered aloud, his eyes moving over the intricate designs on and around the entryway.

"Iron of the Broken Mountain!" A man's voice shouted from behind them. "Face me!"

The unfamiliar voice ripped Hyatt from his fixation on the door and he spun around to search for its owner. Only after he felt the grip of his Cern blade in his closed hand did he realize he'd reached for it out of instinct. Below him on the steps, Jenna's hands were poised to draw her blade and Rellah had half-pulled an arrow from her quiver, while Bex had taken a step down the broad stairs to create space around themself.

Across the open square between the steps to the massive building, a lone figure stood in the lush grass at the edge of the square with his weapon drawn. The sun's rays caught in his prismed blade that bent the daylight in shades of teal like beach glass, and it seemed to glow with the light trapped within it.

"Cern, you don't have to die in Desolate Garden," he called in a clear and certain voice that carried across the space and reached them as if he was standing beside them, "but if you draw your weapons, you'll never see the lowlands of the Reclaimed again."

A few steps below Hyatt, Tobin drew his long fighting knife with one hand and his wire-weapon with the other. "I don't know you – who are you?"

"I am your death," the man replied as he started across the square, the tip of his strange blade inches above the cobblestones. "In four hundred years no Iron has set foot inside the Temple of Sklodowska, and I swear to Her Name you will not be the one to do it now."

If Tobin was afraid, it didn't show in the way he moved down the steps until he planted both boots on the square. He uncurled his fingers and the wire in his hand unfurled, pulled down by the spiked weight on the end until it hung as close to the ground as the man's sword. The Iron began whirling it in a lazy arc, just fast enough to pull the wire taut and make it blur as it passed through the air. Hyatt looked to Rellah who hadn't finished drawing her arrow but also hadn't let go of the fletchings to drop it back into her quiver, while Bex repositioned themself on the steps to be closer to Jenna.

"I am the Iron of the Broken Mountain, and I'm not afraid of you!" Tobin shouted at the advancing stranger.

The man didn't break his stride, moving with a purposeful confidence that reminded Hyatt of the way Iron Delores had moved amongst the chaos of combat. "Then you'll die unafraid."

There was no preamble to the moment they crashed together, no adopted fighting stance or circling in search of an opening. The man's blade came down in fast, iridescent strokes, each one from a different angle that rained on Tobin. The boy deflected the first with his knife and the force of the impact ripped the blade from his hand. He dove aside to avoid being cut in half by the second slash and somersaulted past the man to evade the third, tumbling to his feet as the stranger whirled to face him. Tobin scrambled backward, putting four paces between him and the man who began advancing again with the same self-assured pace.

Hyatt watched the vicious cycle play out, everything in him insisting on action even as his feet felt cemented to the steps. His palm felt warm against the leather wrap around his weapon's handle and all the muscles in his arms and legs were tense as if they were waiting for permission to launch into motion, but his pack-mate's inaction made him move to join Rellah instead of joining the fight.

Tobin launched his wire weapon from his palm with a savage thrust and the stranger canted his head to let it fly past his ear, but the Iron reacted like he'd expected the evasion. He snapped the wire up and down sharply and yanked, and the barbed back of the spike caught against the stranger's shoulder as Tobin yanked the wire taut. The man lurched forward and landed on his face and chest as Tobin pulled with more strength than the boy should have been able to leverage. The stranger retained his grip on his blade and planted his free arm on the cobblestones in search of traction as the Iron began to drag the man toward him hand over hand like he was pulling a wayward boat to shore.

"What rotted..." Rellah murmured as if she was unaware Hyatt had stepped close enough to hear, and when he looked down, her fingers were white from the pressure she gripped her arrow with.

"I know what you are now!" Tobin shouted down at the man he was dragging across the ground with powerful pulls on the wire. "I know!"

The man rolled to his side, elevating his shoulder with the barbed blade of Tobin's weapon in it. As he continued to roll, he brought his blade up under the taut, braided wire and it severed the metal with a snapping sound. The broken tension in Tobin's weapon set the frayed strands of the slashed end flailing like a tentacle. The boy couldn't compensate for the sudden lack of resistance in time and staggered backward, barely finding his footing as the man rose to his feet and ripped the spike from his shoulder with a growl.

"Then you know how this ends, Iron." The man rotated his shoulder, testing its functionality with the deep gash through the meat of it, then grabbed the handle of his translucent blade with both hands.

"What..." Hyatt started, but couldn't choose between the dozens of possible endings to his question that vied for priority.

"He's a Ram," Rellah whispered, as close to reverence as he'd ever heard from her, and her eyes riveted to the fight in the courtyard, "an Iron-killer."

The way she coated her words in respect and awe was as jarring to Hyatt as the stranger's unexpected appearance, and it sifted everything else Hyatt saw in front of him. All at once, Tobin was both an Iron and a little boy about to be murdered in front of him. Rellah was both the unstoppable Cern he fought Heirs with, and the woman about to let Tobin get cut down by a grown man because of some Cern legend. That lens turned inward and Hyatt saw himself with a burning, piercing clarity that seared something deep in his chest.

"Do the Ram have some kind of accord with the Cern, like the Irons do?" he asked, feeling the weight of his sheathed weapon against his thigh with unusual focus.

Rellah's mouth formed the word no as she shook her head slightly. She didn't take her eyes off the Ram's flashing blade as he swung at Tobin, and the boy dove to avoid in an attempt to reach his fighting knife across the square. Hyatt didn't know if she didn't make the sound to go with the movement of her lips, or if he'd stopped listening.

"Good enough." Hyatt pulled his Cern blade and started down the steps, his mind made up.

He wasn't moving quietly and Jenna keyed in on the sound of his boots across the stone, and moved to intercept him. "Stay out of it, Hyatt."

He stepped around her and pushed her aside with his shoulder. "No."

"What are you doing!" She shouted at his back as he reached the bottom of the stairs, following him down two steps before stopping.

He didn't answer her as he turned his weapon over in a single arc, getting a feel for the weight of it as he headed toward the Ram and the Iron. Every step felt better and more purposeful, and he lengthened his stride. Ahead of him, Tobin tumbled to collect his knife but cried out in pain as the Ram's sword caught the back of his calf and sprayed hot blood across the cobblestones. The slash stopped the Iron's leg from supporting his weight as he tried to roll to his feet and faltered, dropping to a knee before forcing his leg underneath him at an angle and bracing his knee with his empty hand.

"Ram!" Hyatt shouted, pointing at him with the tip of his curved blade as he closed the distance. "Fight someone who can fight back, not a fucking child!"

The stranger lifted his blade so it gleamed with blue-white light trapped inside it before he brought it down hard. Tobin's knife wasn't enough to deflect the savage blow but it turned the blade to it landed flat, smashing into the boy's collarbone and driving him to his knees instead of beheading him. With his enemy staggered, the Ram took a step backward to avoid being caught between them as he turned to face Hyatt.

"Are you willing to die for this Iron, Cern?" he asked, a kind of fanatical clarity in his eyes that reminded Hyatt of Delores as much as his movements did, as the Ram brought his prismatic blade to the ready.

"He's a little boy, Iron or not," Hyatt replied as he stepped between the Ram and where Tobin was struggling to stand, turning his weapon over a second time and angling the blade the way Rellah taught him. "I'm not going to let you murder him for a Calling he had no say in."

The Ram took a single step to close the space between them and slashed without another word, his blade coming down so fast Hyatt barely had time to raise his. The impact reverberated through Hyatt's whole body and pain flared in his wrists, elbows, and shoulders from the sheer force of it. He had no time to react as the Ram rained three more overhand strikes on him that made Hyatt feel like his blade was going to shatter under the assault. He managed to keep his weapon up to stop the brutal swings from slicing him to pieces and as the Ram spun in a sudden change of tactic to slash parallel with the ground, Hyatt stepped into it with a forceful block and snapped the handle of his weapon forward. The pommel of the long grip connected with the Ram's cheekbone and nose with a satisfying crunch and he stumbled backward, pressing a hand to the bruised and torn skin under his eye.

"You're going to be remembered as the Cern who tried to save an Iron!" The Ram's words were soaked in unbridled, hateful venom. "Packs will forbid naming children after you. Your jacket will be burned, and your bones will be thrown away!"

Tobin lunged forward from behind Hyatt with his knife out, but his leg gave out halfway through his motion and he faltered. The Ram brought his blade around in a whirlwind, upward swing with both hands, and Hyatt had just enough time to register what was happening without the speed to react. The last two handspans of the translucent blade connected under the point of the little Iron's jaw and bit deep through his skull, coming to a stop in Tobin's opposite eye socket. The weight of the boy's falling body dragged the tip of the Ram's sword to the ground and Hyatt screamed in grief and rage, slashing at the man without aim or finesse.

The Ram pivoted and yanked, pulling his blade free of the dead boy's head and raising it to deflect Hyatt's swing. The weapons smashed together at full force and the Ram stepped back under the assault, but Hyatt kept screaming as he came at the man with everything he had in him. His Cern blade changed angles over and over, crashing down from above, slicing in from each side, upward and downward strokes in random sequences as he tried to kill the man before him. The sheer ferocity drove the Ram back across the square, deflecting where he could and shifting his footing in search of a way to change the momentum of the fight, but every time he tried to circle around Hyatt his blade was there, clanging against the Ram's sword and halting his movement any direction but backward.

Fatigue began to compete with Hyatt's hatred until he could no longer swing with full force, and when the Ram backed up two more paces to catch his breath, Hyatt was too slow to press the attack. The distance between them became dangerous, unbreachable without coming within range of the other's weapon.

"You can't win, Cern," the Ram assured him. "You couldn't save the Iron and you can't kill me. You die today."

Something in the man's eyes and the tone of his voice seemed to bleed into Hyatt, not just through his ears but through his taste buds and pores. It spread through his mind and blossomed into doubt, carried on the current of the Ram's certainty and the way he locked eyes with Hyatt. He felt the aches of his bones and the raw exertion of his muscles move to the forefront of his awareness, drowning more productive thoughts with all the reasons he knew he was going to die.

"Your pack will forget you. Your friends will forget you. Sklodowska will forget you. It will be like you were never alive."

The Ram brought his blade up, teal light washing down the wicked edge of the strange weapon.

Hyatt believed him, and he began to tremble. His own weapon felt heavy, almost too heavy to lift, and he knew that even if he could lift it there was nothing he could do. Every drop of sweat on his body from his fight with the Ram cooled and his skin began to turn clammy, and it felt like he was already dead and his awareness was the last to know. His fingers began to uncurl from around the grip of his blade and he let them, because he knew it didn't matter.

As despair slid through his veins like tar and everything became too difficult, the Ram before him straightened his posture and lifted his chin. A smile touched the man's lips as he turned his weapon in his hand, and took a step into the dead space between them.

The Ram brought his weapon up. "Die without purpose, like you lived—"

His words clipped like a string had been cut as indigo fletchings stopped an arrow from passing clean through the Ram's throat. The man's eyes unfocused. When his gaze broke from Hyatt's, the miring despair that filled him felt like it crystalized and shattered into a thousand little shards. The change was staggering and as he realized he was back in control of his mind, another arrow buried in the Ram's head between his nose and upper lip. The force knocked him over backward and as he landed on his back on the stone tiles, his hand opened and his translucent blade skittered across the square before coming to a stop against Tobin's body.

"You fucking rot!" Hyatt stepped forward, lifted his weapon, and brought the curved edge down in a brutal slash at the side of the Ram's neck.

His blade passed clean through and severed the man's head from his shoulders. The decapitated skull started to tumble but deflected as the arrow through it found purchase on the cobblestones, changing the direction it rolled.

Hyatt plunged his blade into the Ram's stomach hard enough that it could stand on its own, took two steps, and punted the dead man's head as hard as he could. "Fuck you."

"My arrow was still in that," Rellah said from behind him.

He turned to find her passing the dead Iron with her bow under her arm, Jenna and Bex jogging to catch up with their attention turned outward toward the edges of the square in search of other dangers. "I thought you were staying out of it."

"Together after this, until we die," she replied with a shrug, but squinted a little as she studied his expression. "Are you okay?"

Hyatt hadn't found enough equilibrium to think about his condition in the wake of the fight, but her question made him dwell on it. His body felt sore all over, but in a rewarding way, and it felt good to rip his blade out of the gut of the dead man beside him. He dragged the flat of it along the man's shirt to clear most of the gore from the metal and sheathed it with a forceful shove. Having it where it belonged felt good, too.

"Yeah." He adjusted his belt to settle the weapon against his thigh.

She gave him a hard look, asking something with her eyes that Hyatt couldn't read, but only said, "Good. Then go get my arrow."

He nodded and followed the drizzled and dotted trail of blood across the square to where the Ram's head had rolled to a stop. The back of the dead man's skull gave him little to grip as he tried to pull Rellah's munition through the gore and broken bone. Tightening his fingers in the man's hair added torque to the arrow's shaft instead of helping him yank it through. He growled and set the decapitated head on the ground, lifted his boot, and stomped on it four times until he felt it fracture under his force. Every violent smash felt like progress and strengthened a cold, black motivation in him. He reached down, planted his hand on the cracked bone, and ripped the arrow free with a savage yank.

Hyatt shook the gore free as he walked back to Rellah, his eyes following Jenna and Bex as they carried Iron Tobin to the side of the square by the boy's limp arms and legs. "Got it."

Rellah took hold of the arrow but didn't pull it free of his grip until he turned to meet her eyes. When their gazes met, she only held his for a moment before looking down to bury her arrow amongst the rest of them in her quiver.

"What?" He asked, irritation encroaching on the question from every side.

"Be careful what you become okay with," she said, looking up at him again with an intensity that drove meaning straight through his pupils.

She turned to walk away from him, and something boiled in Hyatt. He stalked after her as it bubbled up inside him, rising in his throat until he could feel it build like steam behind his eyes.

"What? No, fuck that!" he shouted at her back when she didn't turn to face him. "He was a monster who murdered a child, Rellah – and you're the one who told me to give the dead more company!"

"But you didn't." She didn't look back at him as she reached the Ram's discarded weapon and knelt, crouching over it and staring down at the strange blade.

Hyatt stopped like her retort had drawn a line across the cobblestones he couldn't step over. "Huh?"

Rellah reached for the handle of the Ram's blade as if it were a wild animal that might spook and vanish if it noticed her movement. Her fingers slid around the grip of the weapon and she closed her hand gingerly. She picked it up and stood with the same care, keeping the blade level and extended at arm's length as she rose to her feet before rotating her wrist to hold it vertically.

"You didn't kill him. I did." She turned to look at him and brought the blade down in a graceful arc, so the tip came to a stop beside her boot without touching the ground. "You cut his head off because you hated him and stuck your blade in him like he was a place to hold it. Animals don't kill like that. Cern don't kill like that."

"Are you telling me you care what happens to his body?" Hyatt was incredulous. "You?"

She walked towards him, then past him as he turned to follow her with his whole body. When she reached the dead Ram, she looked down at the lifeless corpse. An expression crossed her face that Hyatt read as mourning, and it confused him, but it bled away from her cheekbones and lips as she turned to face him.

"No, Hyatt – I don't care what happens to him." Her eyes asked him to comprehend something he couldn't distinguish, and when he didn't, the gleam in them vanished too. "Help me move him."

He didn't know what to say, and a wordless frustration writhed in his gut, but he did as she asked. With the Ram slung between them, they walked sideways across the square toward where Jenna and Bex had deposited Iron Tobin in the grass.

"Do we plant him?" Bex asked as Rellah and Jenna lowered the dead Ram to the ground, looking from him to her and back again.

Hyatt shook his head. "We put him back in the Low Flowers."

"And him?" Jenna asked with a nod to the other corpse.

*Leave him to rot.* The thought came quickly to Hyatt's mind, but it carried a twinge with it that made him hesitate before speaking it aloud. "Keepers burn their dead."

Bex curled their lip in disdain at the barbaric practice. "With fire?"

"It unlocks the knowledge they collect through their lives, so it can be found again," Jenna replied, and shrugged when Hyatt gave her a surprised glance. "I spent time with Keepers before I came to Brathnee."

Her confession brought an equally sharp look from Rellah, but she said nothing that the shake of her head couldn't communicate, and Hyatt shrugged. "I'll find fuel."

By the time he returned with kindling and branches, Rayce and Bex had moved the Ram's body inside one of the nearest buildings and dismembered him. The floor on one side of the large room was drenched in blood, and the Ram's clothes lay crumbled and drenched in a pile against the back wall. Rayce cleaned his blade while Bex fed the severed parts of the Ram's body onto a grate in a large fireplace.

The sight and smell turned Hyatt's stomach, but he crossed the room without vomiting and piled the wood under the fireplace's curved grate. The fuel lit on his first attempt and as the fire grew to consume more and more of the kindling, Hyatt fed the rest of the material into it as the meat of the Ram's limbs began to burn. Around him, Rayce and Bex pulled scarves up over their noses and mouths to block the scent that began to radiate from the immolating corpse.

Hyatt moved back to the courtyard with his pack-mates close behind him, and he spared only a single glance back at the dark, thick smoke that began to rise from the building's chimney. Rellah and Jenna returned to the courtyard and headed their way, Tobin's wire-weapon in Jenna's hand and his Iron bars tucked through Rellah's belt.

"Now what?" Bex asked.

Rellah looked to Hyatt, who turned to stare up the stone steps toward the massive metal doors of the ancient temple. "Now we see what everyone thinks is in there. Kenna is dead, Veck is gone, an Iron and a Ram both died for control of it – whatever is inside, it belongs to us now."

Hyatt crossed the marble courtyard with his eyes locked on the doors of the temple like a predator hunting prey. He felt his pack-mates behind him as much as he heard their boots on the cold stone, and didn't look back as he crossed the inlaid symbol of the world-killer and began to climb the steps. He reached the top and crossed the platform to the doors in search of a latch to open them, but found none. With grim determination, he set his shoulder against the right door and shoved.

The metal doors refused to move or even react to his effort. He frowned and took two steps back so he could throw his shoulder against it with a running start, but the door was immovable. With a wince and a rub of his shoulder, he stepped back a few more paces until he was standing beside Bex and shielded his eyes as he looked up at the giant barrier.

"I don't think it works like that," his pack-mate said, satirically mild.

Hyatt shot them a glare before returning his attention to the large metal doors. "No, I don't think it does."

Bex unwrapped the wax paper around one of their herb-twists and nipped the end between their teeth, the gummy texture making a sticking sound as they crushed it between their teeth. They offered the remainder to Hyatt, but he shook his head and continued to study the structure. Without any obvious gears or levers and with no pull-rings to anchor ropes to, he could find nothing that indicated how the doors could be opened. He crossed his arms and searched for something he might have overlooked, but came up with nothing.

"Any luck?" Jenna asked as she and Rellah appeared around the side of one of the large columns that framed the outer edge of the platform.

Hyatt shook his head in frustration, still studying the ornate doors as they made their way up to join him and Bex. The designs embossed on the door refused to reveal whatever secret they held, immovable and silent.

"Maybe the doors aren't the way in." Bex walked up to the two massive barriers and stood with their back to the doors, shielding their eyes from the sun as they looked out over the square and the Garden beyond. "The way up here was hidden. Maybe the way inside is, too."

"Parts of Keeper maps and hidden tunnels to sky gardens…" Jenna sighed.

"Don't forget Irons and Rams," Bex added, dropping their hand and walking across the broad stone space to the edge of the uppermost stair.

Rayce took his turn at the door, crouching down and tracing his finger along the seam between them. He looked up from where he knelt along the plane of the entrance, then frowned and shook his head.

"I don't see it," he muttered. "It's like this door only opens from the inside."

Hyatt backed away to take in both doors in their entirety, certain he had missed something. Too close to the towering face of the structure to be impressed by its mass, it looked like an impenetrable assembly of stone and metal that offered no vents or hatches to suggest another way in. Even the cold air seemed to deflect off the building.

*We did not come all this way to stop here.* Hyatt breathed into his hands to warm them, then dried them against his shirt beneath his jacket to stop the moisture from freezing on his skin. *You are going to open.*

"I've got something." Jenna took a step back from the column she was facing, her hand half extended as if she'd just pressed something.

Hyatt outpaced the rest of his pack to Jenna's side and saw what she had seen, a depression in the shape of a long blade in the smooth surface of the pillar. "What happened?"

"I pressed on it, and it moved." She stepped forward again and pressed on the indented section of the pillar, and the depression deepened another finger's width with an almost inaudible hiss. "Like that."

At the bottom of the indent, he saw a metal strip inlaid in the pillar had begun to be revealed. Hyatt bent his knees into a half-squat to check the top of the concealed channel, and found a matching band of dark silver inset in the top.

"Where is that blade?" He turned in a circle and moved beyond the pillar to the edge of the stairs, and his eyes swept over the courtyard. "The green one that the Ram had."

"I'll get it." Bex started down the stairs at a brisk trot.

A moment later they returned, the strange glass blade in hand. It fit perfectly in the indent in the column and when Bex seated it as deep as it would go, a mechanical clank reverberated through the stone beneath their feet. Hyatt turned around just in time to see Rayce push against one of the doors, and it swung open as if it weighed nothing at all.

He began walking toward the doorway without a thought, but Rellah grabbed his sleeve and held him back. "Hyatt... wait."

When Hyatt paused and looked over at Rellah, he was surprised at the amount of reluctance he felt coming from her. Her eyes were on the opening between the two doors, and every muscle from her hips up seemed locked rigid.

His eyes moved down to her hand where it opened and closed in anxious anticipation, a gesture he had never seen Rellah make. "What is it?"

"If a Ram guarded this place..." She paused, and swallowed hard, "maybe it should stay closed."

He shook his head and pulled his arm free of her grip, and she let him. "Someday, you're going to have to tell me about Rams – but right now, I'm going inside. I need to know what's in there. You don't have to follow me."

Beyond the doorway, an anteroom with wooden doors inset into each wall awaited him. The slate-gray tiles of the floor and the mint-green walls were offset by cream-colored scarf valances draped through copper rings bolted to the walls, and an area rug in shades of vanilla and spruce blue silenced their steps. The vaulted ceiling was a matching shade of buttermilk with copper flecks throughout, and frosted glass orbs suspended over their heads soaked the chamber in warm light.

"Which way?" Jenna asked as she stepped around him.

Hyatt crossed the room to the door on the opposite side and pressed his hands against its wooden surface. He pushed the door to the side and it slid open, disappearing into the wall until only a sliver of it remained exposed. Beyond, a metal walkway ran in both directions.

Hyatt stepped out onto the catwalk and looked down into a large chamber, both his hands finding the metal railway that protected him from the long drop over the platform's edge. Below, two dozen men and women in dark Keeper robes with their hoods over their heads stood on either side of two long tables, stacks of pages and piles of ancient artifacts scattered between them. Each looked consumed with their task, examining pages in their hands or using mechanical tools to pull apart and reconnect parts of the strange items before them. Freestanding lamps with wide, flat shades on top dispersed yellow-white light over their work, turning their blond and brown hair shades of molten gold and rich chocolate.

He was grateful that he had the railing in front of him to lean on as his mind tried to process what he was seeing, questions cascading into his awareness faster than he could theorize possible answers. The height of the lamps and the way their shades bent light downward created strange, upward shadows, but Hyatt saw no other shapes on the catwalk that ran the perimeter of the chamber and no armed guards moving between the Keepers consumed by their efforts.

"What the compost..." Bex whispered as they joined Hyatt at the railing. "Are they... captives?"

"I don't think so. No guards, no chains..." Hyatt paused, watching one of the Keepers below look back and forth between two pages and a square machine as she took notes. "They're working like... I don't know, not like they're forced to."

He retreated with careful steps to avoid making a sound and when Bex was back in the chamber, he slid the door closed behind them. As he turned around he saw Rellah closing the giant exterior doors, and when she faced him there was no less trepidation in her features, but resolve had mixed in.

"Not that way?" she asked, her voice low.

"There are dozens of Keepers working in there, but I don't think they saw us." Hyatt crossed the room to the next door, and when he slid it open, it revealed shallow stairs that climbed to a corner and turned out of sight. "Let's try this way instead."

# TWENTY-ONE

The stone stairs that rose to another level of the massive structure ended in another small room with two exits, both of which led to corridors with multiple hallways and doors branching away from them. Short, shallow steps continued to change the level they explored, and each room of green and gray was unique but none had a clear enough purpose or marking to distinguish them from one another. It didn't take long for Hyatt to realize he was lost, with no idea how deep in the building they had walked or even which floor they were on.

"What are we looking for?" Rayce asked, his question loaded with the same conclusions Hyatt had reached.

"We're looking for a wall or a door with that symbol from the courtyard on it." Hyatt examined the walls and the three identical doors of the room they were in, but nothing stood out in any way that made it different than the last dozen they had explored. "We'll know it when we see it."

He slid aside the door closest to him, but instead of an empty hallway, three Keepers with their faces masked barred the way. They held strange metal rods with knobs on their ends in two-handed grips, and the closest one thrust their rod at him as if it was a spear. He jumped backward as the end of the weapon passed through where he had been standing, and behind him, he heard the door on the opposite wall slide open.

"On the left!" Jenna called out as she drew her blade and squared herself toward the third entrance to the room as the door opened to reveal more Keepers.

The Keepers advanced from all sides as Hyatt fumbled to draw his blade. They kept their polearms at the ready, brandishing them as they closed in on Hollow Bone to drive them toward the rear of the chamber like they were herding animals.

"Drop your weapons!" One of the Keepers growled through the fabric of their mask.

"Say it with your blood," Jenna snarled back at him, a more primal sound than Hyatt had heard from her since the day they met.

The encircling Keepers reached their limit of advance, unable to push Hyatt and his companions any deeper into the room without starting a clash. As his hand tightened around the grip of his blade, the thought that the Keepers didn't understand Cern tactics flashed through his head, just before Rayce bashed one of the Keeper's weapons aside and used the opening he created to plant a kick squarely into the robed man's sternum that sent him sprawling backward.

The Keeper beside him took a swing to retaliate, but Rellah was already moving and the concave blade in her hands caught the weapon's shaft and slid down until it caught against the knob with enough force to rip it from the Keeper's hands. As the Keeper leaned forward in a vain attempt to recover it, Rellah brought her weapon inside and planted the gleaming tip against the notch in the man's collarbone. She walked forward two steps and drove him back by the pressure on his blade, breaking their encirclement into a line of Keepers that faced an armed and ready pack.

"Enough!" the centermost Keeper shouted, her voice martial and authoritative.

The response from the rest of the Keepers was immediate and almost in unison as they took steps backward, their weapons dipping into lower positions. Hyatt reacted on instinct, moving forward to consume the space created by their marginal retreat, and in his periphery, he saw Rellah and Bex do the same.

The woman who had spoken let go of her weapon with one hand and used the other to lower her mask, exposing younger features than Hyatt had expected and a tuft of auburn hair that escaped her cowl beneath her chin. "You can't win, Lowlanders – there are thousands of us – but you will surely kill some of my Keepers. We can avoid your deaths, and some of ours, if you lower your weapons and come with us."

Hyatt stole a sliver of the moment, as she delivered her ultimatum, to count their adversaries and totaled twelve hoods with one already unarmed. He could envision the carnage to follow, cleaving steel and rended flesh bathing the room in gristle and brain, and every member of Hollow Bone still alive and soaked to their elbows in Keeper blood. The clench in his gut that he expected to feel was replaced by cold stability from his navel to his sternum, and he felt himself smile.

"All of yours," he corrected her, turning his weapon over in a quick spin to ready it. "They may overwhelm us, but all of you are already dead."

He watched his words strike the row of Keepers like arrows from Rellah's bow as they shifted their weight with unease from one foot to the other and adjusted their grips on the hafts of their weapons. Only the unmasked woman in the center seemed unphased by his threat, except for the way her eyes hardened.

"Without our antidote, so are you," she replied without breaking eye contact with him. "How long have you been in our Garden, without a mask, Lowlander?"

Her implication poured mud into his thoughts, and the familiar tension of stress began to spread across his shoulders. He inhaled through his parted lips, and the inward breath felt drier on his tongue than he expected. Hyatt couldn't tell if the air had a unique taste to it, or if the Keeper had created the thought that his senses chose to make real, but as he focused on his breathing, the insides of his nostrils seemed to burn.

"What are you talking about," he forced himself to ask, and he felt his chest tighten in anticipation of her answer.

"Oh, rot..." Bex muttered, wiping their free hand across their mouth and chin like they were clearing cobwebs from it.

When the Keeper spoke again, her same controlled tone had been fortified by notes of certainty. "The flowers in this Garden release toxins that build up in your body. Even if you made it beyond the temple walls, or even back to the Lowlands, you would be dead in days – weeks, at most."

Hyatt studied the woman's face but saw no signs of deception in her direct gaze and solid stance. After a long moment, he glanced over at Rellah and lowered his weapon, and was relieved to see her do the same. The rest of the pack followed her lead.

"Good," the Keeper said. "Follow me."

Her robes swirled around her as she turned and led the way through the doorway into the hall beyond. Four of her fellow Keepers joined her at the front of their procession and the remainder formed a group at the back, with none of them intermixed with Hyatt and his companions. Their path wound through hallways and chambers in a way that felt almost as random as the route Hyatt had explored, but the woman in the lead moved with intention and never hesitated as she climbed and descended stairs, turned corners, or opened and closed doors.

"How did you find us?" Rayce asked the Keepers in front of him as they moved along a broad hallway.

Neither robed figure answered him, and Hyatt exchanged glances and shrugs with Rayce. Behind them, he could hear the raider's cant exchanged between Rellah and Jenna as they walked side by side. The matted consonants of their words did their job well because Hyatt couldn't make out individual words as they talked, and he was certain that the Keepers behind them would have no better luck.

The Keeper in the front of their group stopped before the first pair of doors that were distinct from the dozens of other wooden panels he had seen in the temple. Painted in the deep, burnt orange of the Keeper's robes, perfect lines of embossed symbols within square borders adorned every inch of the exposed surface. Washes of copper paint lingered in the deepest parts of the engraved characters and the depths of their square borders, and only two metal plates along the center seam of the doors broke the rows of characters.

"Wait here." The woman said as she placed her hands on the metal plates.

The Keeper hesitated a moment and Hyatt saw her close her eyes as if she was preparing herself for an examination, then pushed the panel apart, creating enough space for her to sidestep through. Once inside, she turned around long enough to bring the doors together again, and vanished from view.

"Do you think it's real?" Rayce asked as he licked his lips and dragged his hand down across his nose and mouth. "I don't feel anything."

Hyatt had wondered the same thing on their travel through the temple, but could only conclude that it was a risk they couldn't afford to take. Rayce's question pulled it to the forefront of his mind again and he turned it over, thinking about the strange and unfamiliar plants they had seen since entering the garden.

"Where I grew up, there was a job for people who knew all the plants and berries of the Reclaimed. There are noxious plants... Master Petaler Kyled told us about a pink flower with antennae seeds called Somnaletha that would stop your breathing if you slept too close to a bouquet of them. I don't know most of the plants we saw here, but... it could be true."

Rayce's jaw moved like he was chewing on the information, and he nodded. "The Keepers we saw were all wearing masks."

Their conversation faded into reflective silence, and Hyatt leaned against the corridor's wall as he waited for the doors to open. On either end, the Keepers stood in silence facing inward with their hands tucked into their sleeves, their hoods in place, and their masks covering their mouths and noses.

Even in the utter quiet, there was no sound of footsteps to warn Hyatt before the doors slid apart and the woman appeared. She had removed her hood inside and was pulling it into place over her hair as she stepped over the threshold into the hallway.

"The Sentinel Keeper will see you. Touch nothing in this room, and speak only the truth, and he will reward you with the antidotes you need." She paused and looked around to ensure she had the attention of everyone in Hollow Bone Pack. "If you violate either of these conditions, the toxins inside you will end your lives. Now, come with me."

The woman led them into a large oval chamber, the first room in the building Hyatt had seen that wasn't square. Rails set into the floor and ceiling ran beneath bookshelves on either side of a central aisle, and each shelf's end bore a large metal wheel at chest height. At intervals through the aisle, books and papers covered tables in uneven stacks, and a lectern at the far end of the aisle bathed in light that shone down from a glass panel above it.

On the near side of the closest table, a Keeper wore robes that matched every other person they met in the temple except for a simple, woven passementerie at the end of his sleeves and the hem of his robes. He stood with his back to them, a page in each hand, and his hood turned back and forth between the two documents as if he were comparing them. When he finished, he set them down on the workspace and turned around to regard Hyatt and his companions flanked on all sides by Keepers.

"My name is Doveen," the man said, leaning back against the table and clasping his hands in front of him. "I am the Sentinel Keeper of the Temple of the Irradiant Widow, whose gift of knowledge grows in us all. You're not Irons, or Ram... who are you?"

"We were Cern, before. We're Claimed now," Jenna replied, gesturing to everyone else. "What is this place?"

Doveen turned and looked at each of them like he was trying to understand the full makeup of their characters. He made no effort to hide the way his eyes moved from their boots to their weapons, up to their shoulders and then to their faces, taking in every fold of fabric and every crease in their travel-worn skin. When he concluded his assessment of them, he reached up to adjust the way his hood settled on his shoulders.

"There have been four uninvited visitors to the Desolate Garden in my lifetime. We killed three of them. The fourth was a child, too young to remember this place, and given to the Ram. For ten generations, no one who entered the Temple of Sklodowska has seen the Lowlands again." Doveen paused and tapped the side of his index finger against his pursed lips, lost in thought for a moment. "It is strange that you ... Claimed? Is that what you call yourselves? That you Claimed appear in the Garden just as our work is ending."

"If you think you can stop us from leaving, you've never fought Cern before," Jenna warned him, looking over her shoulder with an unimpressed smirk at the two Keepers flanking her.

"Twenty-thousand citizens of this garden tried to leave, in the early days of this History – none reached the lowlands." There was no pride or sorrow in Doveen's voice as he shrugged and walked slowly around the table, putting it between him and them before stacking the scattered pages with attention. "We may not need to see who is right. For now, stay as our guests."

Jenna opened her mouth to argue, but stopped as Bex slipped their fingers through hers and squeezed. Hyatt caught the gesture in the corner of his eye, but as he remembered their need for an antidote only the Keepers could provide, he was grateful for it and kept his face neutral.

"Keeper Halsen, please take our guests to the arboretum," Doveen said.

The woman who had led them to his chamber nodded in a single bow that bent her tall frame at her hips and the base of her neck. "Yes, Sentinel."

He turned his attention back to the Claimed, his gaze shifting from one face to another as he spoke. "Our arboretum should have everything you need for a short stay with us. The fruits, nuts, and tubers are edible, there is space for your bedding, and the temperatures remain moderate. For the days you will be our guests, you should be comfortable enough."

"Days?" Bex repeated, their tone flat.

The Sentinel Keeper turned his back to them and picked up one of the papers he had been examining, then opened the cover of one of the books on the desk and began to turn its pages in search of something. "Fortunately, only days. We'll speak again."

Hyatt felt a thousand questions bubbling up inside him and knew he wasn't the only one, but before anyone from Hollow Bone could formulate the words to express one, the Keepers closed together in a wall of robes between them and Doveen. The woman he had called Halsen gestured to the exit, which was the only direction left for them to move.

The path from the oval chamber to the arboretum was as convoluted and confusing as their last route, but Hyatt had the impression they were higher in the temple than they had been before. Halsen stopped in front of a door that looked identical to every other door they had passed, slid it open, and gestured for them to enter.

Hyatt moved with slow, lingering steps as he entered the arboretum. All around them, elevated plots of earth walled in by white and green stone held concentric rings of plants that began with ground-clinging flowers at the outer edges and rose to trees with tall, twisted trunks at the centers. None of the leaves were familiar to him, but the light that filtered in from the glass ceiling seemed to brighten every color and deepen every shadow, and he found himself staring at every strange fruit and pattern of bark as he moved deeper into the large room.

"I... don't know any of these," Rayce said as he walked by Hyatt's side, but paused to touch one of the low-hanging leaves as they passed it. "I don't even know anything like them."

"They tell you everything is toxic, so you touch the first leaf you see." Bex rolled their eyes.

Rayce shrugged and plucked the leaf and rolled the detached stem between his thumb and forefinger so it twirled in his hand. "They said everything here was edible."

"The berries, nuts, and tubers. The head Keeper said those were edible." Jenna slapped him on the shoulder. "The leaves and flowers are what kill you."

Rayce glared at her, but dropped the leaf. Hyatt watched it flutter down to land on the stone wall surrounding the raised bed before turning his attention to a central space ahead. A ring of wrought-iron benches encircled a low table built around the trunk of a massive tree with smooth bark. The tree towered over everything else in the arboretum with a canopy that cast long lines of shade over the benches below and from that central point, paths extended away like spokes of a wheel and vanished amidst the curated collections of plants.

Keeper Halsen stopped at the edge of the table and turned to face them. "Some of our Keepers will stay with you, in case you have an emergency. As our guests, we request you not leave the arboretum until the Sentinel Keeper sends for you."

Hyatt couldn't recall a time when he heard a request that sounded less like a request. "When do we get the antidote?"

"When the Sentinel Keeper tells us to administer it." Halsen strode along the path they had come from as the remainder of the Keepers in her entourage moved along alternate walkways to disperse into the arboretum. "See you soon."

Hyatt caught Rellah's hand movement as her fingers lingered above the arrows in her quiver, and for a heart-stopping moment, he thought she was going to draw one and bury it between Halsen's shoulder blades. His lungs refused to function until her hand settled over the indigo fletchings and rested there, but even when he could breathe again, his eyes stayed on the singular intent etched into Rellah's features as she watched the Keeper depart.

*That woman will never know how close she came to dying.* Hyatt shook his head and ran his fingers through his hair. *She had better produce that antidote.*

# TWENTY-TWO

The arboretum was everything Doveen had promised, and Hyatt enjoyed the strange tubers that tasted like a cross of corn and onions while his companions sustained themselves on the hard-shelled fruit and giant, husked nuts that grew in tight clusters on the taller trees. Hollow Bone kept a guard schedule while they slept, but nothing disturbed them and the Keepers who remained with them kept to the perimeter. Wherever Hyatt looked in the day that followed, there was always a flutter of Keeper robes in his periphery but never directly in front of him and never looking at him.

On the second day, Bex joined him as he listlessly milled through the spoked walkways and the arcs that connected them between rings of raised flowerbeds. "They have a whole Garden to grow things in... why keep all of these species inside the temple?"

Hyatt thought it over for a moment, studying the plants that lined the nearest stone wall. "We don't know any of these... maybe they are trying to preserve them, or grow enough of them to release in the wild?"

His pack-mate squinted like they didn't like the explanation, but didn't reply. The clouds that had assembled over the glass ceiling released a spatter of flurries, singular flakes that got waylaid by stray breezes on their way to the high panes and tumbled like drunken bees before sticking to the glass. Hyatt frowned and studied the sky, trying to decide if the random snowflakes were warnings of a greater storm.

"How long ago was Rellah Claimed?" Bex plucked a small black berry from the bush beside them, squeezed it until it burst against the pad of their finger, and licked the sticky black juice from their fingertip.

Hyatt watched Bex as they sucked the last of the pigment from their finger and wiped it on their pants, and wondered if they knew he had caught on long ago to the seemingly innocuous things they did when broaching a difficult topic. "Why?"

Bex rubbed their hands together and didn't answer. They continued their stroll between the inflorescence of pale flowers and the slender trees for another ten paces, until Bex stopped to pick up a stray clod of dirt and return it to the raised bed beside them. Hyatt waited until they rejoined him and they started walking again, but his desire to know what Bex was holding inside their head outweighed his resistance to playing along.

"About six months, maybe seven. Why?" he asked again, the unknown entwining with a certainty of something grim to form a knot in his chest.

Bex nodded as if the answer was about what they expected.

"I've been... thinking. Thinking back." Their pause felt like a chair on two legs, about to tip over with a crash. "Something Veck said."

Hyatt pictured Veck silhouetted in the doorway of the room with the contraband weapons and devices. "Bex – I'm sorry about Kenna. I'd do anything to—"

"What?" Realization spread over their face and they shook their head with urgency, turning to grab both of Hyatt's arms and hold him still. "Hyatt, no – you didn't get Kenna killed, and you're not going to get me killed. You don't think that was your fault?"

He didn't expect the heat of tears trapped behind his eyes, or his inability to swallow. "It was my travel plan."

"Oh, for fucking rotted compost – a Veshtrue killed Kenna, Hyatt! She didn't starve, or get lost, or drown. She died with her weapon in her hand, facing a fucking Heir." Bex's voice was stern, but their face was heartbroken for Hyatt. "She had the best death a Claimed can hope for, in combat and in an instant."

He couldn't bring himself to accept his pack-mate's version of events, but every word felt like it was driving an icepick into his own outlook on it. He managed to nod and Bex nodded too before releasing his arms. Hyatt started walking and Bex moved beside him again as they turned along an intersecting path, with different unfamiliar plants channeling them along the walkway. The snow fell in heavier and more consistent flakes and stuck to the clear panes of the arboretum's ceiling, altering the shadows that added texture to the space around them several stories below.

"I wish we'd never come here," he said. "Kenna would be alive, Veck would be here... we shouldn't have come here."

"So you're an Iron now?" Bex asked.

He missed their meaning. "What?"

"You can tell the future now? The Butcher Queen fills your head with visions of who lives and who dies, whose 'story' ends when?" They scoffed. "Or are you just committed to believing every other series of events would have been better – that of all the choices you did and didn't make, you managed to pick the worst combination?"

He knew their point made sense, but it did nothing to change the grief lodged in his chest. "You're right. We're here now. What did Veck say?"

"When an Heir breaks our skin, it can transfer something that stays after the wound heals. We are called Claimed because

Heirs can sense that thing in us – it calls to them like the smell of meat over a fire calls to us." Bex watched Hyatt's face as they talked.

The care with which Bex chose their words and the way their eyes moved over his features made Hyatt wonder what connection he was supposed to be making but was missing. He settled for a nod to signal he was following along and waited for them to continue.

"Sometimes that thing that stays in us... it can be like a toxin. We don't know why, but when some Cern are wounded by Heirs, they develop symptoms. It isn't always right away. It starts with mood swings – too angry, too happy, unable to care about anything..."

Realization came to Hyatt in slow, heavy turns of the gears in his head. "Bex..."

"Erratic behavior, reckless decision making... we call it Blood Ruin." Bex had been trying to hold Hyatt's gaze but what they saw in his eyes overpowered their efforts and they studied the wall of the closest building as they built the resolve to look back at his face. "Rellah has Blood Ruin."

"No – no way!" Even as he protested it, flashes of his time with Rellah since they left the Laybrair came into his mind faster and faster to make Bex's case for them. "She's just carrying a lot – training me, building the pack—"

"I've seen it before, Hyatt." Bex walked a line between tender and firm. "It's going to get worse."

Not knowing how to process what they were saying failed to limit the growing cloud of dread in his sternum that seemed to condense and leak in cold runnels into his stomach. "How do we stop it?"

Bex paused, looking for words, but their resigned sigh admitted their defeat. "It can't be—"

Hyatt started shaking his head, first gently and then more vehemently. "Don't tell me that, Bex – don't fucking tell me there is nothing we can do!"

"—stopped," Bex continued without raising or lowering their tone. "It's part of why Claimed can't stay with their packs–"

"No! We are not going to let this happen!" Hyatt could feel tears welling in his eyes and the poison of grief within them, and he got louder in a bid to keep his voice level.

Bex abandoned the conversation that Hyatt couldn't have and hung their head for a moment, letting the maelstrom of rage and grief churn around them without fueling it. Hyatt didn't realize he needed something to fight against until Bex's silence deprived him of it, and his words turned into a sticky concrete in his chest that refused to form into syllables.

"Will it kill her?" He struggled to keep his voice even.

"Eventually." Bex studied their boots and then squinted up at the sky, as if either could soften the things they needed to say. "Sometimes it's years, sometimes it's weeks."

Hyatt didn't know what to say, so he said nothing. Instead, the future Bex predicted seemed to rattle around inside him like a rock tossed down a mineshaft, ricocheting off his heart and ribs as it looked for a place to settle into existence. They continued walking together, and the Keeper they passed turned his hooded head to track them as they moved through his line of sight, but stayed where he was and disappeared behind them as the strange trees of the arboretum intervened.

"I'm sorry, Hyatt. I know you two are..." Bex broke off, one of the only times Hyatt recalled them being at a loss for words.

He couldn't blame Bex, because Hyatt had no word for the shared existence he had grown into with Rellah. No title or term felt like it carried all the right notes of mentor, friend, companion, and idol. The idea of existing in the Reclaimed without her felt crushing and hollow at the same time, a heavy weight and a total vacuum that shouldn't have been able to coexist in one person but managed in his case all the same.

"She's not going to die." Hyatt shook his head and his voice was quiet, but not quiet enough to hide the way it cracked as he spoke. "We'll find a way."

Bex nodded, and even in the sea of feelings Hyatt was struggling to tame, he knew they didn't believe him but were instead acknowledging how the information existed in his mind. They finished the lap together and Bex broke off toward the central space with the ancient tree. The idea of sitting with the things they had said seemed impossible to Hyatt, so he continued his walk. Above him, snow continued to accumulate and block the light from the sun into the arboretum.

The following morning, Hyatt rolled out of his bedding and as he sat up, he saw Rellah still asleep. The sight of her on her side with her blanket pulled up over her wove anxiety into his waking thoughts as he tried to recall if he had ever seen her sleep later than the rest of the pack, and as he looked around, he confirmed that everyone else had risen already. He found Bex seated at the central table, paring a fruit with their knife, and caught sight of Jenna and Rayce doing pull-ups on a low branch. The snowfall had stopped sometime in the night and most of it slid from the glass panes overhead, letting pale morning light filter down to them.

With a last, concerned look at Rellah, he wandered into the Garden to find more of the tubers he enjoyed. His belt-knife made easy work of separating the long stalks from their bulbed roots, and he bit into one while he collected enough to make a meal out of. Hyatt was on his way back to the benches at the center of the arboretum when the door slid open with a sound that drew the attention of him and all of his pack-mates.

The Keeper in the doorway stood in silence until all of Hollow Bone had migrated to the entrance, and Hyatt saw Rellah wipe sleep from her eyes before shoving her hands into the pockets of her jacket.

"The Sentinel Keeper is ready to speak with the one called Hyatt." When Keeper Halsen spoke, the mask that covered her nose and mouth shifted in a subdued imitation of her lips' movement.

Hyatt rose to his feet and headed toward the woman in the doorway but when Rayce and Bex started to follow him, the Keepers assigned to keep them company in the arboretum began to move on paths to intercept the uninvited Claimed.

"The Sentinel Keeper requires only Hyatt's presence at this time." The Keeper inclined her cowled head as if offering an apology for a miscommunication, but her words lacked any remorse. "You are all invited to remain in the arboretum until he returns."

When it looked like Rayce and Bex had no intention of cooperating, Hyatt slowed down and turned to face them. "It's okay – I can meet Doveen alone. I got us into this place, so I'm going to get us out of here."

Rayce nodded, even as Jenna stood toe-to-toe with one of the armed Keepers on one side and Rellah paced along the other end with her gaze fixed on another robed figure. Hyatt met Bex's eyes and they held his gaze for a moment.

"I'll be right back with the antidote." He knew they didn't need his assurance, but it felt good to say it aloud anyway.

Hyatt followed Keeper Halsen into the hallway, and they began their winding path through the building to the Sentinel Keeper's chamber with two additional robed figures trailing behind them. They lingered far enough behind Hyatt that at first, he thought Halsen had said or done something to relieve them and that they were headed to complete whatever tasks the temple required, but after they descended the second set of stairs with him and Keeper Halsen, he realized his mistake.

He picked up his pace to walk beside Halsen. "Three Keepers for one Cern... I'm not sure if I should be surprised, or flattered."

Hyatt expected an eye-roll or a laugh from the Keeper, but her expression remained neutral and she offered no answer to the question he implied. They turned a corner and passed through a long, rectangular chamber, and when they exited on the far side, they climbed another set of stairs.

"I'm sure these hallways make sense if you grew up here, but I have no idea where I am." He glanced back at the two Keepers trailing behind them, then over at Halsen to gauge her reaction. "Did you grow up here?"

"I did." Her jaw clenched, working hard to prevent any expression from crossing her delicate features. "So did my parents, and their parents, and theirs – and on the eve of the accomplishment we worked our entire lives for, I was given the honor of facilitating your stay."

Her terse tone landed every blow it was meant to land on Hyatt, but he refused to give ground. "Facilitate our stay... because calling us captives would violate the fifth Warning, right? What have you all been doing, all these years?"

Instead of answering, Keeper Halsen stopped in front of the decorative doors of the Sentinel Keeper's chamber. Hyatt looked up and down the hallway, trying to remember which end they had approached the room from on their first visit, but he couldn't recall if the door had been on the left or the right then.

She placed her hands on the door's flat metal panels and paused, then looked over her shoulder at Hyatt. "I cast my vote to kill you and your friends when you reached Desolate Garden before you ever set foot in our temple, and I hope Sentinel Keeper Doveen has come to his senses by now. I don't believe you are the ones we have been waiting for, and I hope you never reach the Lowlands."

"Two of my friends are dead and everyone I love has been poisoned by your dumb-rot Garden," he replied, his tone as matter-of-fact as hers had been. "I hope your temple caves in on all of you, and Sklodowska forgets your name."

She nodded, satisfied they both said what they needed to say, and pushed the doors aside. Her robe fluttered as she stepped into the chamber and when Hyatt followed her inside, the two trailing Keepers took up positions in the hall on either side of the doors. Before him, Doveen leaned against the face of one of the massive bookshelves that lined the room, staring up at the rows of texts on the opposite shelf.

"Sentinel Keeper, I've brought the Cern, Hyatt." She rested her fingers on the giant wheel of the closest shelf and hesitated, then withdrew them as if she had touched something that did not belong to her.

Doveen stepped into the aisle and grabbed the giant metal wheel on the end of the shelf with both of his weathered hands and grimaced in effort as he applied pressure. "Thank you, Halsen. Please, leave us."

The older man built up enough power to turn the wheel, and once it started, it turned easier and easier. As it turned, the entire shelf moved along its tracks until it was abutted against the next one, erasing the aisle where he had been standing.

"Sentinel, I can-" she began.

Doveen released the wheel and turned to face Halsen, and his look stopped her protest mid-thought. She bowed, the edge of her hood concealing her expression, and turned to face the door. Only when she had stepped through the doorway and faced the chamber as she closed the doors behind herself did Hyatt see the hard stare she gave him before she vanished from view.

Hyatt waited until the doors were closed to focus on Doveen, and when he did, he cut straight to the point. "My pack-mates need your antidote, and then we're leaving your garden. We've had enough of your hospitality."

"Yes, I'm sure you have." The Sentinel Keeper chuckled and nodded in concession as he walked towards Hyatt, favoring a slight limp that showed even through the expansive, flowing fabric of his robe. "Strange that you ask about the antidote for your friends but leave yourself out. Have you chosen to stay here with us?"

"No rotted way." Hyatt resisted the urge to close his hands into fists as the Sentinel Keeper drew near. "Are you going to give me the antidote or not?"

Doveen studied Hyatt for a moment like he was committing the creases around his eyes and the scar on his chin to memory. The older man's blue-gray eyes moved with intention from one of Hyatt's eyebrows to the other, down along the bridge of his nose, and back up to his hairline.

"I was ready to meet with you two days ago, but your pack-mates needed more time in the arboretum. The pollen from the tree in the center of that room – the tree you and your pack-mates slept underneath – counteracts the toxins released by the Garden's flora. Follow me, Hyatt of Cern." Doveen turned toward the lectern on the opposite end of the oval chamber and started walking. "As long as you proceed directly to the

Lowlands and do not linger in the Garden, your symptoms will be no worse than muscle aches and head tremors for a few days."

Hyatt stared after him and for a moment, he wondered if the toxins were real. The idea that Desolate Garden grew both flowers that would kill them by breathing their air, but also grew the tree that would cure them in the same manner, was almost too far-fetched for him to accept it. Knowing he might never learn the truth of it only compounded his suspicions.

He followed the Keeper's slow steps and chose to set aside that puzzle so he could focus on whatever battle of wills was required to get his friends away from the temple. Keeper Helsen's wish for his immediate death circulated in his thoughts, and the thought that kidnapping Doveen might help them reach the edge of Bloodstained Mesa alive flashed through his head before he set it aside as well. He tried to take in everything as he walked, his gaze shifting from one shelf to another in the hope of catching something of value.

"What is all this?" Hyatt followed Doveen through the radial shelves loaded down with books and crates of paper toward the podium at the back of the massive, oval chamber. "What have you all been doing up here?"

The Keeper's robes swirled at his ankles like eddies and his sleeves shifted around his wrists as he led the way through the center aisle of the room. "Eleven generations of work. The births, lives, and deaths of hundreds."

As Doveen spoke, Hyatt felt like he could almost see the ghosts of the past moving between the shelves and clutching tomes in their arms like cherished children. The depth of their focus for so many years seemed to thin and still the air, as if Hyatt's breaths brought in less oxygen than they should have. The Keeper reached the lectern and moved behind it, facing the book left open on the lectern's slanted surface that came into view as Hyatt followed him around and stood at his side.

"Do you know what a Warning is?" the Keeper asked, resting his fingertips on the pages of the book.

Hyatt's blood ran cold as the possibilities of what might lie in the pages before him grew more and more narrow with every passing heartbeat. "They're the rules that stop the Ninth History from beginning... the end of the humankind."

"No. A Warning is taking every shade of blood and berry and wine, and reducing it to the word 'red'. It is every joy and pain and hope and fear anyone has ever experienced since the start of time, called 'feeling'." Doveen pulled with his index and middle fingers, sliding the top page across the one beneath it with a smooth hiss before letting it fold along its natural bridge and turning it over to reveal the text on the page below. "It is the smallest expression of the most encompassing thing that remains true."

Hyatt watched as the Keeper turned another page, concealing a page filled from margin to margin with neat rows of script in characters he couldn't read, broken only by graphics of thick lines and thin shading with hexagonal borders. Each new page was covered front and back, and even without understanding the words, Hyatt felt like the book divided all that came before and everything that would come after.

"In the Fifth History, there were three Warnings, then five, and then nine," Doveen said, words crisp with certainty but warm, as if his love for the work that consumed his life spread through them. "Written into the fabric of reality by Sklodowska, distilled through the blood and sacrifice of Keepers, and enforced by the Ram."

The way the Keeper told a narrative Hyatt knew to be wrong with such absolute surety jarred him, but he said nothing as

Doveen continued to sift through the pages of the book, his gaze moving over each line with a kind of adoration that reminded Hyatt of a mother looking at her favorite child.

"Two of the original Warnings were lost to time, and the genocides of the Cult of Ehren. Today, only seven Warnings keep us safe," Doveen hesitated on the last page, his fingertips barely in contact with the textured, cream-colored paper and the copper text in perfect lines across it. "Until now."

Hyatt realized his body was locked rigid with fear and he tried to focus on releasing the clench in his shoulders and legs. The idea of the Keeper turning the last page of the book filled him with a dread he didn't understand, a thing in his blood that threatened to make it still and kill him when it stopped moving. Opening his mouth felt like prying his teeth apart with a crowbar and when he managed, he couldn't speak.

Doveen turned over the final page of the book with the same delicate motion, drawing his fingers across it so the center bowed, higher and higher until the curve of the page was strong enough to carry the edge up over the binding and settle it on the opposite side like a feather drifting to the ground. Perfect, foreign characters covered two-thirds of the revealed left page, and on the right, a single line of text in dark gray, metallic letters spanned the midpoint.

"You're going to carry our work to the Lord Ranger's Keeper, Hyatt of the Claimed." The Sentinel Keeper looked up for the first time, his gray eyes staring into Hyatt's.

Every fiber of his body and mind rejected Doveen's demand. Hyatt's stomach wrenched tight and his throat closed, while a wordless scream radiated through his head with an intensity he could feel in the meat of his brain. He searched for a way to reject the Keeper's instruction but felt cornered by the stacks of papers that all focused on the lectern and the book in front of him that would not be denied.

"There is no Lord Ranger." His technical protest felt weak even as he said it, but it was all he could manage.

Doveen closed the book gently as if it might shatter into a thousand shards if he closed it too quickly or with too much force. His old hands folded the cream cloth that separated the tome from the lectern so it formed a cushion for the dark green cover of the book, the silken material dangling from his hands on all sides like hanging moss. He closed his eyes for a moment and his fingers curled into the fabric, and Hyatt wondered even through his fear and panic if he had ever seen anyone love something so much.

Th Keeper turned toward him, and Hyatt took a step backward out of instinct. "This is what you came here to do."

"That book is going to change the world – I don't want to do this!" Hyatt said, but his tone was more a plea to be released from the fate he felt closing around him. "Give it to one of your Keepers!"

Doveen stepped off the podium, the book held before him like a ring bearer. Hyatt took another staggering step backward and bumped into a table at his back, cutting off his retreat. The Keeper stopped in front of him and extended his arms further, the book held horizontally between them.

"You were born Haleu, became Cern, and now live among the Claimed – only Keepers have no claim to you, but they will read the words and know the truth. We have decided it must be you." Doveen's face seemed at once insistent and entirely content, as if he knew how their conversation would end, no matter what Hyatt said.

"It doesn't work like that," Hyatt insisted. "I'm not a High Ranger or a pack leader – they won't listen to me, just because I show up with a book and claim it has a new Warning!"

"This Warning stands between them and the end of humankind. You'll convince them to listen," Doveen assured him as he pressed the book toward him.

Hyatt recoiled from the book. "I can't even convince you to not give me this task – how am I going to convince the whole world of a new Warning?"

"You must, so you will." The Keeper continued to hold the book at arm's length, his gaze fixed on Hyatt and unwavering in focus or intensity. "Sklodowska will clear your way and imbue you with the ring of truth."

*Sklodowska... this is because I told Tobin to tell you to leave me alone.* Hyatt closed his eyes and squeezed his temple with his thumb and forefinger as he focused his entire mind on rejecting the correlation of events, and by extension, the image of a faceless and primal power smirking at him played through his mind. *I'm not one of your Irons. I don't want to do this.*

"Why can't you do it?" he asked, a spark of hope lighting in the wet despair of his mind. "You could explain where it came from, and help them see –"

Doveen had begun shaking his head as soon as Hyatt started speaking, and raised his hand to cut off the remainder of his thought. "No one born here can enter the Lowlands. You and your Claimed are the only ones who can do what must be done."

Hyatt wanted to argue with the Keeper, but nothing in his face gave the impression that anything Hyatt said would sway him from anything he believed. As soon as he realized it, the absurdity of convincing a fanatical order of Keepers who isolated themselves from the world of anything hit him like someone had dropped a cord of wood on his head. It almost made him laugh, but his body seemed too consumed with alarm and disbelief to remember which reflexes released laughter.

He reached for the book without realizing he had done so, his fingertips finding every texture in the sheer fabric that stood between his fingers and the cover of the text. The Keeper let more and more of the book's weight transfer from his hand to Hyatt's until Doveen could lower his hand from beneath it and leave it in Hyatt's possession. It was denser than he expected.

The light of the chamber seemed to cling to the fibers in the silk as Hyatt wrapped it around the book, smoothing the cloth with his palm and tucking the free ends until it was enclosed like a present in need of a string.  Hyatt tucked it under his arm and looked across the rows of shelves that represented hundreds of thousands of hours of work that led to the book he held and tried to imagine the conversation in store for him when he reconnected with his pack.

As those two thoughts collided, they created an unexpected spark. "This is the largest collection of books I've ever seen or even heard of."

He expected Doveen to acknowledge his statement or to protest it, but instead the Keeper met his statement with silence. The man's robes swirled around his boots as he turned and walked to the lectern and when he reached it, he placed his hands flat on the slanted surface. He looked out over the chamber as if seeing it as Hyatt did for the first time, his gaze drifting along the rows of bound books and stacks of papers. Something in the creases of his eyes spoke of admiration or understanding, but it faded as he looked down to stare at the blank, polished surface of the lectern.

"Your friend has Blood Ruin." Doveen looked over the edge of the stand at Hyatt, and his words found their mark in Hyatt's chest like one of Rellah's arrows. "You want to know if something in all of these books can save her life."

Even muted by the surreal and anxiety-inducing moment Hyatt found himself in, questions burst into existence like popping bubbles in his head. He wanted to know why and how Doveen knew about Rellah's state, and how he knew it was what Hyatt wanted to know. As quickly as his thoughts formed, they melted away as he realized none of them mattered as much as the answer to the question the Keeper had guessed.

"Is there?" With all his consciousness, Hyatt willed the Keeper to tell him there was.

"There was." The Keeper traced his finger along the narrow lip at the bottom of the lectern's surface as if he was checking for dust, then slipped both of his hands into the sleeves of his robes as he stepped from behind it. "It was called Hars Filgrastea, but it has been eradicated. There is nothing that can be done. I'm sorry."

His spark of hope flickered out as quickly as it had formed, and inevitability began to creep into the places in his mind that the flash of possibility had driven it from. "Eradicated?"

"Histories ago." Doveen paused to let his confirmation sink, and when he spoke again, his tone had shifted. "She may still have time left to help you complete your task. This great accomplishment could be how she, and you, are remembered."

A single, dry chuckle found its way through his disappointment, even as he felt a tear leave a wet trail down his cheek and wiped it away with the back of his hand. "I doubt she would agree with your priorities."

The Keeper hung his head in silent acknowledgment, then walked past Hyatt toward the entrance to the chamber. Hyatt turned around slowly, his eyes drawn again to the rows of shelves and the large metal wheels that guided them along the tracks inlaid in the floor, then followed Doveen to the doorway.

"Come with me." The Keeper gestured for him to follow, then turned down the long hallway and looked back to make sure Hyatt was close behind before he continued to speak. "Safe passage from this place requires your agreement to deliver the Warning to the High Rangers of the lowlands."

"I understand." Hyatt looked over his shoulder at the two Keepers who had fallen into step behind them, their strange batons in hand.

"It may occur to you, once you return to the lowlands, to abandon your promise to us, here in the temple, because you know we cannot come after you." Doveen's voice had adopted a professorial tone again and his stride evened out, as if his pace was keeping the cadence of a rehearsed speech.

Hyatt chose not to answer him and followed the Keeper's swaying robes along the hallway in silence. On either side, paintings depicted scenes of conflict and prosperity that he had no frame of reference for, and portraits of people he didn't know. The polished tiles seemed to absorb half the light, reflecting just enough to cause a muted gleam that diffused the edges of their shadows as they walked.

Doveen turned a corner and led Hyatt through a small room to another hallway on the far side that immediately became a downward staircase. The steps turned at right angles down a cubical stairwell, and by the fourth full turn, Hyatt had lost track of how far beneath the temple floor they had gone.

His curiosity finally overcame his silence. "Where are we going?"

"It is important for you to understand what is at stake before you leave this Garden." Doveen reached the bottom of a flight of stairs and instead of a turn to another descending set of steps, only an exit to a hallway remained. "This way."

Hyatt felt his spine tighten and resisted his urge to close his hands into fists. As he followed Doveen through the long hallway without exits or decorations on either side, he tried to picture the two Keepers behind him and whether he could take the baton from one of them without the other striking him with theirs. At the end of the hall, a single metal door blocked their way forward. Above it, a metal sign embossed with the world-killer emblem was riveted into the wall. The sight of it felt like cold water in Hyatt's lungs and he stopped short of it.

"Is that..." He stared at the plain, unassuming door with no markings except the placard above it, and his ability to make words failed him.

Doveen's fingers closed around the door's handle and he turned it downward. "Come."

The door opened to a metal catwalk with a railing and metal stairs that descended to the floor below. At the center, a large metal device unlike anything Hyatt had ever seen took up almost all the room's space. On one side, four Keepers worked on the side of the device from a boatswain's chair suspended from rails that ran the length of the room's ceiling.

"The ones before us called this machine Harmony." Doveen spoke with an almost reverent voice, his eyes fixed on the ancient artifact. "It brought about the end of the Seventh History and killed all but half of a percent of mankind."

Hyatt had no words for the dread and terror that the Keeper's words instilled in him. He stared at the machine without blinking for so long that his eyes began to burn as his gaze traced the curved metal and elongated pipes that made up the machine's exterior. Against the backdrop of the death of Kenna, the impossible Garden, and the new Warning, he felt as though his body should have been wrung dry of emotion with nothing left to give, but the man-made horror before him released fresh waves of fear into his body at a startling rate and volume.

"Why do you have this?" he whispered.

"Harmony is breaking down," Doveen replied. "Nine Keepers have lost their lives this year, trying to repair it, to contain it... horrifying deaths you cannot imagine, memories that no human should be burdened with. The alternative is to let it fail, and erase humanity from the Reclaimed."

Hyatt tried to picture the machine before him, releasing something that would kill every person alive. The image of an explosion that began in the Garden and spread to the furthest reaches of the Reclaimed came to him first but gave way to a flash of the machine opening like a flower and allowing a monster to escape that was more horrific than any Heir. In place of the monster he envisioned a cloud of violet and blood-red smoke billowing from the construct's pipes, cascading down from the mesa and starving everything beneath the canopy of the wilderness from light or air.

Doveen turned his back to Harmony and leaned against the railing, his hands once more vanished into his sleeves where they joined into a single column of fabric in front of him. "Since we cannot come to the Lowlands, we will have to trust that you have honored the generations of lives that have led to your fulfillment of your destiny. Since you will never return to this Garden, you will have to trust that we will be grateful enough for your efforts to continue to our sacrifice in this place to keep your Lowlands safe from Harmony. Do you understand?"

# TWENTY-THREE

When Hyatt stepped into the large arboretum, Bex flung themself at him with an urgency that Hyatt didn't expect and crushed him in a hug that threatened to squeeze the air out of him. The embrace caught him by surprise and he was hugging them back before he realized he'd reacted.

"Are you okay?" Bex stepped back and held Hyatt's shoulders at arm's length, examining him like a concerned parent as the door behind him closed and the sound of the revolving lock clunking into place filled the room.

"Yeah… yeah, I'm okay." He tried to pack as much reassurance as he could into his reply. "The Keeper says we can leave the Garden tonight."

Bex smiled with relief as Rellah and Jenna started toward him from across the room. "Good job."

As his pack-mates joined him, Hyatt looked around in confusion. "Where's Rayce?"

"Rayce is debating Cern lore with one of our guards, behind the flowering birch bushes,' Jenna replied with a bemused roll of her eyes. "They have some strange ideas about our history up here. He can't help himself. What's that, a going-away present?"

He looked down at the book, still wrapped in fabric under his arm. "Something like that."

As they talked, Hyatt tried to discern the meaning of the look Rellah gave him in his periphery. Something in her eyes looked clouded as if she was trying to remember where she knew him from. The way she studied his features, her eyes moving from his forehead to his nose and down to his jaw, unsettled him. He wiped his face with his free hand as if he could wipe away the tangible presence of her attention, but when he stole a glance at her, she was still regarding him with a silent expression somewhere between confusion and curiosity.

From the back of the room, Rayce appeared at a light jog and joined the rest of them. "It's a shame we're captives... these Keepers are... fascinating. Hey, Hyatt."

Jenna rolled her eyes at his wonder and punched Hyatt in the shoulder. "Hyatt has upgraded us to unwelcome guests."

"Oh?" Rayce's surprise was impossible to mistake, but he recovered quickly. "Jenna owes me half her rations. She bet you came back ready for the ancestor-bag."

Hyatt looked at her with sharp alarm, but Jenna laughed at him. "I did not!"

Amidst his pack, for the space of a breath, Hyatt washed in the tide of relief from their warm welcome and pointed jokes. For a moment he wasn't standing directly above a world-destroying weapon, and he wasn't carrying a new Warning under his arm, and Rellah wasn't dying. He just belonged. The feeling filled all the space inside his skin, soaking his bones and saturating his muscles in a restorative flood. It only lasted a moment and Hyatt closed his eyes, trying to hang on to the experience and then the memory of it as it receded.

"Are you okay?" Bex asked, touching his arm again.

He nodded and opened his eyes, as fatigue replaced the floating sensation and weighed his body down like bags of sand. "Just exhausted."

His pack-mate's gesture of concern turned into a pat on the back, while on the far side of the arboretum, Hyatt caught sight through the bushes of one of the guards walking the perimeter of the room. "Come on – your pack's over here."

Hyatt followed them along the tessellated path to a space between two narrow garden beds filled with tall stalks that bore dark honey-gold blossoms. He saw his pack at the end of the row of bags and crouched down beside it, set down the book he carried, and began working the closures of the pack's top flap.

Rellah appeared beside him and crouched down so only they could hear each other. "What did our freedom cost us?"

He wedged the cloth-wrapped text into his pack, rocking it back and forth to work it down into the main compartment. "A lot."

Hyatt closed his pack and adjusted it so that it sat aligned with everyone else's gear, and Rellah waited without another word as he finished fidgeting with his straps and the placement of his pack. He glanced over at her and she was still looking at him, so he shifted to sit with his back against the wall of the garden bed beside his gear which left him looking up at her where she was crouched.

Looking into her eyes, he didn't know how to explain everything that had happened since he had left the arboretum, so he tried to say it all at once. "The Keepers have discovered a new Warning, and I need to deliver it to all of the Gardens and packs. The world-killer is real, and if we refuse, they are going to let it destroy... everything."

Rellah lingered just long enough for him to see the thoughts begin to turn in her irises before her lips started moving to voice them. "You saw it?"

He nodded, trying to come up with a way to explain the machine Doveen had shown him. Every detail felt burned into his memory but defied description, and he wondered if he would ever be able to forget them.

"Can we take it from them?" Rellah asked with a furtive glance over his head to gauge the distance between the nearest Keeper, and lowered her voice into a whispered raider's cant.

"No." Hyatt shook his head, the very thought causing an aching tension in his shoulders and neck. "It's too big – the size of a room. And if we try to move it, it will go off."

Her raised eyebrow at his mention of the size of the weapon was the only indication that anything he had said was outside what she had expected, and she nodded to his pack beside him. "Is that the Warning?"

"Yeah," he replied with a non-committal shrug, "if it even is one."

She nodded and eased herself down onto the ground to sit beside him. Across the tiled path and on the far side of the opposite garden bed, Jenna listened with an unimpressed expression while Rayce relayed a story. Beyond them, the flicker of Keeper's robes between tall, slender trees Hyatt didn't recognize marked the passage of one of their guards.

"They will want to know where it came from." She picked up an errant clod of dark earth from the tile beside her and lobbed it overhand into the flowers in front of them.

He turned to look at her, surprised. "Aren't you going to try to talk me out of it? Are we really just jumping into how?"

It was Rellah's turn to chuckle with a small shrug, a gesture that felt more authentically her than anything Hyatt had seen from her in a long time. "Cern are good at no-win situations. When we can't do what we want, we do what we have to."

Her rationale made sense to Hyatt, and it made him realize how much he had hoped she would have an alternative to provide. The fact that she didn't registered deep within Hyatt, but instead of adding to his dread, it seemed to lessen it by confirming there were no alternatives.

"Okay. We can't tell them about this place – not with the world-killer here. We can bring it to a Keeper... maybe they can confirm it, or something." He tilted his head from side to side, working through the unspoken, component parts of his plan. "That should give it the credibility it needs... maybe. I don't know."

"It's a good idea." Rellah looked over at Bex who was pacing just out of earshot, their hands in their pockets and their gaze shifting around the unfamiliar flora and ornate walls of the room.

Her minimal acknowledgment poured momentum into Hyatt's thinking. "Okay – we get down out of this desolate, rotted garden, find a Keeper to validate the Warning, and head for the Gardens. Can you do something for me, though?"

His question drew her attention, and she squinted at him as turning to look at him exposed her eyes to direct light from the glass ceiling. "What?"

Hyatt worked hard to keep a straight face. "Can you make the travel plan? That job is compost."

Her faint smirk turned into a full smile, and she redirected her attention across the arboretum until she could control it. "I will do that part."

Hyatt smiled too. As it faded, he felt the tide of their reality rise in him. His gaze lingered on Rellah's profile and the knowledge that any given day might be the last time he ever saw her roared in his head like he was standing under a waterfall. The urge came to him to reach out and touch her arm, to feel that she was still real and still with him. As if she could feel it radiating off him, she looked over at him and held his gaze without a word. He stared and didn't look away, trying to commit to memory every fleck in her irises and the width of the ring of hazel that banded the green of her eyes from the whites beyond.

Instead of everything he wanted to express, he said, "Let's get off this mesa."

Rellah nodded, rose to her feet, and offered him her arm. His grip closed around her forearm and he pulled when she did, and in an instant, he was upright and standing in front of her. She stepped forward and wrapped an arm around him, tilted her head forward, and connected her forehead with his in a single thump.

"I'm glad you didn't die."

"Thanks," he replied, trying to keep the choke out of his voice by saying as little as possible. "Me too."

They grabbed their packs, and Rellah led the way back to the central square of the arboretum where she pulled her hands to her lips to emit a quick burst of chirping sounds. Even watching her motion and expecting it, the way her notes sliced through the air grabbed a string between Hyatt's head and his chest and plucked it, and he took a step closer to her before he realized what he was doing. Rayce and Jenna abandoned their conversation and walked over, and from their other side, Bex broke into a jog to close the space between them. The Keepers guarding them abandoned their listless patrols and found places between the raised beds and stands of trees to observe the Hollow Bone assembly.

"We're leaving, but we're not done." Rellah nodded toward the place where they had left their packs. "Nothing from here goes with us – no rocks, no strange plants, nothing. Leave it all behind – we tell no one about this place, ever."

At the last part of her instruction, Rayce and Bex exchanged glances, but everyone acknowledged with nods and grunts of assent.

"These Keepers gave Hyatt a new Warning, and he needs to get it to a Keeper on the ground." She paused there to let her words register with her pack, and Hyatt found himself on the receiving end of their shocked expressions like multiple magnifying glasses pointed between his eyes.

"Can there be new Warnings?" Rayce asked as Jenna lifted her fingers to her temple and rubbed like a headache had just formed behind her left eye.

"Apparently." Rellah shrugged. "Now, get your gear. Time to go."

The six Keepers that had lingered in the distance since their arrival started moving toward the arched doorway of the arboretum by the time Hollow Bone had collected their things and pointed in that direction. The first three stepped into the hallway without a word. One by one, Hyatt's pack-mates made their way into the hall, until it was only Bex and him remaining.

"After you." Bex gestured through the doorway.

He shrugged and stepped into the hall, and heard Bex fall into step behind him. A moment later, the door to the arboretum closed with a solid, mechanical thunk. The scent of the strange flowers and plants in the room lingered in the hallway but faded as Hyatt followed the Keepers ahead of them.

As they turned corners, ascended steps, crossed long hallways, and descended to lower levels, Hyatt became more and more certain that the Keepers who led them were using a different route than any he and his companions had discovered themselves. He tried to imagine finding his way back to either the arboretum or the chamber of the world-killer and realized there was no way he could.

The steps of the Temple of Sklodowska were the same as they had been when Hyatt had climbed them, but the courtyard was devoid of any sign of the fight between the Iron of the Broken Mountain and the Ram. No blood stained the marble, and every bit of debris had been swept from their surface as if it never happened. The Keepers at the front of the procession moved down the steps with their robes trailing over each one like the train of a dress, and when the Keeper at the center reached the courtyard, his companions to his left and right stopped on the last stair.

The Keeper in the courtyard turned around and lowered the mask over his nose and mouth. "I have been given the honor of seeing you to the Lowlands. Please, follow me."

Without another word, he turned around again and started across the courtyard. Hyatt watched him lead the way as his pack-mates continued down the stairs, and he glanced around at the other Keepers who stood with their hands tucked within the sleeves of their robes. Under their hoods and over their masks, he couldn't make out their expressions, but the stillness with which they watched their colleague walk away from the temple felt somehow ominous. As he stepped into the courtyard himself, he looked back to see if any of them had begun their climb back to the doors of the temple, but they continued to stand in silence and watch.

His attention to them slowed his stride enough for Bex to catch up with him, and they followed Hyatt's gaze back to the Keepers on the steps before putting their arm around Hyatt as they walked. "They'll be fine."

He didn't know how to say that his concern wasn't for their safety, so he shrugged an acknowledgment of Bex's reassurance. They crossed the muted gleam of the hexagonal tiles and caught up with Jenna, and by the time they reached the buildings on the far side, they were all together.

Unlike their path through the temple, the Keeper took the shortest and most direct route to the platform that had brought Hyatt and his companions to the Garden. The clouds that had probed the horizon when they had entered the temple had made their way halfway across the sky, filtering subdued afternoon light across the rooftops and through the lattices over the path. They walked in silence, but Hyatt felt like even if he had anything to say, the air would have swallowed the sound and kept the quiet anyway.

The Keeper led the way up the stone steps to the rim of the Garden and didn't move quickly, but his consistent stride spoke to a core strength hidden beneath his flowing robes. By the time they reached the top, Hyatt felt the burn of exertion in his thighs and calves, and his lungs lingered in the space between casual breathing and gasps to provide the air his body demanded.

"This way." The Keeper pointed across the open grass toward the sole structure between them and the outer ring of trees and foliage that shielded the hidden Garden from outside eyes.

"Yeah, we know where it is," Bex muttered beside Hyatt, their words clipped on both ends by their need for air.

Hyatt's chuckled response was more an exhale than a sound. "Give him a break – we're the only people who ever found it without their help."

At the open doors, the Keeper led them over the threshold and onto the metal platform. Once everyone was within the square chamber, he pulled a piece of paper from inside his sleeve and unfolded it. They waited as he turned to let the light from outside the space hit the drawing on the paper, then turned it in his hands to examine it from a different angle.

"Have you..." Jenna paused, then continued. "Have you never done this before?"

The Keeper didn't answer her, his eyes moving in short and rapid patterns over the paper.

"Can I help somehow?" Rayce asked, leaning against the wall behind the Keeper.

The man in the robes folded the paper and returned it to the interior of his sleeve, then moved to the space beside the opening where the two buttons stood out from the otherwise flat wall. From somewhere within the folds of his heavy fabric, he produced a key and slid it into a slot beneath the buttons. Hyatt held his breath as the Keeper held the key in place, pressed the button with his other hand, and turned the key half of a revolution.

The platform underneath them began to rumble, and the floor dropped from beneath their feet. When they caught up with the descending floor, the impact took their feet out from under them and they collapsed against it. The plummet downward felt unrestrained and seemed to gain momentum as it went on, making it harder to struggle to his knees and keep his balance than Hyatt expected it to be. Their stop was just as sudden, and it knocked down Hyatt as well as Rellah and Rayce who had tried to find their footing during their near-freefall.

Hyatt half-stumbled, half-crawled from the open doors onto the ledge beyond. As he staggered to his feet, his companions were getting their bearings and collecting their packs from where the plunge had scattered them.

"Did you know it would do that?" Jenna glared at the Keeper as she rubbed her neck and shoulder.

The Keeper looked at her when she spoke to him, but when she stopped, his attention moved to each face of Hollow Bone pack before focusing on Hyatt. He lowered his mask again and crossed the short distance between them, and touched Hyatt's arm.

"We are counting on you." The man's sincerity radiated from his core.

"Wait –" To Hyatt, the Keeper seemed to move both too fast for him to act, and in slow motion as he let go of Hyatt's sleeve, took two steps, and threw himself off the ledge. "No!"

He lunged and closed his hand in the space where the man's robe had been, but he grabbed only air. Rayce and Jenna were closest and made it to the edge of the ledge before Hyatt did, and they looked down together at the mangled form of the Keeper with his robe crumbled around his body and blood splattered across the rocks below. Rayce shook his head and stepped away first, while Rellah stepped to the edge beside Jenna and glanced over with an unimpressed expression before heading over to examine the rope still anchored to the ledge from their original ascent.

Bex stood behind Hyatt and put their hand on his shoulder as he knelt to stare over the edge at the Keeper's broken and still body. Hyatt didn't know if they were offering support or holding on to ensure he didn't slip over the edge himself, and he was too transfixed by the corpse dashed on the rocks below to dwell on the alternatives.

"Why did he do that?" he muttered, more to himself than anyone else. "Why... why did he..."

"It doesn't matter." Bex patted his shoulder. "Come on. We should go."

# TWENTY-FOUR

"The base of the Bloodstained Mesa felt too exposed to make camp, and Hyatt was grateful when Rellah led them beyond the crater that surrounded the pillar of stone to the welcoming and familiar trees of the Reclaimed. He was grateful to leave the pile of ash that had been the Keeper and the Skarren's hunting grounds behind him, and the hours that Hollow Bone put between the Desolate Garden and themselves felt better and better with every landmark and stop to rest. The sun had long since abandoned the sky and the bitter chill of night had set in before Rellah called for them to halt for the evening.

Even making a fire felt like a familiar pleasure to Hyatt as he piled tinder together in a small pyramid. The darkness that closed around him felt comfortable, and he knew the glow of the campfire would find a balance with the encroaching night that felt right. Against the memory of the silent Garden, a night in a temporary camp in the Reclaimed felt like home. As the shavings and twigs flickered into a blaze, he let himself enjoy the moment for a breath or two.

Bex dropped a pile of branches beside the ring of rocks that enclosed Hyatt's fire. He grabbed the closest one and broke it into three pieces, then stacked them around his growing flame like a fence. While he picked up another stick to continue building a tower around the burning tinder, he glanced over at his pack-mates who were laying out their bedding and positioning their packs. Rellah was the first to finish and she came to join him by the fire. She took a seat beside him with her bow in her lap as Bex wandered off in search of sturdier firewood.

Hyatt expected Rellah to say something, but she seemed content to sit near him and examine the limbs of her bow for marks or scratches. He backed away from the fire and pulled the silk-wrapped tome into his lap, staring down through the fabric as if he could see the words inside through the cloth and the book's hard cover.

"This is all business for Keepers and Irons," Hyatt said at last. "We could turn the book over to them and go home."

Rellah frowned at the mention of Irons, but she nodded as if she agreed. "The Keepers will ask where we found it."

Hyatt knew she was right, and he didn't have a good answer for the same problem that stopped him from bringing it to the Haleu settlements himself. Without the Desolate Garden to attribute the book to, explaining the origins of the Warning seemed impossible, and adding Keepers to the rotation only delayed the inevitable question.

"We could say you wrote it," he replied.

Rellah laughed her single-exhale response, but the joke didn't make her smile and she seemed more exhausted than amused. "Right."

"It doesn't matter. We find a Cloi, give it to the Keepers, and we're done. They can argue about whether or not it's real, and what to do with it if it is – and we can get back to the safe, easy work of killing Heirs."

That time, his remark brought a full smirk to Rellah's face, and she shook her head. Even as he made the joke, it turned to ash in his mouth as Kenna slipped through the shadows of his memory and to the forefront of his mind. Rellah's smile faltered at the corners of her mouth and he wasn't sure if the same thought took hold in her head or if she had caught the shift in his expression, but she said nothing.

Jenna emerged from the dark on his other side and stood with her arms crossed, firelight playing across her features. He nodded a greeting to her and turned to set the book on top of his pack between him and Rellah, but even as his body shifted to square with the fire, his attention lingered on the cloth wrapping around the tome.

"Is it?" Jenna asked.

Hyatt frowned. "Is it what?"

"Do you believe that book is another Warning?"

Hyatt glanced down at the wrapped tome, the firelight deepening the folds in the fabric to pools of impenetrable darkness, before returning his attention to the shifting amber and violet tones of the campfire's coals. "I don't know. I can't even read the thing."

Jenna's jaw worked as if she were physically chewing on his response, then nodded toward the flames with an upward tilt of her chin. "Toss it in."

Her suggestion drew a sharp look from him. "What? No!"

"If it's not real, then—" she reached across him for the book.

Hyatt intercepted her wrist and when she persisted, he lunged to the side to push the wrapped tome off his pack and out of her reach. Jenna gave up on reaching for the book and elbowed him instead, nearly knocking him off his log. By the time he stabilized himself and tucked his arms in to deflect any follow-on blows, she'd settled her elbows on her thighs and leaned forward to study the fire again.

"I don't know that it's not real, Jay-nah." Hyatt imitated Rellah's name-break.

She sniffed and a single tremor of amusement through her. The fire crackled and popped as one of the logs broke apart, settling into the coals and changing the way the light caught against the trees around them.

"You're about to try to convince the Gardens and the Packs that it is," she said, amusement fading from her tone. "You'd better decide."

He nodded, staring into the fire. "This is such compost."

Rayce and Bex found space on the far side of the fire, and for a while, Hyatt was left with his thoughts as his pack-mates talked. Their voices blended and seemed to rise and fall together, making them easy to soak in without focusing on single words or complex thoughts. The voices that didn't join them, Kenna's golden honey notes and Veck's grumble, came to him and once they did it was hard for him to hear anything but their absence. He watched the coals in the fire crackle and flare as Rayce fed another branch to them, and saw the fire turn hot enough to send its smoke straight up to the sky instead of shifting around the edges.

"Tonight Jenna, Rayce, and I will take the guard shifts. Hyatt, sleep for an hour, then head south toward the Cloi before daybreak. Bex, go with him." There was no preamble to Rellah's instructions and instead, she gave them with the assumption everyone would hear her and understand.

Bex rolled to their feet and headed toward their bedding, but Hyatt wasn't ready to walk away from the fire's warmth. Instead he lingered, watching the flame consume the branches and logs they fed to it, and trying to pull as much of its heat into himself as he could as if he could store it for the cold night's walk ahead.

Despite his efforts, the heat fled his body as soon as he stepped outside the glow of the firelight. He carried his pack by hand instead of shouldering it, deposited it beside his bedding, and rolled it around himself to trap in as much of his body heat as he could. He didn't remember falling asleep but knew he must have, because his next memory was Rayce shaking him awake.

"Time to go," his pack-mate whispered, before moving into the darkness to resume his position on the perimeter.

By the time Hyatt prepared his pack and moved to the edge of their camp, Bex was waiting with a half-eaten herb-twist in their hand. They left without a word, moving side by side into the wilderness beyond the edge of the pack's temporary space, and only moonlight filtering through the canopy above them lit their way.

Moving through the dark was slow and Hyatt focused on the scents of the wet, cold ground and the clear air that burned as it filled his nostrils. Without wind to shift the branches over them or the benefit of sights to distract them, even their quiet steps sounded loud. They traded off between paralleling one another and bounding ahead of one another as the Reclaimed became denser in some places and less dense in others.

Two hours into their silent trek, Hyatt spotted a flickering firelight through the foliage, bright enough to stand out against the pre-dawn horizon. "There."

Bex looked where he pointed, and patted him on the shoulder as they moved past him in the direction of the red-orange glow. "Good eyes."

He fell in behind them and they made their way toward the light, and after another thirty paces, Hyatt could make out the grilles over the window that separated the flame from the cold and wet air that surrounded them. He didn't notice until then that he had been unable to smell the smoke or taste it on the air. As he trailed Bex toward the light source, he wondered if his companion would have caught it first with those other senses in play.

They paused together behind a fallen tree whose branches had refused to break when its roots had given up their grip on the ground, concealing Hyatt and Bex from the closest wall of the Cloi.

"I see only one light burning. Do you think they're asleep?" Bex asked.

Hyatt shook his head as he adjusted the strap of his pack on his shoulder, tightening the padded surface against his jacket. "There's always one light and always one Keeper awake at a Cloi. Someone is up."

Bex dropped their pack and wedged it beneath the boughs of the fallen tree, then pulled a nearby branch closer to conceal the front of it. "Ready?"

As he studied the open space between them and the Cloi between the leafless limbs of their hiding place, the realization of how unprepared he was slammed into him like he was caught in an avalanche. Knowing he would have to say something that sounded insane to whoever was inside the structure before them made his throat close up like his body was trying to save him from the stress and anxiety by killing him, and he swallowed hard to clear the lump that threatened to steal his air.

"Yeah, of course," Hyatt lied. "That's why we're here, right? Let's go."

He ignored Bex's smirk and broke from cover, his blade in one hand and the other holding the strap of his pack in place so it wouldn't shift. He abandoned silence in favor of speed and his boots churned the frostbit leaves beneath him as he hurried across the open space to the ivy-covered wall of the Cloi. Bex caught up a moment later and they stood in the shadow of the structure's eves, listening to see if any shuffled steps or shouted alarms gave away their presence. When Hyatt heard none, he put his palm against the door and pushed.

The unlocked wooden door's iron hinges whined in protest of their lack of lubricant, and the friction only let it open two handspans. Beyond the threshold, a red-orange glow promised warmth and light, but it refused to cross the doorway onto the earth beyond.

"Hello?" The man's voice sounded taut and hurried. "Is someone there?"

Hyatt hesitated a moment, but Bex nudged him between his shoulders so he stepped into the doorway and pushed the door open wider. "Hello – I'm coming in."

On the far side of the anteroom of the Cloi, a tall and slender Keeper stood in his robes with a metal pipe in his hands. He visibly flinched as he made out Hyatt's silhouette and for a moment Hyatt saw himself the way the Keeper did, as the shape of a man in a Cern jacket and carrying a Cern blade, emerging from the darkness of the wilderness before sunrise.

"Easy now." Hyatt lowered his weapon and pinned it to his belt by his palm, and stepped away from the doorway into the room along the wall. "It's just me and my pack-mate."

At the sound of Hyatt's recognition, Bex moved over the threshold and waved with an open hand at the Keeper. The man's hood rotated back and forth as he took the measure of each of them. After a moment, he set his pipe down and leaned it in the corner beside him.

"What brings you here at this uncivilized hour?" His voice was still wary but his composure had begun to return, and with it came a hint of annoyance. "We have nothing of value."

"What?" Hyatt asked, confused, then rolled his eyes. "We're not here to steal from you, Keeper. We need your help."

The Keeper lowered his hood to reveal delicate, pointed features and an unkempt mop of brown hair, and to Hyatt, his demeanor seemed to continue collapsing as he felt more assured of his safety. "Asking for assistance is generally a daytime proposition."

Bex crossed their arms and leaned against the wall, and Hyatt could feel the balancing point between their patience with the Keeper and their desire to let Hyatt manage his own affairs become smaller and more precarious.

"This is going to sound..." Hyatt paused, hoping a simple and rational explanation would take the opportunity to appear in his mind, but nothing percolated to the surface. "We have a new Warning, and we need a Keeper to validate it."

He didn't know what reaction he expected, but the Keeper's amicable nod was not it. "Do you have it with you?"

"I, uh... yeah." Hyatt set his pack down and knelt beside it to work the straps open, and squinted up at the nonplussed Keeper as he did. "You don't seem – I mean... does this happen a lot?"

The Keeper smoothed a crease in his robe, his eyes following his fingers along the fabric until they reached their terminus. "Often? No, not often – but more frequently than you might expect."

A knot of consternation formed in Hyatt's sternum and he frowned as his fingers found the edge of the book in his pack. The Keeper's ambivalence made pushing the other contents aside feel less like unwrapping a treasure and more like digging through soiled laundry, and he couldn't fight the defensive bristle he felt as he stood and faced the man.

"This isn't a joke." He held the text out toward the Keeper at arm's length. "We've come a long way to bring this to you."

The man took the book and hefted it to check its weight, then turned it over in his hands like an unfamiliar container without an obvious opening. "I'm usually good with accents, but I'm not sure about yours – are you from Ceojic or Brathnee?"

The question hit Hyatt sharper than he expected it to, and he resisted the urge to snatch the book back from the Keeper's hands.

"Cern." He jammed as much texture and weight into the single word as he could.

The Keeper slid his thumb along the edge of the book's cover, the ridges of his fingerprints bumping over every whipping stitch from the top corner to the bottom. The pressure of his fingertip pulled at each stitch as he passed over it, half-rolling the thread before releasing it to return to its natural lay.

"Maybe, but not originally." He looked up through his eyelashes in unabashed skepticism as he turned the tome over in his hands again, then returned his attention to the book's cover. "Where did you get this?"

Hyatt could feel his frustration with the man's words begin to shift inside him, abandoning specific disliked traits in favor of an aversion to his entire being. The Keeper's question compounded it and he knew it wasn't the Keeper's fault but he began to divide his mental energy between the risks and rewards of punching the man in his face, trying to figure out how far away the next Cloi might be, and keeping his patience.

Bex took a decisive step forward as if they could feel the waves of frustration emanating from Hyatt. They closed the distance between the Keeper and themselves until there was too little for comfort by a half-step, and they rested their hand on their belt-knife.

"He's Cern – not that it matters. Where we got the book doesn't matter either – it's either real or it's not." They met the Keeper's eyes with a direct and unwavering gaze. "Right?"

The Keeper swallowed hard, the first crack in his disaffected and idle disposition that Hyatt could see. "Right."

Bex leaned closer and to the side, halving the distance between their faces so they could speak into the Keeper's ear, but didn't lower their voice to a whisper. "Right... because no Keeper would let a fallacy of logic, or their own ego, overshadow the chance that my friend has unearthed another Warning. That would be dangerous, right?"

The Keeper pulled the book to his chest as if protecting it, with the added benefit of retracting his hands from the space between Bex and himself, and nodded as he tipped his head away from them. "Right."

Bex straightened and shed their intimidating undertone, and smiled at the man as they straightened his robe at his shoulders and clapped him on the arm. "Good. We agree."

"How long will it take for you to review it?" Hyatt asked.

With his recovered space to move, the Keeper lowered the book away from his body and pulled the cover open with his thumb. Hyatt watched as the man's eyebrows registered recognition of some detail before him, but the expression was so fleeting that he couldn't guess what had triggered it. He tried to fortify his patience as the Keeper took his time turning the first four pages, his eyes tracing each edge and along the binding before tracking along the lines of text in a way that looked more like inspection than reading to Hyatt.

"This was written by Keepers." He glanced up at Bex and then Hyatt as he closed the book, before turning his attention to the cover and spine of the text. "Do you know why they rejected it?"

"They didn't –" Hyatt's response was instinctive and more defensive than he had expected, and he clipped the rest of his thought before it could travel to his lips.

The Keeper turned the book over and studied the back cover. "Then why do you need a second opinion? If they said it was a Warning, you wouldn't be here."

*Well you see, there is this secret Cloi inside a Temple to Sklodowska and they wanted me to bring this to a High Ranger that doesn't exist.* Hyatt smashed his thoughts down in his brain like he was trying to stuff a backpack full of too many clothes, and in the space he cleared in his mind, the void filled up with exasperation. Hyatt crossed his arms.

"Look, I don't have any answers for you – just this rotted book. We need to know if it's real. Can you do it, or not?" He tried to matte his words into raider's cant and stared at the Keeper with what he hoped was a defiant expression as if he was daring the man to protest further.

The Keeper balked as he turned the green book over again, opening it to a page near the center that was adorned with rows of text that framed a sketch near the binding. "I can, but –"

Bex cut him off. "No buts. Review the book and we'll be back for it tomorrow."

They turned and headed toward the arched entrance of the room without waiting for the Keeper's reply, and Hyatt fell into step beside them. The night beyond the limits of the Cloi was pitch black in contrast to the firelight of the Keeper's structure, but he was relieved to be leaving the Keeper to his work and returning to the Reclaimed for the night.

"That's not enough time!" The man called after them, a note of stress in his voice.

Bex paused in the doorway and looked back at him as Hyatt walked by. "We will be back with the rest of our pack, so you should have something of value to tell us."

He couldn't fight his smirk as they walked away, but waited until they were a dozen paces into the wilderness before he spoke. "I don't think I've ever seen that side of you."

"That's because it's not real," Bex replied, and Hyatt could almost see their matching grin in the dark. "It's my best Rellah impression."

He barely stifled his laugh. "It's a pretty good one."

They moved far enough to ensure their silhouettes were hidden from the lit structure behind them and then knelt together at the base of a large, vine-encased tree, letting their eyes adjust and listening to the sounds of the Reclaimed. When they could see the starlight filtering through the canopy and the rustles and shifts of the wild became a recognizable orchestra of the forest at night, Hyatt stood and began walking as Bex rose to their feet. With him looking ahead and left, and Bex looking right with glances behind them, they moved through the dark.

# TWENTY-FIVE

No light marked the clearing where Hollow Bone Pack had settled into the underbrush, and only the sound of Rayce's quiet warning call validated that they had traveled on the right azimuth from the Cloi. Bex cupped their hands and returned the call with one of their own, and their pack-mate's form melted into existence from the fork of a tall, slender tree.

"How did it go?" Rayce asked as they approached.

Bex nodded and Hyatt answered him in as quiet a tone as he could. "We'll go back tomorrow night for an answer."

Their companion didn't press for information and turned his attention back to the wilderness as they continued into the space within the stand of trees. Hyatt caught sight of two forms on his left, both cocooned in their blankets in lieu of proper shelters. He searched the gaps between the low brush and deadfall for his own patch of ground and as he eased himself to his knees to open his pack, the fatigue of the day washed through him like he was a campfire that someone had doused with a bucket of water. The straps of his pack seemed more complex than usual and he fumbled with them until they fell open. By the time he pulled his blanket around his shoulders and collapsed onto his side, he was certain he wouldn't remember the cool earth or the chill in his fingertips come daybreak.

When Hyatt opened his eyes, he was reclined on the steps of the Temple of Sklodowska with moonlight and a blanket of pinpoint stars stretching out across the cloudless night sky above with only the foreboding wall of the massive building to block a swath of starlight from his view. The sight of it clenched an iron clamp around his heart and filled his lungs with ice, and he sat up to find himself staring into Iron Tobin's vacant eyes.

"Fuck!' He crab-crawled two steps backward as his vision expanded from the dead boy, taking in the bodies scattered in the Iron's wake.

Lower on the broad, expansive steps, Shelara lay facedown and was struggling to rise to her knees. On the Iron's other flank, Kenna lay on her side with a hand pressed over the gaping hole in her midsection. Beyond them in the courtyard, dozens of men and women with mortal wounds lay on the interlocking cobblestones. Amidst them, Hyatt recognized Iron Sawmet and the Ram, but the remainder of the waking corpses were unfamiliar to him.

"You can't be asleep right now, Hyatt." Tobin patted his hand on his face along the gash torn from his chin to his eye socket, pushing the orb back into place as it started to slip down over his cheekbone.

Hyatt looked over the boy's head, trying to process the horror before him as snow began to fall from the clear sky above. "I... I didn't do that. I don't know them."

The Iron followed Hyatt's gaze to the courtyard. "No, most of them are mine."

"What..." He couldn't process what Tobin said while watching the mangled forms of so many bodies trying to get their bearings.

Tobin wrapped his little hand over his nose so he could hold his face together, and his words were muffled as he tried to speak through his palm. "You need to wake up, Hyatt."

Behind the Iron, Shelara began crawling up the stairs in his direction. Her movements were stilted and jagged but carried her in halting surges up the stone steps, even without her head. Kenna stood but faltered and collapsed, and began dragging herself up the stairs with one arm while she kept the other pressed against her stomach. Hyatt felt the tears tracing down his face as they moved toward him, shallow trails of saline that the chill threatened to freeze in place against his skin.

"I..." Hyatt's seven different thoughts oozed in different directions and left no words on his tongue to express the confusion and grief and stress that vied for control of his mind.

"Hyatt, listen!" Tobin let go of his face to grab him by his jacket and shake him, and Hyatt watched in horror as the two halves of the little Iron's face separated and began to hemorrhage blood and bone through his exposed jaw.

Shelara reached the step just below Hyatt's crawling around Tobin's legs as she reached for his boot. "Time to join us, Hyatt."

"Wake up!" Tobin shouted at him with a clarity that should have been impossible with his mangled mouth and skull.

Kenna ceased her climb and rested her head on the step, snuggling into the angular surfaces of the stairs like they were the most comfortable place she'd ever laid down. "I miss you, becquerel... please come here."

He tried to answer her, but a sob wracked his chest and closed his throat, leaving him only a vehement nod of acceptance to offer her. She looked like she smiled and she opened her eyes, but they were hollow and distant with none of the joy or light that he remembered.

"Hyatt, wake up!" Tobin shouted again as he pulled hard, throwing him down the stairs.

Hyatt spasmed as he woke, his body reacting to the impact of stairs that didn't exist. He was hyperventilating and he forced himself to take a deep breath to stabilize himself. As he exhaled, he saw the night above him shift and caught sight of a Skarren turning on a wing-point in a hunting arc.

His blood froze in his veins as the winged monstrosity devoured starlight and even the moon with its silhouette. The Heir's wingspan stretched so far that on either side, treetops intruded around its edges and Hyatt could only see its full size when it climbed higher and gave itself a wider view of the wilderness below. The silence that surrounded it made it all the more horrifying, as if all the creatures of the Reclaimed and even the wind itself had surrendered to an absolute stillness to avoid the Skarren's attention.

Hyatt blinked and regretted the movement, certain the colossal beast above him would see the flickering of his lashes and plunge into a dive with its talons extended and its jaws gnashing. Instead, it crossed the sky and almost vanished from view. He had just begun to breathe again when it reappeared, flying just above the treetops so that Hyatt saw the studded shell of its thorax and felt the sudden, frozen downdraft of its passage as it streaked by. The gust seemed to cut through bedding, clothes, and flesh to the core of his bones and he felt like he could feel the water in his eyes threatening to freeze.

Every second seemed to stretch on forever as he waited for the Heir to reappear. He lay so still he could feel his own heartbeat, too petrified to move and attract the attention of the beast. He had no idea how long he stared up at the night sky, expecting the stars to vanish behind the Heir's wingspan again, but as he blinked at last and let his fingertips move from their rigid positions where they pressed against the ground, a distant crash and the report of flechette carbines broke the silence.

Across the camp, Hyatt saw Rayce roll to his side and when he came to his feet, his weapon was in his hand. His pack-mate flinched as the staccato crack of three more carbines fired to the east, and the sound of the weapons disappeared behind the sound of ancient trees shattering into matchsticks.

Hyatt rose to his hands and knees and launched into a crouched dash, deflecting Rayce's weapon with a hand as he barreled into his pack-mate. They hit the ground together and tumbled until Hyatt trapped Rayce's blade-arm underneath him and clamped his other hand over Rayce's mouth. They made eye contact and Hyatt shook his head with all the vehemence he could manage, and he felt Rayce relax under him.

He looked over in time to watch Rellah roll toward her bow before Jenna sprawled over her back, her legs wide like a grappler and her arm snaked under Rellah's throat to cut off the air required to make a sound. Rellah spasmed underneath her in an effort to buck Jenna off, but the temporary restraint as Jenna pinned her flat was enough time for Rellah to hear whatever her pack-mate whispered into her ear.

Another shot of the carbine called out through the Reclaimed, and Hyatt gritted his teeth as he absorbed the grim realization that what had been several weapons had been reduced to one. The roar of decimated timbers answered the call of the carbine, and silence followed.

Hollow Bone pack lay still together, and Hyatt could almost feel their pulses and breathing sync as they listened to the intentional silence of everything that surrounded them. The cold crept up from the ground, and they stayed quiet and motionless until the first glow of daybreak began to soften the pitch-black of night into shades of navy and cream.

Rellah was the first to break the stillness and Jenna rolled away to let her up. She found her feet and brushed the earth from her trousers, then ran her fingers through her hair to remove the leaves that sleep had ground into her braids.

"We're not staying here. Break camp." She looked around to find the members of her pack and fixed her attention on Hyatt. "Take Bex and go get the Keeper's answers."

# TWENTY-SIX

"This might..." the Keeper's voice trailed off as he shook his head and ran his fingers through his hair, as if he couldn't believe the words he was about to say. "This might be real."

Bex crossed their arms. "What do you mean, might?"

He nodded as if he expected the question, and led them through an archway so low they needed to stoop to pass beneath it. On the far side they found a workspace with a desk, two tables, and bookshelves on every wall. Loose notes and open texts covered both tables, and the book Hyatt had given to the Keeper stood open on a rehal in the center of the desk. The Keeper pushed a chair aside so he could stand at the desk, and Hyatt and Bex crowded around him at the table's edge.

"This mark here," the Keeper pointed to the serif on the first letter of a sentence on the left page, "denotes an Uncovered Truth. What follows is a statement or function of logic from outside the universal canon that Keepers accept as absolute and do not require additional explanations or evidence."

Hyatt had no idea what the universal canon was and leaned closer to examine the mark, but it looked indistinguishable from the spiraling and jagged entries and exits of the author's calligraphy. The Keeper paused long enough for Hyatt to take a long look at the letter in question, but offered no elaboration and instead turned several pages to reveal a separate excerpt of the text.

"This is a Structured Word – see how the script changes? It mimics the writing style of another author and indicates citation of that author's work. For example, this Structured Word tells us the author is citing Freyal's Record of the Excavation of Joor Mecc." The Keeper let his fingertip linger under the word in the sentence that didn't match the rest, as if studying the font longer would lead Hyatt to a dawning realization about a separate book he'd never read or heard of.

"Ah," he replied.

The Keeper glanced up at him and over at Bex, and when he recognized the lost expression on their faces, he sighed. "Freyal was a Keeper early in our History – this being the Eighth History. Joor Mecc was a ruin from the Sixth History. It was important because... never mind. It just was."

Hyatt bit his tongue at the Keeper's condescension and he caught Bex rolling their eyes, but the Keeper had already turned his attention back to the book.

"Where this gets interesting, is that there are ninety-six Structured Words in the Keeper's Compendium." The Keeper began to flip pages again and then turned them in the opposite direction, his eyes skimming the book as if searching for something specific, then paused and pointed to a word at the bottom of the right page. "This is a Structured Word not included in the Keeper's Compendium. It is a citation to a text that doesn't exist."

He rose to his feet and Hyatt stepped back as the Keeper passed between him and Bex on the way to one of the tables covered in books. He followed the man's rustling robes and found space beside the table as the keeper shuffled the books, bringing a buried text to the surface of the pile. Before he spoke, he moved another pile and turned the pages on a narrower volume near the bottom of the pile.

"Here, and here," he pointed to a place on the open pages of both books, "the same Structured Words appear, but these books were written at the end of the Sixth History. Notice how there are no Uncovered Truth markers? It implies that the Keeper who wrote this text had access to writings that have not existed in two-dozen generations... but your version was bound in this History. As if that wasn't confusing enough, the hot-pressed paper, the lighter weight of the pages, and rubrication patterns used in your book were all abandoned by Keepers in the Seventh History."

Hyatt's mind drifted to the rows of books that lined the shelves of the massive libraries in the Temple of Sklodowska and wondered how many of the texts in that forgotten garden were the only copies in existence. He nodded along as the Keeper explained the contradictions that the new text presented, following the concepts in the abstract even though the details were lost on him.

"You can save the Keeper Trivia," Bex interjected. "What does any of that have to do with the new Warning being maybe real?"

The Keeper had opened his mouth to remark on another facet of the text, but cut off his explanation with pursed lips and narrowed eyes before speaking again. "The author of your text used a framework from the universal canon and supplemented it with Uncovered Truths, which is good. The third kind of information comes from sources that we know to be real, but have not seen – so we have to take the author's word that the material they present is from those sources. That's bad. What works in their favor is that none of those points contradict Uncovered Truths, or the universal canon."

Hyatt frowned. "Is that a long way of saying, it's plausible?"

"I'm saying..." the Keeper paused, looked across the room at the book open on the desk, and shrugged, "I can't prove it's not real."

Inside his head, Hyatt screamed. He hadn't realized until that moment, how much weight he had placed on the Keeper's determination and how much his future hinged on the answer, and hearing nothing definitive made him feel like he was falling from a ledge he hadn't realized he was on.

He didn't know if Bex felt his tension and internalized it, or if it filled them of their own accord, but their words were laced with intention as they put an arm around the Keeper's shoulders. "Knife to your throat, if your life depended on being right – is it a Warning, or isn't it?"

"If I had to—" his sentence broke into a gasp as Bex clenched their fingers into his shoulder, and the Keeper winced as his words ran twice as fast from his pale lips. "It's real enough to ask an Iron!"

Bex let go of his shoulder and the Keeper stepped away from them, rubbing his thumb against his clavicle to soothe the lingering indent of their grip. Hyatt looked back at the book and as he stared at the open pages on the rehal, he knew with a grim and absolute certainty that the Keeper was right. The truth of the man's words seeped into his pores and brought everything into sharper focus, and he hated him for it.

"I've met three Irons, and all three are dead." Hyatt rubbed his face to clear the rising tension in his body and push away the despair that had begun to pool in the cracks and crevices of his brain.

"Hyatt Ironbane," Bex muttered with a dry laugh.

His hands dropped to his sides and he walked back to the desk to stare down at the book, his eyes tracing the lines of text without reading them. "Where do I find one?"

"I don't know." The Keeper's answer drew both Hyatt's and Bex's attention like a magnet, and he put his hands up as he took another step backward. "I don't!"

"You've delayed us a day and been of no use to us, Keeper." Bex took a menacing step towards him. "You need to say something useful. Right. Now."

The Keeper's intimidated retreat bumped him into the edge of a desk and he staggered, catching himself against it. "You can't hurt me! Your pack-master gives us safe passage!"

Bex kicked the leg of the table with enough force to break it free from the bracket that mounted it to the table's surface, and it sent the Keeper's books cascading to the floor as they walked through the disaster they created. "I'm not Cern, and you're not much of a Keeper."

Hyatt couldn't tell if Bex was doing their Rellah impression again or if they planned to harm the Keeper. "Tell them something, Keeper. Anything that can help us."

"What? Wait!" The Keeper backed up and felt a bookshelf at his back, ending his ability to move backward. "I – wait, yes! There's a new Iron, called last season. His Hold is... south! South of here!"

Bex stopped in front of him, opened their hand, and patted him twice on the left side of his chest. "That's better."

Hyatt breathed a sigh of relief and turned his attention back to the open tome. He reached out to close it and just before his fingertips met the edge of the cover, the thought that he could leave it there ripped through his brain and body like lightning and made him pause. He stared at the book and felt like it was staring back at him, gaining more mass and meaning with every passing second. His hands dropped to his sides as the secrets of the book that the Keeper understood, and Hyatt couldn't see even when shown, tumbled in his head like rocks being polished.

Bex had abandoned their intimidation of the wiry Keeper and paused as they passed Hyatt on their way to the low, arched exit to the chamber. "You okay, becquerel?"

He shook his head as if the conflict inside his mind were cobwebs that could be torn apart with a sudden, subtle motion, and he closed the book before tucking it under his arm. "I'm good."

Bex nodded and ducked under the arch, and Hyatt followed them into the room beyond. As they made their way to the Cloi's entrance he glanced back, but the Keeper was no longer in sight. He hurried to catch up with his pack-mate, who was moving with a purpose toward the waiting daylight outside.

They didn't talk as they made their way back to their makeshift camp, and Hyatt didn't know if it was for his sake or theirs, but he found himself grateful for the space to think. He watched the ribbons of sunlight lace through the canopy to form pools on the frostbitten ground, and felt the pockets of warmth as he crossed through them. His arm kept the book close to his body and he found himself turning to prevent it from catching on branches or collecting the moisture of leaves, though he was certain the cover would protect the pages within.

"Tell us it's rot, so we can toss the book in the fire and go set a real camp," Rayce said as they crossed the perimeter into camp. "I would love to take my boots off for longer than four hours at a time."

He smiled at Rayce's request, and Bex broke off to join him. On his other side, Hyatt saw Jenna who looked up from where she sat with her back to a tree, sharpening her blade with a whetstone in her hand, but she returned her attention to her work as he spotted Rellah on the far side of their makeshift campsite. He unslung his pack and set it down in the center of their camp without lingering, and stopped beside Rellah where she stood staring into the wilderness.

"What did the Keeper say?" she asked without looking over at him.

It was impossible for Hyatt to not notice the strain across her cheekbones or the glassy cloud over her eyes, and he wanted to ask if she was okay, but he knew she wouldn't want him to. "I need to take it to an Iron. There's one somewhere south of here."

She swallowed hard, the tendons in her neck straining more than they should have needed to for such a routine act. "You don't need to."

"I do, if it's real," he replied quietly, staring off into the Reclaimed so he didn't have to meet her gaze. "If it could kill all of us…"

She didn't agree with him, but she didn't argue with him either. They stood together, watching the branches shift and sway as the sounds of the Reclaimed surrounded them, the unspoken ramifications of his statement lingering in the cold air around them like the mist of their breath.

"I won't ask Hollow Bone to travel to an Iron Hold. They can make camp somewhere between a Cern pack and Heir territory."

"Okay." Hyatt wished for words to express the black hole that her words opened within his chest, but they refused to form in his mind. "Tell me where, and I'll find you when I finish this."

Rellah cocked her head and squinted at him, then reached up and cuffed the back of his head with her open hand. "Them, you dumb weed. I'm going with you."

He winced and rubbed the back of his head. "What?"

'I'm growing your Cern seed, after all," she replied, the strain in her voice taking some of the humor out of her attempt at a joke. "Unless it's Jenna's?"

"Wouldn't… wouldn't you know?" he asked.

She smiled and her shoulders moved like she had laughed, but no sound accompanied it. "After this, until we die."

She turned her back to the wilds and walked toward the center of their camp. Hyatt watched her and saw the change in the way she moved that matched the tension in her voice and the sheen of sweat on her skin. Her footsteps were still quiet, but her stride seemed less fluid and her shoulders remained raised like she was trying to relieve pressure on her spine.

*An Iron saved her before. Maybe another one can do it again.* He followed her to the edge of the fire pit and stood beside her. *There has to be a way.*

"Gather around." Rellah waited as Rayce, Bex, and Jenna abandoned their seats and made their way to where she stood.

Bex shot a questioning look to Hyatt as he moved to Rellah's side, but he pretended not to notice. As the pack drew close enough to hear her and she had their undivided attention, he kept his case neutral.

"Hyatt and I need to go south to an Iron Hold. Bex will lead, while we are away. Bex, take Hollow Bone pack west. Find a place between Relcora and Cold Water Pack to make camp. Wait for us there, unless you can't."

Before she finished talking, Bex crossed their arms and began to shake their head. "We should all—"

"No." Rellah cut them off. "Rayce is right. It's time for Hollow Bone to mark and hold some space. We will need more Claimed to hunt Heirs, and they will need somewhere to find us."

Whatever Rayce thought of the idea, Rellah attributing it to him took the volume out of it. He nodded his agreement with a shrug and began checking his gear to ensure it was ready to move. Jenna's expression was pure protest, but she held her tongue and put her arm around Bex to lead her away from the campfire.

"Well... that went well," Hyatt muttered.

"They don't have to like it." She headed toward her own gear. "They have to trust me."

Hyatt collected his things and as he was cinching down the straps of his pack, Bex dropped to a crouch beside him. "You should talk her out of this."

He couldn't fight the dry chuckle that rose in his throat. "Do you know anyone who has a long history of talking Rellah out of things once her mind's made up?"

"Yeah. You." Bex stared at him and Hyatt could feel them willing him to look up and meet their gaze, but he refused.

"We'll probably catch up with you by the time you finish making camp." He stood and hefted his pack with a grunt, and it settled onto his shoulders with a familiar weight. "You'll see."

Bex nodded, then stepped forward and threw both of their arms around him in a brief but bone-crushing hug. "You're right. We'll see you soon. Bye, Hyatt."

# TWENTY-SEVEN

In the four days it took to move south and find the Iron's hold, Hyatt watched Rellah's condition improve. By the second day, her form blended with the Reclaimed in familiar ways, and by the third night there was no pallid tint to her features and no sweat matting stray tendrils along her hairline.

"I do not understand Iron territories," she muttered, and her raider's cant sounded cleaner and velvety.

Hyatt ducked under a bough to avoid the moss that clung to it and weighed it down. "No?"

Rellah shook her head.

"There is no sense to where their Holds are, and each one seems to roam the Reclaimed without boundaries." She altered her course to move around a pale green thicket with clusters of small, dark yellow berries, then rejoined him on the far side. "How do they decide where to go?"

*This is your idea of small talk? Okay. I'll play along.* Hyatt shrugged and adjusted the strap of his pack. "Sometimes High Rangers call for them, to settle disputes between Gardens or deal with scavengers and Warning violations. They would probably tell you the Butcher Queen leads them to be where they are needed."

They continued in silence, long enough for Hyatt to wonder if he had answered something wrong to kill their conversation. To their left in the distance, he began to make out the gurgle of a brook tumbling over rocks as it carved a path through the wilderness. He wondered how much longer the cold water could resist the urge to freeze.

The edge of the forest gave way gradually, with denser brush and stands of trees replaced by single ancient trunks and then smaller clusters of saplings. Ahead, the building that occupied the clearing ahead stood out against the intervening branches with its mass and linear angles, more geometric than any natural phenomena in the Reclaimed.

They stopped in the last band of vegetation that offered them any concealment. Twenty paces of grass, flat olive blades that rose higher than the tops of his boots, began beyond the last stand of trees. Stiff amber reeds and patches of rock broke up the field, lending to its natural and unintentional appearance. Beyond the grass, a field of untended Low Flowers blanketed the ground, disrupted by ragged bushes and clumps of weeds. The interlocking metal plates that formed a walkway through the Flowers toward the large stone structure beyond contrasted with the rest of the clearing as the only intentional and ordered part of the expanse.

"It looks... abandoned." Hyatt frowned.

Rellah shook her head. "No. The chimney is smoking."

He winced at missing something that Rellah had seen so quickly and tracked his attention along the top of the building. The wisp of smoke that curled skyward was translucent enough that missing it seemed understandable, but it didn't alleviate the needles that overlooking it drove into his ego.

"Okay, let's go." He started to move, but Rellah grabbed his arm.

"Both of us?" She frowned. "At once?"

Her tone told Hyatt he had made a bad decision, so he paused and tried to look like he was reconsidering the factors of a plan he hadn't constructed at all. "I can go first."

Her frown softened a bit, and she nodded. "I can cover you from here. Did you and Bex walk up to the Cloi together?"

"What? Of course not." Hyatt scoffed, then cupped his hands around his mouth to help his voice carry, and called out, "Hello?"

He saw nothing move in or around the building, and shrugged at Rellah. She frowned and pulled an arrow from her quiver, nocked it, and nodded for him to go forward. Hyatt started toward the edge of the clearing and heard the telltale creak of her drawing her bow. He could picture her at full extension, the muscles in her arm as taut as her bowstring and her eye sighting over the indigo-fletched arrow as she aimed it at the door or window of the Hold. The grass under his boots crunched as the stiffening frost lost the fight against the weight of his steps and he shifted his gaze left and right, half-expecting to hear the thwack of Rellah's arrow racing towards a threat he missed by looking in the wrong direction.

"I'm Looking for the Iron who lives here…?" he called out again, resisting the urge to curl his fingers around the handle of his weapon as the silence leaked into his nerves and played with their endings.

The handle of the door was cold and textured but refused to turn when he tried. He tugged at it and it held fast. He glanced back in search of Rellah, but even knowing where he'd left her didn't help him spot her amidst the trees, so he moved along the narrow band of gravel that covered the ground between the field of Low Flowers and the building's wall. He reached the corner and bent his knees so that when he peaked around the edge, his head wouldn't be at a person's normal height. When there was no enemy to surprise him with a savage attack, he rounded the corner and intentionally crunched the crushed rock as he walked towards the back of the structure and the fence that extended from the back wall, trying to give every indication he was there and avoid startling anyone into a confrontation.

"Iron?" He called out at the midpoint, slowing his approach as he drew closer to the chest-high fence.

Every time he spoke and received no answer, the anxiety in his body felt like it leaked deeper into his bones. Beyond the fence, several metal cylinders stood on end with sides rended open and dark earth spilling from their cores onto the ground. Near one, a man knelt beside the sloping pile of dirt and tilled through it with a tool, collecting something Hyatt couldn't see from within it.

"Hello?" Hyatt called, and raised his hand in greeting when the man looked up.

The stranger rose to his feet, and Hyatt spotted the Iron's bars hanging from his belt as the man dropped his forked tool. The implement landed in the dirt and sank to the handle, and the man wiped his gloved hands on his pants. He started toward Hyatt and gave a sideways glance skyward as he did, as if he was studying the position of the clouds, before returning his focus to him.

"Are you an Iron?" he asked, immediately regretting the question he already knew the answer to.

"I am Iron Mattow, the Iron of the Last Sky," the man replied. "What brings a Cern raider to my Hold?"

The Iron's characterization of him sent a crackle of validation through him, but he fought to keep it from reaching his expression. "I need to show you a book. It might be a new Warning."

The man's eyes narrowed as if he was trying to determine whether Hyatt was joking. He met the Iron's gaze and waited as he watched the man's features shifting from his eyes to his mouth and back to his eyes. Whatever he saw seemed to satisfy him, and he nodded.

"Let's go inside. You can call your friend in." He nodded toward the tree line as he walked along the fence to a gate on the side and manipulated the metal latch that held it closed.

Hyatt glanced in the direction the Iron had nodded but saw nothing in the trees that would have told the Iron where Rellah was hidden. *How did you know that?*

Too late, he realized that his shifting attention confirmed whatever suspicion the Iron had. He mentally kicked himself at falling for such a simple deception as Mattow rounded the end of the fence and strode toward him, the handle of a braided whip slapping against his thigh with the motion of waves lapping the shore as he walked.  The Iron passed him and led the way to the Hold's front door, where he pressed in on the handle before turning it, and it made an audible click as the door opened.

Hyatt paused outside the door and gestured with his whole arm for Rellah to join him, with no evidence that she saw him but no doubt that she did, then followed the Iron inside. The sudden warmth of a wood stove washed over him and twin lamps bathed the room in welcoming orange-yellow light. Mattow hung his short jacket on a peg near the stove at the back of the room and waited as Hyatt's eyes adjusted, then gestured to one of three high-backed chairs around a five-sided stone table.

Hyatt let his pack slip from his shoulder as he settled into the closest chair, and his body seemed to sigh in relief as the dark violet upholstery welcomed his weight. The Iron sat in the chair across from him and gave his attention to the doorway as Rellah appeared in it, her bow tucked under one arm with an arrow in the same fist that held the weapon's handle.

"This is Iron Mattow." Hyatt gestured to the man across the table.

"Rellah." She leaned against the wall beside the table and focused on returning her arrow to her quiver.

The Iron leaned forward to rest his forearm on the table but kept his back straight, and it reminded Hyatt of a man trying to keep his head above water. "Welcome to my Hold."

Hyatt glanced at Rellah in time to see the Iron's manners wash off her like a rainstorm and leave her entirely unaffected, then leaned down to open his pack. He pulled the book from the main compartment and unwrapped the silken material that surrounded it, then set it on the table and slid it across the polished surface toward Mattow.

"This is it." His fingers lingered on the cover for a moment before he withdrew them and looked up from the book to the Iron.

Mattow regarded the book for a long moment without moving or saying anything. When he reached for it, his motion was fluid and without fumble or hesitation, and he picked it up as if he had been able to slide his fingers under it without causing it to shift on the table at all. His hand curled around the binding and his fingers pressed into the cover with a firm grip as he held it less than a handspan above the table, and he closed his eyes. After the space of three breaths, he set it back down and returned his hand to rest near the table's edge.

"It's real." Everything in his tone spoke to certainty.

Hyatt blinked, confused. "What?"

The expression of the man across the table from him didn't change. "This is a new Warning."

"How do you know?" Hyatt hesitated, but he couldn't let the question die there. "Don't you have to do an Iron thing, or something? This is going to change the world – I mean, don't you want to think about it for a little bit? How can you just... know?"

Mattow brought his hands together on the table and laced his fingers. "If it took me longer to consider the consequences, would you believe me more, or less?"

Rellah pushed herself away from the wall and crossed her arms. "So it's real. Take it and do what you need to do with it. Let's go, Hyatt."

She started toward the door and Hyatt followed her with his gaze as far as he could, but kept his seat as his eyes traveled back to the book and then up to the Iron who was studying him from across the table. "What happens now?"

"Now," he replied, "we bring it to the High Rangers and pack-masters of the Reclaimed."

At the Iron's words, Rellah stopped in the doorway and turned to face them. "Not we. You. Warnings are the business of Irons and Keepers. We're done."

Mattow looked over Hyatt's shoulder at her as his hands slid from the table into his lap. "You will be done soon, Rellah - but not yet. You both have a role in this."

"Rot we do. There is nothing you need us to do that someone else can't do. Good luck with your book." The conviction in Rellah's voice was like steel bands that secured her words to one another and made them unbreakable.

Mattow stared at her for a long minute but when he spoke, it was to Hyatt. "I left my gardening tool in the yard, stuck in the dirt. Would you mind getting it for me?"

The Iron's question seemed abrupt to Hyatt and felt more like an instruction than a request, but he nodded and forced himself to his feet. He glanced down at his pack but decided to leave it, and headed for the door.

As he passed Rellah, he bumped his shoulder into hers and spoke with the best whispered raider's cant that he could manage. "I'll be right back."

The cold air outside felt like running into a wall and the sudden chill caused goosebumps to break out across his neck, and he shoved his hands deep into his pockets to shield them from the cold. Wet pinpoints broke across his nose and cheeks, and he squinted up at the white and gray overcast blanket that had closed out the sky while he had been inside the Hold. Against the bleak clouds, he could make out random flecks of snow drifting toward the earth.

He turned the corner and instead of following the wall, he cut across the unkempt grass to reach the gate at the end of the fence. The clinging droplets from melted snowflakes made the metal latch feel colder than he expected as he reached over the gate to release it from the inside. He could tell from the soundless and smooth function of the hinges that Mattow, or whoever had been the Iron of the Last Sky before him, had maintained the gate with routine inspections and grease that didn't gum when dirt or water touched it. The realization made Hyatt recall the mechanical function of the door he thought had been locked, and the silent operation of the mechanism except for the crisp click of the lock disengaging.

*Who puts so much work into the metalwork of their home, but neglects their curtilage?* Hyatt shook his head as he closed the gate behind himself, paying more attention to the fluid motion of the latch as it slid over the retaining hook and dropped into a slot with a definitive click. *What kind of Iron lets their Low Flowers become overrun with weeds and stalks?*

He shook his head and started toward the sloping pile of dirt where he had first seen Mattow. Being alone in the enclosed yard of the Hold felt like it triggered a primordial aversion in Hyatt, a certainty that it was forbidden and dangerous for him to be there and that discovery would lead to a horrible death. He walked with slow, wary steps and looked back over his shoulder, expecting to see the Iron standing at either corner of the rear wall or crouching on the roof like a grotesque with his green eyes fixed on him, but found no one waiting to call out an alarm or try to kill him. He shook his head and wiped the random melting flakes from his hair as he tried to shake the tension that was building in his spine and shoulders.

As he approached the cylinder and the dirt that spilled from it, he noticed details that had been invisible from beyond the fence. The metal canisters stood as high as his chin and were made of curved metal plates riveted together around a diameter just larger than his fathom. The top rims of the cylinders were clean but inset, as if other pieces had once connected to make a higher structure, but the sides where the dirt spilled from had been rended open by a bladed tool with no regard for the canister's structure. The sharp, jagged edges of the opening gleamed with clinging droplets, making them look even more sinister than their dangerous warps and tears already did.

He walked carefully around the dirt slope until he reached the space where Mattow had stood. The Iron's gardening tool was where he had left it, a simple forked instrument with burnt-orange fabric wrapped in identical coils around the handle. He pulled it from the dirt and it carried clods of dark soil with it that showered the pile below as they lost their bid to cling to the metal tool. Hyatt gave it a shake to clear as much remaining earth as he could before starting back toward the Hold.

The transition from the cold to the immediate and enveloping warmth of the structure was welcoming, but not strong enough to prevent him from noticing the change of mood in the room. The taut lines of confrontation had collapsed in his absence and Rellah was no longer standing at the door, but occupying the third chair at the stone table. The book sat closed between them, and they both looked up when he stepped into the room.

Mattow stood and accepted his tool when Hyatt offered it, and he gestured back to the vacant chair. Hyatt gave Rellah a questioning look and she met his gaze with something in her eyes that he couldn't place, a shine that seemed to carry determination and compassion in equal measures, but she said nothing until he took the offered seat.

"We will join Iron Mattow." She nodded to double down on her decision when Hyatt's eyes widened in surprise. "We will bring your new Warning to the Haleu and the Cern—"

"First of all, you can stop with the 'your warning' compost right now," Hyatt broke in. "I didn't write it. It's not mine."

"Think of the legacy for your Cern baby." Rellah's joke had all the necessary words, but there was a hollowness to her ribbing that struck a dissonant chord in Hyatt.

He tried to pretend he hadn't heard the blank space between her words and her expression. "Yeah? What do I sew onto my jacket for 'found a new Warning'?"

Through their exchange, Mattow wore an amused but disengaged expression as his eyes moved back and forth between them. Hyatt felt like he was assessing them, deciding their chances of success or obstacles to their cooperation. Nothing had changed in his features at his companion's mention of a child growing in her, and Hyatt looked over at him before turning back to Rellah.

"Are you sure about this?" he asked.

Her forced smile faltered and her expression matched the hard clarity in her eyes. "Yes."

"Then we are all agreed." Mattow planted his hands on the table in front of him, and pressed down to help himself rise to his feet in a fluid and sharp movement. "We'll leave in the morning – I need the evening to secure the Hold. There are rooms on the second floor, through there. Take any one you want."

He headed for the front door with his gardening tool in hand and Hyatt turned his head to watch until Mattow had stepped outside and closed the door behind himself, before turning to Rellah. "Just like that?"

She nodded, and Hyatt knew that before they had spent months living and fighting together, he might have missed the fact that she was hiding something in her direct eye contact and the deliberate way she kept her expression neutral. He studied her across the table for a moment and she held his gaze, but nothing changed.

"Okay." He picked up the book and turned it over in his hand to look at the back of it, then wrapped the protective cloth around it and shoved it into his pack.

When he stood up, she did too, and he led the way through the opening at the back of the room. The adjacent space was a larger room with faded buttermilk plaster on the walls and couches upholstered in the same dark purple that the chairs at the table had been, gathered around low tables. Hyatt took in the strange metal puzzles that sat on trays on each table and looked unfinished by the pieces and parts scattered around the larger constructs, but left them alone as he continued on to the opening at the far end of the room. On the wall beside it, rivets held a metal placard to the wall with a line diagram of stairs in faded red paint.

Around the corner, broad and gradual steps climbed a stone staircase with no paint or art to disrupt the gray rock on either side. Hyatt climbed the flight of stairs with Rellah behind him and at the top, strode into a hallway with seven doors covering both ends and the far wall. He lingered on the rose-colored carpet as his companion caught up, noting only one door closed and the rest ajar.

"I'm guessing that one is his. Which one do you want?" Hyatt asked as Rellah reached his side.

"Let's take that one." Rellah pointed to the door at the end of the hallway, furthest from the closed door near the top of the stairs.

"Both of us?" Hyatt asked, confused. "There are so many rooms – we don't have to share."

Rellah turned to look at the side of his head and stood there, staring a hole through his temple until he noticed and turned to face her. As soon as he met her gaze, she shook her head and started walking toward the end of the hall.

"You're such a dumb weed."

"What? I am not!" He had let her get a few paces down the hall, and jogged to catch up with her. "What did I say?"

Rellah put her palm on the painted wooden door and pressed slowly, and it swung open in a silent and perfectly balanced arc until it met a doorstop and would swing no further. She navigated the opening to the room like she was searching for enemies and lining up with the doorframe to reveal the interior sliver after sliver until she could see the entire room as she stepped through. Hyatt followed her and his boots sunk into the plush area-rug that covered much of the floor.

A large bed with ornate carvings on the headboard and footboard and posts that nearly reached the ceiling occupied one wall, while a woodstove and two couches filled the majority of the remainder. At the foot of the bed, two wooden trunks with metal bracers on the seams and hinges stood open as if inviting them to secure their things. Hyatt looked over the comforts of the quarters as he made his way to the back of the room, where a window overlooked a terrace on the roof of the building and the rear yard beyond.

"I've never been in a Hold before, except Sawmet's," Hyatt said aloud, half to himself and half to Rellah. "I wonder if they're all so..."

"Soft?" she finished for him. "Unnecessary?"

"Something like that." He didn't resist the chuckle her adjectives caused as he opened the door to the terrace and stepped into the flurrying snowfall and the blast of cold air.

The accumulating snow was too thin to whitewash the gray stone but enough to leave footprints as he crossed to the railing. In the distance, the treetops had begun to surrender their detail to a more uniform silhouette, the first sign that the afternoon light and the gentle fall of snowflakes would give way to darkness and cold sooner than he would have liked. He rested his hands on the carved rail and glanced over at Rellah as she joined him at the edge of the terrace, then turned his attention to the ground below where Iron Mattow sat cross-legged in the center of the yard with his back straight and his hands folded in his lap. A small clay pot stood on the ground before him, a cluster of Low Flowers sprouting from the dirt within.

Hyatt watched him as snow began to accumulate on his bald head, but the Iron made no movement to dislodge it or spare himself from the cold. "Another walk through the Reclaimed with an Iron... is our company the leading cause of death for Iron's, do you think?"

"We should invite them all to dinner." Rellah's tone was flat, but when Hyatt glanced at her again, a smirk twisted the corner of her mouth.

"You know..." He hesitated, but because it was just him and Rellah, decided to finish his thought. "We've seen some strange things since we met, but I still don't know if I believe Sklodowska speaks to them."

He didn't know what he expected her to say, but when she was silent, it made him feel like he should continue explaining his thoughts. In the yard below, the Iron made no movement or sound.

"We're taught growing up that Irons are regular people who she chooses for reasons we can't understand... that she makes them preternatural and speaks to them for as long as they are Irons, and they go back to their regular lives when she releases them." Hyatt paused, considering. "I don't think I know any stories of Irons that made it to that part."

She let the quiet hang for another moment, but when Hyatt added nothing more, she spoke. "We have different stories."

*Ever the storyteller.* Hyatt contented himself with a nod to acknowledge both her sentiment and all the unspoken tales of horror that fueled Cern dreams of the Butcher Queen's assassins. "If we go with Mattow, it will take us further from Hollow Bone – unless we convince him to spread the word to our pack first?"

Rellah shook her head. "Bex knew we weren't coming back. They'll keep the pack together, bring in new Claimed fighters."

"But—" he began.

"We gave them a pack and left them well. This is for you and me to do." Rellah turned and walked back toward the bedroom, leaving him alone on the terrace.

By the time he pushed himself away from the waist-high railing and followed her inside, she had discarded her jacket across the footboard of the bed, opened the door to the woodstove, and begun to feed kindling from a nearby pile into the dark, square opening. By the time he closed the door, the smell of immolating tinder had begun to fill the space. She closed the door to the stove.

He stripped off his jacket and hung it on the free-standing coat rack in the corner of the room. Droplets of water fell from his sleeve and made faint, percussive rings as they smashed against the heavy metal base of the stand. Being free of his jacket sponsored a sudden need to be free of his boots and he crossed to the side of the bed, sat down, and began freeing the laces and straps that held them tight to his calves.

The first wave of warmth from the iron stove reached him, thawing some of the chill that had set into his limbs more than he had realized. He stepped out of his boots and set them together at the foot of the bed, heels aligned with the shadow that the frame cast on the floor. He slipped the buckle of his belt free and set it on the bed beside him, then drove the heavy fabric of his trousers down to his ankles. As he stepped out of them and pushed them to the side across the plush rug, Rellah stepped into his periphery. His eyes moved up along her bare legs to her underwear, over her exposed stomach to her arm where her trousers and shirt were folded and draped. Like a ball rolling too fast to stop, his eyes continued up to her bralette and over her collarbone until they met her gaze, looking back at him with unwavering contact.

Hyatt felt his reaction course through his hips and clench in his stomach, blood leaving his brain and arms in a surge to fill his response to seeing her. His tongue dried and his heart pounded harder, not the indistinguishable whir of a bird's pulse but the repeated slam of a sledgehammer that grew stronger and surer as it found its new, savage rhythm. His lungs refused to expand or contract, but in that moment, he couldn't remember any good that breathing had ever done him.

She took another step toward Hyatt and her bare feet filled the space on the floor between his, the outsides of her thighs so close to contact with the insides of his knees that he could feel the air between them warm. His eyes met her stomach again, a handspan from his lips, and she lowered her arm to let her clothes fall in a pile atop his discarded trousers. Hyatt looked up slowly, every unexplored inch of Rellah's body revealed in part through his eyelashes before being bared to him until his gaze met hers. Rellah looked down with unmistakable intention, and her gaze plunged through his pupils into the molten metal in his chest that was cascading down through his core with need for her.

"Rellah..." Her name was the only word he could form, and her finger pressed to his lips to silence him before she slid her palm out along his cheek to bury her fingers through his hair and clench them in it.

His hand trembled as he lifted it from the blanket beneath him and rested it on the back of her thigh, just above her knee. The euphoric surge of realized desire arced through his spine to explode like a thunderstorm in his mind as his fingertips soaked in the heat of her toned skin, fueling the rush of consuming fire in his entire body. His palm slid up along the curve of her powerful thigh and he heard her exhale. Her fingernails bit into his skull as a shiver ran through her body.

"Take what you want, Hyatt." Even in the dark of the room, her eyes shone with hunger and need like pools of oil ablaze. "Need me. Show me how much... tear me apart."

The roar of his own pulse in his ears was deafening, and he felt like he was reading every movement of her lips as she bent one knee to bring it closer to him until it met his thighs on both sides. Hyatt wrapped his arm around her hips and stood as he lifted her, and her legs wrapped around him without releasing her grip in his hair as he turned and plunged down onto the soft and wide bed on top of her. Rellah's calf slid down his back and stopped at his hip and her free hand grabbed the back of his shirt to strip it over his head. His bare body met hers and her arms came together around his neck, her knee rising to press her inner thigh against him as his demand for more of her pressed into her hips.

"I want every Iron who lives in this Hold to hear the echo of us and smell our sweat, until the end of time." The way her gaze bore into his made space for the raging storm in his body to consume his entire being, and he felt her fingernails sink into the back of his neck. "Make the Butcher Queen forget me because she is certain you killed me tonight. Everything you've ever wanted... give it to me, now."

When day broke through the window that overlooked the yard of the Iron's Hold, it shone on the most peaceful expression Hyatt had ever seen on Rellah's face. The rise and fall of her back as she breathed was unburdened by the lives lost around her or taken by her hand, and no part of her body felt coiled in readiness to face a sudden danger or seize an opportunity. Her hair was damp with sweat and knotted from exertion, but shone in shades and colors Hyatt had never seen in it before.

His attention walked down her back to the short nail marks and fingerprint bruises that spotted her skin, and his fingers traveled along the twine still woven through the braids that had survived. At the end of the strand, his fingertips shifted to her ear to tuck stray ringlets behind it. The sensation teased a sigh from Rellah's lips and she shifted against him, nestling herself back against him and tipping her head to expose her neck as she pulled the bedding tighter around her hips.

Hyatt slid his hand down her arm and across her navel, and tightened his arm around Rellah's stomach, pulling her back against him and leaning forward to feel her hair on his cheek as he spoke softly in her ear. "What did Mattow say to you while I was outside?"

Her legs shifted, the inside of her thigh sliding against his where they were still entangled, and her hair smelled like cardamom and mint. In the silence, he could feel each of her inhales and exhales through her bare back pressed to his chest. He let his palm slide down across her stomach again, his fingers trailing along her skin like individual comets across the skies of her body, until it rested in the crease where her hip joined her thigh.

"He said there were only three futures for us," she murmured, her words muted by lingering slumber, "and the one you survive is the one where we reach Leshtara Garden together."

# THE SEVEN WARNINGS

No individual sources of power

No untethered communications

No turning weapons

No individual transportation

No captivity

No inheritance

No everlasting commitment

# ACKNOWLEDGMENTS

One of my favorite moments in reading fellow author's published works comes in the final pages, when the story is concluded but ahead of their promises of future works and brief biographies. There is something beautiful and scandalous in the act of tracing the lines of appreciation, admiration, and apology that expose the hidden infrastructure that supported the construction of their novel. My love of Acknowledgments gives me pause when writing my own as I face the daunting task of doing justice to everyone who made this work of fiction possible.

In the years between writing The Eighth Warning and completing this novel, Delené Kendrick never let go of the Reclaimed Saga. Through her patience, encouragement, and enthusiasm, she has earned the lion's share of my gratitude. She has been my constant muse and champion, and her excitement for every new scene and character has fueled the engine that has carried this tale from my imagination to the reader's hands. I cannot find words to express how much I love her, and how important her support to this series has been.

Desolate Garden was written in a different chapter of my life than the one from which the Eighth Warning emerged, and so it is appropriate that the cast of characters who have been a part of this project have changed and evolved. What remains the same is the mark that those closest to me have left on the text through their early inputs on the drafts, and how indispensable they have been in honing and polishing the narrative and dialogue into the version in your hands. Jamie Jackson, Michelle Cruz, Cherie-Lee Mason, Christine Fedorchuk, Mikishea Mauss, and Davene Le Grange provided exceptional feedback and insights, and I could not have asked for a better cross-section of my social sphere to engage with the text. Their time, attention, and excitement has been invaluable to me, and I am humbled by their dedication to the success of this story.

If a writer is lucky or intentional, they will find themselves surrounded by friends who are both encouraging and understanding of that writer's passion for the craft and the time it takes to put words to the page. This theory finds corporeal form in questions about "how's the book coming", their excitement to tell others about their "friend who writes books", and their forgiveness for declined invitations in favor of writing in solitude. Chris and Ari Larson, Christine Fedorchuk, Eva Taraseviciute, Jessica McCracken, Jessica Pulz, Jennifer Lemon, Liza-Mae Carlin, Mike Beatty, Nick Heufelder, Taylor Schawang, and so many others have found the perfect balance between supporting my writing through their curiosity and encouragement, and making allowances for my absence so that I could complete it. Without their friendship and patience, this would have been a much longer endeavor both in time and experience.

I would be remiss if I did not take space here to thank my cover artist Izabela Novoselec, who did such a magnificent job capturing the essence of the Reclaimed for this novel and keeping the artwork consistent with the first book in the series, a brilliant cover for which she is also to thank. I am grateful for her patience, dedication, and attention to detail in bringing my words to life with such beautiful artwork.

After a concerted effort to carve out a space all my own to write, it remains true that most of my writing occurs in places more chaotic than the quiet and calm of my desk. From the outdoor tables and cherry blossom lattes of St. Elmo's Coffee Pub to the dimly lit mayhem and roaring karaoke of Rock It Grill in Alexandria, the places and people that surrounded me as I wrote this novel provided the creative atmosphere that enabled me to finish it. In the event that this book finds its way to the hands of the staff who allowed me to enjoy their spaces or the patrons who noticed the novelist with his laptop noticing them, it is only right and just that I express my gratitude for their part in bringing this work to fruition.

In closing, it matters to me that I acknowledge your role in all of this. The story between these covers came from me, but it comes to life and continues to propagate through your imagination. Works of fiction find a life in the hearts of its readers that outshines its cover art and outlasts its pages, and I hope something within this novel lingers with you and inspires you long after you have set it down. Thank you contributing what no amount of imagery or narrative can create, and no amount of marketing can generate – the love of the story that brings it off the page and into memories, fan-fiction, cosplay, and conversation in ways that only you can.

# BOOKS IN THE RECLAIMED SAGA

*The Eighth Warning*

*Desolate Garden*

# COMING SOON

*The Broken Accord: Book Three in the Reclaimed Saga*

*Low Flowers: Tabletop Role-Playing in the Eighth History*

# ABOUT THE AUTHOR

Sam Odiorne was born in New England to a compassionate mother and a logical father, and by all accounts, he has never recovered.

He dislikes talking about himself but when pressed, will tell you that he loves old whiskey, new cities, baby rhinos, and you.

Sam can be found on all the usual social media under his somewhat unusual name, and through his website.

www.samodiorne.com